WHERE WE BELONG

SARAH BENNETT

Boldwood

First published in Great Britain in 2023 by Boldwood Books Ltd.

Copyright © Sarah Bennett, 2023

Cover Design by Alice Moore Design

Cover Photography: iStock, Deposit Photos and Shutterstock

The moral right of Sarah Bennett to be identified as the author of this work has been asserted in accordance with the Copyright, Designs and Patents Act 1988.

A CIP catalogue record for this book is available from the British Library.

Paperback ISBN 978-1-80483-315-5

Large Print ISBN 978-1-80483-311-7

Hardback ISBN 978-1-80483-310-0

Ebook ISBN 978-1-80483-308-7

Kindle ISBN 978-1-80483-309-4

Audio CD ISBN 978-1-80483-316-2

MP3 CD ISBN 978-1-80483-313-1

Digital audio download ISBN 978-1-80483-307-0

Boldwood Books Ltd
23 Bowerdean Street
London SW6 3TN
www.boldwoodbooks.com

For the Straw-Haired Chits x

1

Buzz. Buzz. Buzz. Hope Travers groaned as the harsh sound of her alarm dragged her from the depths of sleep. Having tossed and turned for most of the night, she'd finally managed to drift off sometime after the church clock in the village had chimed a distant single note. There'd been a few complaints about the chimes over the years, mostly from weekend commuters who liked the idea of a pretty house in the country more than the realities of village life, but Hope found them soothing. The alarm buzzed again and she flailed her arm towards the bedside cabinet, knocking her phone off and under the bed in the process.

Buzz. Buzz. Buzz. Muttering something unrepeatable, Hope forced her heavy head off the pillow and fumbled towards the bedside cabinet once again, managing to switch on the lamp this time. Squinting against the glare, she rolled onto her side, one hand groping around on the carpet for her phone. Three tissues, a KitKat wrapper and a pair of tweezers she'd presumed lost later, her fingers found the edge of the annoying device and she slid it out from under the edge of the divan base. After stabbing a finger at the off button before the alarm could buzz again, Hope flopped back against her pillow with a sigh. Perhaps a few more minutes wouldn't do any harm...

A gentle rap against her door was followed by a sliver of light and a waft of familiar White Musk perfume, her Aunt Rowena's signature scent. 'Hope, darling, I'm going to put the kettle on and then I'll make you something to eat. Shall I bring you up some tea?'

Ignoring her gritty eyes and the beginnings of a headache pressing against her temple, Hope forced herself to sit up. 'You should've stayed in bed, Ro. Just because I'm up at some ungodly hour, doesn't mean you have to be.'

The door swung wide and Rowena padded across the room to sit on the edge of Hope's bed. She raised a hand to tuck a few strands of Hope's long dark hair back behind her ear. 'It's an exciting day for you, darling, a busy one too. I couldn't send you off without a bit of breakfast. You'll probably be down at the site all day, so it's important you start the day off right.'

Hope leaned into the gentle touch of her aunt's palm with a smile. 'You're too good to me.'

'Nonsense.' Rowena leaned forward to give Hope a quick hug, her wild corkscrew curls brushing against Hope's skin like a secondary caress. They were magenta this month, a vibrant shade that looked stunning against her emerald-green silk pyjamas. An artist by trade, Rowena's wardrobe was its own palette. With a soft grunt, as though the effort was too much, Rowena pushed herself to her feet.

'Are you okay?' Hope pushed her covers back, ready to climb out and give her aunt a hand.

Rowena waved her off with a smile. 'My back's just a bit stiff. I was working on a new collage yesterday and I spent too long bent over my work bench, that's all. I'll sneak into Meena's Pilates class later and that'll sort me out.'

Another knock on the door had them both turning to see Stevie, Hope's mother, standing in the doorway. 'I thought I heard voices.'

'Go back to bed, Mum,' Hope urged, keeping her voice low before they managed to wake the rest of the family up. She turned to her aunt. 'You, too.'

With an indelicate snort, Rowena knuckled her fists into the base of her spine then headed back towards the door to stand next to her sister-in-law. 'As if we're going to leave our girl to fend for herself this morning, of all mornings. Am I right, Stevie?'

'Of course we're not!' Hope's mother sounded as if the very idea was preposterous. They should've made a comical pair – tall, willowy Stevie in her neutral fabrics and pixie cut salt-and-pepper hair, and short, curvy Rowena with that mass of wild curls tumbling past her shoulders and almost to her waist, but somehow they complemented each other perfectly. And not just in looks. Together they ran the exclusive hotel and spa located in their family's ancestral home and were as close as, if not closer than, blood sisters.

Hope climbed out of bed with a resigned shake of her head. 'You'd think I was five, not twenty-five, the way you two cluck after me like a pair of Rhys's prize hens.' She'd meant it as a joke, but she should've known better. Though they were trying hard not to show it, Hope knew today was difficult for them.

'We don't mean to fuss,' her mother said, a shadow dimming the sweet smile that was never far from her lips.

Rowena spoke almost on top of Stevie. 'It was just an idea, if you'd rather we left you in peace, you just have to say.'

And now she felt like an ungrateful brat. 'It's a lovely idea, and one less thing for me to worry about, so thank you.'

The pair instantly brightened. 'We'll leave you to get ready,' Rowena said as she reached for the door and began to pull it closed behind them. 'No rush.'

Their arrival downstairs was greeted with a chorus of happy barks from the family's motley collection of dogs and Hope closed her eyes in silent apology to her uncles and her cousin. Once the dogs were up, everyone was up. Swallowing a sigh, Hope grabbed a hair tie from her bedside cabinet and twisted her thick hair up into a messy knot on the back of her head. She'd washed it the night before as it took so long to dry these days. She kept promising herself she was going to get it cut off, get something manageable like a chin-length bob or one of those modern takes on a page-boy style with a nice undercut at the back to keep her neck cool during the hot summer days to come. Then something would come up at work and she'd end up cancelling her appointment and trimming the ends off herself.

She wandered across the hall to the bathroom she shared with her cousin, Rhys, and regarded her reflection in the mirror over the sink. With a wince, she tugged at the uneven strands of her fringe. Perhaps taking the kitchen scissors to it the other day hadn't been the wisest idea. Once everything was sorted out, she would book herself a day off and spend it indulging herself at the spa. What was the point of living on the doorstep of the most exclusive establishment in the county if she never took advantage of the facilities there? For now, she'd settle for using one of the never-ending samples her mother gave to her in an effort to persuade Hope to take her skin care regime more seriously. She surveyed her cluttered half of the countertop, her *three-quarters* of the countertop might be more accurate, she thought ruefully, as she eyed the motley collection of bottles, pots and tubes before plucking a pastel-pink tube at random and reading the label. *Brightening and lifting, hmm?* Hope met her tired reflection once more. After weeks doing battle with the planners, the architect, three different building contractors and various members of her family, she could do with all the help she could get.

She squeezed a generous gloop of cream onto one hand then set the tube on the edge of the sink before rubbing her palms together and massaging the cream into her skin the way she would with her usual no-frills facewash. She only realised her mistake when her eyes began to burn and fill with tears. 'Ow! Ow! Ow!' Hope forced one eye open long enough to help her find the cold tap, turning it too far in her haste to wash the mess from her face and sending a jet of icy water over the front of the thin-strapped vest which served as a pyjama top.

'Bloody hell!' Arching her body away from the offending spray, Hope leaned too far forward and banged her forehead on the mirrored front of the cupboard over the sink. The next words that left her lips were even less polite.

'Hope Elizabeth Travers!'

Whirling towards the laughing exclamation, Hope squinted through her agony to make out the familiar shape of her cousin. 'It's not funny!' she snapped.

'I think you'll find it is,' Rhys replied, still laughing as he leaned past her and tugged a towel off the wall rail. 'Here, hold still a minute.' He wrapped a corner of the towel around his finger and started trying to wipe the cream from her face.

'I can do it myself.' Hope snatched the material from his hands and scrubbed her skin clean. 'I'm not five.'

'I'm not five,' he mimicked in the exaggerated voice he'd known since she was that age was guaranteed to drive her up the wall.

'What do you want?' Hope said, trying to cling onto the last vestiges of her temper.

'Well, I was hoping for a shower.' Rhys held his arms out in a look-at-the-state-of-me gesture.

With the last of the tears now wiped from her eyes, Hope was able to focus on him properly. The front of his grey T-shirt was covered in blood and various other bodily fluids, the knees of his old jeans filthy from kneeling in the dirt. 'What happened?'

'Blossom decided 3 a.m. was the perfect time to go into labour.' Rhys gave a rueful shrug as he referred to one of his prize-winning sows. 'I thought I'd be early enough to clean up and get changed before you were awake, but everyone seems to have decided to get up with the larks.'

'We're breaking ground today, so I wanted to try and get myself sorted before the builders arrive.'

Rhys raised a mucky hand as though to slap himself in the forehead, only remembering at the last minute where it had been not too long ago. 'I completely forgot.' Comprehension dawned in his eyes. 'That's why the mothers are fussing around in the kitchen.'

'They decided to make me breakfast.' She knew she sounded ungrateful but there was a fine line between mothering and smothering and just lately it felt like they'd tipped into the latter. She hung the towel back on the rack. 'I'll use the shower in Mum's room.'

Rhys looked relieved. 'Are you sure?'

Hope wrinkled her nose towards him. 'Your need is much greater than mine.'

'Gee, thanks!' Rhys's laughter followed Hope along the landing as she made her way to her mother's room and the tiny en suite her uncle, Ziggy, had installed about twelve years ago in what had once been a walk-in storage space. He'd built it about the same time as he'd decamped downstairs and converted the rarely used dining room into a bedroom and bath-room for himself, having decried the inability to get into the main family bathroom now there were two teenagers in the house. Rhys had moved out of his tiny box room on the third floor and into Ziggy's room, leaving the top floor of the farmhouse to his parents.

Hope paused to look out of the window. Her mother's room was at the front of the farmhouse, offering a gorgeous view across the sprawling parkland of the estate towards the Palladian-style mansion that dominated the landscape. Built in the early seventeenth century and altered and extended by many subsequent generations, the family had decamped from Stourton Hall, or just 'the Hall' as everyone referred to it, when the four Travers siblings had decided it was time for radical change. Their father – Hope and Rhys's grandfather, Monty – had shown zero interest in taking up the reins of estate management from his own father and things had grown rather neglected under his brief spell in charge.

Zap and Ziggy had been barely out of university when they'd confronted Monty about the perilous state of the family finances, not to mention the leaky roof and ancient electrics which were a fire disaster waiting to happen. With barely a murmur of protest, Monty had signed responsibility for the estate over to his four children and he and his wife, Alice, had loaded up their worldly goods in the back of their VW camper and headed off to explore the world. They rattled their way home every now and again, staying long enough to cause chaos and renew their prescriptions before off they went again on a new adventure.

It had been during their last visit home, a riotous and very merry Christmas, that Hope had decided she needed a space of her own. She adored her family, but some days she just wanted to shut the door on everyone and everything, which was simply impossible when you lived under the same roof with five other adults – seven when her grandparents landed. Hope cast one last look at the Hall. When she'd been a little girl, she'd loved to explore the opulent guest suites and imagine one of them was her bedroom. Now, for all they lived on top of each other in the farm-house, Hope was grateful that her uncles and her mother had seized the opportunity and made the most of the family assets. Not only had they saved the Hall from potential ruin, they'd created a huge range of opportunities, for both the family and many of the residents of nearby Stourton-in-the-Vale. Now it was Hope's turn to claim a little corner of the estate for herself. She checked the clock on her mother's bedside table and gasped when she saw the time. So much for getting ahead of things, the builders would be here in less than an hour!

2

Thirty minutes later, a half-eaten bacon roll in one hand and a thermos cup of coffee in the other, Hope rushed out the back door of the farm-house, calling thanks to her mum and Rowena. Sooty and Sweep, her pair of black Labradors, shot out into the yard, determined to join her. It cost her the remains of her roll, but she managed to coax them back inside with the help of Ziggy, who'd been woken by all the kerfuffle just as she'd feared. With a quick apology to him for the noise, she managed to slip back out the door and shut it before her two hellion pups could stage a second breakout. They normally joined her wherever she went and even had baskets in the corner of her office, but there was no way she could take them to the worksite – it just wasn't safe. Still, their desperate yowls and whines at being left behind shredded her heart and she promised to make time to take them on an extra-long walk later.

She made her way over to the small fleet of black Range Rovers, each bearing the discreet logo her Uncle Ziggy had designed on the bonnet and each of the front doors. He'd chosen a sprig of greenery with a bright purple berry next to the words Juniper Meadows in a swirling calligraphy font – the name he and the others had opted for when rebranding the estate. They used it for everything, from labelling the award-winning gin Zap made at their private distillery, to the luxury toiletries available in every guest room in the hotel and spa. It was even on the packaging of the free-range organic meat and dairy products from the estate's farm, which Rhys managed. Hope pointed the set of keys she'd grabbed off the kitchen table and aimed it at the row of cars. The orange hazard lights on the one nearest the gate flashed.

By the time she'd secured her coffee in the drinks holder and adjusted the seat so she could reach the pedals – the perils of being five foot four in a family of six-foot-tall men – Rhys had appeared to unlock the gate for her. His border collie, Samson, sat smartly at his heels and Hope could only sigh at how well-behaved her cousin's dog was. She'd kept meaning to sign Sooty and Sweep up for some training classes, but that was even further down her to-do list than finding time to get a proper haircut. The sight of Rhys's other dog, a miniature dachshund named Delilah, nestled in his arms like the spoiled princess she was cheered Hope up. He might be the dog whisperer when it came to Samson, but Delilah was a diva from the tip of her nose to the end of her stubby little tail. 'Thanks for saving me a job,' she called to Rhys through the open passenger window.

'It's no hassle. I'm on my way back to check on Blossom and her litter, make sure they're all bonding.'

'Take some photos for—'

'The Instagram page,' he said, cutting her off with a laugh. He raised a hand to pat the phone in his top pocket. 'Don't worry, you can rely on me.'

The truth of those words struck her heart like an arrow shot from Robin Hood's bow. Eighteen months older than her, Rhys had been a big brother to her in every way that mattered. They'd been inseparable. Two musketeers. He'd been there to help her with everything from learning to tie her shoelaces, to chasing off unsuitable boyfriends. She hoped her moving out wouldn't change things between them. 'You'll come to dinner all the time, won't you?'

'I'll be there so much, you'll be sick of the sight of me,' he promised with a grin. Leaning down, he rested one arm on the open window of the car, the other still holding Delilah securely against his chest. 'You've got this.'

It wasn't much of a pep talk, but it was everything she needed to hear. 'Thanks, Rhys. I'd better get going.' He stepped back and kept one hand on the gate until she was safely on the other side. Though she knew he would lock it properly, she still watched via the rear-view mirror until he'd secured it and wandered off towards the barn with a wave, Samson close as a shadow. Only then did she turn her attention to the road ahead.

Hope glanced left in the direction of the Hall, then to the right, which would take her towards the main entrance of the estate. The roads around their grounds were never very busy, but it was one of the habits drilled into her when Ziggy had been teaching her to drive, and she'd never forgotten it. More than one visitor to the spa had found themselves nose-to-nose with Rhys's prize herd of cows as they crossed from the pasture to the milking shed.

As she rounded the bend and turned off the long chestnut-lined drive, heading towards the east gate which they used for deliveries and other trade visitors, she focused her attention on the day ahead. The heavy equipment was arriving today and with the compound already set up, she hoped they'd be digging the foundations before lunchtime. She was still some distance away from the east entrance when she spotted a flash of bright yellow and her heart skipped a beat. By the time she'd pulled up in front of the gate, the huge digger dominated her view, its bucket raised high against the pale blue of the early-morning sky. *It's really happening.* Her stomach was suddenly a fluttering mass, and she began to regret the bacon roll. *Get a grip.*

She'd made the decision to project manage the house build herself. It should've been a walk in the park for the operations manager of the family gin distillery, but somehow, she kept finding herself on the wrong foot. The proposed site manager from the first building company she'd spoken to had called her 'Babes' and waved off her request to see his construction plan. The second firm had been impossible to pin down on anything to do with dates, or more importantly costs, and had just kept reassuring her they could do it within budget. She hadn't been reassured. Thankfully, the firm she'd finally signed a contract with had proven sensible and professional, dealing with all of her enquiries – and one or two last-minute panics on her part – with polite and timely responses. Hope pressed a hand to her roiling stomach. Throwing up in front of the site team would not make a great impression. *You've got this.*

Having performed a quick three-point turn in front of the gate so she'd be facing in the right direction to lead the crew through the grounds, Hope climbed out of the car and set her shoulders straight. The first person she saw was Declan, the site manager, leaning against the bonnet of his truck. He straightened up the moment he saw her, and her nerves began to settle. 'Good morning! I hope I haven't kept you all waiting?' she called as she pressed the remote control that operated the gates.

'No, you're fine,' Declan reassured her as he stepped forward and offered her his hand. 'We've only been here a few minutes. I wanted to get the digger off the roads before the local traffic gets busy. The last thing we want is to annoy people before we've even started.'

'That's thoughtful of you.' Hope offered him the remote control. 'Here, while I remember. I've signed it out on your behalf for the duration of the project. If you need any more then let me know and I'll speak to my uncle.'

'Cheers.' Declan tucked the remote into his pocket before he turned to gesture towards the small convoy of vehicles lined up behind his truck. 'One more might be handy in case I'm delayed, but there's no rush for it. I'll introduce you to everyone once we get to the site, if that's all right with you?'

'Sounds good.' Hope tilted her head to see past Declan and waved to acknowledge a couple of the crew, who each raised a hand in greeting. 'Let's get going, shall we?'

Ten minutes later, they were parked up in the secure zone Declan had overseen the building of the previous week. Two large portacabins formed one corner of the compound – a site office and a canteen/welfare unit. Hope had been shown around them and been impressed with the facilities. A bank of portable toilets stood on the far side of the canteen and a large metal storage container for tools and equipment completed the set-up. Through the metal fencing, the coloured flags tied to the stakes marking out the site of what would soon be Hope's new home fluttered in the light summer breeze. Her gaze wandered from the pristine grass to the huge oak tree some distance away and the jumble of fallen stones, half-overgrown, that littered the ground beneath it. The remains were of an old chapel according to family legend, but there was no information about who had built it, or when. It had always been Hope's favourite spot on the estate and one of the reasons she'd chosen this little plot to build her own home. She turned her attention back to the little flags, trying to overlay the architect's vision on the blank turf. As this was a private part of the estate, she'd decided against any kind of perimeter fence so she'd have an uninterrupted view of the oak tree and the ruins through what would be her back patio windows.

'Miss Travers?' Hope jumped at the sound of Declan's voice and when she turned to face him, the quizzical look on his face said it wasn't the first attempt to catch her attention.

'Sorry, I was miles away.' She stepped away from the fence, hoping her face didn't look as hot with embarrassment as it felt.

The site manager smiled. 'Daydreaming about what your new place is going to look like?'

'That obvious?' she replied with a laugh. Looking around, she realised the rest of the crew were watching them, each one wearing a hard hat and a high-vis vest. Her cheeks flushed again. 'I'm sorry, I'm holding you up, aren't I? I'll get out of your way and leave you to get on with things.' She was already fumbling in her pocket for the keys to her vehicle before she'd finished speaking.

Declan's smile softened. 'You're not in the way, Miss Travers, you're the project manager, remember?'

'Well, yes, but that's more to do with managing the budget. What I know about construction work you could write on the back of a stamp and still have room. It wasn't my intention to hang around the site, looking over your shoulder.'

'Well, that's certainly a relief,' Declan said, with a grin that made his white teeth stand out against his tan. It wasn't the kind of skin tone one got on holiday, more that deeply ingrained colour of someone who spent most of their working life outdoors in the elements. 'But you are welcome on site whenever you like, though I'd prefer it if you stuck to the compound unless I'm with you.'

'Of course.' Hope was in charge of overseeing the health and safety at the distillery. The risks were far fewer than on a construction site, but they were very careful about visitor safety during the tours they ran.

Declan nodded in thanks at her swift agreement. 'Look, unless you've got to rush off, I'm about to give everyone a safety briefing and run through the work programme if you'd like to sit in on it?'

'As long as I won't be in the way?'

'I'll get the kettle on,' the man nearest the welfare unit called to them. 'Cup of tea, Miss Travers?'

'Lovely! But you must all call me Hope, please.'

An hour later and Hope was on first-name terms with the entire crew and had admired photos of everyone's children, pets, garden water features and whatever else they'd wanted to show off to her. They'd given her first choice from the biscuit tin and answered all of the questions she'd asked without ever making her feel silly. As they trooped out of the canteen and headed towards the site, Hope found herself smiling as she met Declan's eyes. 'Quite a team you've got there,' she said.

'They're on their best behaviour. It'll be a different story when you're not around.' As though to prove the point, Paul, the operative in charge of the digger, dropped his keys and swore in a manner that was surprisingly inventive, if anatomically unachievable. 'Language!' bellowed Declan, as he gave Hope an apologetic smile.

'Sorry!' A blushing Paul raised his hand before turning and scurrying after the rest of the crew.

Hope laughed. 'I won't faint, don't worry,' she assured the irritated site manager as she followed him down the steps. She didn't add that in his role of surrogate big brother, Rhys had delighted in teaching her rude words and then double-dog daring her to use them in front of the rest of the family. It had cost her more than a few time-outs on the stairs, but a double-dog dare just couldn't be ignored. 'Thanks again for letting me sit in on the briefing, it was really useful.'

Obviously grateful at the way she'd steered the conversation back to more comfortable territory, Declan gave her a relieved grin. 'You're about the only person who's ever enjoyed a site safety briefing. Are you heading off, or do you have time to stick around a bit longer? I thought you might want to watch us officially break ground.'

It was really happening. 'I'd love that, if you're sure you don't mind?'

'Not a bit. Wait here and I'll get you a spare hard hat and a vest.'

With her protective gear on, Hope followed Declan to a spot well clear of where Paul was going through his final inspection of the digger, and promised not to move. She was as close to the perimeter of the site while still being on the working side of the fence. She was too far away to hear the conversation between Declan and the rest of the crew, but that didn't matter, it was exciting enough to be able to witness these first few steps. Tony, one of the other crew, started up a machine that looked a cross between a lawn mower and a quad bike, although he walked behind it, rather than riding it. He crossed the marked-out area, turned and headed back to where he'd started. She watched, puzzled, as he repeated the action a few more times.

As he turned to start another run, a couple of other members of the crew bent down and began rolling up the turf. Within just a few minutes, they'd cleared a good section and tossed the stripped turf into a large skip. Tony and the others moved out of the way while Declan glanced to where Hope hadn't moved from her allocated spot. She gave him a quick thumbs up and, with a nod, he turned and signalled to Paul, who was waiting in the driver's seat of the digger. He started up the engine and the vibration of it seemed to resonate through the ground beneath Hope's feet.

This was it. The start of her journey towards true independence. Head full of dreams of the first supper party she would throw – it would be early autumn if everything went to plan, and hopefully they'd enjoy an Indian summer weekend or two so she could set the table in front of the open patio doors, perhaps even outside – she watched as the first half-dozen buckets of soil were dug up and emptied out into the skip on top of the clear turf. There was something almost hypnotic about the movements of the digger's arm and it was clear that Paul knew exactly what he was doing by the fluid way he steered the big machine.

The bucket dipped again, and a terrible scraping noise filled the air. Declan yelled something over the noise of the digger, his arms waving frantically. The engine cut off, the silence shocking after the heavy roar and rumble of the machine, and Paul jumped down from the cab and jogged over to stand beside Declan.

The two men stared down into the hole, Declan with his hands on his hips, Paul pushing back his hard hat to scratch his brow. Hope popped up on her tiptoes, desperate to see what they were looking at, but it was impossible from her position. She wanted to rush over, but she'd promised Declan she wouldn't move. She settled for calling out, 'Is everything okay?'

Declan raised his head briefly to look at her, but didn't speak, his attention already drawn back to the hole. He said something to Paul, who nodded and hurriedly climbed back into the digger while Declan stepped back out of the way. The digger roared back to life, but only long enough for Paul to raise the bucket and lock it in its highest position before he turned off the engine and clambered down again. When Declan joined him by the hole, the pair of them went down on their knees and Hope watched as the site manager leaned forward until his head and shoulders disappeared from view. He raised his head and called to one of the other crew members who were standing around, their expressions a mixture of concern and curiosity. 'There should be a dustpan and brush in the store, fetch it for me.'

The man hurried off, returning a short time later with the requested item. Ignoring the dustpan, Declan took the brush and leaned back into the hole. The rest of the crew had now gathered round and Hope found herself edging forward, although there was nothing to see beyond the wall of broad shoulders. When her foot caught on one of the boundary stakes, she stumbled and just managed to catch her balance before she fell flat on her face. Chastened, she returned to her original spot and sat down, hands curled around her knees. She wanted to call out again, to demand Declan tell her what was going on, but she forced herself to remain quiet. He knew she was there, and it was better to be patient and get a proper answer about what was going on than to interrupt him just for him to tell her he didn't know yet. That awful roiling feeling in her stomach returned. Whatever was going on, Hope had a bad feeling about it.

3

Dear Dr Ferguson, the committee regrets to inform you that your recent application has not been successful on this occasion.

'Shit.' Cameron slammed the lid of his laptop closed then leaned forward to gently bang his forehead on his desk. 'Shit, shit, shit, shit.'

The door to the cramped square of space the university laughingly called his office swung open to admit the departmental secretary. The briskly efficient Mrs Cotteridge kept watch over Cam and the other junior lecturers in the university archaeology department with the patient exasperation of a veteran sheepdog. A fan of rock and roll, she sported an impressive beehive that never wilted even on a morning so warm Cam already had his desk fan on at full blast. She swept into the tiny office, filling the air with the light floral perfume Cam suspected had been her signature scent for as long as the beehive had been her hairstyle of choice.

'Don't do that, dear,' she admonished gently as she reached for the half-drunk cup of coffee on Cam's desk. 'You'll give yourself a headache.'

'I didn't get the funding,' Cam grumbled, knowing he sounded as hard done by as one of his first-year students whining about a poor grade.

'That's a shame,' Mrs Cotteridge said in the same no-nonsense tone. 'Do buck up, there's a visitor outside and you're the only one available.'

Cam tilted his head up to glare at Mrs Cotteridge. 'I'm not *available*. I've got far too much work to do.' The look he received would've done Medusa proud and he dropped his forehead back on his desk in case she really did have the power to turn him to stone. 'Where's Barnie?' he mumbled, referring to his best friend and former roommate when the two of them had been undergraduates. 'Can't he deal with it?'

'Dr Barnard is busy writing his end-of-term reports, not sulking about like a wet weekend.'

'Ouch.' Sitting up, Cam pressed a hand to his heart. 'Direct hit, Mrs C.'

Mrs Cotteridge clucked her tongue, but her stony gaze softened somewhat. 'I know you were banking everything on that funding for the summer, but perhaps you didn't get it for a reason.' Before Cam could even begin to fathom out her cryptic comment, Mrs Cotteridge raised her voice and called out, 'Dr Ferguson will see you now, Miss Travers.' Giving Cameron a wink – *a wink! Had she been on the gin?* – she turned on her heel and walked the five paces that carried her out of his office.

She'd barely cleared the door when she was replaced by a woman so stunningly pretty that he forgot all about his bitter disappointment over the committee's funding rejection. With her long dark hair bound up in a thick ponytail and her casual T-shirt and jeans, she looked at first glance as though she might be a student. The instant flash of attraction burned to ash. Cameron had very strict rules when it came to his private life. He'd been on the end of more than one student crush, and had found them excruciatingly awkward to deal with.

One of the reasons Mrs Cotteridge was such a godsend was her instinctive radar for such things. She was always kind and protective towards the students involved while gently repelling any requests for one-to-one tutorials and the like. The crushes never lasted long, and Cam didn't flatter himself that he was anything particularly special in the looks department. University was a big step up for many young people and they were bound to try to stretch their wings a little bit.

He studied the woman standing before him with the same eye for small details that he used when out on a dig. There was a confidence to her stance, a tilt to her head that said she considered him an equal and he revised her age up by several years.

Realising he'd been silent for longer than could be considered polite, Cam jumped to his feet, almost knocking his chair flying in his haste. 'Good morning, Miss...' his mind blanked on the name Mrs Cotteridge had given. Damn, damn, damn! *Get a grip, Ferguson.*

'Travers, Hope Travers.' Holding out a hand, she entered his office. 'I'm not interrupting anything important, I hope?' No, whoever she was, she was definitely not a student.

Cam shook her hand and released it, noting in the brief moment of contact how nicely her palm tucked into his own. 'Cameron. Ferguson. My friends call me Cam.' Oh, God, why had he said that? Feeling ridiculously flustered, Cam dropped back into his chair and gestured towards her. 'Please have a seat.'

With a raised eyebrow, he saw Miss Travers take in the cluttered disaster zone that was his office. Books, papers and plaster cast specimens littered every available surface, including, he noticed with a wince, a tottering stack of research books he'd checked out of the library and dumped on the chair he used for visitors. 'Sorry.'

Bouncing back up, Cam rounded his desk and gathered up the pile. He turned in a circle, hunting in vain for an alternative space to put them. 'It's not always this chaotic,' he lied, not wanting her to believe the worst of him. A human chaos bomb, that's what Barnie called him. He did try to keep on top of things, but somehow he ended up getting distracted and before he knew it, things were a mess again. The only place he practised ruthless discipline was when he was out on site. So many of their finds were delicate fragments, easily lost or damaged. One act of carelessness could ruin an entire summer's work. He shot Miss Travers an apologetic smile. 'End of term and all that. I need a good clear-out.'

'It's fine, I'm the one who should be apologising for turning up unannounced.' Miss Travers swept a hand behind her as though she was more used to wearing a skirt or a dress that needed smoothing down rather than jeans and a T-shirt, and sat down, crossing her legs at the ankles. The action drew attention to the heavy work boots on her feet. They looked new, for all the treads on the soles had some mud embedded in them. Miss Travers was a whole lot of contradictions.

Realising he was still standing, Cam hurried back behind his desk, dumping the reference books on the floor for want of anywhere else to put them. Folding his arms atop his desk, he leaned forward and tried to remember he was a professional, even if he'd given Miss Travers no sign of it so far. 'So, how can I help you today?'

Miss Travers rocked over onto one hip, leaning back at the same time to give herself enough room to reach a hand into her pocket. The action pushed her breasts forward against the dark navy cotton of her T-shirt and Cam averted his gaze. What was wrong with him? He'd been alone in his tiny cubbyhole of an office with dozens of women and never once been as aware of them as he was of Miss Travers. Something clicked softly on the surface of his desk and Cam turned back. One glance at the small, dark object Miss Travers had placed on his desk had Cam fumbling in the top drawer of his desk for his glasses. He shoved them on and reached for the object, his fingers freezing inches from the dark, dirt-encrusted treasure. 'Where did you find this?'

He heard rather than saw her sit forward, his eyes still glued on what she'd brought to him. 'Do you know what it is?'

'Possibly.' Spinning around in his chair, he started pulling the kit he needed from the cabinet behind him. A soft toothbrush, a finds tray, a wooden toothpick and a cloth. Setting them before him on the desk, he reached for the object, froze again and looked at Miss Travers. 'May I?'

She gave a little shrug. 'Of course.'

Cam placed the item in the finds tray and studied it for a long moment before he rummaged through the cluttered contents of his desk drawer and retrieved a jeweller's loupe. Using the handheld magnifier, he examined the find once more, flipping it over to check both sides. It was in remarkably good condition, even covered in dirt as it was. Using the toothbrush, Cam began to gently brush the item, the soft bristles following the grooves on the convex side of the find. Swapping the toothbrush for the toothpick, he scraped the underside, loosening the worst of the lump of dirt that had filled the little hollow. It would need a proper clean in the conservation lab, but he'd done enough for now to confirm his first impression. He placed it on the cloth then held it out to show Miss Travers.

'It's a seashell,' she said, voice filled with wonder.

'A scallop shell,' he clarified. 'It's a pilgrim badge, a symbol of St James the Apostle.'

'A badge?'

Cam nodded. 'See the little loop at the top? It would be pinned to a cap or threaded onto a piece of leather and worn around the neck.' He looked up at Miss Travers once more. 'Where did you find it?'

'At home. On a construction site.' She reached for the badge. 'Can I have another look now it's clean?'

He wanted to say no, but he didn't want to risk putting her back up before he knew more about where she'd found it. 'Sure, but probably best to keep it on the cloth. It's made of lead, so you should wash your hands before you eat or drink anything to be on the safe side. I'll also need to pack it properly before it starts to corrode.' When she opened her palm, Cam extended his to meet it, sliding the cloth across until the badge rested in the centre of her hand. The tips of their fingers grazed in the process and Cam found himself curling his hand closed as though he could somehow trap the sensation.

'You said you found it at home, Miss Travers?' he prompted, watching as she turned her hand this way and that, her gaze transfixed on the little shell.

'Please, call me Hope, and yes, I found it on the grounds. I live at Juniper Meadows.' She said it like he was supposed to recognise the name. When he didn't respond, she lifted her eyes to meet his, her lips curled into a smile. 'I suppose someone in your field might recognise its more formal name – Stourton Hall.'

'Stourton Hall?' Cam rocked back in his seat at her mention of one of the finest examples of Jacobean architecture in the region. It wasn't his particular speciality, his personal and research interest being ecclesiastical buildings, but he knew Barnie would chew his own arm off at the chance to have a nose around the Hall. Miss Travers – Hope – had travelled at least a couple of hours to see him that morning. Well, to see someone from the department, he mentally corrected himself because she hadn't come to visit him specifically. The Hall was part of a massive country estate, one of the largest in the area still in private hands. He'd grown up on a very different kind of estate in a little two-up, two-down council house on the outskirts of York. Unless Hope was an employee, she might well be an aristocrat of some description. 'You live at Stourton Hall?'

Hope laughed. 'Not exactly. My family decamped from there when it was refurbished, a few years before I was born. We live in the estate farmhouse and the Hall is a hotel and spa. My uncle thought Stourton Hall sounded a bit stuffy and old-fashioned, so he rebranded when we opened to the public.'

'Juniper Meadows,' Cam said, connecting the dots. He had to agree that it sounded more inviting. Making a mental note to do a bit of research later, he turned the conversation back to his original question. 'You mentioned refurbishments, is that how you found the badge?'

Hope set the badge and cloth down on his desk and sat back in her chair. 'Yes. Well, not exactly. I didn't find it at the Hall.' She laughed. 'Technically, I didn't find it at all, my contractors did. I'm having a house built, you see.'

Not sure he did see, Cam made a non-committal sound and gestured for her to continue.

'It's a bit crowded at the farm and I wanted my own little place. There's a spot I love on the estate with an old oak tree and the chapel ruins. It's out of the way of everything else and I thought it would be the perfect site.'

'Chapel?' Cam sat up at that, his interested piqued.

Hope shrugged. 'Well, that's what I've been told it was, it's now just a few jumbled stones that are mostly overgrown.' She sighed. 'The plot I chose for the house was well away from both the oak tree and the ruins, but not far enough away, apparently.'

Cam held his hand up, thoroughly confused now. 'You found the badge at the chapel ruins?'

Hope shook her head. 'No. I found it at the other ruins, or perhaps it's the same ruins, how should I know? The digger hit something within the first couple of scoops, and the crew stopped work immediately.'

At the mention of other ruins, Cam felt a familiar sense of excitement building inside him. 'I don't suppose you took any photographs of the site?'

'Oh, yes, sorry, that's the first thing I should've shown you!' Looking a touch embarrassed, Hope leaned forward in the chair and pulled her phone out from the back pocket of her jeans. 'Sorry, this whole thing has completely thrown me for a loop. Declan said if we were lucky, it might just be a dumping ground for a few spare stones left over from when the chapel was built.'

'It could be,' Cam said in the most neutral tone he could manage. On the one hand, it would be a relief to Hope if it was just a handful of stray stones so she could get on with her house-building project. On the other hand... 'I can't promise I'll be able to tell anything just from the pictures,' he warned her.

'No, of course not, but you'll surely have a better idea than I do of what we might be dealing with.' She passed him the handset with a rueful grin. 'It just looks like a jumble of old rubbish to me, but perhaps that's wishful thinking on my part.'

The second he laid eyes on the first image, he knew her wish wasn't going to come true. He remained silent, though, taking his time to study each of the dozen images, making sure he wasn't letting his own desire for it to be something of interest unduly influence his opinion. 'And whereabouts did you find the badge?'

Hope reached forward and scrolled back through the images to one he hadn't seen before. It showed the layout of the construction site before the ground had been disturbed. She tapped a finger on a large yellow skip sitting on the far side of the site. 'I don't know exactly. One of the guys spotted it sticking out of the top of the discarded soil.' She gave him an apologetic glance. 'He'd already climbed in and fished it out before I knew anything about it, so I don't have a photo of it in situ.'

Cam gave her a reassuring smile. 'It's not your fault, and if it was sitting in the soil pile, then it would be impossible to tell where it had come from.' He pressed the home button on the phone to close the photo app, an automatic action on his part. He was about to hand it back to her when he noticed the home screen image. It was Hope and a man he guessed to be around the same age. They were grinning into the camera, each clutching an enormous ice cream, their eyes shielded behind sunglasses. The dark-haired man had an arm slung casually around her shoulders. He passed the phone back to her, trying to ignore a pang of regret. Of course someone this pretty was going to have a boyfriend.

'So, what's the verdict?' she asked, having tucked her phone away. When he remained silent, the corners of her mouth slipped down and he hated that he was the one who had chased away that pretty, sunny smile. 'I'm not going to be able to go ahead, am I?'

Cam shook his head. 'Someone will need to come out to site and have a proper look, but it's definitely going to need some further investigation.' He reached into his desk drawer and retrieved the battered organiser he kept all his contacts in. He pulled out a slightly dog-eared card and slid it across the desk to her. 'This is the number of the county archaeologist. He'll be able to advise you further and put you in touch with someone who can carry out a site survey. They'll also need to do a desk survey and search through any archival records your family might have related to the estate. Do you know if you have anything like that?'

Hope looked nonplussed for a moment. 'Well, I'm sure we do, but I'll have to ask my uncle where they are.' She stared at the card on his desk for a long moment, then back up at him. 'Dr Ferguson... *Cam*, I, umm, I rather thought that you might be able to take a look for me.' She glanced back over her shoulder towards his open office door. 'Mrs Cotteridge suggested as much, but obviously I got the wrong end of the stick.' She stood, ignoring the business card as she reached for the badge that was still resting on the cleaning cloth.

She looked so disappointed, and honestly, Cam couldn't blame her. It would likely take the county archaeologist weeks to get around to looking at her case. Not for want of effort, but because, like so many other public sector resources, his department had been cut to the bone. As her fingers touched the badge, Cam found himself placing his hand atop hers, holding it in place. When her eyes met his, there was the slightest flare of her pupils, the black widening to swallow the inner edge of the vibrant blue of her irises.

'I have some time this weekend,' he found himself saying, ignoring the weight of all those unwritten end-of-term reports. 'I can at least take a look and try to determine if there really is a need for further investigation.'

4

'She definitely said to turn left at the previous junction,' Barnie said as he turned in his seat to look back the way they'd just come.

The 'she' in question was the sat nav and this wasn't the first time it'd sent them in the wrong direction. The overgrown hedgerows loomed closer to the car and Cam tapped the brake, easing their already slow speed down to below thirty. 'Keep your eyes peeled for somewhere we can turn around,' he muttered. Beyond the hedgerows, it was agricultural land as far as the eye could see. If they encountered a tractor around one of these blind bends, they were done for.

Beside him, Barnie was fiddling with his phone. 'No signal, of course,' his friend sighed as he held the phone up towards the window as though he could coax a bar or two to appear. 'Who lives where there's no 4G, anyway?'

'No one, by the looks of it,' Cam observed dryly as he surveyed the open fields around them before turning his attention back to the road. They rounded the corner and were almost plunged into darkness as hedgerows gave way to an avenue of tall trees. The branches on either side curled over the road, the canopy all but blocking out the sun. Cam shoved his sunglasses up on his head, blinking to adjust his eyes to the abrupt change in the light. The trees stretched on and on, one of those stray patches of ancient woodland that had somehow survived when everything else around had been cleared for farmland. Cam glanced down at the sat nav and groaned. The screen was blank apart from two words: NO SIGNAL. There wasn't much he could do about that now. They'd have to hope the tree cover cleared and they could pick up a signal again. As he drove through the dappled light, Cam gave up looking for a turning spot and just focused on the road ahead. It had to lead somewhere, eventually.

After what seemed like forever, but was probably less than a couple of miles, the wooded area ended as abruptly as it started, and Barnie raised a hand to point in front of him. 'A spire! Over there on the left. Civilisation!' He made it sound as though they'd been navigating through the heart of the Amazon rather than meandering along a country road for a few miles.

'Looks like I won't have to eat you to survive,' Cam said with a wry laugh.

'Not if that pub does some decent grub,' Barnie replied with a grin, pointing ahead of them again.

Cam rolled up to the junction and stopped. There was no traffic behind them, so he took his time to look around and try to get their bearings. The lane appeared to have led them into the heart of a village, complete with chocolate box cottages. With their honey-coloured stone walls, lichen-stained tiled roofs and gardens brimming with rose bushes, lilac trees and hollyhocks, it looked more like the set of a Sunday evening television show than a real place. A pub stood a short distance from the row of cottages. Well, it more sprawled than sat, the original structure having been extended on both sides over the years. The Stourton Arms, proclaimed the long black sign with gold text over the front porch of the pub. A smaller sign to the right of the door promised local ales, good food and a warm welcome. When she'd given him the postcode, Hope had mention that Stourton-in-the-Vale was the village closest to the Juniper Meadows estate. It didn't take Sherlock Holmes to work out that this had to be the village pub – or at least one of them. 'Looks like we're in the right place. We can't be far from the estate, so we can pop in for a spot of dinner on the way home.'

'We could have a little sampler now,' Barnie said, voice hopeful. 'For quality control purposes.'

'And turn up at Juniper Meadows with you half-cut? What kind of an impression would that make?'

'The right one?' Barnie grinned, not in the least bit apologetic. As he stared at Cam, the grin turned into something sly. 'What kind of an impression were *you* hoping to make? Or should I say, is there someone in particular you're hoping to make an impression on?'

The gleam in his eyes made Cam want to squirm in his seat. 'We're going to offer our professional opinion to the Travers family, so please, try to remember that you are capable of behaving like a professional.'

Trying to ignore Barnie's laughter, Cam focused on the task in hand. The main road through the village looked a lot wider than the country lane they'd approached from, much to his relief. Glancing left and then right, he searched in vain for a signpost that might give him a hint of which direction he should go. The sat nav had woken up and was indicating he should turn right, but he didn't have much faith in the blasted thing. 'Left or right?' he asked Barnie.

'The sat nav says right, so given how useless it's been so far, I say left towards where we saw the spire. If we can find the church, there's bound to be a signpost nearby, or at least someone to help with directions.'

Cam gave the sat nav screen one last look then tugged the connector out of the socket. 'Left it is, then.'

There was no traffic so they were able to edge through the village at little more than a crawl, giving them both time to have a good nose around. To their left stood a row of shops. To Cam's surprise, there was a family butcher, an independent greengrocer and a village store. Round where he lived, the only shop was a late-night convenience store that sold mostly booze and junk food. The Cotswold stone buildings all had what looked like their original wooden windows and there was no sign of the ubiquitous chain logos which had crept into most places. Beyond the village store was a café, the blackboard on the pavement outside advertising afternoon cream teas.

'I could just nip in and ask for directions,' Barnie said, fooling no one about what was really on his mind. Honestly, for a man who seemed to be ruled by his stomach, Barnie had no right to be in such decent shape.

'Or we could ask this chap who's just come out of the village store,' Cam pointed out.

'Spoilsport.' Barnie lowered his window. 'Hello! Excuse me? Can you help us with some directions?'

The man paused in the act of untying the lead of a small terrier from a little rail outside the shop and looked up with a smile. 'Hello! Hello! Lovely morning for it, hey?'

Cam wasn't sure what it was a lovely morning for, but he gave the man an encouraging smile as he leaned his head towards Barnie's so they could both look up through the open window. 'We're trying to find Stourton Hall. Do you know where it is?'

The man threw his head back and roared with laughter as though Cam had made the funniest joke in a year. 'Know where it is?' he sputtered through tears of mirth. 'Goodness, lad, I can tell you're not from around here. Know where it is, indeed.' He muttered the last almost to himself.

Cam cast a quick glance at Barnie, who gave him a nope-no-idea-what's-going-on smile. 'We have an appointment with Miss Travers and our sat nav sent us on something of a magical mystery tour,' Cam said to the man, who continued to chuckle to himself. 'We... er, we don't want to be late.'

'I should think not,' the man said. 'Wouldn't do to keep Miss Hope waiting, no, not at all.' The man turned away and untied his dog's lead from the rail.

'Stourton Hall?' Barnie prompted and though his tone was polite, Cam knew him well enough to catch the impatient edge to it.

'Why are folks always in such a rush, Paddy?' The man tutted as he leaned down to straighten the dog's collar. Perhaps he'd caught the edge in Barnie's voice as well. Paddy – well, Cam assumed that was the dog's name – gave a little bark as though in agreement. When he'd finally finished fussing with the dog's lead and adjusted the newspaper under his arm (and Cam had ground his back teeth until his jaw ached), the man turned back to face them. Raising his hand, he pointed in the direction the car was facing.

'You'll need to turn around, so best thing to do is head up that way until you see the village green then do a circuit of it. When you get back to the road, just keep going straight, you can't miss it. Come along, Paddy.' With a click of his tongue, the man led the little dog away.

Barnie pressed a finger to the button to raise his window, waiting until it'd finished closing before he turned in his seat to look at Cam. 'Ask him for help, you said. Better than the sat nav, you said.'

They looked at each other a moment before they burst out laughing. 'Round the village green it is,' Cam said as he put the car in gear and pulled away from the kerb. The circuit took them past more cottages with immaculate gardens and Cam felt a twinge of envy. He could barely keep a pot plant alive, and no one was putting pretty tubs of plants out the front of the utilitarian block of flats he lived in – not unless they wanted to provide a free urinal for the students on their way home from the city centre pubs. Stourton-in-the-Vale looked like an advert for one of those Best Kept Village competitions.

Barnie pressed his face to his window as they drove past the Stourton Arms for the second time. 'We could've popped in there for a half and not lost any time.'

He sounded so forlorn, Cam couldn't help but laugh. 'Did I mention that Hope is the operations manager for their family gin distillery? Maybe they'll have some samples.'

As he'd suspected, that cheered Barnie right up. 'Why didn't you say so before? An ice-cold G&T could be just what the doctor ordered.' He turned to beam at Cam. 'Lucky we're both doctors, eh?'

Cam was saved from responding to the terrible gag by the sight of a huge sign on the side of the road declaring 'Juniper Meadows Next Right'. Each corner of the sign was decorated with the same purple berry and twig logo as the one on the business card Hope had left with him.

Barnie looked from the sign to Cam and back again in a double-take worthy of a cartoon. 'Juniper Meadows!'

Cam shot him a confused look before he focused on the road. 'I told you that's what the family called the estate, didn't I?' There was another white sign in the distance and Cam sped up a little, relieved they were almost there.

'No, because if you had, I would've been even more keen to accompany you on this trip! Juniper Meadows is one of the best brands of artisan gin on the market. I can't believe I didn't make the connection immediately when you mentioned the family run a distillery.' Barnie snorted. 'Why am I even bothering when I'm speaking to man who stocks his drinks cabinet with supermarket own-brands?'

'That brandy I got for a tenner was pretty smooth,' Cam protested as he indicated then steered the car onto the wide gravel driveway.

'Only if scraping your throat with sandpaper is your idea of smooth!' Barnie said with a grin.

'It wasn't that bad,' Cam grumbled. It wasn't that he was tight with his money, he'd just never escaped the mindset of not spending more than you needed to. His parents had worked hard to provide for Cam and his younger sister, Nora. There had always been food on the table, and they'd never had to forego necessities, but no one would ever have described the Ferguson family as being well off. Holidays had been in a caravan on the coast and most of the tins in the cupboard had supermarket value labels on them.

When he thought about his childhood, Cam never remembered feeling jealous of his friends who got to jet off to Spain or Florida during the school holidays, though he was sure there were times when he'd wished his dad had a better car, or he had access to the latest computer games console. His abiding memories were filled with the sound of his mother's laughter, of chasing his sister along the beach and helping her build her first sandcastle. Though his university salary paid enough for Cam to have built up a nice little savings nest egg, he'd never got over the lesson of making his money stretch as far as possible.

They turned off and the road instantly narrowed. Recalling the winding route through the wood, Cam hoped they weren't about to embark on another mystery tour of the Cotswold countryside. Trees lined the road, but they were spaced out in a more uniform manner, as though deliberately planted rather than the wild spread of nature. The road sloped upwards and, as they crested the top of the hill, Cam's foot found the brake without any conscious thought at the view laid out before them. A high stone wall stretched in both directions as far as the eye could see.

An impressive stone archway stood over the road, set with an enormous pair of wrought-iron gates. The gates stood open and framed in the far distance was what must be Stourton Hall, the golden honey stones of its edifice glowing almost white in the sunshine. 'Wow,' Barnie murmured. 'That's one hell of a view.'

Cam started forward, the smooth tarmac beneath the car's wheels giving way to the crunch of a broad gravel driveway. Although there were no other vehicles in sight, Cam stuck to the left-hand side and kept his speed low. His car wasn't new by any stretch of the imagination, but he still took good care of it and didn't want to risk dinging the paintwork. The driveway wound through an expanse of open parkland dotted with enormous trees. The width of their trunks spoke of their age and Cam doubted he and Barnie could span the largest ones with their arms joined. A glistening thread of blue snaked along the edge of the parkland, something between a stream and a river, and a large expanse of water sparkled to the left of the Hall, an ornamental lake, perhaps?

As he followed the road, the Hall disappeared from sight. Whoever had laid the route hadn't been a fan of straight lines. They turned another bend and were faced with a crossroads. Left was signposted Juniper Meadows Hotel and Spa and Cam recalled Hope's reference to that being what the Hall was used for now. The sign pointing right was for the distillery and something called The Old Stable Yard. Hope had said she'd be working and would meet them in the car park by the distillery, so Cam headed right.

To his surprise, the car park was huge, with enough room for at least a couple of hundred cars, he reckoned, based on how many were parked there already and how much empty space was still available. He slotted in at the end of the third row and he and Barnie got out. In front of the car park was a large courtyard filled with people wandering in all directions between the collection of buildings that surrounded three sides of it. The row on the left had signs for a shop and a café. There were smaller signs over several open doorways along the back of the courtyard, but they were too far away for him to make out what each one was. A taller building filled the right-hand side, a pair of large arched doors indicating it might once have been a carriage house, though now it housed the distillery. Cam took out his phone and searched through his contacts for the number Hope had given him. It rang a couple of times before her mellow voice filled his ear. 'Hope Travers.'

'Hope, hi, it's Dr Ferguson, uh, I mean Cam. From the university. We're here. Outside. In the car park.' God, it was like he'd forgotten how to speak in proper sentences. He risked a quick glance at Barnie, then wished to hell he hadn't bothered because his so-called friend was grinning like a loon, clearly enjoying Cam's discomfort.

'Oh, you found us okay, then? I wondered if you would because sat navs get a bit confused with all the little local roads. We say on the website to stay on the main road until you see the signs for the estate, but I forgot to mention that when I saw you the other day.'

Cam laughed. 'That was definitely information we could've done with, but we made it in one piece with the help of someone in the village.'

'Great! Well, as long as you made it, that's the main thing. Look, I know we said we'd meet at eleven but Zap's having a meltdown over a dodgy batch of rose petals and I need to speak to the supplier and get it sorted out. The café's open and they do a lovely lemon drizzle cake, or you could have a browse around the workshops if you prefer.' She sounded tired, and a bit flustered.

'Take your time, we've got all day,' Cam reassured her.

'We?'

'Yes. I brought a colleague of mine along for a second opinion. I hope you don't mind?' Cam began to worry that perhaps he should've mentioned it earlier.

'Oh, not at all! Honestly, the more the merrier if it means we can get to the bottom of things. Damn, that's the supplier on the other line. I'll be with you as soon as I can.' The phone went dead before he could reply.

'Everything all right?' Barnie asked, his earlier smirk replaced by a frown of concern.

'Yeah, fine. Hope's got to sort out a problem, something to do with someone called Zap and some rose petals.'

'What kind of a name is Zap?'

Cam shrugged. 'No idea, mate. What I do know is that Hope said we should check out the lemon drizzle cake in the café and she'll meet us in there when she's ready.'

Barnie slung an arm around his shoulders. 'Well, this day just gets better and better.'

5

Having extracted an apology from the supplier and a promise to replace the faulty batch of petals with a new delivery first thing on Monday morning, Hope let herself out of the side door of the distillery and made sure to lock it behind her. Even with a 'Private – No Entry' sign on the door, they'd had a curious visitor or two poking around where they shouldn't be on more than one occasion.

Tucking her keys away, Hope reached up and tugged the band from her hair, quickly smoothing the wisps that had escaped and refastened her ponytail high on her head so only the end of it brushed her shoulders. She smoothed the front of her fuchsia-pink Juniper Meadows branded polo shirt, then wondered why she was fussing over her appearance. Cameron Ferguson was here to give the remains she'd found the once over, not her. Heat suddenly suffused her cheeks at the realisation she wouldn't mind if he did.

Where had that come from?

Sure, he was attractive if tall, blond and bookish was one's type. Okay, yes, that *was* definitely her type, but it still didn't explain why she'd caught herself staring into space on several occasions over the past few days thinking about the slightly roughened touch of his skin as he'd covered her hand with his own. She was being ridiculous. She'd just been on her own for too long and had grown unused to physical contact.

Her previous relationship – if you could call three months of twice-weekly dinners occasionally followed by some rather disappointing sex a relationship – had ended on Valentine's Day. Rupert had promised her a romantic, candle-lit supper, only he'd left it too late to book anywhere decent and they'd ended up in a Wetherspoons around the corner from his flat. To add insult to his choice of a chicken vindaloo, he'd started bleating on about her not having time to see to his needs properly when she'd taken an urgent phone call about work. Rising from the table, Hope had dropped her napkin next to her half-eaten chicken korma and told him in her sweetest voice that it was very difficult to see to anyone's needs properly in under three minutes and walked out.

'You need to get laid,' Hope muttered to herself as she wove her way across the busy courtyard towards the café. 'And by a man who knows what he's doing.'

'I beg your pardon?' A woman Hope supposed was around the same age as her mother swung around to give her a shocked glare.

'I said a couple of these cobbles need to be re-laid,' Hope said, scuffing her boot over one of the tightly packed stones. 'There's always maintenance that needs doing.' Hope tapped the company logo on her shirt and hoped her face wasn't as pink as her top.

The woman was suddenly all smiles. 'That's why we love coming here – the staff are always so conscientious. I hope your boss appreciates you!'

Thinking about Zap sulking in his little office tucked behind the main distillery tanks, Hope rather doubted it. She decided it was probably best to keep that to herself, though, and opted for a diplomatic answer. 'Thank you, we do our best.' With a quick smile at the woman, Hope hurried away before she could get herself into any more trouble.

The café was busy, but it wasn't hard to pick out Cam. Even seated, he was taller than most of the other visitors. He must've been watching the door for her arrival as he was rising from his seat before she even had chance to wave hello. He was dressed a little more casually than he'd been in his office – a checked shirt open over a black T-shirt and jeans that looked as well-worn as her own. Hope wove quickly between the busy tables and stopped in front of him. 'Hello, I'm so sorry I kept you waiting.'

'It's fine, not a problem. I was worried that I was going to keep you waiting!' They laughed, with only a touch of awkwardness.

'No one seems to mind if I was kept waiting,' a voice drawled from behind her, and Hope spun around, face flushing as the second man at the table also rose to his feet. Goodness, was it a prerequisite of the university's department of archaeology that everyone who worked there had to be good-looking? Though he wasn't as tall as Cam, the dark-haired man was broad through the shoulders and chest. Dressed in a similarly casual outfit, the sleeves of his shirt were folded up high enough to display a glimpse of a pair of impressive biceps.

'This is Barnie,' Cam said. 'He thinks he's funny.' Hope swung back in time to see him shooting a glare at his colleague.

'Dr Barnard.' The dark-haired man extended a large hand towards her. 'But you can call me Barnie as I'm already sure we're going to be very good friends.'

Hope shook his hand, trying not to smile when he held it for a fraction longer than necessary. Dr Barnard was nothing if not a very practised flirt. 'It's a pleasure to meet you, Barnie, and I am very sorry to have kept you waiting.' She did smile then. Her very best client-charming smile and didn't miss the teasing glint in Barnie's eye.

'You didn't keep anyone waiting,' Cam insisted. 'Please, have a seat.' He'd actually moved around the table to hold the back of the empty chair next to him. Brownie points for that, Hope thought as she sat down. Some women might baulk at such behaviour, deeming it sexist or old-fashioned, but Hope attributed it to good manners. Her cousin Rhys would do the same. 'Can I get you a coffee?' Cam asked.

A shot of caffeine sounded like just what she needed, but she was conscious of the time. 'Don't you want to get to the site?'

'Oh, we've loads of time for that,' Barnie said, his tone breezy as he raised a hand. 'And I for one could do with another slice of that delectable lemon drizzle cake.' He directed the last comment at Sandra, one of the staff who'd approached at his wave.

'I made that one myself,' Sandra said, with a smile as she pulled her notepad and pencil out of the pocket of her apron. 'Do you want another cappuccino to go with it?'

'You made it? Then I insist you marry me at once!' Barnie pressed his hands to his heart.

'Well, if I wasn't old enough to be your mother and a lesbian to boot, then I'd consider that the best offer I've had today.'

The rebuff didn't stop Barnie for a second. 'Well, I'll just have to settle for the cake then. Your partner is a very lucky woman.'

'Yes, she is, and I make sure to tell her that every day.' Sandra turned to the rest of them. 'Same for everyone, is it? Oh, hello, Hope! I didn't realise these gentlemen were guests of yours.'

Spotting a hint of panic in Sandra's eyes, Hope leaned on her elbows and gave her a conspiratorial smile. 'No lemon drizzle for me, but I will take a sliver of black forest gateau if there's any left.'

Sandra beamed back at her, all traces of worry wiped away. 'Penny's already put a slice by for you. I was going to pop it over later, but you've saved me a walk.' She glanced around as though missing something. 'Where are the boys?'

'I left them with Zap. He's taking them and Hercule for a long walk. Hopefully he'll come back in a better temper.' A tromp around the woods with the three dogs in tow would hopefully help him clear his head.

Sandra smiled. 'I've baked some biscuits for them. I'll drop in on Zap later with an extra-large latte and some shortbread, that should cheer him up.' She turned to Cam. 'And what can I get for you, dear?'

'Just a coffee, thanks, Sandra.'

The woman glowed at the fact he'd taken the trouble to read her name badge. 'Coming right up.'

As she walked away, Cam turned to Hope with an odd look on his face. 'If you have a childcare issue, we can do this on another day.'

What on earth was he talking about? 'It's hard to have childcare issues when you don't have children,' she said with a laugh.

He shot a quick puzzled glance over his shoulder towards Sandra's retreating back. 'But when Sandra mentioned your boys, you said Zap has taken them for a walk. I just thought, given you mentioned him being stressed out about a supplier problem and everything, that he might not be in the best frame of mind for looking after them.'

Hope giggled. He'd clearly put two and two together and made babies. 'Oh, goodness, I can see why you might be confused. The boys in question are two very unruly puppies I made the mistake of adopting earlier this year.' She shook her head. 'I didn't mean that – I wouldn't be without them even if they are a bit of a handful.'

Cam had gone bright red, his distress palpable as he began to stutter out an apology. 'I... I'm so sorry! I shouldn't have assumed...'

Hope found herself reaching out to cover his hand with her own. 'It's really not a problem,' she promised. 'Like I said, I can understand where the confusion might have come from.'

He shifted in his seat, still clearly uncomfortable. 'Still, it wasn't appropriate of me to speculate.'

Barnie leaned forward. 'Tell us a bit about the set-up here at The Old Stable Yard. How did the workshops come about?'

From the quiet sigh of relief beside her, Hope could tell she wasn't the only one who was grateful for the timely intervention. This felt like much safer ground than her personal life and she was so proud of what they were achieving on the estate. She could wax lyrical about it for hours. 'My uncle, Ziggy, came up with the idea. He was looking at innovative ways to provide employment for the local community, but wanted to offer something more than service jobs, which is of course a large part of running an estate like this.' Hope paused as Sandra approached and set down their drinks and two slices of cake. 'I said a sliver,' she admonished Sandra fondly when what could only be described as a slab of black forest gateau was put in front of her.

'I know you won't stop for lunch today. You'll be wasting away at this rate.' Sandra patted her shoulder before moving off to serve another table. Hope twitched her lips at the comment. A skipped meal here and there wasn't going to do her any harm. She wasn't bothered about the shape of her body, had come to terms with the fact she would never squeeze her bottom into a pair of size twelve jeans and had embraced it. She got plenty of exercise. It was impossible to work somewhere as large as Juniper Meadows and not spend half your time on your feet. Although the distillery was her primary responsibility, she was the one Ziggy tended to call upon when he needed something sorting out. Rhys couldn't leave the animals on the farm to look after themselves, and Rowena and her mother had their hands full with the day-to-day running of the hotel and spa. Zap had to keep an eye on his latest brewing batch. Hope could take her phone – and therefore her office – anywhere.

Noting there were two forks on her plate, Hope took one and used it to cut the slice in half before pushing the plate between her and Cam. 'Help me out?'

He hesitated a moment before picking up the other fork and taking a piece. 'It'd be rude not to.' He closed his eyes as the first hit of rich chocolate reached his taste buds. 'Oh, wow,' he mumbled around the delicious mouthful. 'That's bloody fantastic.'

'And one of the reasons I'm never going to be a catwalk model,' Hope said with a wry grin as she forked up a piece for herself.

'You look great just the way you are,' Cam said, his gaze fixed on hers.

Okay, she was going to file that away to think about later. Breaking eye contact, Hope looked towards Barnie. Yes, he was handsome, but he didn't have that same level of quiet intensity that made her feel a little too aware of herself that Cam did. 'As I was saying, my uncle—'

'What is it with the names in your family?' Cam interjected, instantly drawing her attention back to him. Not that she minded an excuse to look at him again. 'You said he was called Ziggy, right?' Cam continued. 'And you mentioned someone called Zap was having a problem in the distillery...'

Hope laughed. It never took people long to ask. 'My grandparents are a little eccentric, part of the tune-in, drop-out generation. They named my mother and her brothers after their favourite musicians – Stevie, Zappa, Ziggy and Dylan.'

'Ah, parents and their penchant for unusual names.'

There was a touch of something dark in Barnie's tone, not bitter exactly, but a definite edge that seemed out of place from his usually light-hearted demeanour. Hope cast a questioning look towards Cam, who mouthed, 'Later,' before saying out loud, 'You were saying about your uncle wanting to create better jobs for people?'

Hope gave him a grateful smile. 'Oh, yes. As I said, a place as large as this needs a lot of help in general supporting roles – cleaners, groundskeepers and what have you, and plenty of people are happy with those as we give them flexible working hours so they can fit them in around other responsibilities. But Ziggy wanted to do more, so he set up a bursary programme so local people can have the financial support they need to study something that interests them which can also benefit the estate in the longer term. We don't force people to work here afterwards, but we ask them to consider it. Most of the therapists who work at the spa have come through the programme, for example. We've got a trainee accountant, who supports Ziggy in the estate office. She is studying through day release to college.'

'That's very generous of your family,' Cam said as he took another piece of cake.

Hope shrugged. 'We couldn't survive without the support of the local community and we ask a lot from them, particularly when we put big events on that bring a lot of traffic to the area.' She picked up her coffee and took a sip, trying not to think about how much there was left to sort out before they had a handle on the sound and light show planned for the late summer bank holiday. It wasn't on her to-do list today. Her top priority was to find out what her building contractors had uncovered and how much of a problem it was going to cause to her plans. Raising her cup once more, she drained the rest of her drink. 'If you're ready, I'll take you to the worksite now.'

The two men scrambled up, Barnie stuffing a last bite of lemon drizzle into his mouth. 'Ready when you are,' was his slightly cake-muffled response.

Hope led the way out of the café. 'It'll probably be easier if you leave your car here. I'll drop you back when we're finished if that's okay?'

'Sure, whatever you think. I've just got a few things I need to grab from the boot,' Cam said, pulling out a set of keys.

She followed them to the visitor car park where Cam unlocked an old hatchback. He and Barnie rummaged in the back and when they straightened up, they were both holding well-worn rucksacks. Barnie plonked a battered leather hat on his head, the style more than a little reminiscent of the fedora favoured by Indiana Jones. Hope resisted the urge to point it out and instead gestured towards the distillery. 'I'm parked around the back there.'

They followed her around the side of the distillery, through the padlocked gate marked 'staff only' and over to a pair of matching Range Rovers. Hope pointed her key fob and unlocked the one on the left, heaving herself up into the raised driver's seat and leaving it to them to sort out who would join her in the front. She hid a smile when Cam opened the door beside her and climbed into the passenger seat with a lot more ease than she had just managed.

A service road connected the private car park to the main estate road and when Hope approached the simple barrier, Cam was already unfastening his seat belt. It was certainly much easier to negotiate the route with helpful passengers on board and she gave him a smile of thanks when he climbed back in. 'The gates are a pain, but they're enough of a deterrent to keep people to the spaces open to the public,' she explained. It didn't stop everyone, however. Even though they offered a space for people to camp and hard standing for a dozen caravans or campervans, they still found a few waifs and strays who'd decided to try and set up elsewhere. The groundskeepers had a handful of quad bikes which they used to patrol the likely spots. She pointed out the road that led to the camping grounds as they passed.

'I'm surprised there's a demand for camping with the hotel,' Barnie observed from the back seat.

'We try to offer something for every budget. The hotel is definitely aimed at the luxury end of the market. We offer day passes for the spa to anyone who camps, though, and Rhys is working on a plan to expand the camping side of things into the glamping market to cater for people who want the option to self-cater but want something special.' Hope followed a bend in the road then pulled over to the side to let them take in the full majesty of their first proper view of the Hall. 'There she is.' Hope couldn't keep the note of pride out of her voice. They might not live there any more, but she felt the pull of connection to the place nonetheless. Her history was here – in every brick and every stone as much as beneath the elaborate mausoleums and wall crypts in the family chapel and graveyard which were tucked behind the ornamental gardens at the rear.

'A grand old lady,' Cam said, earning himself a smile. He understood. It wasn't just a building, the Hall was a living entity, deserving of admiration and respect.

'I'll take you for a tour some other time, if you like?' she offered.

His face lit up. 'Yeah? I'd love that.'

'I'd love that, too,' Barnie said, leaning forward between their seats. 'Assuming the invitation extends to me as well, of course.'

'Of course!' Hope blurted, though, if she was honest, she'd forgotten he was there for a minute as she and Cam had shared that moment of reverent appreciation. 'Right, let's get over to the ruins, shall we?'

6

The ruins turned out to be the remains of two connected walls. The larger stood around waist height and extended about twenty feet. The shorter part of the corner ranged little more than a couple of feet and half a dozen stones high. The uneven ground around spoke of more remains beneath the turf, or perhaps the roots of the old oak. The location near the river suggested the site had been chosen to provide access to fresh water. Nothing about it screamed ecclesiastical to Cam, but there wasn't enough visible to make a snap judgement.

Cam pulled a laser measure from his rucksack and aimed it from his spot in the centre of the ruins towards a marker left by the construction team that was close to the open excavation. If the stones there were part of the same building, or even the same complex, then it was a site of some status. 'And you're sure this was the original chapel?' It was a long way from the Hall and the quick glimpse he'd caught of the current chapel as they'd driven past had looked of a similar age and design to the imposing building. Why would they need a second, separate chapel, unless there was an older house predating the Hall? A familiar buzz of excitement started in his mind, that tantalising feeling he always got when he knew he was on the trail of something.

Hope shrugged. 'I'm not sure of anything. We've just always called it the church or the chapel.'

Cam's head snapped up at that. 'The church or the chapel, which one is it?'

She gave him another confused lift of her shoulders. 'Aren't they the same thing?'

Reminding himself that not everyone was a history geek with a side interest in religious buildings which some might consider obsessional, Cam reined in his impatience and smiled. 'Sometimes, sometimes not. Let's have a look at these stones you found.'

As they made their way to the excavation site, Cam silently counted off the paces he took, mentally verifying the laser measurement reading. The ground here was much flatter than that around the chapel, an open expanse of meadow that extended between the riverbank to the east and the woods to the west. He could see why the spot had appealed to Hope.

The contractors had left a set of barriers around the hole, but they were easy enough to shift to the side. Dropping his rucksack down beside him, Cam went down on his knees and studied the jumble of stones and dirt. His first thought was they were definitely of an age with the walled remains; his second that they were too uniform to be a natural feature or even a dumping ground for leftover building material. There was something different about the colouration – something not quite right.

Hope crouched down beside him. 'What do you think?'

Not ready to answer yet, Cam pulled a leather tool case from his rucksack and rolled it out. It was a mismatched collection of things he'd put together over the years. The various sized trowels, picks and brushes were mostly courtesy of his local DIY superstore. He selected a narrow pointing trowel and began scraping the loose dirt away from the stones. He'd have to take measurements later, but they appeared smaller than those used in the wall – a floor, perhaps? Whatever he was looking at, the stones were too tightly packed and even to have fallen like this. He spent a few more minutes cleaning the area in front of him. The colour was definitely off. Taking a thin pick from his kit, Cam scraped the corner of one of the stones then raised the tool to examine it. He rubbed the end of the pick between his fingers and noted the black residue, not dirt, more like soot.

Had this been a kitchen, perhaps? Were the stones the remains of a fire pit or an oven of some type?

Cam sat back on his heels. The uncovered area was too small to make a proper judgement. He glanced around him, looking for any features in the landscape that might suggest the presence of more buried walls. Technological advances made a lot of things easier, but so much about his job was about observing the land, getting a feel for the terrain, and ultimately getting down on his hands and knees in the dirt. They'd have to walk the full site and note any features in the landscape. He would also need a proper survey trench, maybe two or three given the size of the area. A geophys survey would be useful...

'I'm not going to be building my house any time soon, am I?'

Hope's quiet question drew Cam back to the reality of the situation. 'It's too early to give you a definite answer,' he hedged, not wanting to upset her. He really needed a second opinion. 'Where's Barnie?' His friend had wandered off as soon as they'd arrived.

He was mostly wondering out loud, but Hope raised a hand and pointed off towards the right to where Barnie was crouched next to the river, a couple of hundred metres away. 'Hey, what was going on with him earlier in the café? He got a bit weird about names and you said you'd tell me later.'

Cam huffed a soft laugh. 'It's a bit of a sore spot for him, personally.'

Hope cocked her head to the side. 'Barnie's not that odd of a name, unless he got fed up of being compared to a big purple dinosaur.'

'Barnie comes from his surname, Barnard. When his mother was pregnant, she had to go on bed rest for a while and developed a mild obsession with Jilly Cooper novels. Barnie's real first name is Lysander, after her favourite character.'

Hope did her best to smother what he was sure was a laugh with a polite cough. 'He doesn't look much like a Lysander.'

Cam grinned at her, not sure he could picture what exactly a Lysander was supposed to look like. 'Don't tell him I've told you, whatever you do. He'll never forgive me.'

Hope made a zipping motion across her lips with her fingers. They watched Barnie in silence as he leaned forward so far Cam worried he might lose his balance and tumble into the river. He dropped back on his haunches and pulled what Cam knew was his sketchpad onto his lap. Head bent, arm whizzing back and forth, Barnie was oblivious to their attention. Hope nudged Cam and raised her fingers, miming unzipping her lips. He couldn't help but laugh at the sweet silliness of it. 'What's he doing?' she asked.

'Barnie's an archaeological surveyor. He takes in the bigger picture, tries to identify natural versus man-made features in the landscape. Anything that catches his eye, he makes a sketch of it and then he tries to find maps or photographs in the archives that match what he's spotted. He's like a bloodhound and always manages to sniff out details other people miss. That's why I asked him to come along today. If anyone can figure out the scale of any settlement here, it'll be him.'

She swung to face him, all sign of her earlier humour gone. 'Settlement? That sounds significant.' A deep frown was etched between her brows, and he could tell the word had sent her mind leaping to all sorts of conclusions.

Damn. He needed to guard his tongue better, not just keep blurting the first thing that came into his head. 'It could be something, or it could be nothing,' he said, trying to sound reassuring. 'Sites of religious worship often date back to beyond the Christian era. The church had a habit of taking over pagan sites. Rivers and streams were often used for offerings and rituals dating back centuries and it may be that's what we have here – a local area of significance that was claimed by an enthusiastic evangelical.'

Hope didn't look convinced. 'Settlement implies something more than that, though. Do you think that people lived here?'

It was Cam's turn to shrug. 'Honestly, it's too early to tell. I was speculating rather than interpreting the data. I should've kept it to myself.'

She straightened her spine. 'No. I'd rather you kept me in the loop right from the start. I don't want you to feel like you need to shield me from anything because you are worried about how I will react. I want to build a home of my own, and yes, this is my preferred location, but I won't risk destroying a piece of my family's history just to suit my own selfish desire.' There was something in the way she said the last couple of words that made him hesitate. She hadn't struck him as being selfish – determined, perhaps, certainly persuasive because hadn't he given up his Sunday to come grubbing around in the dirt for her? It sounded more like she was repeating something someone else had said.

Cam shook his head. Whatever it was, it was none of his business. 'It needs proper analysis but the blackening on these stones looks and feels a lot like soot, so I was wondering if this is the base of a fire pit or some other kind of heating or cooking facility.'

'Which would mean people lived here.' Hope held her hand up when he opened his mouth. 'I know, I know, it's too early to say.' She sighed. 'I knew the moment the digger scraped on these stones that it would be a complication.' Before Cam could offer his sympathies, Hope rolled her shoulders and straightened her spine. 'That's that then.' She turned towards Cam. 'The estate is plenty big enough for me to find somewhere else if I need to. I want you to do a thorough investigation here, not a rush job that risks missing something important. Take all the time you need.'

Cam raised an eyebrow at that. 'Look, I agreed to come here and have a look around and give you my opinion, but that's all. I have a commitment to my students.' Sure, he'd been thinking about test trenches and getting a geophysical survey done, but not with any real seriousness. There was a mystery here to be solved, but it wasn't one he would be unravelling.

Hope put her hands on her hips and cocked her head to one side, a considering expression on her face. 'Isn't it the end of the summer term in a few weeks?'

'Well, yes, but my job doesn't just stop when the students go home.' He didn't tell her he'd planned to take an eight-week sabbatical to tour the Norman churches of the low countries – plans that were now in tatters because his funding application had been turned down. He could still go, of course, but only if he was willing to decimate his savings in the process. 'Besides, it's too short notice to be able to put together a team, never mind paying for it.'

'Paying for it isn't an issue.' There was no arrogance to Hope's statement, it was just a matter of fact to her, and Cam was reminded once again of the gulf between their lives and upbringing. 'I'll have to speak to my uncle, but we have reserves to cover unforeseen contingencies and I'd say this qualifies. If there's something of significance here, then perhaps we can turn it to our future advantage by creating a new attraction to draw more visitors to the estate.'

'You're very practical, aren't you?' Cam meant it as a compliment. He liked the way she took everything in her stride and didn't seem afraid to make decisions. Not that he knew much about things outside his rather sheltered academic existence, but he doubted you became the manager of something like the distillery – even if it was a family business – at Hope's age without having a pragmatic approach to things.

Hope looked at him in surprise. 'What did you expect me to do? Sob into your shoulder because my plans have gone awry?' She shook her head. 'I don't do self-indulgence, I'm afraid.'

'Don't get me wrong,' Cam said, quickly, worried he'd offended her. 'I like it. I wish I could be a bit more decisive myself sometimes.'

Hope sat back, bracing her arms behind her, her toes hanging over the edge of the shallow excavation. 'Well, now's your chance. Come and work for me this summer. Help me figure out what's going on here.'

He wanted to say yes so badly, he could all but taste the word on his tongue. Spending the summer at Juniper Meadows would be no hardship. Having the chance to put together his own team and run a dig was a dream come true, and could be the next step forward in his career – especially if the site turned out to be something significant. He glanced at the woman beside him, feeling once again that instant tug of attraction he'd felt when she'd appeared in his office doorway. The chance to get to know Hope a bit better would be the icing on the cake. She raised her eyebrows, a challenging look in her eyes, and he knew she thought he was going to bottle it and turn her down again.

'Okay. I'll do it.'

'Good.' Hope jumped to her feet and brushed off her jeans. 'Make me a list of what you think you'll need in terms of equipment and accommodation and send it over. I'll speak to my contractors and see if they can help with site clearance. They have the professional skills and training to dig trenches and make sure everything is safe. I'd prefer someone I trust, if that's okay with you?' Cam nodded, slightly stunned at the barrage of words. She was already a dozen steps ahead of him, it seemed. She proved as much when she continued speaking. 'We might as well hang onto the cabins as you'll need welfare facilities. I'll speak to Rhys and see if we can allocate an area of the campsite for you and your team – I assume you'll be wanting to stay on site rather than traipse backwards and forwards every day?' Without waiting for a response, Hope pulled out her phone and started tapping notes. 'I'd better go and speak to Ziggy and get his sign-off, and I'll ask him about the family records while I'm at it as I'm sure you'll want to have a look at those.'

Cam stared up at her, getting the distinct feeling he'd been played. 'Do people always end up doing what you want?'

'Not always.' The grin she gave him suggested otherwise. 'Are you staying here for a while, or do you want me to drop you back at your car?'

Cam put his tools away and stood, hooking his rucksack over his shoulder. If he was really going to do this, then he needed a plan – and fast. There wasn't much more he could do here today. 'I think we'll head back.' He glanced around for Barnie and was relieved to see him already making his way towards them.

'What did I miss?' his friend asked as he lifted his hat long enough to ruffle a hand through his damp hair.

'Cam's coming to work for me for the summer,' Hope replied, that same cat-that-got-the-cream gleam in her eyes.

'Are you now?' Barnie's grin was far too knowing for Cam's liking.

'*We're* coming to work here for the summer,' Cam corrected, delighting in Barnie's shocked expression. Before his friend could come up with an excuse, Cam dangled the bait he knew would get Barnie on board. 'And Hope is going to arrange for us to have full access to the family archives.'

Barnie's face brightened immediately. 'Does that come with a guided tour of the Hall?'

Hope grinned at him. 'You'd probably need to stay there while you are going through them.'

'Hang on a minute,' Cam interjected. '*He* gets to stay in Stourton Hall, and I get a pitch on the campsite?'

'Those are the breaks, my friend,' Barnie said, clapping him on the shoulder. 'Those are the breaks.'

'So what is your family connection to the Hall, exactly?' Barnie asked as Hope was driving them back to collect Cam's car.

Cam caught Hope giving Barnie a puzzled look via the rear-view mirror as she steered them back along the winding estate road. 'What do you mean?'

It was a valid question. What did Barnie mean? Cam tugged his seat belt loose so he could half-turn to face his friend as Barnie elaborated. 'Well, unless I'm mistaken, isn't Stourton Hall named for, well the Stourton family? How do the Travers fit into that mix?'

Hope laughed. 'Ah, I see why you might be confused. We *are* the Stourton family – the Stourton-de-Lacey-Travers if you want to be exact. My grandfather, Montague Stourton-de-Lacey, married Alice Travers and he took her name.' She cast a quick glance between the two of them before she turned her attention back to the road. 'Monty has never been comfortable with his legacy and has done everything he can to distance himself from the rather large silver spoon he was born with. He refuses to use the family title and would've sold the estate off if my uncles and mother hadn't intervened and taken it over.'

Family title. Cam had already thought Hope a lady because of her manner, perhaps he should've considered her more as the Lady of the Manor. He shot a quick look at Barnie – he would probably know the correct terminology.

Hope pulled into the same parking spot behind the distillery and turned off the engine. She unfastened her seat belt and turned to face them, a wry but affectionate smile upon her face. 'The responsibility gene in our lineage definitely skipped a generation with my grandfather.'

Cam released his own seat belt, thinking about everything he had seen that day, how many diverse income streams there seemed to be on the estate and knowing they'd only scratched the surface of what the Travers family did. 'It seems like everything is in safe hands now.'

Hope nodded. 'Ziggy is the glue that holds us all together. Without him, none of this would exist and Stourton Hall would either still be mouldering and neglected or taken over by the National Trust. It's strange, really. He's the one most devoted to the family and yet he's never married or had children. The title will be his when my grandfather passes as he's the older of the twins by all of ten minutes. Unless he has a sudden urge to procreate, it'll pass to my cousin afterwards.' She shook herself, an embarrassed little smile quirking her lips. 'Goodness, you don't need to know the ins and outs of all of that.'

'If you want us to do a thorough job of things, then I'm afraid we'll be rooting around in all your family's secrets.' Cam knew Barnie was making a joke, but he didn't miss the slight flinch from Hope.

'Anyway, if you're sure you are finished for the day, I ought to get back and see how Zap is getting on in the distillery.' Without waiting for a response, Hope let herself out of the car, leaving them no choice but to do the same.

'Nice one, Barnie,' Cam hissed under his breath, using the noise of closing his door to muffle his words.

Barnie gave him a 'what did I do?' gesture which only irritated Cam more. He had a heart of gold, but his tendency to speak before thinking was not one of his best traits.

Leaving his friend to sort himself out, Cam rounded the car and held out a hand to Hope. 'I'll get back to you as soon as I can with a proper plan of action.'

'Thank you.' She shook his hand, and he couldn't help but notice once again how well it slotted into his larger palm.

'And don't pay any attention to what Barnie said about us digging around, we'll be discreet,' Cam assured her, with a smile. 'Besides, it's the past we're interested in, not you.'

Her eyes widened a fraction. 'Of course. Well, if you'll excuse me, I'll let you find your way back to your car.'

Cam realised what his words must've sounded like, but before he could salvage the situation, Hope spun on her heel and walked briskly towards the distillery.

'Smooth, Cam, really smooth.'

'Oh, shut up and let's get out of here.' Cam wasn't sure what was worse, Barnie's mocking tone or the knowing grin he was shooting his way as they returned to the visitors' car park.

7

Hope was sitting at the kitchen table with Ziggy, sharing a pot of tea and giving him an update on Cam and Barnie's visit to the building site, when Rhys let himself in the back door, Samson as ever at his heels. She'd left Zap at the distillery hard at work on a new batch to replace the one he'd ruined due to the substandard rose petals. While out on his sulk-cum-walk with the dogs, he'd concocted a new flavour combination to try, and when she'd returned that afternoon, he'd been full of his usual fire and enthusiasm. The poor dogs had been less excited, more exhausted from the long tramp around the woods, especially poor Hercule, her uncle's little Brussels Griffon, who couldn't hope to keep up with two boisterous Labrador puppies. All three of them were flopped now in the corner, snoring their heads off.

Hope watched as Rhys toed off his boots before setting them carefully on the sheet of newspaper that Mrs Davis, their cleaner, had placed there for that purpose. She was a great believer in newspaper, using it for everything from protecting her freshly mopped floor from the horrors of dirty boots, to polishing the windows and using twists of it to light the enormous inglenook fireplace in the parlour. Hope watched as Samson left a trail of muddy paw prints between the back door and the giant cushion pile in the corner. Sadly, Mrs Davis hadn't been able to train the dogs to use the newspaper. There was a bit of whining as Samson disturbed his doggy best friend, Delilah, who'd taken advantage of his absence to hog the biggest cushion. Sooty raised his head briefly before flopping down again, while the other two dogs didn't even stir. Once Samson got himself settled, Delilah snuggled against his fluffy belly with a sigh and promptly fell back asleep. Soon the air was filled with the familiar sound of snuffles and doggy snores which had been the backdrop to Hope's life for as long as she could remember.

'Is there enough in the pot for me?' Rhys asked as he collapsed more than sat in the chair opposite. He looked shattered, the circles under his eyes dark as bruises.

Hope lifted the knitted cosy and touched the side of the pot before lifting the lid to check the contents. 'It might be a bit stewed? I can brew a fresh one.'

Shaking his head, Rhys slid an empty mug towards her. 'As long as it's warm and wet, it'll do.'

Hope filled the mug, added a generous dash of milk and passed it back while Rhys and Ziggy discussed a problem with one of the cows. He'd been out with the vet when Hope had got up that morning, out half the night according to Aunt Ro, who'd been making up a flask and a bacon sandwich to take out to him. Wondering if he'd even found time for lunch, Hope got up to fetch the cake tin. She eased the lid gingerly, but in that sixth-sense way of dogs when it came to anything they weren't supposed to eat, there was an instant stirring from the cushions. Ignoring the clack of doggy claws on the floor tiles, Hope kept her attention on the tin. There was always a selection of treats in there from Sandra and Penny at the estate café. Surveying the contents, Hope placed a rock bun and thick slice of ginger cake on a plate and placed it in front of Rhys before gathering up the teapot and setting about making a fresh brew.

Sweep was the bravest of the dogs, nudging her calf for attention as the pack followed her around the kitchen as she moved between the kettle and the sink and back again. 'No.' She kept her voice quiet, but her tone was firm. Sweep backed away with a soft whine to join the others who were milling around and licking the floor searching for non-existent cake crumbs. Only once she'd finished making the tea did Hope reach for the box of doggy treats and carry it over to their bowls. The one rule everyone in the family stuck to without fail was not feeding the dogs at the table. She dropped a handful of biscuits in each bowl and stepped aside just in time to avoid getting knocked over by the melee.

'Lord, you'd think we never fed them,' her uncle observed with a rueful chuckle.

By the time she returned to the table, Rhys had eaten two-thirds of the ginger cake and drained his mug. She refilled it, before setting the pot in front of Ziggy and retaking her seat. Her uncle refreshed his mug then recovered the pot with the cosy, giving Hope's hand a quick squeeze of appreciation before he turned back to what Rhys was saying. Hope didn't mind the interruption any more than she'd minded being the one to make the tea. It was turn and turn-about in the Travers household, with everyone doing their fair share. If one or other of them needed a bit of extra support, it was there before they could ask for it. It was just what they did – they looked out for each other.

'I'll pop out after dinner and make sure everything is okay, but hope-fully she's past the worst of it.' Rhys raised his mug and took a long drink before sitting back with a sigh. 'But enough of my troubles, how did it go today?' Hope pulled a face that coaxed a sympathetic laugh from her cousin. 'That good?'

Hope shook off the beginnings of another pity spiral. 'Cam is going to put together an action plan and send it over to me so I can start putting some costs against it. They won't be able to start until the summer holi-days, but he's agreed to lead the dig.'

Rhys rocked his chair back on two legs and whistled. 'A dig? As in an archaeological dig? That sounds pretty full on for a few stones.'

Hope shrugged. 'Looks like there's more to it than that. He doesn't know how much more, but either way, we need to find out – and I want it done properly.'

Ziggy leaned forward, resting his clasped hands on the table. 'Hope wants to treat this as a positive opportunity, and I'm inclined to agree with her. If they uncover something of significance, then it could add to the visitor appeal of the estate.'

Hope nodded, seizing on the threads of the upbeat attitude she'd adopted earlier. 'If it is something big, then it might be something we can extend beyond the summer. I know I'm probably running before I can walk, but if they find it is a site of significance then we could look at experience packages where people who are curious could come and volunteer at the dig and learn more about archaeology.'

'No one's ever going to say you lack vision, Hope,' Rhys said with a grin. His features grew sombre. 'I guess this means the house project is on hold.'

Hope's positive resolve began to waver again, but she refused to let it overtake her. 'It's not the end of the world. I'll have to have a think about where else might be a good spot to build, that's all. Cam mentioned needing to do one of those ground survey things, so perhaps I can persuade them to survey other potential sites once they have the equipment here.' She tried to laugh, but it came out a bit wonky. 'At least Mum will be pleased that I'm sticking around here for the foreseeable future.'

Rhys reached across the table and patted her arm. 'There's always one of the lodges if you need it.' Lodge was a very modest word for the couple of luxury rentals he'd recently had installed in the woods near the campsite. They were the first stage of what he hoped to develop into a glamping business, although looking at how exhausted he was, Hope wasn't sure how he was going to take on board any more responsibility on top of managing the farm.

'I was going to ask you about one of them, but not for me. Cam will need somewhere to stay for the duration of the dig. I know it's a lot to ask...'

Rhys smiled. 'Consider them both yours to use for the duration. Honestly, you'd be doing me a favour because I haven't even had time to set them up on the website. There's bound to be some snags that won't come to light until someone stays in them so you could be my guinea pigs.'

'I'll pay you for them,' Hope insisted which only made him laugh.

'That's just robbing Peter to pay Paul. Why add costs to your project to boost my revenue?'

His jaw all but cracked on a huge yawn and Hope pushed her own worries aside. 'You're all done in. Dinner won't be for a couple of hours yet, so why don't you try and catch up on a bit of your missed sleep? I'll give you a knock when it's ready.'

Rhys rubbed his broad palms over his face. 'It's my turn to cook.'

'Oh, rubbish,' their uncle said, rising from his chair. 'I'll make dinner and Hope will lend me a hand, won't you, sweetheart?'

'Of course I will.' Not waiting for a reply, she stood and gathered Rhys's empty plate and mug. 'On your bike.' She gestured towards the hallway with a thrust of the plate.

'Okay, okay, I can take a hint.' Rhys pulled himself to his feet with the effort of a man trying to drag himself from quicksand.

Having set the washing up in the sink, Hope followed her cousin into the hall but only as far as the sitting room. Opening the door, she whistled once. The patter of claws on tile soon followed as the dogs appeared, recognising the summons. 'In you go,' she urged Sooty when he stopped in front of her with an expectant look upon his sweet still puppyish face. 'You know the rules.' With the help of the gentlest of nudges from her knee, the Labrador padded into the sitting room where a pile of cushions even larger than the one in the kitchen was spread out in front of the empty fireplace. She'd let them back in later, but it would take twice as long to prepare dinner with one or other of them chancing their luck and pestering for more treats. She closed the door and returned to the kitchen, rinsing her hands beneath the tap before she filled the sink with soapy water and tackled the few bits of washing up.

'Chicken or beef?' Ziggy asked as he surveyed the contents of the fridge.

Hope considered the options for a moment. It was a warm day, so nothing too heavy, but Rhys at least would need something substantial to keep him going. Catching sight of the makeshift herb garden on the windowsill in front of her, she had a flash of inspiration. 'Chicken. We could grill it and let it cool and make a nice pesto pasta salad to go with it.'

'Great idea. There's loads of salad stuff in the fridge boxes so I can throw a big bowl together and Mrs Davis has put a couple of fresh sourdough loaves from the bakery in the bread bin.' He began setting things out on the countertop.

With the dishes dried and put away, Hope plucked a handful of fresh basil leaves, rinsed them and set them on a clean tea towel to dry. They liked to cook from scratch, so the walk-in larder was a cornucopia of ingredients. And cooking with her uncle was one of her favourite things in the world. They'd always had a special relationship; with her father dying before she was born, Ziggy was the only father she'd ever known. Zap was amazing too and she loved working with him, but Ziggy was always the one she'd turned to. As she'd grown older, she'd often wondered why her uncle had never married when he had so much love to give, but she'd never quite found the words to ask. She'd learned as a child that there were just some questions you kept to yourself, because asking caused tears.

She remembered being four or five and coming home from school with a homemade Father's Day card and asking her mother if they could send it to her daddy in heaven. Stevie had rushed from the room in tears and Aunt Ro had done her best to comfort a confused Hope. When they'd made cards the next year, Hope had given hers to Ziggy. She still gave him a card every year, and did her best to ignore the blank space in her memories where her father should've been. As she'd grown older, the space hadn't shrunk at all, she'd just become better at ignoring it.

'Where have you drifted off to?'

Startled from her daydreaming, Hope realised she was standing in the doorway of the larder, staring at nothing. For a moment, she considered asking her uncle if he knew anything about her father, but how to explain her thought process without spoiling the moment? 'I was just thinking how lucky I am to have you in my life,' she said, ignoring the little stab of disappointment that once again she'd chickened out.

'Oh, get on with you.' Ziggy flapped at her with a tea towel, but there was no hiding the pleasure in his smile. And just like that, the blank space didn't matter so very much. Whoever her father had been, he could never have loved her more than this man in front of her did. *Count your blessings, not your hurts.* It was something her Aunt Ro had told her when she was little, and it was a motto Hope tried hard to live by.

Grateful that she had far more blessings than hurts, Hope ducked into the larder to fetch a jar of pureed garlic. It was a lazy choice but so much better than the stink of it clinging to her fingers even after multiple washes. After a brief perusal of the shelves, she grabbed some pine nuts and a bottle of lemon juice and carried them all back to the stove. It only took a matter of moments to toast the pine nuts and whizz all the ingredients in the blender, together with some fresh parmesan. Setting it to one side, she took the tray of chicken breasts her uncle had trimmed and rubbed with a little oil and placed it in the top oven to cook.

The pasta she would leave until the last minute and give people the choice of having it warm or cold before she stirred in the pesto. 'What else?' she asked Ziggy, who was surveying the array of salad items he'd pulled out of the fridge.

'You can chop these, if you like.' He pushed a tray of tomatoes, half a cucumber and some spring onions towards her. They worked side by side for a few minutes. Ziggy was humming something under his breath and it made her smile and chop a little louder to drown it out. If she wasn't care-ful, she'd be trying to work out what it was and then she'd be stuck with the song in her head. Her uncle was notorious for picking up ear worms from whatever he'd been listening to on the radio in his office and passing them on to the rest of the family. She'd finished the tomatoes and cucumber and was just starting to top and tail the spring onions when the humming stopped. 'Hope...'

There was a surprising note of hesitation in her uncle's voice, enough to make her set down the knife and turn to face him. 'What is it?'

He glanced down at the knife in his own hands before setting it down on his chopping board with a sigh. 'I'm going to say something, and I want you to please think about it.'

Not sure she liked the sound of that, Hope gave him something of a non-committal nod. 'Okay.'

Ziggy fidgeted around for a few more moments, the behaviour so out of character for him that Hope began to worry that there was something seriously wrong. When he did speak, however, it was all she could do to suppress a sigh. 'I'm not sure you moving into one of the lodges is a good idea.'

'Why not?' It was hard not snap because honestly, she expected this from her mother, and even from Aunt Ro, but Ziggy was usually more chill about her spreading her wings than this. 'It's probably going to take months to sort out whatever is going on up near the chapel. Even if the investigation works come to nothing and I end up being able to build there, it won't be any time soon.'

'It was going to take months to build the place, anyway,' her uncle pointed out, his tone and point so reasonable, Hope wanted to gnash her teeth at him.

'But now I need to keep an eye on what's going on with Cam and the rest of his team and Rhys said I'd be helping him out by checking out the lodges first hand.' Feeling like she had the upper hand with that, she quickly doubled down. 'You saw how knackered he was just now. Running the farm is a full-time gig and he's spreading himself too thin. If I'm at the lodge, I'll be on hand to keep an eye on things at the campsite and run some interference for him. I can do a morning and evening check on everything, make sure things are running smoothly.'

'That's very altruistic of you, darling, but you could do the same job just as well and still live here for now. After all, you practically have to drive past the campsite on your way to and from the distillery, so it would just be a case of dropping in before and after work.'

Hope sighed. The problem with accepting Ziggy as a surrogate father was it gave him the right to have an opinion when he thought she was doing something wrong. 'Has Mum put you up to this?' Turning so his back was to the counter, her uncle folded his arms across his chest and gave her the kind of look that would've had Hope squirming a few years ago. She wasn't the little girl who'd skipped doing her homework to go climbing trees any more though, no matter how much she loved him. 'Well, did she?'

Ziggy shook his head. 'Your mother loves you.'

'I know that, and I love her too, with all my heart and soul but she's...' Hope groped around for the right word. 'She's stifling me.'

Ziggy scrubbed a hand through his still mostly dark hair. 'She's just worried about you.'

'I understand that, but I can't allow the fact she lost my father to allow her to keep clipping my wings like this. She can't mourn him forever!'

'Is that what you think? Bloody hell, Hope, it's nothing like that at all!'

Hope could count the number of times Ziggy had raised his voice to her on the fingers of one hand. The blank space seemed to yawn like an endless void before her. If her mother hadn't refused to speak about her father because she missed him too much, Hope couldn't begin to fathom what had kept her silent all these years. 'Then what is it like?' she demanded, letting the years of frustration leak into her voice.

'It's not my story to tell, but all I will say is he's not worth your time wondering about him.' Ziggy didn't sound angry any more, just sad and tired. 'Look, if it was up to me, then you'd have been told everything a long time ago, but Stevie made us all promise.'

Hope sagged back next to him, the frustration leaking away until she felt as flat as a week-old party balloon. 'How bad can it be? You make me wonder if my father was an axe murderer or something.'

Ziggy chuckled, though there was little mirth in the sound. 'Not that bad.' He edged closer to Hope, nudged her shoulder with his. 'We love you, kiddo. Love you and Rhys more than either of you could possibly know. Zap and I, well, we've always tried to do our best to fill the gap, to give you everything a father could give their child. I'm sorry if you feel like it hasn't been enough.'

Oh, God, is that what he thought? Swinging around, Hope threw her arms around her uncle's neck and hugged him tight. 'You couldn't have been a better father,' she said, voice fierce as she pulled back to look up at him. 'You and Zap both have been amazing. I don't care who my father was, that's not the main issue here. I just want to know why Mum feels like she can't tell me the truth, especially when he's been dead all these years. Whatever it is, I'm strong enough to take it.'

Her uncle was silent for a long time. 'Perhaps you need to consider whether she's strong enough to deal with it. You don't know what it was like when she came back to us. I sometimes think if it hadn't been for you...' Trailing off, he shook his head. 'No, that's not fair. Stevie was fragile for a while, but she's made a wonderful life for the two of you and the hotel runs like clockwork because of her hard work.'

Hope smiled, almost against her will, as old memories came flooding back. 'I loved it when she let me sit in her office during the holidays and I could watch her working. I wanted to be like her when I grew up, to be like both of you,' she said, giving her uncle another hug. 'You both inspired me.'

It was her uncle's turn to smile. 'I was worried about how gung-ho you were in the beginning. I didn't want you to feel like you'd been pressured into working here.' His expression dimmed as he glanced towards the ceiling. 'I wonder sometimes if we should've done more to encourage both you and Rhys to strike out on your own. It feels selfish of me to have burdened the two of you with so much responsibility, especially on days like today when Rhys is exhausted, and you're trying to manage half a dozen different things and take on the responsibility for this dig.'

This wasn't the first time he'd expressed similar reservations, and now, just as before, Hope only had one answer for him. 'I love my job. There isn't anywhere else I'd rather be, no other career I would choose for myself, and I know Rhys would say the same thing.' She shook her head. 'My wanting to move out isn't because I'm feeling tied down, or resentful of my place here. I just want a little space to call my own, a bit of privacy.'

'Room to breathe,' Ziggy added, as he reached for her hands and squeezed them gently between his own. 'You're our girl, Hope. Our little ray of sunshine after so much darkness. From the day you were born, you filled all our hearts with so much joy. I suppose we've all clung on a bit too tightly for your comfort, not just Stevie.'

Darkness? The use of such a foreboding word only served to increase the unease about who her father might have been. 'You mean because Mum was having such a hard time?'

Her uncle shook his head. 'It wasn't only her.'

'Dylan,' Hope guessed, and knew she was right when Ziggy's face shut down, his brows pulling low enough to almost shield the familiar blue of eyes so like her own. Her wayward uncle's departure was another thing shrouded in mystery.

'Amongst other things.' Here it was, a chink in his armour. Perhaps he'd finally put his guard down enough to share some of the family secrets that had bothered Hope for far too long. Before she could push for answers, her opportunity was gone. Straightening his shoulders, her uncle plastered on an exaggerated smile that didn't touch his eyes. 'Don't mind me, I'm just being a gloomy old fool. Every family goes through the odd rough patch, that's all I meant. Let's leave the past where it is and focus on

the future. And the most immediate future is getting these dinner preparations finished before everyone else gets home.'

Ziggy didn't quite meet her eye and Hope wanted to scream from the
frustration of being fobbed off yet again. Turning back to the chopping
board, she took her anger out on the poor, unsuspecting spring onions.
'The trouble with this family,' she said through gritted teeth as bits of
green flew everywhere under her rapidly slicing blade, 'is that there are
too many bloody secrets.'

8

Cam sat at his desk the Thursday afternoon following his trip to Juniper Meadows, his glasses perched on the end of his nose as he squinted at his computer screen. With a click of his mouse, he enlarged the document he was trying to decipher, squinted again and then shoved his glasses on top of his head with a tired sigh. The recent efforts to digitise historical records should in theory have made life easier for everyone, but the quality of the scans varied greatly and when the original records were written in tiny, cramped script like the one on his screen, they were little more than a recipe for a headache. He added the reference number of the document to his notepad, then clicked it closed.

Tugging his glasses back down again, he returned his attention to the index list to see if he could find anything else that might be relevant. When he told people he was an archaeologist, the first questions were either something about Indiana Jones, or for those of a certain age, *Time Team*. The popular TV show had turned archaeology into mainstream entertainment. It had started airing a couple of years after he was born and his parents had watched it religiously throughout its twenty-year run. Cam could remember sitting cross-legged on the rug by the electric fire, eyes glued to the screen as Tony Robinson and his team rooted around in the mud and wove incredible stories of ancient lives – often from little more than a handful of pottery shards and a few marks in the ground. It had seemed like a form of magic to Cam and he'd been fascinated by it.

It was only once he'd begun his studies that Cam had come to understand, if not always appreciate, how little time was spent on actual field work. Desk surveys, such as the one he was doing, were the usual starting point. Digging around through county and national records, trying to piece together an occupational timeline, was tiring and often frustrating, but it was an essential part of his toolkit, just the same as his trusty trowels and brushes. Cam had already copied a number of documents to the shared drive he had set up for the not altogether imaginatively named Project Juniper. Together with Barnie, Cam planned to return to Juniper Meadows tomorrow evening and stay the entire weekend. They'd been promised full access to the family's archives and Cam was much more hopeful of finding something that might help them pinpoint what they were dealing with.

He ran his eyes down the index one last time before concluding there was nothing else there of potential interest, then closed the page. He and Barnie had split the survey work, divide and conquer being their only hope of getting through everything in time. Cam focused on ecclesiastical and parish records while Barnie tackled the history of Stourton Hall and the family history. It made sense to do it that way, with Cam's specialist religious knowledge. Besides, he hadn't felt all that comfortable digging around in Hope's past. He wanted to get to know her better, rather more than was sensible given he was technically working for her now, but not via the impersonal tool that was the internet. Hopefully she wouldn't be too busy over the weekend.

The end of term was rushing towards them and between final assessments, dealing with anxious students panicking about their imminent exams and the endless form-filling the university bureaucrats demanded, there simply weren't enough hours in the day. He'd barely seen Barnie all week, a brief encounter – so to speak – in the department kitchenette on Tuesday, an agreed lunch meeting that had ended moments after Cam had sat down because a tearful undergraduate had spotted him. An hour and one very damp shoulder later, Cam had left the girl in the safe hands of the pastoral team while she waited for a chat with one of the university's mental health counsellors. He'd returned to his office to find Barnie had left his abandoned sandwich on his desk, together with two apples and a banana arranged in a rude formation. It had been just the laugh Cam needed and he'd been reminded once again how lucky he was to have a friend like Barnie. Having opened the drive and updated the results of that afternoon's search, Cam decided to have a quick check on his friend's progress. He'd just opened Barnie's notes when there was a knock on his office door. Suppressing a sigh, Cam reminded himself that his students were the priority. Turning away from his computer, he set his glasses to one side. 'Come in.'

There was a long pause and Cam was about to call out again when the door opened to reveal the last person he'd expected, or wanted, to see. Scott Willoughby was a second-year student, and a thorn in Cam's side. He'd been in Cam's tutor group for his first year until Cam had caught him cheating on his final written assessment. It wasn't the first case of plagiarism he'd come across, pressure to succeed and temptation were an intoxicating partnership for many students struggling to cope with the realities of university life, but he'd never witnessed anything as blatant as the paper Scott had turned in. Huge chunks of the text had been copied and pasted and the few lines inserted to stitch them together had been desultory at best. Cam had had no choice other than to recommend the boy be sent down.

Scott's father, a university alumni and very wealthy donor, had intervened. His not-so-veiled threats to withdraw his funding for a new library had sent the powers-that-be into a tailspin and a desperate compromise had been reached. Scott had been given the opportunity to redo his essay. Cam had stood his ground and refused to have anything to do with it, leaving the head of the department to do the marking. Scott had passed with flying colours, though Cam wasn't sure if that was down to hard work or his father's bullying and threats. When he'd returned for his second year, tutorial responsibility had been transferred to Barnie. By all accounts, Scott was a model student and had given no cause for concern with any of his other assignments. He'd done his best to stay out of Cam's way, until now.

'Scott. What can I do for you?' Cam kept his tone polite, though he really didn't have time to spare. Scott glanced to the floor, his hesitation on the threshold the picture of reticence Cam well remembered from their previous encounters. He'd hoped Barnie might have had more luck bringing the boy out of his shell, but apparently not. Mind you, given what Cam knew of the kid's father, it wasn't any surprise if he couldn't say boo to a goose. Swallowing a sigh, Cam reached for his reserves of patience and sat back in his chair and gestured to the visitor's chair. 'You can come in, you know?'

Scott flashed him a quick smile and scurried over, dropping into the seat with a sigh of relief. 'Thank you, Dr Ferguson. It's just that Dr Barnard mentioned the project you're both working on and it sounds great, only... I... well, I wasn't sure you'd want to see me again, given everything that happened.' He dropped his gaze to his lap and Cam could see he was twisting his fingers together, clearly still nervous. Scott's head shot back up, his brown eyes wide. 'Not that I would blame you, of course!'

Having had quite enough of the student's squirming discomfort, Cam held a hand up. 'What's done is done. Dr Barnard tells me you've applied yourself very well this year, which is to your credit. Now, you wanted to talk to me about the Juniper Meadows project?'

Scott nodded with more vigour than that cartoon dog Cam used to see on TV advertising some insurance brand or other. If he wasn't careful, he'd do himself an injury. 'Yes! Dr Barnard said you were looking for volunteers to take part over the summer and that there might be the chance for an extra course credit.' He gave Cam a bashful smile. 'I can do with all the credit I can get, if I'm honest.'

'You want to be considered for a role on the team?' Cam wasn't sure what to make of it. Scott had all but turned tail and run in the other direction whenever he'd spotted Cam, so it must've cost him a lot to come here today and face him. He wondered what his father would have to say about it. Perhaps he didn't know? Barnie had mentioned the lad had moved into a shared house with a few others on the course, so perhaps being out from under his father's direct influence had something to do with it.

Scott nodded again. 'I don't mind what I do. You can give me the dirtiest, most boring job going, I'd just really like the chance to experience a proper dig from start to finish.'

It was true that the project at Juniper Meadows would offer the students a unique experience. Most had been on short digs or on visits to other projects but nothing on the level Cam was planning. He'd agreed with Hope they'd carry out a full geo-phys survey of the area and would do a full excavation on all sites of interest, not just exploration pits. He also had permission to fully uncover what there was of the existing ruins so they could be properly mapped and recorded. It was ambitious to say the least, but she had insisted that no stone was to be left unturned, so to speak. She'd even dangled the possibility of the project extending over more than one summer if their initial work warranted it.

As he watched Scott wilt before him, Cam realised he'd been silent for a bit too long. His instinct was to refuse and to continue to keep Scott – and his awful father – as far away from him as possible. That might be the pragmatic thing to do, but as Cam watched the boy all but curl in upon himself, he felt his heart go out to him.

'If I accept you on the team, you'll be a full member and treated just the same as everyone else. You'd be given the chance to learn as many different skills as possible. There'll be crap stuff to do, and you'll have to do your share, but no more and no less than anyone else on the team, me included. When I said what's done is done, I meant it. I'm not one to bear grudges, that's just not who I am.' The fact he suspected Scott's father of being the sort of man who *would* bear a grudge, Cam kept firmly to himself. Maybe a summer free of Willoughby senior and working as part of a team would help Scott to continue to grow up.

'No, of course not. I just meant that I'd be happy to do anything that's required of me,' Scott said, his expression all but pleading at this point.

'There will be lots of hard work and some of it will be boring as hell,' Cam warned him, conscious he was already speaking as though he'd agreed to allow the young man to participate. 'And you'll be camping out for the duration,' he added, wanting to make sure Scott understood there would be no special favours, regardless of who his father was. 'Miss Travers, the project manager, has kindly agreed to allocate us some pitches on the estate's campsite so there'll be access to proper toilets and a decent shower block, but it'll be camp beds and sleeping bags and four-person tents.'

'Dr Barnard made all that clear when he was briefing our class the other day. I won't expect any kind of special treatment, that's not who I am.'

It was the first flash of anything resembling a backbone and Cam steepled his hands in front of his face to hide a smile. 'Why did you come to me rather than speaking to Dr Barnard about it?'

The fact Cam hadn't slapped him down for turning his own words back on him seemed to boost Scott's confidence further. Sitting up straight, he looked Cam square in the eye. 'The problem was between you and me. I didn't want you to think I was afraid to face you or that I was using Dr Barnard as an easy way in.'

Good for him. Cam found himself nodding with something close to approval. He still wasn't convinced anything that risked bringing the boy or his father back into his orbit was a wise idea, but what the hell. 'Let me speak to Dr Barnard about it. If he thinks you are up to it, then you've got yourself a place on the team.'

Scott jumped up so quickly, he almost knocked over his chair. He thrust a hand towards Cam, who couldn't suppress a smile as he shook it. 'I won't let you down, Dr Ferguson, I promise.'

'See that you don't. I'll let you know my decision on Monday.' As though he was worried Cam might change his mind, Scott left as quickly as he'd arrived, all but babbling his thanks. Rocking back in his chair, Cam stared after him, hoping like hell he wasn't making a big mistake.

* * *

'At least we know where we're going this time,' Barnie pointed out the following evening as he steered his car off the motorway and into the leafy back lanes of the Cotswold countryside. They'd waited for the worst of the Friday night rush hour to clear before setting off and had had a decent run down the motorway. It was that funny time of a summer evening where it wasn't quite full light and no one really knew whether or not to switch on their headlights, so the passing traffic was a mix of the over-cautious and the confident.

Cam checked his watch. Hope had invited them for supper, saying the family tended to eat late anyway and everyone wanted to meet them. He was glad Barnie was driving because he'd spent most of the journey wondering about the kind of things the Travers family might ask him and conducting imaginary conversations in his head. 'Don't forget you're heading for the side gate, rather than the main one,' he reminded Barnie as they neared the outskirts of Stourton-in-the-Vale.

'The tradesmen's entrance, you mean,' Barnie said with a laugh. 'We know our place.'

Cam grinned. 'I think the family use it as well so I'm going to consider it privileged access. You can't pretend you're being hard done by when one of us is getting put up in the hotel and bloody spa!'

'Miss Travers clearly recognises class,' Barnie said, sitting up straighter in his seat. 'Which is no doubt why you're staying in some shack in the woods.'

A few years ago, that kind of jibe might have put Cam's back up. Barnie came from a solidly middle-class background, his parents both working professionals with enough money to have afforded them a sprawling villa in Portugal for use as their private holiday home. When they'd met on that first day at university, Cam hadn't been able to stop himself from comparing his meagre belongings, unpacked from a canvas holdall that had seen better days, with Barnie's array of grand possessions. He had every gadget imaginable, including a brand-new iPad, while Cam was coping with a third-hand laptop his dad had managed to secure from a sale of hardware at the company where he worked as a security guard. Technically speaking, he hadn't been entitled to the discounted sale as he was employed by a third-party contractor, but his dad was well liked at work and had been so proud of Cam for being the first in the family to stay on through A levels, never mind secure a place at university.

Cam remembered looking at his dated laptop and across at Barnie's iPad and feeling embarrassed and envious. It shamed him now to think back on it, because his parents had made so many sacrifices to enable him to get there. Thank God he'd grown up and been able to recognise it and thank them, though he still felt a twinge of guilt about the shallow boy he'd been. With his heart of gold, Barnie had never once made Cam feel any less of an equal and had shared everything, from his superior technology to his extra allowance, with such natural grace and charm, it had been impossible for Cam to feel patronised by him. More used to hard work and far more aware of the cost of failure, Cam had helped Barnie in other ways, curbing his tendency to procrastinate and instilling a healthy study routine for the both of them. Those early bonds had solidified into a friendship they both relied on.

Leaning back in his seat, Cam folded his arms and grinned at the information Hope had sent him about his 'shack'. 'I'll be weeping into the hot tub on my private deck tonight as I think about you in your stuffy hotel room.'

'Ha! I'll be in there with you, pal. Those beers in the boot aren't going to drink themselves.' Barnie flicked a sly glance at Cam. 'Unless, of course, you're planning on a rendezvous with the delectable Hope, and then just say the word and I'll keep a low profile.'

An image flashed into Cam's head of a smiling Hope with all that glorious dark hair, wet and slicked back from her face while the bubbles of a hot tub obscured her body from his view. Was she a beer drinker? He rather doubted it and quickly swapped the bottle in her imaginary hand for a slender flute of golden champagne. Perhaps she'd prefer a gin and tonic, though, given she ran the distillery. He'd never really developed a taste for the stuff, though he'd be willing to submit himself to Hope's tutelage. He'd be willing to submit himself to a lot of things, if he was honest with himself.

'Earth to Cameron!' Barnie took one hand off the wheel and waved his arm in front of Cam's face. 'I'd ask for a penny for your thoughts, but I'm not sure they would be repeatable given the glazed look in your eyes!' Barnie cackled with laughter, clearly enjoying himself. 'Cam's got a crush,' he continued in the annoying sing-song way he'd used to tease him when they were undergraduates and Cam had spotted a pretty girl in one of the student bars.

'Piss off, you idiot,' Cam grumbled, but he knew he had been caught bang to rights. What on earth was he going to do about this attraction he felt towards Hope? *Ignore it.*

'Come on, Cam, don't be like that, you know I'm only messing around.'

'You'd better be.' Cam sat up straight, his voice growing serious. 'I mean it, Barnie. This project could be really important, and I can't afford to muck it up or upset Hope and her family with any suggestion of impropriety.'

'I swear I'll be on my best behaviour,' Barnie assured him. 'But I think it's a shame. She's got brains as well as beauty. Breeding too, from the research I've been doing.'

'Well, that's definitely put a scotch on things because if she's from a fancy bloodline, they won't want to pollute it with common stock like mine.' Cam laughed as he said it, but there was still a touch of truth in his words. Hope Travers might be everything he'd look for in a woman, but they were from very different worlds. 'How posh are we talking?' He hadn't meant the question to slip out, but he told himself it was research rather than personal curiosity.

'Grandfather's a baron. The title itself dates back to the first half of the sixteenth century.'

'Henry VIII?' Cam tugged his seat belt loose enough he could turn in his seat to look at his friend.

Eyes on the road, Barnie nodded. 'You know what that might mean...'

Cam blew out a breath. He knew they were leaping to all kinds of conclusions, but he couldn't help it. 'So, the ruins could be something to do with the dissolution of the monasteries?'

'Ding! Ding! Ding!' Barnie flicked another grin towards him before returning his focus to the road. 'Look, I know it's way too early to make that kind of claim, but it's definitely something to keep in mind.' Before he could speculate further, the sat nav announced they were approaching their turning. 'Oh, nearly there, let me concentrate so we don't end up in the middle of nowhere again.'

The rest of their journey was uneventful, but Cam was happy to keep quiet and let Barnie navigate his way there in peace. As he stared out of the window, Cam let his mind wander. The dissolution – and in some cases – destruction of many religious institutions, as Henry VIII wrestled power from the papacy to found the Church of England, had been a time of great upheaval. Noble families, and those looking to make a name for themselves, took the opportunity to purchase the extensive lands and estates seized from the church and consolidate their power. If Hope's family were newly ennobled, then it was entirely likely the estate had come into their possession at the same time. The granddaughter of a baron and the son of a security guard and a school dinner lady... Cam shook his head. Well, that definitely put paid to any foolish thoughts he might have entertained about Hope Travers. He wasn't ashamed of his parents, they were kind, decent people and he adored them both. But he wasn't naïve enough to think blood and heritage didn't matter in the kind of families who could trace their roots back over half a millennium.

His phone pinged and he checked the screen to find a message from Hope.

Just checking on your ETA.

Cam glanced at the sat nav then tapped in a reply.

We should be there in the next ten or fifteen minutes.

Three dots bounced in the corner and then another message popped up.

Fab! Supper's at nine so plenty of time. Use the fob I gave you to open the gate and head straight for the Hall. I'll meet you there.

'That was Hope,' he said to Barnie as he tucked his phone back in his pocket. 'I've told her we'll be there in about quarter of an hour.'

As they drove through the village this time, Cam used a more forensic eye as he studied the buildings around them. The first time, he'd been caught up in the chocolate box whimsy of the place – all warm honeyed stone, thatched roofs and hanging baskets. This time, he tried to look past that, to seek out the anomalies, to look at the story the buildings were telling him by their style and location. 'Can you swing past the church?' he asked his friend as he spotted the signpost for St Swithin's.

'We don't want to be late,' Barnie cautioned, though he flicked on the indicator and followed the sign.

'Hope said they're planning supper for nine and it's not even eight

o'clock yet. We've got time for a quick once around the block,' Cam said. 'I
want to check out the architecture near the church as that's likely where
the oldest dwellings will be located.'

'Good point.' The village was as quiet as last time, meaning Barnie was
able to slow the car to a crawl. 'Look there, on the right,' he said a few
moments later. 'That cottage, see how rough the stonework is?'

Cam craned across his friend. There was enough ambient light for him
to see what Barnie was pointing at. Ideally, he'd like to get out of the car
and have a proper close-up look, but there wasn't time, and tramping
through people's front gardens wasn't a great way to introduce themselves
to the village they were going to see a lot of over the next few weeks.
Unlike the neat, almost uniform blocks of the cottages along the high
street, this one looked like it had been thrown together from any old bits of
stone the builder had been able to lay their hands on. Not unusual, but
there were some very large blocks mixed in, particularly on the lower level,
which might suggest reclamation or reuse from a previous structure. As
they did a slow circuit of the roads around the church, they spotted at least
half a dozen other homes with a similar hodgepodge construction. 'Interesting,' was all Cam allowed himself to say as Barnie steered them back
onto the high street and towards the estate.

'Indeed.'

9

Hope didn't recognise the red saloon circling slowly around the ornamental fountain in front of the Hall. The light had shifted in the past few minutes, the dark edges of twilight softening the horizon and casting deep shadows beneath the trees. Making sure to stand well clear, Hope raised a hand in cautious greeting. The car slowed even further and a familiar face poked out of the open driver's window. 'Only us!' Barnie called in a cheery voice.

Hope bent forward so she could see both Barnie and Cam, sitting in the passenger seat next to him. 'Hello! Sorry, I didn't recognise the car.'

'I volunteered to drive, which is why we've made it in good time,' Barnie said with a grin.

Hope watched as Cam rolled his eyes. 'It's called a speed *limit* for a reason,' he said, before turning the full effect of his blue eyes on her. Even in the fading light, there was something almost hypnotic about them. 'How are you, Hope?'

'I'm good, thanks. No dramas at the distillery.' She instinctively raised a hand to her forehead to touch wood as she said that. 'So I'm all yours for the entire weekend.' Catching what she'd said too late, Hope felt her cheeks begin to glow. 'Well, I'll be around if you need anything. Oh, you know what I mean.' *Shut up, shut up for goodness' sake, before you make a complete arse of yourself.* 'Anyway!' she continued in much too bright a voice. 'You can leave your car here and we'll get you checked in, Barnie, shall we?' She turned away, trying to ignore how loudly her boots seemed to crunch over the gravel. She was a successful business-woman, not a simpering idiot and Cameron Ferguson wasn't *that* good-looking.

As she waited for Barnie to unload his things, Stevie appeared and began walking down the steps to meet them. Hope locked her car, ignoring the forlorn whines from Sooty and Sweep in the boot, knowing that by the time she'd let them out, it would be time to get them back in again. Pressing a button to lower all the car windows so the dogs had plenty of ventilation, Hope hurried to meet her mother as she reached the bottom of the steps. 'Are you sure you don't mind?' Hope asked, not for the first time that day, as she pressed a quick kiss to her mother's cheek.

'Of course not, darling. I'm quite excited about the whole thing. I always wanted to know more about the family history. Unfortunately, your grandfather couldn't have given two hoots about it all and your great-grandfather was an old stick in the mud who thought girls were only good for marrying off. The two of you would've loved each other,' she added, casting a mischievous grin at Hope.

'I can only imagine,' Hope said with a grimace, thankful her grandparents had had a far more modern outlook on life and had raised their children accordingly. She turned her attention to Cam and Barnie, who were waiting for them at the bottom of the steps. 'Mum, may I introduce you to Dr Cameron Ferguson and Dr Ly—' she caught the warning flash in Cam's eyes just in time. 'And Dr Barnard. Cam, Barnie, this is my mother, Stevie Travers.'

In full hostess mode, Stevie swept forward, holding out her hands to first Cam and then Barnie. 'Welcome, both of you. Hope has got us all enthralled about what you might uncover up at the chapel, I must say!' She tucked her arm through Barnie's, who Hope noted was already looking a little starry eyed. Her mother on full charm offensive was a glorious sight to behold. 'And you, Dr Barnard, though of course we shall be great friends, so I shall call you Barnie, are staying with us for the week-end, I believe?'

'Umm, yes, that's right,' Barnie said, already caught in the full tractor beam of her mother's personality.

'Marvellous! I've got a lovely room set aside for you. It's on the ground floor and just a stone's throw from the library. I've got the key for what used to be my grandfather's study and I thought you could use that as a workspace. It's got an interconnecting door with the library, so you'll be able to come and go as you please and store whatever documents you are working on without worrying about tidying up every evening. If you let me know your schedule for the summer, I can set aside your room for the duration.'

'Oh, I couldn't possibly!' Hope had to suppress a smile as Barnie cast a rather wild glance over his shoulder at them.

'Of course you could! Now come on, let's get your bags and I'll show you to your room.' Stevie turned to Hope and she spotted the slightly impish light in her mother's eyes. Clearly enjoying herself, Stevie continued, 'Hope, darling, why don't you take lovely Cameron here to the lodge and we can all meet up at the house in a bit.' Reaching up, she patted Barnie's biceps with her free arm. 'You'll give me a lift when we're ready, won't you?'

Recovering his composure, Barnie placed his hand over Stevie's. 'It would be my pleasure.'

'You'll have to put your bags in here unless you want the boys to chew everything,' Hope said as she pulled open the passenger door on her Range Rover for Cam to store his luggage.

'No problem.' After he'd stowed his things, Hope liked the way Cam leaned further into the back so he could greet the dogs and offer them his hand through the protective grill so they could catch his scent. 'They're gorgeous animals,' he said, though she didn't miss the discreet way he wiped a bit of dog slaver off his fingers onto his jeans.

'I love them to bits,' Hope said as she circled the car. 'They're still very much puppies, though, so don't let their size fool you. I almost went flying this morning when they spotted a rabbit and wanted to give chase.' She made another mental note to sort out some training classes before all hope was lost – so to speak. Standing on the running board of the car, Hope called a quick farewell to her mother and Barnie, who had almost reached the top of the stairs. Their heads were bent together, like a pair of old gossips, oblivious to Hope and Cam's imminent departure. 'Those two are going to get on like a house on fire,' Hope observed with a grin as she dropped down into her seat.

'I can see where you get it from.'

The quiet observation had Hope spinning in her seat to face Cam. 'Get what from?'

He had a grin plastered across his face, his attention on his window where he was watching Barnie hold the door of the hotel open for her mother, the pair of them laughing about something. 'The force of personality that gets people to do what you want them to,' he explained with a nod up the stairs.

Not sure she liked the sound of that, Hope turned to put on her seat belt, yanking it with too much force and causing it to jam. 'You make me sound manipulative.'

'Persuasive,' he corrected, his voice still mild. 'And it was meant as a compliment. You have that same warmth and welcome about you, it makes people want to cooperate.' Feeling somewhat mollified, Hope slotted her seat belt into place then glanced up to see his smile broaden. 'I bet you're lethal in meetings.'

He sounded like he wanted to be a fly on the wall in one of those meetings and Hope couldn't help but laugh at his rather over-inflated sense of her business achievements. 'It's true people sometimes underestimate me, but unfortunately they don't all roll over as quickly as you did.'

Cam barked a laugh as he secured his own seat belt. 'I guess I asked for that.'

He glanced back up the stairs and Hope wondered if she'd miscalculated in not offering Cam a room in the hotel. 'You don't have to stay in the lodge, if you'd prefer to be here instead?'

The look he shot her was quietly amused. 'Do I look jealous of Barnie's preferential treatment, then?'

Her instant reaction was to leap to her own defence and deny it, but then she realised he was teasing her. 'I think you should wait and see your accommodation before you judge which of you is getting the preferential treatment.' Not wanting to say any more and spoil the full effect of the lodge, she put the car in gear and drove off.

'It's just a couple of minutes' walk from here,' Hope assured Cam as she pulled into the car park next to the campsite. 'There's a shop there that serves the site, which you are welcome to use,' she added, pointing to a squat single-storey structure opposite. 'It's open for a couple of hours morning and evening to allow people to pick up a few essentials and to collect larger orders made via the village store.'

'I'll check it out, thanks,' Cam said as he hauled his bags out of the backseat. 'But I shouldn't need much. Barnie and I are planning on a repeat visit to the pub for dinner tomorrow night. We had a fabulous meal there on the way home last time.'

'At the Arms? I haven't been there for a while, but they've got a really good reputation.' Hope popped the boot open with the remote and the two Labradors leapt out before she had a chance to grab their leads, never mind clip them on. Slamming the boot closed, she rushed around to rescue Cam, only to find out there was no need. Abandoning his bags, he'd crouched down and had a firm hand on each collar and was laughing as he tried to avoid their enthusiastic licks of greeting.

'Sorry!' Kneeling beside him, Hope fastened on the dogs' leads and tugged them gently towards her so Cam had room to stand up. He showed no sign of being in any rush, taking the time now his hands were free to ruffle ears and scratch each dog in turn.

'It's not a problem, really,' Cam said, giving each dog a bit more fuss before he straightened up.

'You seem very relaxed around dogs, which is just as well!'

Cam shouldered his two bags and tucked a small pack of beer under one arm. 'I love dogs. We always had them when I was growing up, and I really miss having one around. I live on my own and spend so much time at work that it didn't seem fair to get one.'

Hope locked the car and began to stroll towards the woods, the puppies bouncing around her ankles. 'Well, you'll get as much of a doggy fix as you could possibly need while you're here. There are currently five canine members of the family.' A thought struck her. 'I hope Barnie is okay with dogs?'

Cam shrugged. 'As far as I'm aware, he's not got a problem. He stayed with my folks a few times when we were at uni, and he was fine then.'

'I hadn't realised you'd known each other that long.' It certainly explained the easy way they had together.

'Best mates since we were eighteen.' Cam laughed. 'God, it's hard to remember being that age. Every year, when the new students file into my lecture theatre, they look so young.'

'Or perhaps you're just getting old,' Hope suggested, not being able to resist the chance to tease him.

'Ouch!' Cam staggered as though she'd struck him. 'You're probably right, though!'

As soon as they were clear of the car park, Hope unclipped the dogs and let them have their freedom. They bounded off, happy to chase either other and snuffle around at whatever scent caught their attention, but they never went out of sight for more than a moment or two, and they understood enough to wait when she called them. 'It's not too much further,' she said to Cam, gesturing towards a narrow path off the wide avenue they'd been following. 'Just through here.'

They reached a deviation in the path and a low signpost that read Cosy Canopy to the left, and Woodland Wonder to the right. Hope fished a set of keys out of her pocket. 'I'll show you Woodland Wonder, but you are welcome to choose whichever one you would prefer. Rhys has decided against renting them until he can get a proper site manager in place, so you'll be able to use whichever one you choose for the entirety of the dig. Between the farm and the campsite, he's already stretched a bit too thin to manage everything and he really wants these to be a VIP experience and not just a bit of upmarket self-catering.' Hope stopped herself with a laugh. 'That was probably a lot more information than you needed.' She gestured for Cam to go ahead of her. 'After you.'

Without the small path to follow, it would be hard to know there was anything other than a dense coppice of trees in amongst the rest of the wood. It was only as they got up close that the privacy fence became visible, and give it another couple of years for the new planting to thicken out and the building would be completely hidden. Hope knew the moment

Cam had spotted the lodge itself because he stopped dead in his tracks. 'Bloody hell.'

Hugging herself with delight at his reaction, Hope put on a straight face by the time he spun around to look at her. 'It's not bad, is it? The entrance is around the other side.' She pointed to a couple of narrow, high windows. 'The lodge has been designed for maximum privacy, so it's much more open to the rear.'

'Not bad? It's like something out of a fairy tale!' Heedless of the bags he'd set on the ground, Cam moved forward, reaching out to run a hand along the moss-lined wall. 'It's real,' he said in a voice full of wonder.

'Amazing, isn't it?' Hope followed Cam as he walked along the side of the building. The architect had designed the lodge to adapt to the natural environment and not the other way around, so the walls curved rather than following straight lines to ensure the ancient giants of the forest were protected. 'The moss acts as a camouflage, helping the structure to blend into the environment and also provides excellent insulation. It's a great thermoregulator and will keep guests cool in the summer and warmer in the winter. There's a heat pump for water and state-of-the-art underfloor heating – not that you'll be in need of that if this glorious spell of weather continues.'

She watched as Cam gazed up into the thick branches overhead, the dappled evening light casting his face into unreadable shadows. 'It's another world, like I'm miles from civilisation rather than a short stroll from the campsite,' he said, that note of wonder still in his voice.

'It's so peaceful, isn't it?' Hope felt a yearning in her heart and wondered again about whether she should take up Rhys's offer and spend a few weeks in the lodge next door. It was of a similar design, but the layout was different, as nothing about the woods themselves was symmetrical. After Ziggy's quiet request, she hadn't raised the issue with her mother, but she was feeling more unsettled than ever since he'd shrugged off her questions with one too many platitudes. There were things about her past she needed to know, but how to raise them without hurting anyone? It simply didn't seem possible, so for now, she was trying to hold her tongue.

Not wanting to let those unwelcome thoughts intrude on the evening,

Hope reminded herself she had guests to look after. If they wanted to make it back in time for supper, she needed to show Cam around the place. 'Come on, I'll take you inside.' She whistled for the dogs, who were snuffling along the edge of the building. Sweep came at once, the more reluctant Sooty eventually following when Hope called his name in a low no-nonsense voice. With their leads secured, she followed Cam.

She led the dogs towards the wide low wooden steps at the back of the lodge, tying their leads in a loop and giving them enough extension to nose around without causing trouble. 'What do you think?' she asked Cam as she led him up the stairs and onto the semi-open deck. There were doors currently in a storage area underneath which could be fitted to turn the deck into an all-weather conservatory for the winter months, but for now, the overhang from the first-floor balcony provided shade and shelter for the outside furniture and the round hot tub in the corner. Cam paused at the top of the steps, a lopsided grin on his face. 'I thought you were kidding about the hot tub.'

Hope laughed. 'Nope! I bet you can already picture yourself soaking in it after a long day at the dig, can't you?'

Cam wandered over, lifting the edge of the cover to reveal the steaming water inside. Rhys had found time earlier in the week to check it over and get it up and running while Hope had arranged for Mrs Davis to give the rest of the place the once over and make sure everything was spick and span. Hope had been into the village and picked up some treats from the bakery and the village shop. Cam had mentioned he wouldn't need much, but she'd wanted him to feel welcome on his first visit. It was also a way to thank him for taking on the dig at such short notice. 'It's going to get a lot of use, for sure,' he said, trailing his fingers through the hot water before letting the lid fall closed again.

Hope unlocked the door and pulled it open, standing back to let Cam go in ahead of her. 'You can either leave the doors open like this, open them halfway or fold them all the way back. I'll show you when we've got more time, but you can basically have the whole of this area open to the elements if you want to. It's the same upstairs in the bedroom.'

Cam was nodding, but she wasn't sure he was actually listening as he turned in a slow circle as though trying to take it all in. While Rhys had kept the outside neutral and natural, the inside of the lodge was the epitome of luxury, with deep cushioned sofas, and rugs so thick Hope wanted to slip off her shoes and flex her toes in them. There was a small dining table and chairs, all made by one of the craftsmen who worked out of a unit in The Old Stable Yard. Beyond that lay the open-plan kitchen with its sleek modern units and brushed stainless-steel appliances. All the plug sockets had USB ports and there was decent Wi-Fi connection thanks to the large booster they'd installed for the campsite nearby. A flatscreen on the wall could be switched to a variety of screensavers, including artworks or a photographic montage of shots captured around the estate, when not otherwise in use. Stairs in one corner led to the upper floor which was occupied by a huge bedroom with an en suite bathroom, complete with a copper roll-top tub and a huge walk-in shower.

'I got a few things in, just to say thank you for agreeing to do this,' Hope said as she skirted around Cam and moved into the kitchen to open the fridge.

Cam stirred from his reverie and came to join her. 'Wow, what a spread. I can't possibly eat all this on my own. Why don't you come and join me for dinner tomorrow?'

Hope's tummy gave a funny little turn at the thought of sitting out on the deck with him, watching the sun set as they gorged themselves on the cheese, meats and other deli treats she'd filled the shelves with. There was a nice bottle of white wine already chilling which would be the perfect accompaniment. She was about to accept when she remembered his earlier comment. 'Oh, I thought you and Barnie were having dinner in the pub tomorrow?'

Cam frowned, and she wondered if he was feeling anything like as disappointed as she was. Damn, she should've just accepted the invite and kept her mouth shut. 'We were planning to, but it seems a waste of all this lovely food. We can go to the pub another time, there'll be plenty of opportunities. He can come here and I can make him green with envy about having this place to myself. You're still welcome to join us both, of course.'

'I'd like that very much, thank you.' She'd have liked it even better if it was just the two of them, but she couldn't exactly say that now, could she? She cast a glance at the illuminated digits on the microwave set into the wall. 'If you are happy with everything here, we should probably head over to the farmhouse for supper.'

'Happy? I'm beyond ecstatic, but are you sure Rhys is happy for me to stay here? I can camp with the rest of the team, you know?'

Hope smiled, appreciating his thoughtfulness. 'You can speak to him yourself and get all the reassurance you need. You'd be doing us a favour. You can keep an eye on the place and also be a bit of a guinea pig for us, make sure everything is working as it should.'

Cam nodded. 'Sure, sure, whatever you need.' He paused. 'What about next door?'

Hope hesitated. 'I was thinking about staying there myself, but...' she trailed off, not wanting to bog him down with family business. Especially when she didn't know what the hell was going on with everything herself. 'Come on, let's go and get some supper.'

10

Hope was quiet on the short drive from the campsite car park. Cam had got the feeling she'd been about to say more about the possibility of her staying in the lodge next door to his but then she'd so deliberately changed the subject, he decided it was best to let things lie.

He couldn't deny it would be nice to have her staying there. Not 'nice', he corrected himself, useful, because they'd be able to chat about the dig as the work progressed and resolve any issues face to face rather than over the phone or WhatsApp. He wasn't a big fan of using social media to communicate but he'd already been asked by several of the students taking part when he'd be setting up a group, so it was one of the tasks on his list for the morning. It was what one got used to, he supposed, and it would be a handy way to coordinate information in one place. They arrived at a metal farm gate and Hope jumped out to open it before Cam had chance to offer. He followed her out, though, so he could close it behind them.

'Thank you,' she said, giving him a sweet smile that he felt down to his toes as he climbed back in. 'We keep talking about automating it, but somehow never get around to it. Which reminds me, do you know how many access fobs you'll need for the east gate? Do you think you can manage with a couple between you for the whole team?'

Cam nodded. 'Two will be more than fine and I'll try and make sure either Barnie or myself are there to make sure the gate is secured afterwards.'

'I'm sure your team can be trusted, but the fobs just have a habit of going missing and then Ziggy has to recall them all and reprogramme them which is a pain. There's a pedestrian access gate by the main entrance which is a much quicker walk to the village. It has a four-digit code which we change every couple of weeks. I'll make sure you're included in the staff WhatsApp group so you get the new code.'

Cam laughed. 'I was just thinking I need to set up a group for the dig team. Whatever did we do without mobile phones?'

'Had a much quieter life, I'm sure. It has its uses, but it's hard not to feel a prisoner to my phone, sometimes.' Hope put the car in gear and drove them slowly down the side of a large stone yard and around a metal-sided barn, the front of which was open to show a varied collection of tractors and other farm machinery parked in a neat row. Beyond the barn, another courtyard opened up in front of a sprawling building he assumed was the farmhouse. It was such a mishmash of architectural styles, it was impossible for him to begin trying to date it, but he promised himself a good look around at some point.

Cam found buildings like this so much more interesting than grand structures like the Hall. Oh, there was no denying the impressive mark the grand building made in the landscape, but the farmhouse wore its history like a much-loved patchwork quilt, the signs of use, repair and extension of the original structure everywhere he looked. The door was open and a heap of colourful cushions had been placed outside, on which a number of dogs were snoozing happily in the last of the evening sunshine. Hope added her Range Rover to a little row of matching vehicles under an all-weather shelter on the far side of the yard and they got out. Sooty and Sweep were already pressed up against the rear window, their breath fogging the glass as they panted to be let out. The moment they were released, they raced across the yard to engage in a doggy dance of barks and greetings before they and their companions flopped down in a pile of tails and noses in the middle of the cushions.

A man with an impressive salt-and-pepper mane of hair flowing down to his shoulders appeared at the door holding two champagne flutes. He was dressed casually in a pair of faded jeans and an open-necked shirt. His feet were bare, and several beaded bracelets clacked together on one wrist. 'Ah ha! I assumed the racket just now was to announce your arrival.' He handed the first flute to Hope in exchange for a kiss on the cheek. 'Hello, darling. You'll be pleased to know that final batch came out perfectly.'

He turned to Cam then, offering him the other glass while extending his free hand for a crosswise shake. 'You must be Cam! What did you think of the lodge? Bit fancy, eh? Rhys has done a grand job with them, I must say. Come in and meet everyone!'

Warmed by such an effusive welcome, Cam accepted the drink and the handshake and allowed himself to be ushered into what turned out to be a massive kitchen, the back wall dominated by one of those fancy cooking ranges which would take up most of the space in his mum's little box of a kitchen. The walls had been painted a bright, sunny yellow and the wooden cupboards had the patina of age and use. They were too imperfect in shape and size to be anything other than handmade – none of the easy uniformity of an off-the-shelf package from a DIY store – which only added to the charm of the space. A table big enough to seat a dozen people filled the centre of the room, several of the chairs already occupied, including Barnie, who was deep in conversation with a man who would've been the mirror image of the one who'd just greeted Cam if his hair hadn't been cropped close to his scalp. *Zap and Ziggy*, Cam mentally reminded himself of the family's penchant for odd names.

'Look who I found!' Zap declared, at least Cam had assumed it must be him because he was the one who worked with Hope at the distillery and had mentioned a batch to her.

Stevie, who'd had her back to the room, turned with a smile. 'We were about to send out a search party!' she exclaimed, before coming around the table to greet both Hope and Cam with a kiss each on the cheek. Clearly the Travers family were not ones to stand on ceremony, regardless of their heritage. 'Have a seat,' she said, as she breezed back around the table. 'Rowena and I are just throwing together a few nibbles.'

The other woman in the room turned to give them a quick wave over her shoulder. 'We'll be two ticks,' she said, her round face creasing into a smile that immediately warmed something inside Cam. 'Rhys is upstairs having a shower.'

'I'm not, I'm here,' a tall man around the same age as Cam said from the doorway opposite, one hand raised to his head as he towelled off his hair. 'I heard the cork pop and knew I'd better get a move on before you lot drain the bottle.' He padded across the room into what Cam thought might be a utility space from the quick glimpse before returning without the towel. He offered his hand to Cam. 'Hiya, it's great to meet you.'

There was no mistaking him. He was the man from the photo on Hope's phone who'd been sharing ice cream in the sunshine with her. Cam was surprised by a sudden jolt of jealousy, but he made himself smile through it as they shook hands. No ring on his finger, Cam noticed, same as Hope, but they obviously lived together and he was part and parcel of the various businesses here. 'Thanks for the loan of the lodge,' Cam said, reminding himself that he was there to work and that this man had been incredibly generous already.

'Hey, it's not a problem. I'm sure Hope explained to you that I decided against renting them out this summer, so you're doing me a favour, really.' Rhys raised his glass as though in toast before taking a sip.

'I think we're going to have to agree to disagree on that,' Cam said with a grin as he returned the toast. The golden champagne fizzed on his tongue as he took a drink. Champagne on a Friday night? This really was a case of how the other half live. His impression of grand living wasn't diminished in the slightest when Stevie and the lady she'd called Ro placed several platters on the table. Nibbles in the Ferguson household were a bowl of salted nuts and a few crisps – maybe sausage rolls if it was a special occasion like Christmas because they were his dad's favourite. Eyeing the array of cheeses, charcuterie, olives and other treats like stuffed peppers and vine leaves, he doubted the Travers family knew one end of a frozen sausage roll from the other.

Stevie did another trip from the countertop to the table to fetch an enormous basket of baguette slices before taking a seat beside Barnie and urging everyone to sit down. Cam pulled out the two chairs nearest to him and when Hope took one, he gestured for Rhys to take the other. 'No, you're fine, thanks,' the other man said. 'I've been crouching most of the day, so my knees are not keen on bending any more.'

'Oh, darling,' Rowena said, sending Rhys a beaming smile. 'As you're up, can you fetch my rings off the windowsill?'

Cam watched as Rhys did as he was asked, and Rowena slid on a thick gold band and a ring with what looked like an enormous opal surrounded by diamonds from the way it caught and shimmered in the light. He wondered at the size of it and whether it was a family heirloom. It would be nice to get a closer look, but he couldn't think of a polite way to ask.

Rhys dropped a kiss on top of Rowena's head. 'You'll lose them one of these days.' Cam had always considered his family affectionate, but the Travers were very demonstrative. He hadn't known what to expect, a bit more of a stiff upper lip, perhaps, given their heritage. He smiled to himself, at that bit of inverse snobbery.

Rowena laughed. 'It hasn't happened yet, touch wood.' She quickly tapped her fingers on the wooden table. 'The setting takes forever to clean, so I have to take them off when I'm cooking.'

'Well, then the sacrifice will be worth it because this looks fabulous, Ma.' Reaching past her shoulder, Rhys took a handful of olives and retreated to lean his back against the sink. 'You'll have to come to dinner more often, Cam, if it means we get a spread like this.'

Cam was still trying to process the implications of Rhys calling Rowena 'Ma', so all he managed was a half-smile, while both Rowena and Stevie protested his cheekiness. 'You make it sound like we live on scraps,' Stevie said with a frown before she turned to smile at Cam. 'We just thought it would be nice to welcome both you and Barnie and to have a little celebration for what we hope will be an exciting summer.'

'It's a wonderful welcome,' Barnie said smoothly, giving Cam a sharp look at his lack of response.

'Y... yes, thank you so much,' Cam managed to get out while his brain still whirled with calculations as to who was really who in the Travers family. Raising his champagne flute to his lips, he peered at Rhys over the rim. He didn't know how he'd missed it before, but there was no mistaking the same solid jawline as the two older men at the table. So, if he was either Zap or Ziggy's son then he must be Hope's cousin rather than the romantic partner he'd mistaken him for. The wave of relief that moment of realisation brought should've set off a big warning siren in his head, but Cam didn't care. And that in itself should've sounded another alarm.

'Can you tell us about your progress so far?' Stevie nudged one of the plates towards Cam with an encouraging nod for him to help himself. 'Or is it too early to tell anything yet?'

Taking a couple of pieces of bread, Cam offered the basket to Hope as he pondered how much to say. Some of the speculations he and Barnie had made on the drive down were exactly that and it would be unfair, not to say unprofessional, to share their slightly wild theory about the site being linked to the upheaval following the religious reformation. 'I've been working on a desk survey,' Cam settled on saying.

'Which is exactly as boring as it sounds,' Barnie put in dryly, earning a few chuckles.

'It's not the most exciting thing in the world,' Cam conceded with a grin as he added a sliver of brie to his plate and again passed the plate in Hope's direction, then accepted the charcuterie board from Ziggy with a nod of thanks. 'But it's a vital part of the archaeological process. We have access to a huge range of records and databases and it's a case of combing through them, trying to find information that might be relevant. With a site of significance like a stately home we have a great place to start, but it's important to look beyond those records as well.'

Ziggy nodded. 'My grandfather was something of an obsessive about the title and family history, so there are boxes of records in his old office. I've given Barnie permission to dig through the lot.'

'It's always good to have at least one obsessive in the family – makes my job a whole lot easier,' Barnie said with a grin. 'As I was saying to you earlier, it looks like the barony dates back to the court of King Henry VIII, so I'd love to find out the back story to that, unless you already know?'

Ziggy shook his head. 'My grandfather probably told me, but I'm afraid if he did, it went in one ear and out the other.'

'He was always banging on about the family,' Zap muttered, not looking too happy at the memory. 'Ziggy, thank God, shouldered his way out first so he was the golden child. I, being merely the spare, was left in relative peace.'

'He was only trying to do what he thought was right by the family,' Ziggy said. His voice was light, but it didn't match the shadows in his eyes and Cam got the impression their grandfather might have been hard work.

'Don't you dare defend him!' Stevie burst out, shocking the entire table into silence. 'Not after what he put you through.'

'Stevie, we have guests.' Ziggy's tone was mild, but a muscle twitched in his cheek as though he was clenching his jaw. Cam fixed his eyes on his food and wished with all his might he was somewhere else.

'Ah, yes, propriety at all times,' Zap murmured. 'Grandfather really did train you well.'

'Have some more bread, dear.' Rowena all but shoved the basket under Cam's nose, leaving him no choice but to accept a slice, even though he still had two pieces untouched on his plate.

'Thank you.' Cam flashed her a quick smile, saw the slight panic in her eyes. 'This really is delicious.' Though his appetite had deserted him at the sudden tension around the table, Cam added a piece of brie to the slice and forced himself to take a large bite.

'I'll take a slice,' Barnie said, reaching across to snag one. 'And some of those delicious-looking pickles too, if I may.' God bless his friend for trying, but Cam could tell he felt just as awkward.

He shot a quick glance at Hope, who was staring between her mother and her uncles with a mystified expression on her face. 'What on earth is going on?' she demanded.

'It's nothing,' Ziggy said with that same tight smile.

'Isn't it always?' Hope didn't sound at all happy and Cam couldn't blame her. He raised his brows at Barnie and gave his head the slightest tilt towards the door in a should-we-go gesture.

Barnie raised a hand as though to scratch an itch on his face, lifting his shoulders in a shrug hopefully no one but Cam had caught. 'I'm looking forward to getting stuck into the archive tomorrow,' Barnie said to no one in particular. 'I'd love to be able to build a family tree if you don't already have one. I have a computer program that makes it easy to plug in the data as I come across it.'

'There might be something like that already,' Ziggy said. 'As I said, I didn't pay close attention to that side of things as I was busy trying to get up to speed with learning how to run the estate.'

'Only because Daddy let him dump it all on your shoulders, it wasn't fair the way the two of them treated you.' Stevie was fiddling with a pendant around her neck, her earlier cheer having completely given way to agitation.

Ziggy raised a shoulder as though it was no big deal, but his eyes were still troubled. 'Someone had to step up. Regardless of Grandfather's methods, it was the right thing to do. We wouldn't have what we do now, and I wouldn't go back and change a thing.'

'Not anything?' Zap asked him. 'What a saint you are, big brother.'

'Better that than someone who gives into their feelings, no matter who gets hurt in the process,' Ziggy snapped back. A shocked silence settled over the group and Cam wished a hole would open up beneath the table and swallow him. The conversation was beyond uncomfortable now, but the family seemed to have forgotten he and Barnie were there and he couldn't see an easy way to escape without making even more of a scene.

'Hold on a minute, how come I've never heard about any of this before? I thought you all agreed to take over the business because it was what you wanted to do. No one told us anything about you being put under pressure.' Rhys looked across at Hope. 'Did you know anything about this?'

'No.' Hope's ponytail bounced as she shook her head. Cam had had enough. Whatever was going on with this family, it was none of his business. He pushed back his chair and was about to stand when Ziggy spoke again.

'What's past is past.' Ziggy set down his glass as though to emphasise the topic was over. 'What's important is how we do things now.'

Hope muttered something that sounded like 'more bloody secrets' and Cam closed his eyes for a moment. There was no way he and Barnie could leave without making things even more awkward. They would just have to try harder to change the subject. He turned to Hope and sent her a pleading look. 'I can send you a copy of the desk survey results, if you like? I still need to finalise a few things, but I'd be very happy to share it once it's completed.'

Hope nodded, looking relieved. 'That would be great, thank you.'

'I can take you through it in the morning, show you what we've found out so far. We also need to finalise the timetable for the dig, and some other bits and pieces of admin. As you're the project manager, I'll leave it to you to decide how often you'll want a progress update, and what level of detail you'll want. I've brought a few examples of different kinds of reports I've done in the past so you can choose what you think works best.' Some of the tension around the table seemed to dissipate as he rattled on and on, reminding the family of his presence, begging them silently not to continue what was clearly brewing into a fight – no matter how polite everyone sounded.

Hope's shoulders relaxed and Cam sent her an encouraging smile. 'That sounds good,' she said. 'I'll bring along my work diary as well, and a copy of the summer events we've got planned for the estate. It's mostly smaller-scale stuff, visitor days at the distillery and a few child-friendly activity days centred around The Old Stable Yard. The only really big thing we have planned is a sound and light show for the late bank holiday weekend. We're using the Hall as the backdrop for the projections and there's going to be a live orchestra playing.'

'That sounds fantastic. I've got a month pencilled in for the dig, with a couple of weeks spare for tidying up and securing the site, so we should be out of your hair by mid-August at the latest.' It was Cam's parents' anniversary that weekend and he was planning on a trip home to see them before the new term started, so it sounded like things were already falling into place.

Barnie picked up the conversation and started asking Rowena questions about the sound and light show and Zap soon joined in. Ziggy said nothing, his eyes fixed on something in the middle distance, the fingers of one hand drumming on the table the only remaining sign of tension. Those stilled when Stevie reached out and placed her hand briefly over her brother's before she got up from the table to cut some more bread.

Dinner progressed with everyone doing their best to pretend everything was normal. The starter platters were supplemented with salad fresh from Rowena's kitchen garden and a delicious dressing Ziggy whipped up at the table. Cam was happy to graze and let the conversation carry on around him as he continued to try to understand the Travers family dynamics. Whatever had been said earlier about Ziggy being the one selected by their grandfather to run things, it struck him as a pretty egalitarian set-up. Each member of the family appeared to have autonomy over the part of the business they ran, and Cam recalled Ziggy's comment about what mattered being how they ran things now. The champagne had been substituted with a delicious elderflower and lime pressé, which given the previous tensions was probably a sensible idea. Cam accepted a glass from Zap, who explained he'd been working on some non-alcoholic lines to expand the distillery's range.

'Isn't it fabulous?' Hope asked as she offered him a refill from a large glass jug beaded with condensation. 'I can't decide if this one is my favourite or the raspberry and mint.'

Cam wasn't sure what he thought about that as a combination, but he guessed you didn't run a successful distillery without understanding what flavours worked together. 'I'll take your word for it, but I'm very happy with this. Thank you.'

Zap beamed with obvious pride. 'I'll sort you out a couple of bottles to take back to the lodge, unless you'd rather have some gin? I've got a few quarter bottles here I make as samples.' He was already rooting around in one of the cupboards before Cam could say anything. Something caught his attention, a movement on the edge of his peripheral vision and he turned to see Barnie gesturing, a frantic thumbs up to indicate he should accept the offer of the gin.

'I think you've got a taker for the gin over there.' Hope's words were followed by that lovely rich laugh.

'Barnie is much more of an expert on gin, I'm sure he'll be happy to accept,' Cam agreed, sharing a conspiratorial smile with Hope.

'Honestly, it's the only reason I agreed to get involved in the project in the first place,' his friend said, rising to accept the two bottles Zap offered to him without a trace of shame. 'I'd love a look around the distillery sometime as well, if that'd be possible.'

'The chance to talk someone's ear off about gin?' Rowena glanced back up at her husband with a gentle smile. 'Sounds like your idea of heaven, darling.'

Bending down, Zap pressed a quick kiss to her lips before straightening up with a grin. 'I'm surrounded by philistines, so it'll be wonderful to share my unappreciated skills with a true connoisseur. You can come down tomorrow if you like.'

Hating to break up what looked to be the start of a beautiful friendship, Cam intervened. 'We've got a lot of work to do this weekend, but I'm sure there'll be plenty of time over the summer to arrange a visit.' He turned to Hope. 'I wouldn't mind a look around myself, if that's okay?'

'Of course. We can work out a date tomorrow when we go through everything.' She raised a hand, stifling a yawn. 'Oh, excuse me! I'm so sorry.'

Cam checked his watch and was surprised to see it was after ten. 'Look at the time, we really should be making a move.' He caught Barnie's eye.

'It's been a wonderful evening,' Barnie said, tucking one of the small gin bottles in the pocket of his linen blazer so he could shake hands with Zap and then Ziggy. 'Really great.'

'I'll give you both a lift back if you like,' Rhys offered. 'I put the long-wools in a new grazing paddock this morning and I want to check they're doing okay.'

Cam glanced down at Hope. They would have plenty of time to talk tomorrow. 'It saves you turning out as well.'

'I can do it,' Hope said as she stood. 'You've had a long day, Rhys, I'm sure you must be tired.' Cam felt something soft and warm glow inside him at the thought she might want to extend their evening together a little longer too. The next minute, her entire face was scrunched in another enormous yawn.

'You can barely keep your eyes open.' Placing a gentle hand on her shoulder, Cam urged her back into her seat. 'I'll see you in the morning.'

She raised a hand to cover his. 'I'll be over straight after breakfast so we can get cracking. Is half-eight too early?'

He wanted to stare at where her hand covered his, to turn his palm up so their fingers would slot together. Instead, he reminded himself that this was a family who were free with their touches, and she likely meant nothing by it. Across from them, both Stevie and Rowena were exchanging cheek kisses with Barnie, as though to prove his point. Like a whisper of silk against his skin, her touch slipped away, leaving him wondering for a moment if he'd imagined it. 'I'll have the kettle on ready,' he promised, making himself take first one and then a second step away from the table.

The women stayed inside, but both Zap and Ziggy came outside with them to move the dogs and their cushions back into the kitchen. A little dachshund walked on dainty paws towards Cam and leaned against his leg. Bending down with just a hint of a groan for his aching limbs, Rhys scooped up the dog with a laugh. 'You're such a little flirt,' he said, as the dog curled up in the crook of his arm. 'Come on, let's get you inside.' Rhys pointed the remote in his hand towards the bank of Range Rovers and the hazard lights flashed on one of them. 'I'll be with you in a sec, just let me get madam here settled.'

Cam and Barnie let themselves into the back of the car, Barnie's gin bottles clanking together as he sat down. 'Well, that came very close to being a disaster,' his friend said with a grimace. 'Well done you on saving the day.'

'It was all a bit tense for a moment,' Cam agreed. 'We'll have to tread carefully when it comes to the archive. Maybe talk things out just between us before we share stuff with the family, especially around this grandfather of theirs.'

His friend nodded. 'He sounded like a right piece of work. There's a lot going on we don't know about. I mean they're nice enough people, but talk about having to walk on eggshells.'

'More like tiptoeing through a minefield, I reckon,' Cam said, thinking about the tension between the older Travers siblings and Hope's muttered complaint about secrets. 'Well, whatever is going on with them, it's none of our business. We're here to do a job for them, so let's try and not ruffle anyone's feathers.'

11

Hope lay on her back, staring at the thin sliver of light shining across the white plaster through the crack in her curtains from the security light in the yard below. She should get up and close them properly, but she was too tired to bother moving. Tired, but not sleepy – was there anything worse? She could feel the weight of exhaustion tugging at her, the pressure of a headache starting, that dry, stale feeling in her eyes.

Everything felt sluggish apart from her mind, which was darting around like a squirrel. Bits of the half-argument between her uncles and her mother kept popping up. She hadn't known her great-grandfather personally, but she'd never heard anyone say much about him before. Nor had Rhys, from what he'd said. Certainly nothing along the negative lines of him bullying Ziggy into taking on responsibilities his father had shirked. She knew Monty hadn't been interested in running the estate, but she'd always been led to believe Ziggy, Zap and her mother had taken over things by choice rather than obligation. How had she never known?

Secrets. Always secrets.

With a frustrated sigh, Hope threw herself onto her side with a huff and forced her eyes shut. That lasted all of about thirty seconds before she decided her pillow was too high and she raised herself up on one elbow and punched the pillow flat with the other fist. She settled down again and started one of the counting and breathing exercises from her relaxation app. Two slow exhalations later and her brain was off again. Why had she all but held Cam's hand like that? God only knew what he must think of her! The way he'd tried to ease his hand away without saying anything. Her face felt like it might burst into flames as she recalled that slow slide of his fingers from beneath hers. How was she going to face him in the morning? She rolled back over and stared once more at the sliver of light. Rhys must still be out checking his sheep because the last person in for the night always turned off the outside light. Hope fumbled for her phone and checked the time. It was only ten minutes since she'd turned her light out, but it felt like an hour or more. She chucked it onto the bed beside her with a groan as the squirrel started repeating phrases over and over.

Don't you dare defend him...

What a saint you are, big brother...

What's past is past...

Feeling like she wanted to scream, if only to drown out the nonsense in her head, Hope sat up with a jolt and flicked her light on. Grabbing one of the spare pillows from beside her, she propped herself up then retrieved her Kindle from the bedside cabinet. Perhaps if she read for a bit, she could turn off that mental loop, and make herself sleepy in the process. She'd barely scanned the first couple of lines, trying to remind herself where she'd left off in the book she was reading, when there was a tap on the door. Mum poked her head in, saw Hope was sitting up and let herself into the room, closing the door behind her.

'I was just on my way to bed when I saw your light come on. Is everything all right?'

Hope lowered her Kindle to rest on her lap. 'I couldn't sleep so I thought I'd read for a while.'

Her mother nodded but didn't make any move to leave. 'I was talking to Ziggy just now. He said you were thinking about moving into the spare lodge next door to Cameron.'

'I haven't decided yet,' Hope said, keeping her tone neutral. 'I wanted to wait until Cam has his team finalised, as it may be that someone who is participating in the dig might need something more comfortable than a tent to sleep in.' That was true, but she'd also listened to Ziggy's advice and decided not to rush into anything. So, why had he raised the subject with Mum, and what else had they been discussing? No doubt they'd waited until both she and Rhys had gone to bed before they'd revisited that scene at the dinner table earlier. The thought didn't do anything to reduce Hope's growing annoyance at being kept out of things once again.

Her mother's smile was soft and a little sad. 'You're staying here because of me, aren't you?'

Now the door was opened, Hope decided to lean against it, just a little. 'You haven't exactly been enthusiastic about my plans to move out.'

With a sigh, Stevie crossed the room and flopped down on the empty side of Hope's bed. 'Ow, what's that?' She shifted almost immediately and retrieved Hope's phone, holding it out with a rueful grin.

Hope took the phone and set it on the bedside cabinet together with her Kindle and then settled down on her pillows so she and her mother were facing each other. 'The last thing I want is to upset you, Mum, but I can't stay cooped up here forever.'

Reaching out, her mother tucked a strand of Hope's hair out of the way, turning the gesture into a caress of her cheek. 'I know, my darling, and I'm the one who should be apologising because you are the one who's been upset, and I've been a terrible coward about everything for far too long.'

Taking a deep breath, Hope asked the most pressing question on her mind. 'Are all these secrets you and the others have been keeping something to do with my father?'

Her mother nodded, then rolled on her back to stare at the ceiling. 'Turn the light out, will you? Some things are easier to share in the dark.'

With trepidation causing her stomach to clench, Hope turned out her lamp then settled back on her side, tucking her hands under her cheek. 'I'm here, Mum, you can tell me anything.'

The room was quiet for a long time apart from the restless shuffle of her mother moving against the sheets, as though she was trying and failing to get comfortable. Hope schooled herself to keep silent, giving her mother time to settle.

'Of the four of us, I was the one most like Daddy. I was the one who wanted to be outside all the time, building dens, climbing trees, getting the others into trouble in the process. Your grandparents didn't believe in discipline, they claimed it was all about letting us express ourselves, but I don't think they could be bothered, so we ran wild at first. All that changed when they packed us off to boarding school because they wanted to go travelling. It wasn't so bad for the boys, as they all went to the same place, but I was completely alone for weeks at a time. My grandfather would sign exeat slips for Ziggy to come home at the weekends, but the rest of us had to stay in school until the holidays. I didn't understand why at the time, I just remember hating Ziggy because he got to come home while I was cooped up in that horrible place.'

'Oh, Mum.' Fumbling in the dark, Hope reached out and grasped her mother's hand.

A soft chuckle was followed by a reassuring squeeze of her fingers. 'It wasn't that bad. The teachers were nice enough and the house matron couldn't be kinder to me if she tried. It wasn't even that I wanted to be back here, I just hated seeing the other girls go off with their parents for week-ends and day trips. I used to sit at the window for hours, hoping to see that bloody rainbow-striped VW van bumping along the drive.' She went quiet again. 'Of course, it never appeared. I always wonder why my parents had so many children when they didn't seem to be interested in us. They didn't neglect us. We were well looked after in a physical sense. But they've always been so desperately in love with each other, it's like they just don't have enough room in their lives for their children.'

'No wonder you were horrified when I said I wanted to go to boarding school!' Hope said with a sigh, thinking back to how exciting she'd thought it would be.

'I blame those *Malory Towers* books you devoured when you were little,' her mother said with another little laugh. 'That and the fact I was probably suffocating you even back then.'

Hope sorted through the jumble of her emotions and tried to find the right words. 'I can't blame you for wanting to make me feel secure after the way you were treated.'

'I suppose that was part of it, but that was never the real reason.' Stevie fell silent again.

Hope gritted her teeth. Come on, come on. You owe me the truth.

Just when she was ready to climb the walls, her mother spoke. 'I was terrified that if I let you out of my sight, your father would somehow find out about you and snatch you away.'

'Snatch me away? What on earth do you mean?' Hope sat up, reached for the light and then stopped herself. This was more than her mother had ever shared with her before. If she changed the atmosphere, then Stevie might clam up again. She forced herself to settle back down. 'Tell me, please. Help me to understand.'

'If I'm going to explain properly, I need to tell you it all.' The bed dipped as her mother shifted once more. 'I thought everything would be different when I finished school and came home, but I was just as lonely. Ziggy and Zap were off at university and Dylan was still away studying for his exams. No one was interested in me here and I had nothing to do. When I asked my mother for advice, she laughed and told me I had the whole world at my feet and I should go out and see it for myself. I took her at her word and packed a bag that night and caught a train to London the next morning. I found a cheap hotel and did all the tourist things first and then started going around the galleries and museums. I met a group of people my own age at the National Portrait Gallery and found out they were studying at the art school at St Martin's. They seemed so cool and glamorous, and I felt like a total country bumpkin. We ended up in a pub over the road from the gallery and I drank far too much cheap wine. I was very grateful when one of the lads in the group offered to see me safely back to my hotel.'

There was a crack in her mother's voice and Hope gripped her hand tight. 'You don't have to tell me, Mum,' she whispered, not knowing if she could bear to hear the next bit.

Her mother returned the pressure. 'Yes, well, I'm sure you've worked out what happened next. I woke up the next morning with a terrible pain in my head and a crumpled receipt on my pillow with a phone number scribbled on it, so I suppose he thought the evening was better than I did. I stared at that number for ages, feeling more and more disgusted with myself because I couldn't even remember his name. Eventually, I scrunched it up and threw it in the bin and ran for the bathroom to be sick.

'Afterwards, I scrubbed myself in the shower until my skin turned red, but it didn't help. I just had to get out of that room. I didn't know where I was going, only outside where I could breathe. I walked for hours and even when it started to rain, I couldn't make myself head back. I thought I'd sit on the tube for a while where at least I'd be dry, but I got halfway down the stairs and then I remembered the night before when I'd been lolling all over the place while that lad held me up. I stopped dead and someone behind banged into me, almost knocking me down the stairs. I remember staring up into a pair of dark eyes under even darker brows that were drawn down into a deep scowl. He told me off for acting so foolishly, even as he steadied me on my feet. When he let go, my legs wouldn't hold me up and then I was crying.'

Hope felt wetness on her own cheeks. 'Oh, Mum,' she whispered.

Her mother made a half-laugh, half-sob. 'I don't know who was more embarrassed at the time, your father or me. He marched me up the stairs and into a nearby McDonald's where he bought me the most disgusting cup of coffee I've ever had in my life. It was hot, though, and I was so cold inside that I drank every drop while he just sat there quietly. It was only when I'd finished that he asked me what he could do to help me and the whole tale spilled out. When I told him I couldn't face going back into that hotel room, he walked me back through the rain and made me wait in the lobby while he went upstairs and packed my things for me. I was in such a daze, I didn't realise until afterwards that he'd settled my room bill as well.

'He recommended another hotel which he used for clients and got me a preferential rate on his account. It was much nicer than where I'd been staying and although he wouldn't accept money for the bill he'd paid off, he didn't argue when I said I wanted to check in for myself. I only planned to be there for a couple of nights, just to get my head on straight and then I'd decided I was going to go home. He called me the next day and asked to take me out for lunch, and then for dinner and then...'

'You didn't come home,' Hope said, filling in the gaps.

'No. He was a bit older than me – more than a bit, but he was so calm and capable and honestly it was just so nice to have someone looking after me. Six weeks later, we were married at the register office.'

'You married him?' Hope couldn't stifle a gasp. She'd always assumed she'd been the result of a fling gone wrong, but this was something completely different. Her parents had been married, and yet Hope didn't even know her father's name...

'Your uncles were furious when I told them, but my parents just laughed and said it was like history repeating itself because they'd fallen in love almost at first sight.' Her mother's laugh was bitter. 'It wouldn't have mattered if they had protested because I was convinced I'd met the perfect man. It didn't take long before the honeymoon was over. What had started out feeling like I was being taken care of morphed into something much darker and controlling. Your father was a successful businessman and we had to go to lots of dinners. I wanted to look my best for him and tried so hard to entertain his clients and colleagues. At first, he thought it was sweet when I asked him to brief me beforehand so I knew what to talk about, but then we'd be in the taxi on the way home and he'd start grilling me about what had been said, why'd I'd been laughing, or telling me off for spending too long speaking to one person. It was always the men he quizzed me about.

'I couldn't understand it because he was the only man I was interested in, and I was only doing it to try and help him in his career. When I tried to explain that, he laughed in my face. He told me I was an embarrassment, a hindrance rather than of any use, so then of course I didn't want to go out any more because I believed it must be true. So I stayed at home and did everything I could to keep him happy that way, but somehow that was all wrong as well. He was so cruel, and it wasn't just words. I...'

Her mother gulped loudly then let out a final rush of words. 'I lost a baby when he pushed me down the stairs, so when I found out I was pregnant again, I knew I had to get away and keep you safe from him.' The rest of her words were lost under a series of convulsive gasps.

'Oh, God, no wonder you didn't want me to know about him!' Hope shuffled across the covers so she could rest her head on her mother's shoulder. 'I should never have pushed you into telling me.'

'I tried to save you both, but I couldn't. My Ben, my poor baby,' her mother said between sobs, breaking Hope's heart into a million pieces. To have been far enough along to have thought about names and to lose a child in such terrible circumstances? It was beyond Hope's scope of comprehension.

Sitting up, Hope gathered her mother into her arms, reversing their roles as she rocked her gently and did her best to offer the comfort she'd been lucky enough to be able to rely upon every day. 'Shh, it's all right, Mum. Don't cry, it's all right.' Eventually, the desperate tears subsided and her mother's breathing settled into a deep, regular pattern. Hope eased her mother gently down upon the pillows and with a little bit of effort managed to get the quilt out from under them both and tucked her mother in. Rolling onto her side, Hope closed her aching eyes and settled in for a long, sleepless night.

Perhaps some things were best left in the past.

* * *

Feeling like she'd barely had a wink of sleep, though she was sure she'd dropped off for an hour or two at some point, Hope slid quietly from her bed at the first sign of light creeping through the crack in her curtains. Her mother didn't stir, so Hope gathered her clothes as quietly as she could and tiptoed down the hall to shower and change.

The hot water made her feel slightly more human, and as she wove her hair into a loose plait, she tried to push aside the ghosts of the past and focus on her task for the day. She owed both Cameron and Barnie an apology for having to sit through what came as close to a family argument amongst the Travers as they ever had the previous evening. She hadn't missed the way both of them had tried to salvage the situation and she could only imagine how embarrassing it must've been to witness. God knows she was cringing at the thought of addressing the matter with them. Best to tackle it head on and get it over with and then she could give them both the attention they deserved after being so good as to give up their weekends to help her.

Her positive attitude lasted about as long as it took to get down the stairs, where she found Aunt Rowena hovering by the kettle, looking pensive. 'Oh, Hope, I thought I heard you up and about! Have you seen your mother? I popped my head in to see if she wanted a cup of tea, but her bed looks like it hasn't been slept in.'

Hope gathered her aunt in for a reassuring hug. 'She slept in my room last night.'

Aunt Rowena stepped back and stared up at Hope. 'Is everything okay? Is she poorly? Are you?'

'We're both okay, well, physically at least.' She sighed. 'We had a long talk last night about what happened with my...' She hesitated over the word father because she didn't want to have any connection with someone capable of the terrible things he'd done to her mother. A father was someone who picked you up and kissed the grazes on your knees, who checked under the bed when you were frightened of the monsters under it, who pushed you that bit too high on the swings until you screamed in equal parts fear and delight. Ziggy. Zap. They were what fathers were, even if Ziggy had never had a child of his own. Hope had everything she needed in the two of them and she wouldn't give credit to the man who gave her half her genetic material. 'She told me about what happened when she moved to London,' Hope settled on, trusting her aunt to understand. 'And why she left.'

Rowena's expression crumpled in sadness and understanding. 'Such a sad time, but, for all that hurt and pain, your mother ended up with you, and you are her greatest joy.'

Hope hesitated, wondering if she should mention the thing that was most playing on her mind. Her mother and Rowena were as close as blood sisters and she was already married to Zap by the time her mother must have returned home. Hope doubted there were any secrets between the two women. 'She told me about Ben, as well. I feel so bad for her.'

'She *told* you about Ben?'

Aunt Rowena sounded so shocked that Hope found herself going on the defensive. 'Why wouldn't she? I'm not a child, I can deal with the emotional fallout of the fact Mum had a miscarriage and I'll give her all the support she needs to finally come to terms with it. She's held all these secrets in so long because she was trying to protect me, and that's not fair on her. She was so upset last night, Ro. It was absolutely heart-breaking.'

'Yes, yes, of course.' Seeming to have recovered from her shock, Aunt Rowena opened her arms. 'And what about you, my darling? This must've been all very upsetting for you too.'

Hope moved into the familiar, comforting warmth of her aunt's embrace. 'I knew it must be something awful, that *he* must be something awful for her to have avoided telling me for so long.' Again, she resolved she would have nothing to do with the man who had caused such pain. 'Perhaps I should've left well alone.'

Rowena squeezed her tight. 'You have every right to ask those questions and I know Stevie has wrestled with herself over when to talk to you and how much you needed to know.'

Hope hugged her back. 'I know what's important and that's Mum, you and the rest of this family. I have everything I need right here under this roof.'

'That's my girl.' Rowena pressed a kiss to her cheek, then let her go. 'I'm not sure you quite have everything you need, though. There's the matter of a certain tall, blond and bookishly handsome archaeologist. He might be on the quiet side, but *phew!*' Rowena fanned a hand in front of her face, her eyes dancing with laughter. 'The way I caught him looking at you a couple of times last night. All I can say is that still waters run deep with that one!'

'Stop it!' Hope could already feel the heat rising on her throat at the idea that Cam might have been looking at her with interest. 'He's here to do a job, that's all. Besides, it wouldn't be appropriate.'

Her aunt made a rude noise to show what she thought of that. 'All work and no play makes Hope a very dull girl. You are in the prime of your life, darling, you should be out there having fun, not worrying over balance sheets and monthly accounts.'

'You make me sound so boring,' Hope protested.

'Not boring, just a bit single-minded in your focus, that's all. I know how hard you work at the distillery because Zap tells me almost every day that he wouldn't know where he'd be without you. And I know Ziggy relies on you more and more as well.' Stepping forward, Rowena cupped her cheek. 'You are incredibly capable, you and my Rhys, both, but I worry about how much the pair of you are taking on.'

As her hand fell away, Hope reached for it, grasped it tight and smiled. 'We're fine, Ro. It's lovely of you to worry, but you don't need to.'

Rowena frowned for a long moment before she shook her head. 'As if you're going to listen to what I have to say! You've always known your own mind, ever since you were a little tot running around the place. Still, you can humour an old woman and pretend to pay attention when I tell you that Dr Ferguson has taken quite a shine to you, so if you've got even an inkling of the same kind of attraction towards him, you should make the most of the opportunity. Intelligent, handsome, *kind* men like that don't grow on trees, you know.'

Hope grinned. 'I'll take it under advisement.'

12

Cameron was just rinsing his breakfast plate under the tap when the sound of a dog barking warned him of Hope's impending arrival. Grabbing a tea towel, he quickly dried off the plate and his hands then refilled the water tank on the coffee machine beside the sink. The patio doors were already pushed wide to let in the cool early-morning air. According to the weather app on his phone, they were in for another scorching day. The way things were going, it was looking like it would be one of those long, hot summers that led to hosepipe bans and crowded beaches.

He'd never been one for lazing around in the sun, but for all the trouble a dry spell brought to farmers and gardeners proud of their pristine lawns, it could be a great aid to archaeologists. As the ground dried out, lost treasures could sometimes be revealed. He remembered a summer about five years previously when records had been set and all sorts of wonders had been visible from above. Long-forgotten prehistoric barrows, the ghost outlines of Roman villas and lost Tudor ornamental gardens, the land had given up its secrets. The eager patter of claws on the wooden planks of the decking stirred Cam from his thoughts and he hurried across the cool tiles of the living room area just in time to bend and greet Sooty and Sweep.

'We're a bit early, I hope you don't mind.'

Cam raised his head to welcome Hope, the words he'd been about to say dying on his lips. Her voice had sounded bright and cheery, but there was no mistaking her pale skin nor the dark shadows marring the delicate beauty of her eyes. *Is everything okay?* He swallowed back the question and pushed himself to his feet, the dogs still milling around his ankles looking for attention. 'I was just going to make a coffee, so you're right on time.'

Hope's smile was a pretty good effort, but it didn't quite mask the strain etched on her features. 'It's a shame you're not a medical doctor as I could do with a drip so you can feed it straight into my veins. I didn't have a great night's sleep.'

So, there was something. Still, he knew the last thing any woman wanted was to be told she looked a bit rough around the edges. 'I can't manage a drip, but there's a drawer full of coffee pods so I can keep brewing as much coffee as you need.'

'That'll do nicely.' Hope clicked her fingers at her dogs. 'Come away, you two and leave poor Cam alone for five minutes.'

The dogs roundly ignored her and Cam couldn't help but grin. 'Those training classes…'

Hope held up a hand. 'I know, I know! There just aren't enough hours in the day at the moment.' Stepping forward, she took both labs by their collars and pulled them back. 'Leave him alone, I said.' Sooty whined, while Sweep managed one of those absurdly innocent looks only dogs who knew they were in trouble were capable of.

'Honestly, they're fine. I'll get a couple of bowls of water for them and I'm sure they'll settle once they get over the excitement of being around someone new.' He hesitated halfway to the kitchen, thinking about the pristine new furniture. 'Should I fetch a towel or a blanket to cover the sofa?'

She laughed, and it lifted the tired lines from around her face, the sound filling the room with sunshine. 'They're naughty, but not *that* naughty. If you can get that water, I've got some treats in my bag that will keep them quiet for a bit.'

Cam returned with the bowls to find both Labradors sitting at Hope's feet, their attention rapt on the two rubber Kong toys she was holding. He didn't think he'd seen the puppies that still before, although Sweep's – at least he thought the one with the streak of white across his eyebrow was Sweep – tail was hammering a tattoo of excitement on the tiled floor.

'Good boys,' Hope said with the kind of affection that made Cam consider sitting at her feet as well, before she set the two toys on the floor beside the open window. The dogs flopped on their bellies, one paw curled around each of the toys as they worked to try to retrieve whatever treats she'd stuffed inside it. 'There, that'll keep them busy.' Hope dusted off her hands and rose to her full height beside him. 'Now, didn't you promise me a coffee?'

They were on their second cup and halfway through a packet of custard creams Cam had found in the cupboard when they finally settled at the dining table in front of his laptop. A stack of documents he'd retrieved from his bag sat to one side, but they were both focused on his screen.

'This is the timetable I've mapped out. The first few days will be tied up with getting everyone settled in and familiar with the site and the rules. Then we'll move on to a full walking survey by one team while the other focuses on carrying out a geophysical one. Barnie's going to lead the walking team and it'll be a good chance for some of the newer students to learn how to read the land, look for signs of previous developments, scour around for any surface finds.'

'Do you pick much up from the surface?' Hope asked him, the tiredness chased away by her obvious interest in the topic.

'You'd be surprised. If the land was ploughed, then we'd be bound to find all sorts of things – flints, maybe even the odd shard of pottery or a bead.'

'We've got some agricultural land but that's outside the main boundary of the estate.' Hope gave him a half-smile. 'The family owns several of the farms in the surrounding area.' She looked a bit embarrassed, like she should apologise for her family's good fortune.

'That's too far. Does your cousin ever use the area we're interested in for grazing? That disturbs the ground enough to unearth things now and again.'

Hope paused to consider the question. 'Not recently, but I can check with him if you like because he may well have done in the past?'

Cam shook his head. 'It doesn't matter to the survey, I was just pointing out reasons why there might be things to find on the surface. That badge you found wasn't too deeply buried in the soil if the digger turned it up in the first couple of shovels.'

'Speaking of which, I had a chat with Declan, who was the site manager for my house project. He's happy to come along with a small team to handle whatever groundworks you might need. He's also had a chat with his boss and can make himself available as the site manager for the duration of the dig if that would be useful for you. He's got all his health and safety qualifications and he'd be happy to work with you on risk assessments, supervision of works, under your lead, of course.'

It was the kind of help which could prove invaluable and would certainly free up Cam to be able to focus more on the archaeology. 'It's not something I'd budgeted for.' He had a line in for the groundworks, but not a fully qualified site manager.

'If you want him, then cost isn't a problem. I want this to run as smoothly as possible and while you and your team are on our land, then you are my responsibility. I'd feel better if there was someone around whose sole focus was on the safety and security of the site and everyone working on it.'

Cam's shoulders relaxed. 'Then I'd be delighted to have him. Honestly, it'd be a huge weight off me, thank you.'

He watched as Hope made a note in the planner she'd brought with her and marvelled at the neat rows of script, the divided sections of a to-do list, appointment reminders, even a little shopping list. He smiled to himself as he spotted the words 'dog trainer' and a number that had been underlined three times and he wondered how many pages she'd carried that over from. It surprised him she was so low-tech about things when his entire life was managed through the phone resting on the desk beside him. It linked to his office calendar, which the formidable Mrs Cotteridge maintained for them all. No one was allowed to add anything without funnelling it through her, which Cam had found annoying at first until he'd circumvented her system and double-booked himself for two equally important meetings and had to go begging to her for help on how to fix it. When Hope reached for her phone and repeated the note, he couldn't help himself. 'Isn't that a bit of a waste of effort?'

Hope set her phone aside. 'Only if you've never lived in the middle of nowhere and a storm took out the local mobile phone network the day after a contractor managed to dig up the village's main internet cable while trying to repair a broken water main. We had to rely on the landline and our memories because we'd automated everything.' She closed her planner and patted the pretty floral cover. 'Plus I get to indulge in my love of gorgeous stationery. Right, how about you show me what you've found in your desk survey?'

They spent the next half an hour going through the timeline of the estate that he and Barnie had been piecing together, opening up copies of records he'd found online to support their findings. 'Barnie's the genealogy expert and he's found the establishment of your family title dating back to the reign of Henry VIII. As he said last night, hopefully he'll be able to fill in the gaps once he's had a chance to go through your family archives.'

Hope pulled a face. 'About last night. I owe you an apology for the way my family behaved. I don't know what got into them, to be honest, because they're normally so good at keeping up appearances.'

He didn't miss the hint of sarcasm in her tone and he recalled again how she'd muttered about secrets. There was definitely something going on beneath the surface with her and her family and he reminded himself to tread carefully. Knowing she was waiting for a response, he opted for the truth. 'I did feel a bit awkward, but more for your sake than mine. I know I can speak for Barnie when I promise you can trust us to be discreet.'

'Thank you.'

'The same applies to whatever we uncover through the archives and from the dig itself. We're working for you on this project, and though I might be interested in publishing something should we uncover anything of significance, you would have final sign-off on any reports or papers produced.'

'That's reassuring, I guess.' Hope hesitated. 'Although it does rather make me worry what you're expecting to uncover if you think I might want to veto it!'

Cam couldn't help but laugh. 'If it's any consolation, there isn't a noble family in the land that got where they are through altruistic means. Power is seized by force, held by force, consolidated by force, or at least the threat of it. The history of this nation is steeped in blood and destruction.'

'You don't have to sound so excited about it!'

Cam was relieved when he glanced at Hope to find she was giving him a wry smile which took the sting out of her words. 'Sorry. I think I told you before I'm particularly interested in the history of the church and let me tell you, that's a very murky topic. One of the reasons why many of the ordinary population were so willing to embrace the overthrow of the Catholic faith was due to the corruption of local priests and monasteries who held the lands they worked on. Promises of salvation were sold like any other commodity and the rents and tithes imposed by the church could be crippling.'

Hope's mouth quirked. 'And along came people like my ancestors to fill the void and those poor people ended up crushed under a different kind of system. I remember at least that much from my school history lessons.'

'Got it in one.' When she continued to look troubled, Cam wanted to reach out and take her hand, but he settled for giving her shoulder a gentle nudge. 'Hey, we can't help the family we are born into, all we can do is try to make things better with what we have. Your family seem to be doing a hell of a lot to support the local community with jobs and opportunities like that training scheme you said your uncle set up.'

Hope nodded. 'Yes. I suppose that's true. So, what about you? What's your family history?'

Cam was a little taken aback by the question, but supposed it was nothing more than natural curiosity on her part. 'Not as interesting as yours.' He shook his head. 'No, that's not fair. My family aren't going to be mentioned in connection with royalty anywhere, but every life should be considered of value. My great-grandfather worked in the pits, my mum's family are from a rural village and their name is in the parish records going back generations. Dad's a security guard and Mum is still a dinner lady at the same school I went to.' He let himself remember the pride in her eyes as she poured a ladle of custard over his bowl of treacle sponge. 'She was always on puddings. My mates used to get an extra big portion now and then, but she was careful never to show me favour.' He laughed. 'I also couldn't get away with anything because if word got to her that I'd been misbehaving or not done my homework properly, then I'd get a lecture for it all the way home. I wouldn't be where I am today without them.'

'She sounds fabulous, I'd love to meet her one day.'

Cam grinned at the idea of driving his mother through the gates of the estate and watching her expression as she took in the imposing sight of the Hall dominating the landscape as far as the eye could see. She'd probably sniff and make some comment about being glad she didn't have to worry about heating or hoovering a place that size. 'I think the two of you would get on like a house on fire.'

'So, you've looked into your family history, then? What did you use? One of those genealogy websites?'

'Not exactly.' Turning the laptop slightly so the keyboard was in front of him, Cam brought up his list of saved links. 'We have access to all sorts of different services via the university including access to the General Records Office. Most people don't realise that a lot of those popular ancestry research websites are basically front portals for information that is held by the GRO. They're a bit more user friendly and have nice add-ons where you can build a family tree and stuff like that, but anyone with a bit of computer know-how and some patience could do it all themselves. The university also has access to parish records where they've been digitised and a good database of contacts, so we can get help looking at manual records as well.' Cam glanced at Hope and gave her an apologetic smile. 'Sorry, I went into lecturer mode for a minute then.'

She grinned and shook her head. 'No, you're fine. I like listening to you explain things, you have a really easy way about you which I'm sure your students appreciate. You were telling me about your family...'

'Oh, yeah. Anyway, I did the whole family tree thing for my parents for their last big anniversary. They are hopeless to buy for, as they always insist they have everything they need and don't think I should be spending my hard-earned money on them.' He sighed. 'I've tried to explain that I wouldn't be earning half what I do if it wasn't for the two of them, but they won't have it. I decided to put the skills their support helped me to get into creating something unique for them. I made an album and got copies of marriage and birth certificates, war records for my grandfathers and my great-grandfathers, anything I could get my hands on.'

'That sounds like a really thoughtful present. I hope they liked it.'

Cam nodded, thinking about the stunned look on his mum's face when she'd understood the significance of what he'd given them. 'I wanted to show them how proud I was of not just them, but all of my family.'

'No robber barons in your bloodline then?' Hope sounded rueful again.

He laughed. 'I found a lots-of-great-times-uncle who was transported to Australia for being a thief. Someone on my mother's side did time for assaulting a policeman. There was a distant cousin who was jailed for being part of the suffragette movement. She smashed the windows of the local magistrate's house.'

'She sounds like a hero, not a villain.' Hope still sounded despondent, which hadn't been Cam's intention at all. She fiddled with her pen. Tugging the lid on and off, flipping it around in her fingers then setting it back down, only to start the whole routine over again. He wondered if she even knew she was doing it because the movements looked involuntary, like a tic or a stress-coping mechanism. Rather than draw attention to it, he tried again to ease her feelings about her own ancestors.

'Look, we all have good and bad people in our families because they are just people at the end of the day, regardless of whether they're born with a silver spoon or a wooden one. I'm sure there'll be some other philanthropists in your family history, just wait and see what Barnie unearths once he gets going.'

Rather than reassuring her, his words only made Hope look more stressed. He remembered how tired she'd looked that morning and wondered if the family had revisited their discussion about her great-grandfather after he and Barnie had left with Rhys the night before. 'Is there something specific that's bothering you?'

Hope glanced up at him, shook her head and reached for her pen. 'No. Everything is fine. Let's go over the timetable one more time to make sure we're not missing anything.' Cam could spot a polite version of being told to mind his own bloody business when he saw one, so he flipped to the tab with the timeline he'd drafted on it and they went through it from the start.

By mid-afternoon, they both had a to-do list worked out, and Cam was confident they'd be in really good shape by the time he and the team arrived on site. Hope had called Declan and he'd agreed to come over in the morning and meet Cam so they could discuss the site set-up and management. He reached for the custard cream packet, only to find it empty, and checked the time on his laptop screen. 'Hey, it's almost three. You must be starving.'

Hope glanced up from her planner, the dark shadows beneath her eyes even more pronounced. 'I could definitely eat.' She reached around to knuckle the small of her back. 'And I definitely need to stretch my legs.'

While she took the dogs out for a walk, Cam made himself busy clearing off the table and setting out a selection of the goodies from the fridge. His phone rang and he knew who it was before he'd glanced at the screen display. 'Hey, Barnie. How are you getting on?'

'Great, thanks. My God, Cam, there's so much stuff here, I could spend the next month wallowing in all this lovely information like the proverbial pig in shit.'

Cam laughed. 'You always have such a charming way with words about you. Found anything that might be of use regarding the church?'

'Not so far.' Barnie's voice sounded muffled as though he was talking and eating at the same time, which knowing him, he probably was. 'But I did find a stack of diaries which might have some juicy scandal hidden in the pages.'

Mindful of his conversation with Hope, Cam warned his friend. 'Let's try not to yank too many old skeletons out of the family closet, eh?'

Barnie laughed. 'Point taken. How's it going with Hope?'

'We've made some good progress this morning.'

'Oh, really?' Cam could picture Barnie waggling his eyebrows or giving some grotesque wink as he said that.

'Shut up, you perv. We've been through the work schedule timeline and tightened it up a bit. The site manager who was here to build Hope's house is coming on board to oversee safety and what have you, and his groundworks team will do whatever mechanical digging we need too. I've got a meeting with him about it tomorrow.'

'That's a bonus because you were still waiting for some quotes to come back about that, weren't you? And one less thing for us to worry about. We should dig out those departmental risk assessments and send them over to him, see what he thinks.'

'Good idea.' Tucking his phone between his shoulder and his ear, Cam grabbed a pen and added a note to his to-do list. 'We lost track of time so we're just about to have a late lunch. What time are you planning on coming over for dinner? There's a steak in the fridge with your name on it and a mountain of salad and stuff.'

'Ah, about that... I was thinking I might leave you to it.'

How many times did they have to go over this? 'There's nothing for you to leave us to. There's nothing going on between Hope and me. Not now, not ever, so stop with the bloody matchmaking.'

A burst of laughter filled his ear. 'Look, mate, no offence but it's not your love life I'm interested in, it's my own. I met this absolutely gorgeous girl on my way to breakfast this morning. She's the yoga teacher here and I've persuaded her to join me for a drink in the pub later. If I play my cards right, I might be able to talk her into extending it into supper.'

Bending over, Cam knocked his forehead against the kitchen counter in mild despair. 'I can't leave you alone for a minute! What the hell is Stevie going to think about you trying to seduce one of her staff?'

'I'm not trying to seduce her! All I did was ask her out for a drink. You make me sound like a sex pest or something.' Cam had been half-joking, but Barnie sounded really hurt.

'Ah, mate, I'm sorry. I don't think anything of the sort. You are about the best person I know. I just don't want any complications this summer.'

Barnie huffed a sigh. 'I know you're right, but Cam, you didn't *see* her. I'll be on my best behaviour, I promise. And I won't say anything else to you about Hope either. It'll be like last night when I never said a word about the two of you all but holding hands with each other.'

He might have known Barnie wouldn't stay down for long. 'We weren't holding hands, you idiot. I'm hanging up the phone now.' He cut Barnie's laughter off with a quick jab of his finger and tossed the phone down.

'Sorry, I didn't realise you were on a call.'

Cam spun around to find a slightly pink-cheeked Hope standing in the doorway, the two panting puppies at her heels. 'It was just Barnie,' he said, wondering how long she'd been standing there. Long enough to catch the comment about them holding hands, or rather *not* holding hands, by the looks of it. Desperate for a distraction, he decided the only thing for it was to drop Barnie in it. He deserved it, after all, for embarrassing poor Hope like this. 'He's cried off dinner tonight because he's taking some yoga teacher he met up at the Hall out for a drink.'

'Meena?' Hope's expression immediately brightened into a wicked grin. 'Oh, I almost feel sorry for Barnie.'

'Why? What's wrong with her?' As much as it would be good to have his friend taken down a peg or two, he didn't want him getting mixed up with someone who would give him grief.

Hope laughed. 'She's lovely, all five feet two of her. I'm sure Barnie was taken in by her delicate looks, but she doesn't only teach yoga. She's also an expert in martial arts and was shortlisted for the national judo team for the last Commonwealth Games.'

Cam grinned, imagining Barnie being sent flying by a tiny woman. 'He's promised me he will be on his best behaviour.'

'Well, let's hope for his sake that's true.' Having settled the dogs back by the door to enjoy the water Cam had put out for them, Hope surveyed the table. 'This looks great, I'm starving.'

'To be fair, it's mostly down to you because you're the one who filled the fridge. All I did was put everything out.'

'Still, it looks good. Shall I start dishing up?'

'Yes, please. I'll sort out some drinks.' Cam returned to the fridge and studied the contents. 'I've got some of that lovely cordial your uncle gave me, wine, beer, more coffee?' He glanced back over his shoulder at her. 'What do you fancy?'

Hope tilted her head to one side as though considering it. 'No more coffee because I've had too much already. If I'm honest, I really fancy a glass of wine. Is that awful?'

'Not at all, we've achieved more than I'd hoped for today, so we deserve a break. Besides, it'll give me an excuse to have a beer. We can take it out on the deck if you like?'

'Oh, that sounds like a great idea. I'll take the plates out.'

By the time he'd joined her with the drinks, Hope was settled on one of the pair of sun loungers with her shoes kicked off to display a set of scarlet-varnished toenails. The heat of the day was at its peak, but thanks to the surrounding trees and the overhang from the balcony, the patio was a shady oasis. Cam nudged his lounger so it was angled more towards Hope, then handed over her drink before settling back with a sigh. 'I could get used to this,' he murmured, letting his eyelids drift closed for a moment as the drowsy warmth soaked into his bones.

'You've got all summer to enjoy it.' Cam cracked one lid open, but Hope had her head tilted back, eyes closed too, so he settled back again and just let himself relax into the moment. He might have dozed off if a fly hadn't buzzed past his nose. He opened his eyes just in time to wave it away from the plates. Hope's hands were resting on her stomach, her fingers wrapped around the base of a wine glass that was starting to lean at a precarious angle. Swinging his legs around to sit up, Cam rescued her wine before it could spill and Hope's eyes jolted open.

'Did I fall asleep?' she asked, voice as drowsy and warm as the gentle breeze.

'Just for a second.' Cam held out her glass and she sat up to take it. 'Have something to eat and then have a nap. You look done in.'

She looked like she might argue for a second then nodded. 'I didn't sleep much last night.'

It was the second time she had mentioned it and he wanted to press for information, to see if there was anything he could do to help. But she'd already made it clear earlier she wasn't in the mood to talk, so he settled for small talk. 'This really does look good, thanks again for filling the fridge up.'

'It seemed like the least I could do when you are giving up your weekend for me.' She was right, he realised with a jolt. Even if he thought the site was a bust, he would've happily come here for the simple excuse of getting to know her a little better.

They ate in silence, but there was nothing awkward about it. It was enough to enjoy the good food, the better company. Nothing stirred in the heat of the afternoon. Even the leaves on the trees seemed too lazy to be bothered to flutter in the sultry air. The only sound was the occasional scrape of a fork on china, a snuffling sigh from one of the dogs as it shifted in its sleep.

'It feels like the whole world's stopped,' Hope murmured.

'Or we've stepped through a portal or crossed a fairy ring into another world,' Cam mused as he stared out over the green canopy.

Hope laughed softly. 'That's a rather fanciful thought for a man of science.'

It was his turn to chuckle. 'I deal in fantasy as much as reality. We had to study this book at school called *The Go-Between*. The opening line was something about the past being like another country where they do things differently. That's what my job is – visiting a different land where I don't speak the language and know nothing of the customs.'

Hope did that funny little head tilt she seemed to always do when she was considering something. He found it surprising, encouraging even, that he'd already begun to understand some of her unspoken cues. 'And you don't have the luxury of being able to observe the people of that place going about their daily business the way I do when I go somewhere on holiday. All you have is whatever you dig up out of the ground and any records you can uncover.'

Cam nodded. 'And until someone invents a time machine, we have to do the best with what we've got. Technology has helped us understand so much – carbon dating, geophysical surveys, digital software that can help us build 3-D models.'

Setting aside her almost empty plate, Hope curled up on her side to face him. 'What do you think it would be like if you could travel back in time?'

'Smelly,' Cam said, making her laugh. 'I'm serious! Look, I love a historical TV show as much as the next person, but the one thing I can't get out of my head is how clean everyone and everything is. We take so much for granted, but we have a romanticised view of the past. Take the levels of disease—'

Hope pulled a face. 'Do I have to? We've just had such a nice meal.'

God, she was adorable. Setting down his own plate, Cam lay down so he was mirroring her, the space between them separated by a small table no more than a foot wide. Hope's lashes drooped, fluttered down until she forced them back up. 'It's okay,' Cam murmured, keeping his voice low. 'Let the world stop for a while and rest.'

13

Hope came awake in stages. The first thing she was aware of was a numbness in her hand. She tried to move it, but it was trapped under something. She tugged again and her head jolted, bringing her close enough to consciousness to realise she'd been lying with her hand trapped under her cheek. Opening her eyes, she rolled from her side to her back, not the easiest thing to do on the narrow sun lounger. Sun lounger? That was enough to wake her up properly and she sat up, massaging her dead hand to get the blood circulating.

'Ow!' She winced as pins and needles tingled painfully. Once the feeling had returned, she rubbed her cheeks, trying to rid herself of the lingering sluggishness from her nap. *What time was it?* The patch of sun on the end of the patio had definitely moved around. There was no sign of Cam, nor their plates or glasses. Looking over her shoulder, she saw he'd pulled the patio doors closed. The dogs were still curled nose to tail on the tiles inside, clearly not bothered by her absence.

Standing, she did her best to check her reflection in the patio door and quickly retied her plait, which had started to come loose. She didn't think she'd drunk more than half her glass of wine, but her head felt as muzzy as if she'd downed the bottle and her mouth was sandpaper dry. Beyond her shadowy reflection, she could see Cam sitting at the dining table, his gaze focused on his laptop screen. She slid open the door, then froze when she heard him talking to someone. The movement was enough to disturb Sooty, who opened one eye and gave her a little bark of greeting.

'Shh!' Hope dropped to her knees in time to catch the puppy as he bounded over. 'Be good now,' she murmured.

'Hey! It's all right, I'm just having a quick chat with my mum.'

Before Hope could answer, he'd turned his laptop towards her and she could make out the figure of someone on the screen. 'Hello.' Hope waved. 'Sorry, I didn't mean to interrupt.'

'You aren't interrupting, love, we were just saying our goodbyes.' The voice from the laptop was faint, but Hope caught the strong rhythms of the northern accent which she'd noticed in Cam's speech from time to time.

Cam turned the laptop back towards him. 'I'm sorry I missed Dad. Tell him I'll send him a text later and I'll speak to you both next weekend.'

'All right, love. Bye-bye.'

'Bye.' Cam shut the lid and turned to Hope. 'Did you have a good sleep? You were out like a light and I didn't want to disturb you.' He seemed to hesitate for a moment, then added. 'You looked like you needed it.'

Hope buried her wince in the thick fur at Sooty's neck. Was that his polite way of telling her she'd been looking rough all day? She'd dabbed on some brightening cream from the samples her mum was always giving her, but it obviously hadn't made a difference. 'Yeah, like I said, I didn't get a great night's sleep.'

'Well, I hope you feel better for it. Can I get you a drink?'

'Just some water, please.' Her fuzzy head was probably due to the gallon of coffee she'd drunk earlier. If she had any more, she definitely wouldn't be sleeping again. She wondered how Mum was feeling and a pang of guilt lanced through her. She should've checked on her earlier. Giving Sooty one final hug, she rose and crossed to the table to retrieve her phone. When she checked her messages, there wasn't anything from her mother, which only made her feel worse. Did Mum think she'd been ignoring her all day on purpose? She started tapping out a message and then thought better of it and pressed the dial button.

'Hello, darling. I was just wondering how you were getting on.' Her mother sounded as tired as Hope felt.

'I'm fine,' she fibbed. 'We had a really productive morning and a late lunch so time's kind of run away from me.' She decided to skip over her impromptu nap.

'Oh, that's good. Are you eating with us tonight? Rowena and I have decided we can't be bothered to cook so we're going to get some fish and chips – it's been an age since we had a takeaway. I only ask as I saw Barnie a little while ago when I popped up to the Hall and he was under the impression you might be having supper with Cameron.'

Hope glanced up as Cam placed a tall glass in front of her. She smiled her thanks at him and took a sip, then smiled again. He'd made her a glass of cordial rather than just water straight from the tap. 'Mum wants to know if we're eating here or with them tonight. She and Aunt Ro are doing a fish and chip run later.'

Cam shrugged. 'Whatever you'd prefer. There's some nice steak in the fridge. I was going to do them on the barbeque, maybe put a couple of jacket potatoes in foil and tuck them in the coals.'

'That sounds nice, as long as you don't mind cooking again?'

He laughed. 'Putting a few things on the table hardly constitutes cooking, but if you'd rather have something from the chip shop, I'm easy.'

Hope shook her head. The idea of a takeaway was always more appealing than the actual outcome. The last thing she wanted was a load of greasy batter, even though the chip shop made everything fresh. 'Steak sounds good.'

'Well, I'm glad that's sorted,' her mother said with a soft chuckle into the phone.

'Sorry, Mum, I didn't mean to keep you hanging on. I need to pop home and feed the dogs, so I'll see you in a few minutes.'

'Okay, darling. See you soon.'

Hope hung up and reached for her keys. 'I won't be too long,' she said to Cam. 'I might leave the car there and walk back, though, as I could do with some fresh air.' She was still feeling a bit groggy and the exercise would hopefully perk her up. If she had any sense, she'd call off dinner, go home and flop down in her bed, but she was also worried her mother would take it as an opportunity to revisit their conversation from the night before and Hope needed some more time to process everything. She'd been doing her best to ignore it all day, but ignoring it wasn't going to resolve anything. A walk in the woods would give her a bit of time and space to start to come to terms with what she'd learned about her father. Plus, she didn't like the idea of leaving Cam on his own all evening. He was easy company to be around, and he didn't seem to mind if she wasn't in the mood to talk much. A quiet dinner, just the two of them, would be the perfect opportunity to relax and get to know each other a little better.

'Do you mind if I come with you? I haven't had time to explore and it'd be great to know if there's a shortcut between here and the farmhouse.' Cam's expression grew concerned. 'Unless you were wanting a bit of peace and quiet and now I've just gone and invited myself along.'

He looked so downcast she couldn't help but laugh. 'I'd like the company, and it's a good idea for you to get your bearings a bit.' Okay, perhaps she was avoiding dealing with all the confusing family stuff, but she'd gone twenty-five years without knowing anything about her background, so it could all wait another day or two. It'd be better to deal with it once Cam and Barnie had gone, anyway. She glanced towards Cam's laptop. Mind you, he did have the know-how to find some of the answers she was looking for. He'd put together that family tree for his parents. Now she knew her mother and father had been married, how hard would it be for Cam to track down a name using that website he'd mentioned?

'Shall we get going then?' Cam had gathered the keys for the lodge and was standing next to the open patio doors with an expectant look upon his face.

'Sure.' Hope ushered the dogs out and filed away the idea of looking up her father for another day.

* * *

The kitchen was the usual pleasant chaos. Mum and Aunt Rowena were sitting at the table, sharing a cup of coffee with Mrs Davis, the cleaner, who'd just popped in to drop off some dry cleaning. Zap was sitting at the other end from the ladies with a pair of headphones on. He was something of a podcast addict, though Rowena reckoned he wasn't listening to anything half the time and it was just an excuse to block out whatever she was saying. Hercule was supine in his lap, his scruffy head resting in the crook of Zap's arm like a baby.

Hope's plans for a quick dash in and out were thwarted as Mum introduced Cam to Mrs Davis, who of course had a million and one questions about the upcoming dig. 'You'll be wanting a hand to keep your place nice for the duration of your stay. I've an hour free on Tuesday mornings and a couple more on Friday after lunch. You can leave me a list on the table of anything you want picking up, or any specific jobs you want doing.'

Cam looked somewhat taken aback. 'Oh, I hadn't really given any thought to having a cleaner.'

Mrs Davis eyed him over the rim of her mug. 'Well, now you won't have to, will you?'

'No, I guess not.' He shot a pleading glance towards Hope, which she studiously ignored. It was easier to argue with a stone than Mrs Davis once she got an idea in her head.

'Right, well, I've fed the dogs so now we're going to head back, if that's okay?' Hope directed the question at her mother, who gave her a smile. She'd done a better job than Hope of hiding the ravages of the night before, but there were lines of strain around her eyes. Needing her to know things were all right, Hope leaned down and gave her a kiss on the cheek and squeezed her shoulders. 'I'll see you later, Mum, enjoy your fish and chips.'

Her mother's smile chased away some of the strain. 'You two have a nice evening. Have you got a torch with you in case it's dark when you walk home?'

Hope tugged her phone out of her pocket and held it up. 'I'll make sure it's fully charged before I leave as well.'

'I'm making a fuss, aren't I?' her mother said with a laugh.

'I wouldn't have it any other way.' It was the truth, for all she had chafed so long against it. Now she understood what lay behind her mother's protectiveness, she knew she needed to give her a little more grace. They still needed to find a balance. Hope was determined to move out once the dig was over and she could turn her focus back to building her little house, but she would find a way to do it without hurting her mother further. God, it was just as well she hadn't asked Cam to research who her father was, because she wanted to kill him for what he'd done.

She and Cam had just turned for the door when a glowering Rhys came stomping in and threw himself down in his chair. 'Bloody, stupid bloody man! Why did he make me do it?'

The noise of his entrance disturbed Hercule who jumped down off Zap's lap and ran away to hide amongst the cushion pile. Zap tugged off his headphones with a frown. 'What's got you in such a mood?' Hope was wondering the same thing, too, because it took a hell of a lot for her cousin to lose his cool.

'Keith bloody Riley,' Rhys growled, bending down to unlace his boots. 'Samson was digging at something in the hay in the back of the cowshed earlier. When I went to see what he was doing, I found a stash of empty bloody vodka bottles buried in the straw! We're just about to put half a dozen pregnant cows in there. What would've happened if one of them rolled in the hay and smashed the glass?'

'My God, that's awful,' Aunt Rowena said with a gasp. 'And you're sure that it's Keith that's been hiding them there?' Hope wasn't the only one who turned an incredulous glance her way. Keith Riley was a notorious drunk who'd been making his wife and his daughter's lives a misery for as long as Hope could remember. He'd used up every bit of good will around the village and been turned off every job he'd ever had. Rhys had taken him on as a last resort as a personal favour to Amelia, Keith's daughter. Keith had sworn he'd turned over a new leaf. Another lie. Rowena held up a hand, her cheeks reddening. 'I know, I know. Poor Daisy.'

'She should've shown him the door years ago,' Rhys snapped.

Hope couldn't blame him for his anger. She knew he was bound to be feeling guilty about having to front up to Amelia about it. They'd been close once. Sure, it was a long time ago, but Hope wondered sometimes if he still kindled a little flame for her. 'He was already on his last warning,' she reminded her cousin gently.

Rhys sighed. 'That's true. God knows I did my best by him, but I can't help the man if he won't help himself. And I won't have anyone on the farm who puts my animals at risk.'

'Of course not,' his father said, his expression furious. 'Where is he now?'

'I chucked him off site and told him not to come back. I'll have to have a word with Ziggy about changing the code on the gate.'

'Don't worry about that,' Zap said, reaching out to cover his hand. 'I'll sort that, you worry about the herd. Take a breath, have a cup of tea and then I'll come out to the barn with you and we can check all the stalls to make sure they're safe. The cows will be all right outside for a day or two more.'

'Cheers, Dad.' Rhys covered his face with his hands. 'What the hell am I going to tell Amelia?'

'You don't need to tell her anything, lad,' Mrs Davis said in her no-nonsense tone. 'Because she knows better than anyone what he's like.' She turned towards Hope's mother. 'I'll speak to Daisy on the quiet and give her some extra hours.'

'Yes, that's a good idea,' Stevie agreed. 'I'll speak to Ziggy and see if there's anything else we can do.'

'We'll need someone to help keep the site office and welfare block up to scratch once the dig starts.' Until Cam spoke up, Hope had all but forgotten he was there. When everyone turned to look at him, he raised one shoulder in an embarrassed shrug. 'Sorry, I didn't mean to butt in. I'd normally get the team to do it on a rota basis, but I can find some flex in the budget to take someone on for a few hours a week. It's not a lot...'

Touched at his kindness, Hope reached out and squeezed his hand. 'That's a really good idea, and it'll be easier to sell to Daisy so she doesn't think it's a case of us taking pity on her.'

'With that and the cleaning at your lodge, it's a start,' Mrs Davis said then she reached around and rubbed her back. 'Plus my sciatica's been giving me terrible trouble so I'll have to be on light duties around here.'

Hope bit back a smile because Mrs Davis was as fit as a butcher's dog. 'Right, if that's sorted, we'd best be getting back.' She hesitated, looking towards Rhys. 'Unless you need a hand in the barn?'

Her cousin shook his head. 'No, you're fine. Dad and I can check the stalls tonight and then I'll give the rest of the place a thorough going over tomorrow.' He shook his head. 'Let's hope that was his only stash and I'm not going to be turning up the contents of an off-licence by the time I'm finished.'

'I have some free time tomorrow morning, so I'll lend you a hand.' She turned to Cam. 'You don't need me for your meeting with Declan tomorrow, do you?'

'No, that's fine. You know what we're going to talk about, and I can update you afterwards.'

'Great. Come on. Let's get out of here.'

14

They walked in silence for a while and Cam was content to focus on their surroundings and make a mental note of the route they took in the hopes he'd be able to remember it. Once they were away from the farm, it was easier as there were signposts dotted around pointing towards The Old Stable Yard, the hotel and spa, the campsite. As they reached the edge of the forest, Hope paused in front of a large board which showed a basic map of the estate. As well as marking out the main features, there were three suggested walking routes indicated with green, amber and red dotted lines, for difficulty or duration, he presumed. Hope tapped the green line. 'We're going to follow this one as it leads to the campsite, but I'll show you where you can turn off the path and cut through to the back of the lodges.'

Cam was glad to see the discreet wooden posts spaced at regular intervals with a reflective green stripe around the top. With the torch on his phone, he reckoned he'd have no trouble finding his way even on the darkest night. It also meant he wouldn't have to worry about his team finding their way back after their inevitable trips to the local pub over the duration of the dig. He made a mental note to add an orientation tour to his list of things to do with them on arrival, then let himself relax and just enjoy the shady peace of the early evening. The green route had been cut back so they didn't even need the signposts to guide them for the most part. Here and there, Cam noticed trampled-down areas leading off under the trees where intrepid walkers had ventured away from the route to explore beneath the trees. Hope pointed towards one of the more well-trodden paths. 'There's a lovely glade through there, perfect for a picnic. Mum used to tell me it's where the fairies live.' She smiled as though recalling a memory and Cam could almost picture her as a little girl, racing around the woods with her long hair flying as she hunted for fairies.

'The drainage at the bottom of our garden isn't very good, so it gets a bit boggy in the autumn and winter. I'd often spot mushrooms or toad-stools growing down there and Mum used to tell me that's where the pixies lived.' God, he hadn't thought about that in years.

Hope glanced up at him through the thick weight of her fringe. 'Not such different lives, after all.'

He had to admit that she had a point. He'd been a bit overwhelmed by the material gulf between their upbringings, but some things were universal. Children had the same imaginations and willingness to believe in magic whether they were gazing out of the misty window of a two-up, two-down terrace or across acres of parkland.

'My mum always said I could travel the world in the pages of a book, and she was right. My favourite day was Wednesday as she'd take me to the library on our way home from school. Dad wasn't into fiction much, but I used to always pick a reference book or a travel guide and he'd sit on the end of my bed when he came home from work and we'd read it togeth-er.' It hadn't occurred to Cam at the time, but his dad must've been tired most days from a long shift. He never showed it, though, or perhaps Cam had been too wrapped up in his books to notice.

'That must've been nice for you both.' There was something wistful in the way Hope said it that had him wondering about her own situation. There was no sign of her father, no mention of him either, only her mother, Stevie.

'I don't think I took him being there for me for granted,' Cam said, his head once more in the past. 'But I'm not sure I ever told him how much it meant to me either.' Plenty of the kids he'd been at school with had been from single parent homes. Sure, his dad hadn't been one of those who was marching up and down the touchline at every football match, but Cam hadn't minded that given the way some of the other dads had bellowed and bullied if they didn't think their kid was trying hard enough, or the ref had made a bad call. He knew his dad needed to work, had never been in any doubt about where the food on the table or the clothes on his back had come from. Those quiet hours, just the two of them, had been a really special gift, he realised now.

'I'm sure he knows,' Hope said, her voice soft.

Cam nodded. 'Yeah. He works some funny shifts so it's not always easy to catch up, but we do our best. He's recently discovered GIFs.' He laughed as he said it because it was fun to watch as his dad tried to find the right meme for every occasion. He didn't always understand the context behind some of the clips, which only added to the humour of the messages they exchanged.

Hope swung to face him. 'Thanks for weighing in earlier with that suggestion about a cleaner for the site offices.'

The abrupt shift in the conversation took him aback for a moment. 'I hope it didn't feel like I was poking my nose in, I just saw an opportunity to help.'

She nodded. 'It's a tricky situation, especially for Rhys, as he's been close friends with Amelia for a long time. He only took Keith on as a way of trying to help her and her mum out and now it's blown up in his face.'

Cam could see how it would make things awkward. 'If it's an ongoing issue with her father, then it's probably not going to be that much of a surprise for her.'

'True.' Hope wandered on for a bit, then turned back to face him. 'Family is such a lottery, don't you think? They shape everything about us and yet we get no say in it until it's often too late.'

'There are lots of different kinds of a privilege, just as there are many different types of deprivation. My family didn't have a lot of money, but I grew up in a stable household full of love and laughter. I saw a lot of my school friends go off the rails because they weren't so lucky.' He thought about Scott, who had all the advantages his father's wealth could buy him but not the one thing the poor kid craved – approval. 'It's not about being rich or poor, either, well, not always, although financial stability isn't something to be taken lightly.'

'Some of us get dealt a handful of aces from the start, and I've always been aware of that,' Hope said, her expression thoughtful. 'I know I have more than most people ever dream of.'

'And yet?' He didn't know what had made him ask the question, only that she seemed to be searching for something.

She hesitated, then sighed. 'My father died when I was young. I never knew him – not even his name. It didn't bother me when I was little because I always had Ziggy around to fill the gap. I went through a phase of being curious when I was a teenager, even went so far as to search for my birth certificate, but his name was never recorded. I hadn't even realised until last night that my parents had been married at some point.'

The reason for her sleepless night began to dawn on him. 'And now we've come along and started poking around in your family history, it's making you wonder about him?'

Hope started to nod, then shook her head. 'I finally got Mum to open up about him and it's... well, let's just say it's a lot to get my head around. And then there's whatever was going on between her and Ziggy last night about my great-grandfather.' She rubbed her forehead. 'I want to know and yet given some of the stuff Mum told me last night, maybe I'm better off leaving it alone.'

'I hate to see you so stressed out. Look, if you're worried that Barnie is going to uncover something that you don't want anyone else to know about, then just say the word and I'll call off his search through the archives. We can just survey the site and try and uncover whatever is there and report our technical findings. We should be able to at least date what we find to a reasonable approximation and find out whether it's connected to the rest of the ruins up there. Whatever connection your family might have to the site can be left for another time. Or we don't have to try and tie the two things together – even presuming there is actually a connection. Like I said before, the stuff Barnie and I have been thinking about is definitely on the wilder side of the speculation index.'

'But would you be happy with that?' Hope asked, folding her arms around her middle. She looked tired and fragile, and he wanted to pull her close.

'I'll be happy with whatever makes you comfortable with us being here,' he promised her. Sure, he'd harboured hopes of finding enough of interest on the estate to publish his findings, but some things were more important than his career ambitions.

She seemed to consider that for a long time before she tilted her head to look up at him. 'I didn't mean to drag you into my personal drama.'

Unable to help himself, Cam reached out and brushed aside a hair that had got caught on her eyelashes. 'I can handle a little drama, don't worry.'

'I'm glad one of us can.' She locked eyes with him, and Cam wished he knew what to say. He wanted to offer her comfort, to reassure her once again that her secrets were safe with him, to put his arms around her and pull her close because he didn't think he'd seen anyone more in need of a hug than she was right then. He did none of those things, however, because it wasn't his place. After a long moment, Hope set her shoulders and the tiredness seemed to melt off her. 'Come on, if that offer for dinner is still open, I'm starving.'

She held out her hand to him and it felt like the most natural thing in the world to take it. She kept their fingers entwined for the rest of the walk back to the lodge, only letting go so they could fold back the patio doors. Without discussing it, they made their way into the kitchen and started preparing dinner, moving in a rhythm that made it seem like it was something they'd done a hundred times before. Hope scrubbed the potatoes while he took the steak out of the fridge to take the chill off before they cooked it. He was out on the patio lighting the barbeque when she came out with the steak and potatoes on a plate, a beer bottle and a tall glass balanced in her other hand. He took the beer with a smile of thanks then set the plate on the table next to the barbeque. 'It needs a few minutes yet, do you want me to sort out some snacks?'

Hope shook her head as she settled back on her lounger. 'No, I can wait.' Cam bent to sit on the lounger next to hers, but Hope shifted her legs to the side and patted the edge of hers. 'Come and sit with me.'

He perched on the side of the lounger, facing towards her, his free hand braced on the other side of her legs. 'I'm not sure this is a good idea.' He gestured between them with his bottle of beer.

'No, you're probably right.' Hope took a long sip from her drink, then set it aside. She regarded him for a long moment. 'If you're worried this is about me using you because I'm in need of comfort, then don't be. I like you, Cam, and I think you like me too. Are we really going to spend the whole summer pretending otherwise?'

Cam's gut clenched in response while his brain ran a quick pros versus cons exercise. Pros – she was gorgeous, smart, funny and intriguing. Cons... *come on brain, list those cons...* All he could come up with was the difference in their background and the fact she was technically going to be his boss for the next few weeks. The background thing didn't need to be an issue if he didn't make it one, and she along with the rest of her family had been nothing but welcoming to him. He thought about the way her mother and her aunt had been sitting at the kitchen table having a coffee with their cleaner; about the things Hope had said about her uncle's altruism and determination to run the estate for the benefit of the whole community, not just to boost the family coffers.

Hope gave him a wry smile, shaking her head as she reached for her drink again. 'I won't be offended if you say no.'

Cam took her hand before she could grasp hold of her drink, brought it to his lips and pressed a soft kiss to the centre of her palm. 'I wasn't working out how to say no, I was working out what I'd be saying yes to.' He turned her hand over in his, stroking his thumb over the spot where he'd just kissed her. 'I don't want things to get complicated between us and put the project at risk.'

'I'm not talking about anything serious,' she interrupted and scooted down the lounger until they were sitting hip to hip. 'I just thought we could have a little fun together, that's all.'

It would be so easy to let himself believe her. To fall into a kiss, into the heat of her, and not give a damn for the consequences. He wanted to, God knows, he wanted to more than he'd wanted anything before in his life. But he couldn't pretend this would be something casual for him. He'd been there, done that and he was tired of meaningless flings. He liked Hope, liked her a lot and he wasn't prepared to pretend otherwise, even if that meant missing out on any chance of being with her. Reaching out, he took a stray curl and brushed it back behind her ear, letting his fingers steal a caress of the soft skin on her neck. 'But I'm not sure I can do this and not get serious about you,' he murmured. 'What I'm starting to feel for you is—'

Whatever he'd been about to say vanished in a flash of heat as Hope leaned forward and pressed her lips to his. Cam froze for a second, letting the reality of the moment sink in before he curled his hand around her nape and let the ebb and flow of their kiss wash his lingering doubts away. Maybe it was risky given how closely they'd have to work together over the coming weeks, but as she opened beneath him and he deepened their kiss, he couldn't bring himself to care. She felt so good in his arms, like it was where she'd always belonged.

When they broke for air, Hope looked a little dazed and Cam couldn't help a little smile of satisfaction that he'd been the one to put that expression on her face.

'Rowena said you were a still-waters-run-deep kind of man, and she was right.'

Cam huffed out a laugh, pushing out some of the tension in his body at the same time. He wanted to take his time with Hope, really enjoy getting to know her rather than falling into bed straight away. 'You've been talking about me, have you?'

Hope flopped onto her back with a laugh. 'Maybe.' She held out her hand and though he wanted to accept her invitation more than anything else right then, he forced himself to his feet. 'I think we should finish getting dinner ready, don't you?'

When she gave him a puzzled frown, Cam leaned down and pulled her to her feet. 'I'm trying very hard to be on my best behaviour,' he told her, before dropping a teasing kiss on her mouth. 'Let me prove to you I know how to be a gentleman.'

She cupped his cheek. 'You have nothing to prove to me, Cameron Ferguson.'

'Well, let me prove it to myself, then.' He lowered his forehead to hers. 'I haven't felt like this in a very long time. I don't want to blow it.'

She tipped her head back to stare up at him. 'I get it. We've got the whole summer to get to know each other – I'm happy if we take a little time.'

'Not too much time,' Cam blurted, making Hope's sunshine laugh fill the air.

'Definitely not! Now, if we're not going to satisfy one appetite, you owe me dinner in compensation.'

Cam stole one more quick kiss then let her go before he undid all his good intentions.

15

The next fortnight passed in such a whirl that Hope almost didn't have time to miss Cam. He was up to his eyes in work, juggling the final preparations for the dig while trying to keep on top of all his usual end-of-term responsibilities. They'd managed to speak most evenings and he found time to text her at random times during the day. Sometimes it was just to say hello, but now and then he'd send her a Spotify link for a song he'd heard on the radio that made him think of her, or a promo link for a film or a TV show he wanted them to watch together. Who would've thought such a romantic heart hid behind that sensible façade? It was enough to make a girl swoon.

Things were just as hectic for Hope at Juniper Meadows. It was the height of the wedding season and both she and Zap were flat out at the distillery, creating, bottling, and sending out custom-designed gins. Hope had a love/hate relationship with the miniature bottles they'd procured for use as wedding favours. She loved how popular they were, what with couples always on the lookout for something unique to offer their guests as a memento, but she hated how bloody fiddly they were to fill. They had a machine that could handle the normal full and half sizes they offered to the mainstream market, but if the favours proved to be more than a fad, she was going to have to invest in some specialist equipment that could automatically fill the miniatures. One must exist because how else did all those hotel minibars get stocked? She'd scrawled a huge reminder on her office whiteboard, but hadn't had time to properly research and cost it.

Cam and the team were due on site in less than eight hours to get everything set up and Hope wanted everything to be perfect, which was why she was sitting in bed updating the project costs tracker at 1 a.m. She'd tried to settle earlier but ended up switching the light back on five minutes later. *Cam would be here in the morning.* When had she ever felt this giddy over a man? Never was the simple truth of it.

Her phone flashed in the dark and she picked it up to read the notification, already knowing who it would be from. At least she wasn't the only one who was having trouble sleeping.

Are you in the tracker? I'm locked out.

Lord, he was as bad as she was. Grinning to herself, she tapped out a reply.

What are you doing still awake? It's going to be a long day tomorrow.

The response came back almost instantly.

I could ask you the same thing!

He added an emoji of a little face with a monocle casting a quizzical look upwards as though it was reading what she'd just written.

I'm just checking everything over. I'm too excited about tomorrow to sleep.

I know the feeling! We'll both be fit for nothing though if we don't get some rest.

He was right.

Five minutes and then I promise to shut my laptop.

Good! Get some sleep. Can't wait to see you tomorrow x

Her stomach did a little flip.

Me too. Sleep tight x

Hope set her phone on the bedside cabinet then turned back to the tracker before admitting to herself that she'd only been fiddling around with it as an excuse to stay awake just in case Cam messaged her. Giving herself a mental side eye for being a soppy idiot, she saved and closed the file and placed her laptop on the floor well away from where she might accidentally step on it if she got up. With a quick fluff of her pillows to get comfortable, she closed her eyes and was asleep within moments.

She woke the next morning feeling surprisingly refreshed and a quick blast of cold water at the end of her shower chased the last of any tiredness away. The forecast on her weather app said they were in for another scorcher, so she dressed in thin linen trousers and a vest with a long-sleeved cotton shirt over it to protect her skin from the worst of the sun. Declan had ordered a massive supply of sun cream for the site welfare office as well as cheap sun hats and baseball caps. Hard hats would be required whenever the groundcrews were working, but he'd wanted to make sure everyone had a head covering at all times. With her hair plaited and pinned in a coil at her nape, Hope plopped her own sun hat on and headed downstairs with her laptop under one arm.

As she neared the kitchen, she could hear voices and was amazed to walk in and find the whole family gathered around the table, all dressed in similar comfortable clothing. 'What's going on here?'

Rising to fetch her a mug from the cupboard, Rhys set it down in front of her usual seat with a grin. 'You'll need some extra bodies today to help everyone get from place to place, so we thought we'd volunteer.'

'Your mother and I are going to make sure everything runs smoothly at the campsite,' her Aunt Rowena said, pushing the toast rack and the butter towards her. 'We also wondered about throwing a barbeque here in the yard later, to welcome everyone and have a bit of an ice breaker in case there are people who don't know each other.'

Hope pressed a hand to her chest, touched at the thoughtfulness of the gesture. 'That's so kind of you. I don't want to put you to any trouble, though.'

'Nonsense,' Stevie said. 'You've had more than enough on your plate. You'll always be my independent little miss...' The sweetness of her smile told Hope it was a compliment, not a criticism. 'But you don't have to do everything yourself.'

Hope nodded and looked around at the familiar faces. 'Thank you. I really appreciate your support.'

It was Ziggy who responded. 'Zap, Rhys and I will each take a vehicle up to the gates and act as escorts as people arrive.'

Hope reached for her phone. 'I've got an email here somewhere from Cam with a timetable showing where everyone is coming from and their best estimate at when they expect to arrive.' She found the message and forwarded it to her uncles and her cousin. 'There you go.'

Zap picked up his phone when it pinged and glanced at the message. 'And I didn't think it was possible for someone to be even more of a planner than you,' he said with a chuckle. 'You really are a match made in heaven.'

'Zappa!' Rowena hissed at her husband.

'What?' He looked around, face bemused as though he couldn't work out what he'd said wrong.

Hope poured herself a mug of tea from the pot, and gave herself time to process the fact she and Cam had obviously been the subject of some family speculation. Raising the mug to her lips, she blew on her tea before surveying her mother over the rim. '*Mum?*'

Stevie's cheeks flamed in an immediate tell-tale blush. 'I might have observed that Cameron's a nice young man and pointed out how well the two of you have been getting on together. I didn't mean anything by it!'

'Hmm.' Hope turned her gaze onto her aunt next. Rowena was much less of a soft touch than Stevie and the look she returned had more than a shade of defiance in it. 'If you think I'm going to ignore the bloody obvious and pretend the two of you aren't half-smitten already, then you don't know me at all.'

'I'm not asking anyone to pretend anything of the sort,' Hope said firmly. 'But I do expect that you won't interfere. Cam and I are perfectly capable of managing our relationship without any assistance.'

'So, there is a relationship.' Her aunt exchanged a look of triumph with her mother. 'What did I tell you?' With a sweep of her colourful kaftan, Rowena rose from the table and headed to the kitchen sink. 'We'll say no more about it. Bring your cups and plates those that have finished,' she said as she tugged off her rings and set them on the windowsill.

'Not another word, I promise!' Her mother's face was a picture of delight and Hope knew she had to nip things in the bud before they got out of hand.

'Don't start getting excited, we're taking things very slowly and it might not even come to anything...' Hope trailed off because her mother was already across the kitchen and whispering with Rowena.

'Big mistake.' When she glanced around at her cousin, it was to find Rhys grinning at her without an ounce of sympathy. 'You never, ever let your guard down with them. Haven't I taught you anything?' Rising, he gathered his mug and plate. 'A hundred quid says they'll be picking hats out within a fortnight.'

'By the way, Rhys,' Aunt Rowena said without bothering to turn around, 'I spoke to Mrs Davis yesterday and Daisy Riley has come down with an awful cold, so Amelia is going to be helping out around the place instead.'

'Oh, I haven't seen Amelia in ages, it will be lovely to get the chance to catch up with her, won't it?' Hope aimed a beaming smile at her cousin as she watched the back of his neck redden. She knew she shouldn't encourage her aunt's dream that one day Rhys and Amelia would get over themselves and realise they were still in love – that ship had long since sailed for both of them – but he deserved it after his smug remark just now.

'I... er, I need to go and clean my teeth,' Rhys muttered, turning on his heel and all but bolting for the stairs.

'You shouldn't tease the boy, Ro,' Zap said as he carried his breakfast things to the sink. 'You know they're just friends.' He softened the mild criticism with a kiss to her cheek.

'I know,' she admitted, pushing her wild hair out of her face with a dry bit of one soapy hand. 'But I'm worried about him. That farm is tiring him out and now he's a worker down after that mess with Keith, he's taking on even more of the load.'

'I'm in the process of sorting out some extra support for Rhys,' Ziggy said from his usual spot at the head of the table. 'The agency sent some CVs over and we're going to go through them next week.'

Rowena turned to her brother-in-law with a smile. 'I might have known you'd already have things in hand.'

Ziggy raised one shoulder in a kind of 'what did you expect' gesture then continued speaking. 'Plus, Mikey popped over yesterday to catch up. He's finished at Cirencester for the summer and is more than happy to put his studies into practice and put some money in his pocket at the same time. He's starting on Monday.' Michael Dobbs was another one of Ziggy's success stories. A few years younger than Hope, he'd started to go off the rails after his father left home and his mother had struggled to cope with him acting up. Ziggy had stepped in, taking the boy under his wing. Hope didn't know exactly what had gone on between them, but Mikey had eventually turned a corner and knuckled down at school. He'd come away with top grades and a bursary from Ziggy's fund to study at the nearby agricultural college.

Hope's phone buzzed and she checked the screen, only slightly disappointed to see the message was from Declan rather than Cam. 'Declan's just arrived, so I'm heading up to the site,' she said, swiping two spare pieces of toast to take with her. Splitting one slice in half, she offered the pieces to Sooty and Sweep. 'Come on, you two.'

Declan already had the welfare office unlocked and the kettle on by the time Hope arrived. He stood in the open doorway of the cabin and beamed down at her. 'Lovely morning for it.'

'Isn't it just.' She moved around to the back of the Range Rover. 'Can you give me a hand to get these two settled?'

'Sure.'

Having the puppies with her had never been a problem at her office, but she'd been at a loss at what to do with them over the summer when she'd be back and forth between there and the site. It wasn't fair to leave them at home all day. Ziggy had said he would look after them, but she hadn't wanted to burden him when he was already taking back some of the stuff he'd normally rely on her to do so she would have more time to focus on the dig. A chat with Declan about site safety had resulted in him constructing a little doggy den in between the two cabins. Secured with Heras fencing on all sides, he'd constructed a sunshade from some old pallets and Hope had brought up a couple of their old doggy pillows and water bowls. This way, Sooty and Sweep could see what was going on, had enough space to wander about and still be kept safely out of the way.

'In you come, lads,' Declan said as he lifted the front fence aside to let the dogs in the compound. Rather than close it up immediately, he bent to accept their licks of greeting, laughing when they showed a great deal of interest in one of his pockets. 'Can't hide anything from you, can I?' Declan pulled a couple of chews out and tossed them onto the pillows in the shade. The dogs dived for the treats and were settled in moments, gnawing away at the rawhide treats.

'You'll spoil them,' Hope admonished as he secured the fence behind him, though she said it with a smile.

Declan gave her a sheepish grin. 'What can I say? I'm a soft touch. I'll take them for a walk later once we've got the morning arrivals briefed and I'll make sure they run it off.'

She could've told him he didn't have to do that, but it had become clear he was as much of a dog person as Cam was, so if he wanted to take the dogs out now and then, she wasn't going to stop him. 'That would be great, thanks. While I remember, we're throwing a barbecue later to welcome everyone – it's a bit short notice because Mum and Aunt Rowena only came up with the idea this morning, but you should come too as you're very much part of the team.' He wasn't staying on site like the others as he lived less than twenty minutes away, but Hope wanted Declan to feel included.

Declan shook his head. 'Any other time, but I've promised my wife I'd take her to the cinema later.'

'Oh, that's a shame.' Hope thought about it for a moment then offered a possible solution. 'Could your wife not come and meet you here? You could eat with us and then head off to see the film afterwards, if it's a late enough showing, that is.'

'We were planning on eating beforehand, so let me check with her and see what she says.' Declan's smile was warm as he gazed down at her. 'That's really thoughtful of you, Hope, thanks.'

She was spared the embarrassment of replying by the sound of a horn beep-beeping behind them. Turning, she spotted her cousin waving out of the window of his Range Rover, a convoy of half a dozen vehicles behind him. She recognised Cam's rundown hatchback and Barnie's smarter car in the little queue and couldn't stop the fizz of excitement in her stomach. 'Here we go.'

'I'll get those teas and coffees made,' Declan said, but she shook her head.

'No, let me sort that out. This is your site to manage, so you should go and greet them. I don't want the lines of who's in charge getting blurred.'

'Well, as long as you're sure?' When she nodded, Declan ducked into the cabin and returned a second later with a hardhat on and carrying a high-vis vest, which he slid his arms into as he marched with purpose towards the site entrance gate.

Hope climbed the steps into the cabin and tossed her sunhat on the table. She bypassed the kettle to fill the large hot water urn and switched it on to heat up. They'd decided on reusable mugs to cut down on waste, so she set them out on the counter and opened a box of tea bags and a jar of coffee, which she placed next to the urn so people could help themselves.

She was just checking the fridge had enough bottled water when someone rapped on the open door and a familiar voice called out. 'White coffee, two sugars for me!' Turning with a laugh, Hope found herself almost nose-to-nose with a grinning Barnie. 'Hello! Hello! Well, here we finally are!'

'Hello!' She leaned forward to kiss his cheek and laughed because he'd thrust out a hand. 'There'll be no standing on ceremony here,' she said.

'Well, if you're not going to accept a kiss, get out of the way so I can at least claim mine,' a familiar voice said from behind Barnie's shoulder.

Barnie rolled his eyes at her, before pecking her cheek and edging past her on the steps. 'I'll get my own drink then, shall I?'

'Whatever you like,' Hope murmured, not really listening to him because Cam had taken his place on the steps. It was silly to feel so shy, but she couldn't seem to calm the butterflies in her stomach all of a sudden. 'Hello.'

'Hello. Everything okay?' He reached up to tuck away a stray curl that had escaped her plait and it was as though his touch broke the spell.

'Everything's great.' He was one step below her, which set him at the perfect height to claim the kiss she'd been anticipating all week.

'It is now,' he murmured against her lips. In a normal voice he continued, 'I'm sorry we're a bit earlier than expected, but everyone was so keen to get going that they were already waiting in the car park at the university when I arrived.' Slipping an arm around her waist, he turned to face the people waiting at the bottom of the steps. 'This is Hope. She's the reason we're all here today, so be nice to her, okay?'

She laughed as half a dozen greetings rose from the gaggle in front of her. Most of the team looked to be undergraduates, but there were a couple of faces that were older, maybe even around her age. 'I just want to say how grateful I am to all of you for giving up your time to help me solve the mystery of whatever I accidentally uncovered.'

'Is it true you were building a house?' one of the young men asked. His cheeks reddened almost immediately and there was something of a look of panic as he looked past Hope towards Cam. 'Sorry, I hope that wasn't inappropriate of me to ask. Dr Ferguson has already told us we should respect your family's privacy.'

'It's fine,' Hope assured him. 'I don't mind answering questions about what happened.' She gave them a quick rundown of what had happened, then cast a quick glance up at Cam, who had stiffened a little beside her. 'It's fine,' she repeated so only he would hear. 'They're bound to be a bit curious.'

Cam nodded. 'I meant what I said before, though, so let me know if anyone starts poking their nose in where it's not wanted.'

'I will. Come on, I'm sure everyone could do with a drink.' She led the way into the cabin. It was a bit of a tight squeeze with everyone inside, but thankfully, Barnie took control. He soon had a little production line set up by the urn. He took orders, dumping either a teabag or a spoonful of coffee in mugs and passed them to a handsome Asian man with a fringe that dangled in his eyes who added hot water from the urn. A pretty blonde woman next to him added milk and sugar as required. With a mug of tea in hand, Hope followed Cam outside and soon the others had joined them in a loose circle.

'Five minutes, everyone, and I'll start the safety briefing.' They turned to see Declan standing on the steps of the site office.

'Thanks, we'll be there in a minute,' Cam assured him. He turned back to the group. 'Remember what I said: Declan is in charge of everyone's safety and security, so I want you all to play close attention to what he has to say, okay?' The group nodded and began to break up as people finished their drinks and a couple of them began returning the dirty mugs to the welfare unit.

'I'll wash up afterwards,' said the Asian man with the long fringe.

'Cheers, Adam.'

'Scott will give me a hand, won't you?' Adam asked with a grin at the young man who'd questioned Hope about how she'd uncovered the site.

'That's me volunteered, I guess,' Scott said, though he was smiling rather than disgruntled at the thought. Hope was getting a good feeling from the little group already.

They were about to head to the site office when a phone started ringing. Scott pulled it out of his pocket, his happy expression swallowed by a frown as he looked at the caller ID. 'It's my dad,' he said, staring at the phone like it might bite him. 'That's the third time he's called me this morning.' He made no move to answer it and it seemed to take forever for the noise to stop.

'Is there a problem I need to be aware of?' Cam's question sounded casual enough, but Hope could sense a sudden tension in his body.

Scott raised his head, his expression one of such abject misery that Hope wanted to reach out and hug him. 'He's really mad at me for coming on the dig. He'd lined up a summer job for me at his company. I've told him a million times that I'm not interested in working in the leisure industry, but he just won't listen.' The phone began to ring again, and the poor kid looked close to tears of frustration.

Reaching out, Cam took the phone from Scott, pressed the button to reject the call and tucked it away in his pocket. 'New site rule. All phones are to be handed in and locked away in the site office. I don't want anyone distracted, is that understood?'

The relief on Scott's face was like the sun breaking out from behind a dark cloud. 'Understood, Dr Ferguson.'

He turned to go but Cam called him back. 'You're not a child, Scott, and we're not in school, so you should call me Cameron or Cam.'

'O... okay, Cam. Thanks again.' Scott's smile this time was sweeter, and a little shy. 'I'll make sure everyone is ready for the briefing, shall I?'

As he loped off, the phone began to ring again. With a muttered curse, Cam tossed it into the boot of his car, slammed it shut and locked it. 'Controlling bastard.'

It was the first time Hope had heard him swear, certainly the first time she'd seen him angry. 'Is there a problem I need to know about?'

Slinging an arm around Hope's shoulders, Cam sighed. 'Scott's father and I have a bit of a history and let's just say I'm not his favourite person. He likes to throw his weight around, that's all. We're going to have to keep a close eye on Scott for the next few weeks. Adam's already taken him under his wing, it seems, so I'll ask him to make sure Scott isn't getting too much of a hard time from his dad.'

Hope leaned her head against him. 'You're a good man. I'm sure that with a little guidance from you, Scott will find a way to deal with it.'

He gave her a quick squeeze before his arm fell away. 'I hope so. Come on, Declan's already giving us a death stare and I don't want to annoy him on the first day.'

After the briefing and a quick tour of the site, Hope led the convoy of cars around the estate to the campsite and left the students in the capable hands of her mother and Rowena to get them settled in and make sure they had everything they needed. By the time she returned to the site compound, another couple of cars had arrived and she was just in time to exchange a word with Rhys, who was heading back out. 'There's only one more person arriving today, so I'm heading back to the farm,' he said. 'Z and Z seem happy enough to hang about by the gate and wait for them. They've set themselves up with a couple of camp chairs and a picnic.'

Hope grinned. 'They're probably enjoying the peace and quiet.' She glanced towards the two cars and the noisy group who were spilling out of one. 'Can't say I blame them.'

Rhys laughed. 'They'll calm down a bit once everyone is settled in. See you later!'

He drove off with a wave, leaving Hope to negotiate her way to a parking spot without running anyone over. She'd just parked and got out when a pretty blonde jumped out of the second car and made a smiling beeline for Cam. His face lit up the moment he saw her and he swept her up into a tight hug. Hope might have felt a bit awkward at their apparent intimacy if Cam hadn't immediately raised his head and called out to her. 'Hope, hey! Come and meet one of my favourite people in all the world.'

Well, with an invitation like that, how could she refuse? Intrigued to meet another one of Cam's friends, Hope walked over to join them. 'Hello.'

'Hello.' The blonde gave her a speculative look before turning back to Cam. 'Well, introduce us then!' she said, giving him a little poke in the middle with one finger.

Cam batted her away. 'Behave! Hope, this is Cassie. She and I go back a long way. Cassie, this is Hope.'

Well, that wasn't much of an introduction. 'Hope Travers, it's a pleasure to meet you,' Hope said as they shook hands. 'My family own the estate and I'm the one who accidentally uncovered the ruins. So, how exactly do you two know each other?'

'We were undergrads together,' Cassie said. 'And we've been friends ever since.' Her tone was just bland enough that Hope couldn't help wondering how close their friendship might have been.

Cam curled an arm around Hope's waist. 'Cassie left me for another man when we were first-year students, but I'm just about over it now.'

Cassie threw back her head and laughed. 'Oh, what absolute rubbish! You and I were the most unsuitable match going.' She turned to Hope, mirth shining in her eyes. 'He actually thanked Ed for taking me off his hands during his best man's speech, can you believe it?'

Hope grinned, liking this funny, bubbly woman already. 'Shocking behaviour! I'm appalled.'

'Oh, I *knew* I was going to like you!'

'Did you now?' Hope looked up at Cam. There was a hint of a blush on his cheeks. Had he been talking about her with his friends, then? Well, well, well. Holding out a hand to Cassie, Hope drew her arm through hers. 'Let me make you a coffee and you can give me all the inside info I need on Dr Ferguson.'

'It would be my pleasure,' Cassie said, giving her arm a squeeze. They took one look at the rather discomforted look on Cam's face and both burst out laughing. Hope would make it up to him later, but it wouldn't do any harm to make him sweat a bit in the meantime.

16

Cam led the excited group along the trail from the campsite towards the farm, pointing out the landmarks he'd used to help memorise the route as well as the little marker posts. He was that strange combination of exhausted and hyped up. After their early start, it had been a long day and part of him wanted to stay in the peace and quiet of his lodge and chill out on the patio with nothing but the sound of the birds and the breeze rippling through the trees – and Hope by his side, of course.

He wasn't a naturally outgoing person and one of the biggest challenges he'd had to overcome to do his job was being the centre of attention. On a one-to-one basis or leading a small discussion group, he had no problems with his confidence. The first time he'd had to stand in front of a full lecture theatre, though? He'd thrown up before, almost during, and several times afterwards. His nerves had become so bad, one of the senior lecturers had suggested he do some cognitive behavioural therapy to conquer them.

It was during that process that he'd come to understand it wasn't just because he was a naturally reserved person. Though he'd challenged it at first when his therapist had raised it, he'd slowly come to accept that part of his lack of self-belief was to do with his working-class roots. He'd mistakenly believed the therapist had been insinuating he felt some kind of hidden shame towards his parents, but she'd carefully explained it was more to do with him unconsciously taking on the lack of expectation society had towards boys like him being able to succeed. Throughout his education, he'd been treated as something of an anomaly by his teachers. A poor white boy who came from a strong, stable home where both parents worked and encouraged his love of learning. That didn't match the messaging at all. He wondered how many of his peers had lost out on opportunities to excel because they were written off before they had a chance to get going.

He looked around the group and was saddened to be reminded that not one of them was from a background like his. Those students were off working for the summer, earning as much money as they could to shore themselves up financially for the coming academic year. Cam had been able to eke out a small stipend from his budget for everyone coming on the dig, but it was only enough to cover food and basic essentials. Even the most frugal of them would struggle to have anything left at the end of the summer. It was something Cam should've thought about before, he was dismayed to admit to himself.

'Which way now?' someone asked.

Lost in his thoughts, Cam hadn't realised they were this close to the edge of the woods and the people ahead had already reached the cross-roads. Deciding he would try to have a chat at some point with Ziggy and ask him how his bursary scheme worked, Cam wove through the milling group and pointed to the right. 'We're going to cut across here and then we'll meet one of the estate roads that will take us directly to the farm.'

Letting the group go ahead of him now they were confident on the directions, Cam waited to make sure no one was left too far behind. He was pleased to see Scott chatting away with Adam Lau and his girlfriend, Zoë. Scott hadn't asked him for his phone back yet, and though Cam had retrieved it from his car boot and charged it up, given the number of missed calls and messages from Scott's father which had popped up on the notification screen, he'd decided to *accidentally* forget it. Scott would want it back eventually, of course, but if Cam could give him the rest of the evening to hang out and relax with his friends, then it seemed like a small gift. If there was any blowback from Willoughby senior then Cam would deal with that as well. The man had already learned once that Cam was not easily bullied, he would have no problems in serving him a reminder of that fact.

Cassie was at the back of the group, talking into her mobile. Usually so animated, her rigid posture and pulled-down mouth had him concerned there was something wrong at home. He caught her eye and waggled his thumb in and up-and-down gesture. She grimaced before giving him a thumbs up and began walking towards him. As she grew closer, he caught her words and understanding dawned.

'Don't cry, baby, don't cry. You are going to have such a lovely time with Granny and Granddad. Daddy said you're going to the beach tomorrow. You love it at the beach.' She threw Cam a helpless look and he moved to her side, curling an arm around her shoulders to offer what comfort he could. 'I love you, sweet girl, night night,' she said, looking like she might burst into tears too. Her tone changed then. 'Oh, bloody hell, Ed. I don't think I can stand it.'

Cassie sniffled as she chatted to her husband and Cam hugged her tighter, wishing there was something more he could do. 'Really?' Cassie's voice sounded brighter. 'You're not just saying that to make me feel better? That little minx!' Cassie glanced towards Cam and rolled her eyes as she turned the phone away from her mouth. 'Ed says she's been fine all day. Barely even mentioned me or looked at him because she's been so wrapped up with his parents... What?' she addressed the last into the phone. 'Oh, Cam's here being my emotional support stand-in. We're all on our way to a welcome barbeque the lovely people who own the estate are throwing for us. Oh, and guess what! I met Hope and she's *lovely*.'

Cam shot her a warning look, which only made his friend grin wider as she blew him a kiss. He should be relieved, he supposed, that Cassie and Hope had hit it off so well, but when they'd disappeared off together earlier, he'd worried about exactly how much Cassie would reveal. Resolving to have a chat with her later, Cam let her go and walked ahead so she could finish her chat with Ed in privacy.

He'd been gutted when Cassie had broken up with him halfway through their first year at uni, but it had been the right thing to do. She and Ed were much better suited, for one thing, Cam having struggled a little with Cassie's need to be the centre of attention when he was happier sitting on the sidelines. He'd never wanted her to dim that bright light of her personality, but he hadn't been comfortable being dragged into the spotlight either. Ed was much more like Barnie in that respect and happy to throw himself around on the dancefloor or join the million and one causes and committees Cassie had got involved with. It had all worked out perfectly as far as Cam was concerned because he'd gained another friend after Ed and Cassie had got together, and a beautiful goddaughter a few years later. He adored Fleur, their vivacious little three-year-old, who was already showing every sign of being as full of personality as her mother, and spent hours in the run-up to her birthday and Christmas trying to find the perfect gifts for her.

'Ed says hello,' Cassie said, curling an arm through his as she moved up beside him.

'I take it Fleur turned on the waterworks?' Cam asked.

'That girl of mine is going to win an Oscar when she grows up,' Cassie replied with a laugh. 'I could hear her giggling in the background while Ed and I were saying goodbye, so she's absolutely fine.' But there was no mistaking the tiny bit of doubt in her voice as she said it.

'This will be the longest you've been apart from her, won't it?' She might be big on personality, but he knew Cassie well enough to know when she needed a shoulder to lean on. Ed was due to join them tomorrow, which he hoped would make things easier for her, but he understood it was going to be tough for Cassie having to be apart from Fleur.

Cassie nodded. 'She goes to both our parents for holidays, but we've never left her for longer than a week before.'

'If it gets too much, then you only have to say the word.' Cam would struggle without his friends to help guide the younger members of the group, but he and Barnie would handle it if they needed to. Some of the recent graduates like Adam and Zoë would likely relish the chance to step up and take on more responsibility.

'I know, and I appreciate that, but it's been so long since I've been able to commit to some field work, and besides, I want Fleur to be confident and capable. I don't want her clinging onto my hand and afraid to try new things.'

Cam doubted any child with parents like Cassie and Ed would be a shrinking wallflower. 'There's a spare lodge next to mine. I could have a chat with Hope later and see about whether your in-laws could come up and use that for a few days. There's loads of space for Fleur to play during the day and she'd get to see you both in the evenings.'

Cassie's megawatt smile all but lit up the early evening. 'Do you think that would be possible?'

Cam shrugged. 'I don't know without talking to Hope, but if it's a problem, then I will happily move into one of the tents for a week and they can use my place instead.'

Cassie leaned her head against his shoulder. 'You really are the best guy I know,' she murmured.

Cam pressed a kiss to her temple. 'Second best. You married the best. Come on, let's go and chat to Hope about it now.'

When they arrived at the farmhouse, the family were still in the process of setting everything up. Before Cam could suggest they help out, several of his students were already in motion, taking plates and dishes off Stevie and Rowena before they could take more than a couple of steps out of the kitchen door. Barnie was halfway up a stepladder stringing fairy lights along the back wall, a petite dark-haired girl bracing the bottom step as she instructed Barnie to rehang the string about six inches further along. Meena, Cam assumed. Hope was behind a group of trestle tables organising the food being ferried from the kitchen, so he made a beeline towards her. 'What can I do?'

'Zap's sorting out drinks inside, can you see if he needs a hand?'

'Of course.' He was going to suggest Cassie come with him, but she'd already circled the tables and was shuffling plates around to make more room for the seemingly unending stream of food. Hope gave her a small frown but didn't say anything and Cam wondered if she preferred to do it herself. Too many cooks and all that... Deciding they were more than capable of sorting it out between them, Cam beat a not quite hasty retreat towards the kitchen, forgetting all about his earlier concern about Cassie spilling too many of his secrets.

Stevie met him at the threshold. 'Cam, darling, your students are simply the most charming bunch! Rowena and I can't lift a finger without one of them volunteering.' She nodded towards the sink, where Scott was already elbow-deep in washing-up suds, with Adam beside him wielding a tea towel and Zoë following instructions from Rowena about where things could be put away. Zap was supervising a couple of the other students as they filled jugs with ice and either mint, slices of lemon and lime or chopped fruit. He then poured in the requisite measures of alcohol before Ziggy added the mixers.

'Hope sent me in to give Ziggy a hand, but I see I'm pretty much surplus to requirements,' Cam joked.

'Rhys is looking after the barbecue,' Stevie said. 'Why don't you go and see if he needs some help?'

'Okay.' Cam doubted Rhys needed his help, but he knew when he was being politely dismissed. Spotting a metal tub filled with cans and bottles, he grabbed a couple of beers from it and wandered over to where Rhys stood behind a pair of enormous gas barbecues.

As Cam had suspected, he had everything under control, but he accepted the beer with a grin of thanks. 'Perfect timing.'

'I have my uses,' Cam said with a laugh. 'Mostly they involve keeping out of the way.'

'That's a useful talent,' Rhys replied, surveying the people milling around the yard. 'There's a reason why I'm hiding behind here.' They clinked bottles and shared a smile.

A few minutes later and the atmosphere in the yard switched from a frenzy of activity to something altogether more chilled out. Zap had set up his cocktails on one of the tables and was doing brisk business dishing out mojitos, Pimm's and some kind of gin and prosecco cocktail that Cam thought he might have to sample before the evening was out. The fairy lights flicked on, their pretty sparkle greeted with a cheer, and Cam watched as a grinning Barnie took a bow. When their eyes met, Cam raised his beer in toast and his friend returned his greeting with a wave. A few moments later, he joined them, clutching his own beer.

'Nice work,' Cam said. 'Though I think that's probably down to your supervisor.' He nudged Barnie with his elbow. 'I thought you were going to play it cool.'

'I tried,' Barnie said, raising his hands in protest. 'But the gorgeous

Meena finds me inexplicably irresistible, and I am but a weak man in the face of her beauty.' As though she'd sensed him talking about her, Meena glanced up from her conversation with Hope and Cassie and sent them a wave. Barnie waved back, the expression on his face that of a man completely smitten, and Cam hid a smile. It looked like Juniper Meadows was weaving a spell on his friend as well.

'Oh, here we go,' Rhys said, drawing Cam's attention back to them. Rowena was approaching, Scott at her side, both of them carrying plates filled with burgers, sausages, meat and vegetable kebabs. 'Veggie stuff that side,' Rhys said, nodding towards the grill on the right.

Scott set his two plates on the extended stand on that side and stepped back. 'Is there anything else you need me to do?'

Rowena shook her head. 'No, darling, you've done more than enough already. Go and get yourself a beer and enjoy yourself.'

Scott ducked his head, as though unused to the praise. 'I was happy to help. Just give me a shout if you need anything.'

Rowena reached up and brushed a strand of hair off his forehead. 'You'll be the first person I ask. Oh!'

'What is it?' Scott's expression was instantly concerned.

Rowena laughed. 'Oh, nothing! I just forgot to put my rings back on. I'd better go and find them before Zap notices. Even after thirty years, he still gets grumpy when I'm not wearing them.'

'I saw some on the windowsill when I was washing up, was that them? I'll go and fetch them.' Scott was loping across the yard before Rowena had time to reply.

'What a sweet boy he is,' Rowena said, turning to them with a smile, though Cam didn't miss the slight pinched look around her eyes. 'Strikes me as a bit of a worrier, though.' She hesitated as if perhaps she'd spoken out of turn.

'His dad's an overbearing prick,' Barnie said before taking a hard swig of his beer. 'That boy's half-suffocating under the weight of parental expectation.'

Rowena's face creased with concern. 'Ah, that makes sense, I suppose. Why some men choose to behave like that, I'll never understand.' Cam saw her glance towards where her husband was chatting quietly to his twin

and he remembered what Stevie had said about their grandfather trying to
control Ziggy. 'Well,' she said, turning back with a smile. 'We shall have to
see what we can do to make that boy feel appreciated, won't we?'

True to her word, when Scott returned a few moments later, she showered him with affection until the young man's face glowed with embarrassed pleasure. Hooking her arm through his, Rowena took Scott off to
sort him out a drink and a few moments later, she had him secured
between herself, Zap and Ziggy, the four of them laughing together.

'Your mother should be available on the NHS,' Barnie observed with a
wry smile as he raised his beer towards Rhys.

'She's all right.' Rhys's laconic response was at odds with the broad
smile on his face as he started to place food onto the grill with a set of
tongs.

'We need to keep an eye on Scott,' Cam said to Barnie as they stepped
back to give Rhys room.

'He's a good kid!' Barnie protested, eyes hot. 'Can't you give him a
break?'

'Hey!' Cam held up his hands to placate his friend. 'I meant we need to
look out for him for his own welfare, not because I'm worried he'll do
anything wrong. I took his phone off him earlier because his dad was
harassing him. He's really not happy about him being here, is he?'

Barnie shook his head. 'I still don't understand why he twisted so many
arms last year after you caught Scott cheating. He hates that Scott defied
him by choosing archaeology, so you'd have thought he'd have been
pleased when you threw him off the course.'

Cam had been thinking along similar lines. 'Perhaps it's a pride thing?
His father strikes me as the kind of man who cares more about his status
than anything else. Having his son sent down must've been a terrible blow
to his ego.'

Barnie sipped his beer, eyes thoughtful. 'That must be it. I still can't get
my head around why Scott cheated in the first place, though. It wasn't lack
of ability on his part, that's for sure. That second essay he turned in was
one of the best I've seen from a first year and he's always one of the best
contributors in class discussions. It seems like it was an act of total self-
sabotage.'

It was definitely a conundrum and one Cam wondered whether he should discuss with Scott now they were back on speaking terms. It pricked his conscience that he hadn't seen deeper into the matter in the first place, had dismissed Scott as an over-indulged rich kid rather than seeing the unhappy young man beneath the surface. What did it say about Cam's own personal prejudices? Nothing good, that was for sure. He glanced towards Scott once more, saw the happy glow on his face and made a decision. Best to leave him be for now and let him relax and enjoy his summer. Whatever guilt Cam was feeling over the way he'd handled the situation, it was for him to deal with, not for Scott to alleviate.

17

Hope sipped her cocktail, enjoying the sweet-sharp burst of Zap's bestselling 'Very Berry' gin mixed with prosecco and soda. It was a favourite of hers and felt like the very essence of summer in a glass. She found a quiet spot on one of the benches beneath the fairy lights and watched contentedly as the party swirled around her.

The volume of conversation had risen, a combination of relaxation as people got to know each other better and a bit of competition with the music someone had put on. There was a short line at the barbecue, where Rhys was holding court with Barnie, and little groups of three or four people had sprung up as her family mingled with their guests. The twins, her mum and Rowena were all in host mode and it was fascinating to watch them work. Though each of them appeared completely absorbed in their current conversations, she didn't miss the way Ziggy would scan the crowd every couple of minutes, nor the effortless way her mother gathered a lone person into her little group. Hope knew she should be playing her part to make everyone feel welcome instead of hiding away in the shadows, but she'd been around people all day and she wanted five minutes alone to recharge her batteries.

Like the moths irresistibly drawn to the glow of the outside lights,

Hope found herself scanning the crowd for Cam. It didn't take her more than a couple of seconds to pick him out. Even with his back to her, she recognised him. She wasn't aware of purposefully studying him to the point she felt like she knew every line and angle of him, but somehow he'd imprinted on her until she had an innate awareness of his location at all times. He was chatting to Cassie, and Hope couldn't help trying to picture them together.

Though they'd teased Cam about planning to gossip about him, Cassie had spent most of the time telling Hope about her little girl, Fleur. It was clear she was madly in love with both her husband and her daughter, so there was no reason to be jealous about what she might have meant to Cam in the past. Still, she was intrigued about the dynamic between them. It must've been a case of opposites attracting, she supposed. Cassie seemed the type to throw herself into everything, as she had earlier when she'd helped Hope setting up. She hadn't asked, she'd just seen what needed to be done and got on with it. She'd chattered a mile a minute, a babbling brook of enthusiasm for the estate, for the excitement of starting work on the dig the following morning, for life in general. Cam was much more like Hope. He watched and waited rather than diving in. Or perhaps Hope was projecting that onto him because she wanted them to be a better match?

As though sensing her eyes upon him, Cam glanced over his shoulder and Hope couldn't help the warm glow inside as his expression lit up. He said something to Cassie then began weaving through the crowd towards Hope, a broad smile on his face. 'So, this is where you're hiding!' Bending down, he pressed a lingering kiss to her lips. He tasted of gin and a heated promise. She'd wondered if perhaps he would play things cool around everyone, particularly his students, but he'd made no attempt to hide his affection for her.

'Come and hide with me.' Hope patted the bench.

Instead of sitting beside her, Cam stretched out on his back, his head in her lap as he smiled up at her. 'Are you having a nice evening?'

'It's looking more promising with every moment,' she said, leaning down to claim another kiss.

'Mmm, definitely.'

The desire in his eyes was enough for Hope to be grateful they were somewhat hidden on the bench. 'Don't look at me like that.' She raised the cold surface of her glass to her face and pressed it to her hot cheek.

Cam's smile deepened. 'What should I look at instead?'

God, he was incorrigible. 'Look over there.' Hope tilted his head towards the other party guests, only to find her mother watching them with a knowing smile. 'Maybe not over there,' she amended quickly, turning him back to face her. 'Why don't you look at the stars? It's a very pretty night.'

'I'd rather look at you,' Cam grumbled, but he rolled his head until he was staring straight up. 'Oh, this is a much better view.'

Hope poked him in the ribs, making him giggle and squirm. Hmm, a ticklish spot, she'd have to file that away for later. As he settled back down, she tipped her head back until they were both looking upwards. The sky was every shade of dark blue from sapphire to the deepest indigo and covered in an over-blanket of glittering stars.

'I never really think about the effects of light pollution in the city until I come to the countryside and it's like being in a planetarium or something.' Cam's voice had taken on an almost dreamy quality and she wondered if he was exploring those distant galaxies in his imagination. 'What I wouldn't give for a telescope right now.'

She'd never really thought much about the view above her being something other people didn't get to experience all the time. How many times had she got lost in the dark walking home from the village with a phone battery too flat to work the torch function? She'd have given anything for a few streetlights then. 'I didn't know you were a stargazer,' she said. 'I thought you were more interested in things under the earth.'

Laughing, Cam sat up and twisted around so his feet were resting on the ground, the heat of his body mere inches from hers. He slung an arm along the back of the bench, sliding close until there wasn't a whisper of breath between them. His fingers toyed with the ends of her ponytail, their tips brushing her nape in a way that was so distracting, Hope almost missed his next words. 'I'm definitely drawn to what's below rather than above, but when the night puts on a display like this, it's hard not to be in awe.'

Hope knew she should get back to the other guests, but she couldn't resist the urge to cuddle against him, using his solid chest as a cushion for her head as they watched the milky way dance and sparkle overhead. 'Are you all set for the morning?'

Cam curled his arm around her as though he too was trying to hold onto the moment. 'As ready as we can be. I've already had a quiet word with Declan before he and his wife headed off for the evening and I've promised him I'll start rounding people up soon before we risk too many sore heads. I want everyone on their game tomorrow. We won't be digging, but still, I don't want anyone hungover.'

Hope nodded. 'Zap watered all the cocktails down, so unless someone has necked half a dozen, then they should be okay. Perhaps I should swap them all out now and just leave the soft drinks?' She stirred reluctantly but it didn't take much more than a flex of Cam's arm for her to settle back against him. 'Five more minutes,' she murmured.

He dropped a kiss on her head. 'Everyone here is an adult and I expect them to be able to behave responsibly. Anyone who isn't fit in the morning will be sent back to their tent with a warning.'

Hope looked at the party before them. Dirty plates and half-empty glasses littered the tables, and she felt a tug of conscience. 'I need to start tidying up.'

'Can't wait to get away from me, huh?' There was a teasing note in Cam's voice that let her know he was joking.

'Invite me over tomorrow evening and we can snuggle in peace for as long as you like.'

'Now that sounds like a plan.' Cam eased her off his chest, stood and held out his hand. 'Come on, then. Once we make a start, I'm sure the others will get the hint.'

As he'd predicted, Hope had barely picked up the first stack of dirty plates when Adam spotted her and held out his hands. 'Here, let me.'

'Thank you. Take them into the kitchen and you can just leave them on the table.'

'Well done for getting things started.' Aunt Rowena appeared at Hope's side and gave her a quick squeeze. 'Your mum and I will sort out in the kitchen if you can handle things out here?'

'Thanks. Hopefully it won't take too long to sort everything out.'

Rowena nodded over to where Cam was organising the students. 'How are things with Mr Still Waters?'

When Hope swung to face her aunt, she was faced with a knowing grin. 'There's a ripple or two,' she conceded.

Rowena laughed as she nudged Hope in the ribs. 'Just wait until the flood gates open.'

'Ro!' Hope's half-horrified, half-amused gasp had several heads turning in their direction, including Cam's.

'I'll go and pop the kettle on!' Rowena declared, her expression now one of complete innocence before she turned on her heel and left a blushing Hope to deal with the curious watchers.

'No coffee for us,' Cam said, coming to her rescue. 'We're heading off as soon as everything is cleared away.' It was enough to get the others moving again.

Hope reached for another stack of plates, but Cam intercepted her hand and tugged her away from the table. 'Where are we going?' she asked as he continued to draw her further away from the party area and into the darker shadows of the yard. 'What about the clean-up?'

'It's under control.' Cam halted around the corner of the farmhouse. They could hear the chatter from the open kitchen window, but tucked against the wall, it was easy to pretend they were alone. 'Come here.' He slid his arms around her back, pulling her against his chest.

Hope found herself grinning from ear to ear. 'Aren't you afraid of setting a bad example to your students?'

'No.' His face was half-hidden in the shadows, but the light spilling out of the window was enough for her to catch the humour around his lips, the banked heat in his eyes. 'There's an old saying you might not have heard of – what happens on a dig, stays on a dig. Now put your arms around my neck,' he urged.

'I'm not sure I like this new bossy version of you,' Hope lied as she slid her hands up over the firm contours of his chest, earning a sharp indrawn breath as her reward. Good. He should feel as unsteady as she did, as foolish and giddy and ready to tumble headlong into whatever the future held for them both.

Cam ducked his head so his next words were a whisper over her lips. 'I think you like it just fine.'

As she opened her mouth to welcome his, she had to admit he was right.

18

Cam woke the next morning with a smile on his face and the memory of the sweet kiss Hope had given him when they'd said goodnight. They'd smooched against the kitchen wall like a pair of teenagers until Stevie had come looking for them. He hadn't been sure who was more embarrassed, himself or Hope, but her mother had just said 'Oops!' and disappeared with a laugh. At least there'd be no chance of them being interrupted when Hope came over this evening... The alarm on his phone went off and there was no more time for daydreaming.

Ten minutes later, he was showered, shaved and just pulling on his T-shirt when he heard a bark outside. Hurrying to the balcony doors, he pulled them open and stepped out into an already warm morning. Holding the rail of the balcony, he looked down to see a grinning Hope standing in the little garden below, Sooty and Sweep sitting expectantly at her feet. They were being suspiciously well-behaved until Cam noticed the large paper bag Hope was holding. 'I brought breakfast,' she said, holding the bag a little higher.

'I'll be right down.'

Cam took a quick diversion into the kitchen to switch on the coffee machine before he unlocked the patio doors and pushed them wide open. The dogs pattered in and settled in what had already become their regular spot on the cool tiles. Hope, on the other hand, remained on the patio. 'Are you waiting for an invitation?' he said with a smile.

'I was waiting for you to say hello,' she said, with a teasing glint in her eye.

Stepping through the door, Cam folded her into his arms and gave her the kiss he'd just been thinking about since he'd woken up. 'Hello,' he said when he settled her back on her feet with a pleasing flush on her face. 'Do you want to come inside now?'

'You just want your breakfast,' she accused him with a laugh that was just a touch unsteady. Good. He wasn't feeling all that steady himself.

'Maybe?' He stroked her cheek with his thumb. 'Although what I want even more than that is to kiss you again.'

Her lashes lowered then flicked up to reveal pupils grown wide. 'I'd like that too.'

Cam bent his head and their lips were less than a breath apart when the phone in his back pocket started ringing, startling them both. He wanted to ignore it, but the moment was gone. 'It might be important,' he said, with an apologetic smile as he pulled it out and checked the screen. Seeing the caller's name, he answered immediately. 'Hi, Declan, everything okay?'

'I'll sort breakfast out,' Hope whispered, and he gave her a nod in reply.

'Have you been up to the site since we locked up last night?'

Declan's gruff question chased all thoughts of a relaxing breakfast and perhaps getting that kiss from Hope. 'Nope. No one has, as far as I'm aware. We all walked back from the farmhouse last night and straight to the campsite.' The only person who hadn't been with them was Barnie, but he'd sloped off early with a giggling Meena, so Cam doubted they'd been headed anywhere other than straight to bed. 'What's happened?'

'I'm not sure, but the pedestrian gate is unlocked and I can see the door to the site office is open.'

Something inside Cam went cold. 'Hold on, I'll be there in five minutes.' He turned the phone away from his mouth to speak to Hope. 'We'd better make that coffee to go, there's a problem up at the site.' He missed what Declan had been saying in the meantime. 'Sorry, say that again?'

'I said I'm going to have a look around and check things out,' the site foreman repeated.

'I'd rather you waited for me. I'm sure it's nothing, but let's not take any chances.' He expected Declan to argue with him, but when he agreed to wait, the unsettled feeling in Cam's gut increased. 'Five minutes,' he promised, then hung up.

'What's happened?' Hope had filled a couple of insulated travel mugs and was clutching them and the bag of pastries.

'Not sure. Declan just arrived and found the pedestrian gate unlocked.' The only people who had the code were the members of the dig team. Had someone made an early start without letting him know? It didn't seem likely. 'I've asked him to wait for us before he goes in.'

'Good idea. I'll call Ziggy and get him to come up as well.' She handed Cam their breakfast and he stowed it quickly in his rucksack and slung it over one shoulder, then grabbed the dogs' leads and clipped them on their collars. 'He's on his way – he'll probably get there before us.' Cam didn't mind that because at least it meant Declan wouldn't be on his own if he did lose patience and decide to go investigating. Cam wanted to tell himself that he was overreacting to the situation, but something didn't feel right.

By the time they'd reached the car park, Cam had disturbed a still-sleeping Barnie, who confirmed Cam's suspicions about his nocturnal activities. His next call was to Adam, who promised to do a quick check around and call him back. They were just climbing into Hope's Range Rover when Adam called back. 'No one's left the site all night other than Scott. He wasn't at the shower block when I came back ten minutes ago, so I'm not sure where he is.'

'Okay, well, you guys sit tight until we've checked things out,' Cam told him as Hope reversed out of their parking spot.

'Okay. Are you sure you don't want me to come up, though?'

'No, we'll be fine. Why don't you make sure everyone is up and sorted so we can be ready to start as soon as we know everything's all right?'

'Sure thing. Oh, hang on, here comes Scott now. He's been for a run by the looks of things.' Cam heard him call out an enquiry to Scott, but couldn't catch the reply. 'He's been round the woods,' Adam relayed a few moments later. 'Said he did a couple of laps of the yellow route and didn't see anyone.'

Cam tried to recall the map Hope had shown him a couple of weeks ago. He couldn't remember the exact layout of either the yellow or the red routes, but neither of them went anywhere near the dig site. 'Okay, thanks. I'll give you a call back ASAP.'

Hope paused at a junction, turned to look at Cam and he shook his head. 'I don't like this at all,' she muttered as she crossed the main road and began to follow the gentle incline up towards the site. Well, he supposed it was some comfort that he wasn't the only one feeling uneasy.

They arrived to find Ziggy and Declan deep in conversation in the middle of the compound. Ziggy had his phone out and was typing something into it.

'Is everything okay?' Hope called out.

'You'd better come and see for yourself,' Declan said, his expression grim.

Cam exchanged a worried look with Hope as he held open the pedestrian gate for her to enter. They followed the foreman as he led them over to the cabin they were using as the site office. 'Someone forced the door,' Declan said, pointing at the jamb. 'There's scratches here from a crowbar or something similar.'

'Have they taken anything?' Instead of answering, Declan stood to one side so they could see inside the open door.

'Jesus Christ.' A scene of absolute devastation greeted them. The chairs and tables had been upended and stuff was strewn everywhere.

'I haven't gone further than the top step because I didn't want to touch anything,' Declan said from behind Cam. 'Whatever they used to force open the door has been used to break into the lockers as well.'

'Oh, God, that's awful!' Hope exclaimed. 'Have they taken anything?'

Cam turned away from the mess to see Declan shaking his head. 'I don't know. It looks like whoever it was has dumped the kit, but I don't know if any of the kids left their valuables. There was a petty cash box in the desk with about a hundred and fifty quid in it. I couldn't spot it in amongst all the mess, but as I said, I haven't been inside.'

'I've spoken to the police,' Ziggy said, coming to join them. 'They're going to get someone from the investigation team to give me a call. I'm not expecting much of a response given how many people have been in and out of the office. As soon as I've got a report reference for the insurance company, I'll get onto them. Do we know if the cabin door can be secured?'

'I haven't tried yet as I didn't want to touch anything,' Declan replied.

Ziggy nodded. 'Let's leave it as is until the police call me back and we'll go with whatever they advise.' He huffed out a breath. 'I'm at a bit of a loss as to what to do because we've never had anything like this happen before.' His phone began to ring and he walked away to answer it.

'Who the hell would bother to break in?' Cam wondered. 'Apart from the cashbox and whatever they found in the lockers, there's nothing of any real value.' The main equipment was kept in a secure container at the other end of the compound and Cam spun towards it.

'This is the only unit they've damaged,' Declan said, as though reading his mind. 'I would've said it was kids up to no good, until I checked the lock.' He reached into his pocket and pulled out the code lock Cam recognised from the gate. 'There's no sign of tampering, so unless we didn't lock it properly last night, it must have been someone who knew the code. I'd better make a list of everyone I gave it to.'

Cam closed his eyes, trying to picture leaving the site the previous evening. Declan had already gone to meet his wife ready for the barbeque, so Cam had closed up. He'd been chatting with Cassie, but he was sure he'd secured the lock behind them, but maybe he hadn't? He'd rather it was his error than consider someone they thought they could trust was responsible. 'I can't be 100 per cent about the lock, but I'm pretty sure I closed it as we left. We all walked back to the campsite afterwards, and everyone was together when we went to the farmhouse and back. I spoke to Adam earlier and the only person who left the campsite since then was Scott and he only went for a run around the woods. I don't for one moment believe anyone on my team would be capable of something like this.'

'Oh, I'm sure it's no one involved with the project,' Hope agreed. 'Everyone was so excited last night, I can't believe they'd risk sabotaging things.'

'Plus they'd know there was nothing of value in the office,' Declan added. It wasn't exactly an endorsement, but the site manager didn't know them as well as Cam did, so he let it go. Declan frowned. 'The only other person I can think of is that lass who's doing the cleaning. I forgot to give it to her when she dropped by, so I sent her a text with the code on it.'

'Lass?' Hope looked surprised. 'I'd hardly call Daisy Riley a lass.'

'The Riley bit's right, but the girl who showed up here was called Amelia. She had all my details from Mrs Davis and came at the pre-arranged time for her safety briefing.' He turned towards Cam. 'You remember her popping in, right?'

Cam shook his head. 'Can't say I do, but there was a lot going on yesterday.'

'Amelia is Daisy's daughter,' Hope interjected. 'Daisy's come down with a cold so Amelia is filling in for a few days. Sorry, I should've mentioned it to you both.'

Declan didn't look happy, and Cam couldn't blame him. The site manager took his job very seriously. 'Well, she never said anything about that yesterday when she signed the risk assessments. I can't have one person signing on behalf of another, even if they're only coming to do a bit of cleaning. The insurance would have a field day if something happened.'

Hope shook her head. 'I've known Amelia all my life and she's not the type to deliberately mislead anyone. There's a lot going on with her family, so don't be too hard on her, please. When Daisy is well again, you can run through everything with her.' Hope glanced towards her uncle. 'I'll talk to Ziggy, and we'll try and get an update on the situation.'

As Hope walked away with a frown on her face, Cam turned back to the problem at hand. 'If the lock still works, will the cabin be safe to use?'

Declan shrugged. 'I'll have to talk to the hire company once we've got the go-ahead from the police. They'll probably want to swap out the unit, which will be a pain in the arse, but not the end of the world. I'll see about getting a stronger lock for the gate and I think we should install a security light and an alarm on the compound. It'll be up to them, I guess, as they're the ones footing the bill, but that's what I'd recommend.' Declan nodded towards Hope and Ziggy.

'Can you cost it out when you have time and then we'll suggest it to Hope? And we'll keep the code for the new lock to ourselves for now. If the cleaner needs to come in, then one of us can let her in and stick around while she works.' It would be a small inconvenience and Cam could as easily sit in the office and write up his daily reports. 'Would you have any objection to me getting the team up here?' Cam was still worried about who'd broken into the compound, but he didn't want to lose a day before they'd even got started. 'We can keep them away from the site office until the Travers decide what they want to do, but I'd like to at least get the surveys underway.'

'Fine with me. I've got the groundworks crew booked for a week on Monday, so if we don't know where to start, that'll be a waste of time and money to have them standing around.'

'Good point. I'll give Adam a call and get them heading up here.' He'd just finished his call when Hope and Ziggy came and joined them. 'Did you manage to sort things out?'

Hope nodded. 'I had a quick word with Amelia to see how her mum is. From the sounds of it Daisy's going to be out of action for a while as her cold has developed into a chest infection.' She quirked her lips in a sympathetic twist. 'Poor Amelia's run ragged trying to keep on top of everything. She's got a full-time job of her own as well as trying to cover for her mum here, and she'll have to keep things running at home. That father of hers is no use to man or beast, so it's all fallen to Amelia.'

'He's the one Rhys had to let go for being drunk on the job?' Cam recalled and Hope nodded.

'Yep. According to what I could get Amelia to admit, he's all but taken up residence in the Arms. Useless git.'

Ziggy put an arm around her shoulders. 'I'll speak to Iain on the quiet and see about getting him to bar Keith, at least temporarily.'

'So then he'll just drink more at home and make Daisy and Amelia's lives even more of a misery,' Hope protested.

'I'll have a word in the shop as well. If we cut him off from any local supplies of booze, then perhaps he'll sober up long enough for us to be able to talk some sense into him.' Ziggy didn't look too hopeful about it, but Cam had to admire the man for being willing to try.

'It's better than doing nothing,' Hope agreed. 'Now what did the police have to say?'

Ziggy sighed. 'The officer was sympathetic but not overly interested, as I suspected. He'll be out later today to do the report, and he's going to request a technician to come with him. The bad news is that the forensic lab is backed up for weeks and we'd be a low-priority case so he couldn't say when any results might come back. I had to mention to him that we weren't 100 per cent sure the site was fully secured.'

Cam felt sick at the thought he might be responsible. 'I'm sorry about that.'

'Don't be daft, I'm not blaming anyone other than whoever bloody did this.' Ziggy shoved his hands on his hips and huffed out a breath. 'The campsite is almost full and I wouldn't even know where to start with questioning guests about their whereabouts last night without causing serious offence – or making people worry about their own security. What a bloody mess.'

'It's a bit of a trek up here from the campsite,' Cam pointed out. 'I can't see someone roaming this far on a whim, especially as there's no lighting in this part of the site.'

Ziggy nodded. 'I'm inclined to keep it between us for now. Boost the security where we can without making guests feel like they're being watched 24/7. If there's any more sign of trouble, then I'll have a chat with some of the estate workers about doing a few night patrols. I'd rather not have to get in a specialist security firm because it doesn't look good, for one thing. I want our visitors to feel safe and secure and having a load of uniforms wandering around could end up leaving the opposite impression.' A beep of a horn alerted them to the arrival of Adam and the rest of the team and Declan went to unlock the gate and let them in.

'Right,' Ziggy said. 'I don't think there's anything more I can do here for now, so I'm going to head into the village and see what can be done about Keith.' With a wave, Ziggy headed off, leaving Hope and Cam alone together.

'Do you think it was kids?' Hope asked.

'I really hope so.' Cam folded his arms around her for a quick hug, needing to reassure himself as much as her. If it wasn't, then the only other possibility was someone had deliberately targeted the dig. He watched as

his team climbed out of their cars, the atmosphere subdued compared to
their excitement of the previous day. *Please let it be a one-off. Please.*

* * *

With the site office being the only one targeted, the team were free to crack
on with both the walking survey and the geophysical one. Barnie had
arrived not long after the others and after a few choice words about
whoever had wrecked the site office, he gathered the bulk of the team
together for the walking survey. They headed off towards the river,
carrying everything from sketchbooks to compasses, pegs and string to use
as markers and even a measuring wheel to help calculate distances.

Once they were out of the way, Cam and Adam got to work setting up
the magnetometer. Cam always thought it looked like something from a
Wallace and Gromit cartoon knocked together from an old bicycle frame
and a few plastic poles. Regardless of appearances, it was actually an
incredibly sophisticated piece of kit and the data they could gather in a
matter of hours was invaluable. Adam was going to do the first section, so
Cam made sure he was strapped into the harness which carried the power
supply and then positioned himself at the opposite end of the area they'd
chosen to map so Adam had a target to aim for.

After about thirty minutes, they swapped places, and it was Cam's turn
to trudge up and down the wide green space between the ruined walls of
what Hope knew as the old chapel and the spot where Declan and his
team had uncovered the new stonework. There was something about the
area which kept nagging at the back of Cam's mind as he walked. It was too
flat, he realised after a while. The wheels of the pushcart rolled too easily
over the ground. They'd had the area mowed by the estates team the
previous week, but even so, Cam would've expected the terrain to be much
more uneven if it was an area that had previously been built upon. Maybe
he was wrong and the two sites weren't connected, or the stone in the new
trench was some rubble which had been dumped when the old chapel
had been destroyed.

The samples he'd taken had contained high levels of soot, which indicated a fire of some description. While the fire could've been started acci-

dentally by a lightning strike or a stray candle, it had often been used on churches as an easy way of melting the valuable lead from the roof and other fixtures. He pictured again the size of the blocks he and Barnie had seen used in those cottages in the village. Whatever the land was telling him to the contrary, there'd been something substantial on this site at some point. He'd have to trust his gut and wait until they could download the data from the survey. Lifting the cart by the handles, Cam nudged the kickstand up with his foot and carried on walking.

He was about three-quarters of the way through his section when he noticed Zoë waving to catch his attention. He re-engaged the kick stand and unhooked himself from the harness, setting it carefully on the ground so the battery didn't become disconnected from the data recording block. He jogged over to where Zoë was showing something on her laptop to Adam. Neither of them looked happy. 'What's up?'

Zoë shook her head. 'There's something wrong with the magnetometer. The results I'm getting don't make any sense at all.'

Cam circled around so he could glance over her shoulder at the laptop screen. Instead of a mostly pale background with potential darker markings to reflect disturbances in the ground that might be signs of previous excavation and building work, the entire thing was a mass of dark interference, like an old-fashioned TV which had lost its signal. 'Are you sure the data is downloading correctly?'

Looking miserable, Zoë nodded. 'I checked in case I'd somehow corrupted the data, but I'm getting the same result every time. It doesn't make sense,' she repeated.

No, it didn't. 'Come on, let's check we wired everything up properly when we set the frame up.' When she still looked dejected, Cam laughed and patted her shoulder. 'Shit happens, Zoë. If you let every little set-back get you down, you're in for a long summer.'

She nodded. 'I know you're right, but I was just so excited to finally get started.'

They disconnected everything, set the magnetometer up again and Adam did a trial survey of part of the area they'd previously covered. After an anxious wait for the data to download, Cam was disappointed to see the same fuzzy mess as the first set of results. 'If I didn't know better, I'd say this looks like the whole area has been disturbed at the same time. Let's take a quick break and then we'll see what the earth resistance survey has to show us.'

The resistance equipment was slower than the magnetometer as it couldn't cover the same area with each pass, but until they could work out why they weren't getting decent data from the other equipment, there wasn't much point in carrying on. After a quick drink, they started over from the beginning, Adam going first again. He set the small frame onto the ground, waited for the meter to beep to confirm it had sent out a pulse, took two strides forward and lowered the probes again. Beep. Two strides, pause, beep. Up and down. Cam knew from experience that once you got into a rhythm with it, there was something almost meditative about the experience, but standing around watching was an exercise in managing his own impatience. While he waited, he glanced around the site to see Barnie's group had split off into twos and threes. A couple of students were sitting near the chapel ruins, sketching by the looks of things. Another pair were measuring off something near the riverbank using the meter wheel. Cam watched them for a few minutes, wondering what had caught their – or likely Barnie's – attention. *Where was he, anyway?*

Cam turned a slow 360 and finally spotted a small group quite a long way up from the site where the river curved in a lazy arc before it followed the natural slope of the land. He spotted Barnie amongst them, his broad frame and dark hair easy enough to pick out. He watched as Barnie reached down then stretched his arms high. Why was he taking off his shirt? 'I'll be back in a minute,' he called to Adam before breaking into a jog up the incline.

He arrived just in time to see Barnie sit on the edge of the riverbank and lower himself into the water. He straightened up, hands still pressed firmly on the bank, only letting go when he had a sure footing beneath him. The water covered him almost to mid-thigh, turning the bottom of his khaki shorts a dark brown. 'What on earth are you doing?' Cam asked.

It was Scott who answered him. 'There's an anomaly in the water,' he said, pointing a little upstream from where Barnie was standing. 'I noticed it earlier and thought perhaps there was a large rock or something that was diverting the water, but I couldn't see anything, so Dr Barnard decided to check it out.'

'You just wanted an excuse to go swimming,' Cam said, as he adjusted the sweaty brim of his hat against his forehead.

'Well, that was one temptation for sure,' Barnie said with a grin. 'But Scott's right, there's something here that's changing the current.' With care, Barnie lowered himself to his knees, the water swirling up his chest almost to his shoulders. The lack of rainfall over the summer had lowered the level of the river, but even so, Cam didn't want to take any risks.

'Scott? How well can you swim?'

'For God's sake, Cam, I don't need a bloody lifeguard. It's not exactly the Niagara rapids,' Barnie scoffed.

Ignoring him, Cam turned back to Scott. 'Well?'

'I'm a strong swimmer,' Scott said, already toeing off his shoes. 'What do you want me to do?'

'Just stand downstream and brace Barnie's weight a bit so he doesn't topple over.' He turned back to his friend. 'What are you looking for, anyway?'

'I'm not sure.' He glared up at Scott. 'Hurry up then, if you're coming in. These stones are killing my knees.'

Scott eased himself into the river and took up post, one hand braced on the bank, the other holding Barnie's shoulder. 'How's that?'

'Ask nanny over there,' Barnie grumbled, his attention turning back to the bank.

Cam didn't say anything, just gave Scott a quick, reassuring nod and they both turned their attention back to Barnie, who was running his hands along the inner edge of the bank. His hands dipped lower, the water rising almost to his chin, and Scott had to bend at the waist to keep hold of the other man's shoulder. 'What the hell is this?' Barnie said in a wondering voice. 'Hang on a sec.' Before Cam had a chance to ask him what he was planning, Barnie sucked in a deep breath and ducked down below the water, almost pulling Scott off balance in the process.

'Bloody idiot,' Cam muttered. 'Are you all right, Scott?'

'I'm fine. I've got my leg braced against him.'

Barnie bobbed up above the surface, shaking the water from his head

like a dog. Cam was about to tell him off for acting the fool, but one look at
the beaming smile on his friend's face and all thoughts of safety flew out of
his head. 'What is it?'

'Stonework.' Barnie was still grinning like a Cheshire Cat.

Cam frowned. 'What, like something to shore up the bank, you mean?'

Barnie shook his head. 'Better than that. There's an opening in it. If I
put my hand in front of it, I can feel the water flowing in that direction.'

Cam felt a familiar thrum of excitement in his blood. 'Like it's feeding a
well?' He glanced around. Why would anyone need to build a well when
they were so close to a source of fresh water? It would be a hell of a lot of
work when they could as easily walk down and dip a few buckets.

Barnie shook his head. 'I don't think so, because the movement would
indicate that if it's coming in here then it must be flowing out somewhere
else, otherwise there'd be signs of flooding.'

'A drainage system, then?' Cam stared back over his shoulder and
looked towards the lumps and bumps of the chapel ruins. 'How sophisticated would this complex need to be to require a drainage system?'

He hadn't realised he'd asked the question out loud until Barnie
heaved himself up onto the bank beside him and sprawled on his back,
still grinning like an idiot. 'Now isn't that the million-dollar question?'

19

Hope had left as soon as the site surveys began. Although she was interested in what everyone was doing, the mood was understandably flat and she'd decided the best thing she could do for now was leave them in peace. Besides, with the police still to make their visit she hadn't wanted to let the dogs out of the car, even with the little compound Declan had built for them. She headed back to the farmhouse to catch up on some paperwork. If she turned up at the distillery, Zap would think she didn't trust him to keep an eye on things, which wasn't true. He'd be fine handling the orders and sending out invoices, but he hated chasing customers for payment. She'd spend a couple of hours going through the most recent bank transactions then send out a few polite email reminders after lunch.

She'd just finished the bank reconciliation and was contemplating heading down to the kitchen for something to eat when her phone pinged with a message from Cam.

Everything okay?

She rolled her shoulders. Working sitting on her bed was not good for her posture, but it was the quietest spot in the house. She could take the dogs for a walk after lunch – a bit of exercise would do her good. Carrying her phone with her, Hope paused at the top of the stairs and typed out a quick reply to Cam.

Fine thanks x Just been catching up on a bit of work but I'm taking a break for lunch. How are things with you?

The three dots bounced for what seemed like ages as Cam typed his reply.

Barnie's found something we don't understand and our first geo-phys results were a mess. Adam's just finishing off so I'm hoping I'll have something more to tell you later. Dinner tonight? Xx

Hope's stomach did a little flip.

Sounds good x I'll pop down the shop and pick us something up. Send me a text when you're done for the day.

Cam sent her three kisses in response.

Hope tucked her phone away and all but bounced down the stairs with excitement over the thought of a whole evening, just the two of them.

'Mind the floor!'

Hope froze with barely one toe touching the wet tiles. 'Sorry!' Her head snapped up as she registered who the desperate cry had belonged to. 'Amelia? What are you doing here?' Her friend looked terrible – that was the only word Hope could think of to describe her. Her usual vibrant gold-blonde hair looked dark with grease and was scraped back from her head in a lank ponytail. The shadows beneath her deep-set eyes gave her already too-thin face an almost skull-like appearance and the angry red spot was the only other bit of colour on her otherwise pale skin.

'What does it look like?' Amelia brandished the mop at her, before bending over and pushing it over the tiles.

'Well, I can see what you're doing,' Hope said as she picked her way across the drying patches of the floor towards the table. 'What I mean is why are you doing it now? Aren't you supposed to be at work?' Having turned down the chance of one of Ziggy's scholarships, Amelia had taken a job in the nearby town straight after they'd finished their A levels. She'd worked her way up to be the office manager, but Hope knew she hated admin almost as much as Zap did. She'd always been so creative – brilliant at art, when Hope could barely draw a straight line even with the aid of a ruler. Every time she saw her, which wasn't as often these days, Hope realised with a pang of guilt, Amelia looked smaller and paler, as though that spark within her was slowly being extinguished.

'Like I said on the phone earlier, with Mum out of action I can't manage everything, so I've taken a couple of weeks off. We couldn't afford for her to lose the hours she was doing before, never mind the extra Mrs Davis managed to conjure out of nowhere.'

'She did say something about her sciatica playing up,' Hope said, quickly, scrabbling for the excuse her mum and Mrs Davis had come up with.

Amelia stopped working the mop long enough to give Hope a hard stare. 'I'm not stupid, just desperate.'

Hope closed her eyes for a long moment. 'I know, I'm sorry.' Sliding into one of the kitchen chairs, she pushed the one beside it out with her foot, ignoring the freshly mopped floor. 'Leave that a minute and sit down and talk to me. You shouldn't have to give up your leave to do this! Tell me what I can do to help.'

Amelia looked like she would refuse, but eventually set the mop aside with a sigh and flopped into the chair. 'I don't think there's anything to be done.' She drew her already raw-looking lower lip between her teeth and began to worry at it.

Reaching out, Hope took her hand. 'Rhys did everything he could to keep your dad on.'

Amelia swallowed hard. 'I know. I don't blame him for kicking him out. I'd do the bloody same if I could, the bastard.' She sounded so desperate and furious that Hope felt her own anger rising to match it.

'Your mother should be the one to do that.' Hope knew it was harsh, but they'd all danced around the problem for too long as it was. 'She should've done it years ago.'

'She tried,' Amelia said softly. 'It didn't go well.' She stared at Hope, the bleakness in her eyes conveying something terrible.

'Oh, no, I'm so sorry.'

Amelia shrugged. 'I can't do anything about it until she's fit and well again but once she's over this damn chest infection, I'm going to do whatever it takes to get rid of him once and for all.'

For a moment Hope was truly worried about what she might mean. 'You... you won't do anything stupid?'

Amelia laughed, a harsh bark. 'Don't worry, I won't make you follow through on the pledge that you'd always help me bury the bodies.' It was a silly promise they'd made to each other when they were young, a way of saying they'd always have each other's backs. Only things had changed once Amelia had started work and Hope had gone off to university. When she'd come back in the holidays, it was to find Rhys and Amelia had started dating and that had driven another wedge between them because the last thing Hope had wanted to hear was all the gory details of what went on between her erstwhile friend and her cousin.

Still, Hope wanted to reach for that old connection, to let Amelia know that however far they'd drifted, she still cared for her and would do what she could to support her now. 'Oh, I don't know,' Hope said, in a deliberately off-hand voice. 'What with the excavations and everything, I'm sure we could find a quiet spot to dump his useless carcass.'

Amelia's eyes widened as she stared at Hope in disbelief and then she sputtered out a laugh. It sounded rusty, almost painful, and Hope wondered how long it was since her friend had last found something to laugh about. The sounds coming from her throat changed an instant later, and Hope ran around the table to gather Amelia close as her body racked with sobs.

'It'll be all right,' she promised Amelia, even though she had no idea what she was going to do.

Though it had taken some persuading, Hope had eventually encouraged Amelia upstairs to her room for a lie down. The exhausted woman had fallen asleep almost as soon as her head touched the pillow, so Hope had settled in the rocking chair beneath the window with her laptop and worked quietly. A couple of hours later and she had everything up to date. Amelia hadn't stirred, not even to turn over, so Hope tiptoed out of the room and downstairs. She was just finishing off cleaning the kitchen when Ziggy came in, his expression grim. He stopped at the sight of Hope wiping down the large table. 'Everything okay?'

Hope nodded. 'Keep your voice down.' She pressed a finger to her lips then pointed above them. 'Amelia is asleep upstairs. She's taken a couple of weeks' holiday to keep on top of Daisy's cleaning hours while she recovers from a chest infection.' She thought about mentioning Amelia's determination to get Keith out of their lives, but she knew Rhys would wade in and probably make things worse. He and Amelia might be just friends these days, but he was still fiercely protective of her.

Her uncle sighed. 'The village is rife with gossip about Keith and his antics. Iain didn't need any persuasion to ban him from the pub. He was already on the verge of doing it because of the size of the tab Keith's run up. It's the same in the shop – their bill hasn't been paid in weeks. Rumour has it they're on the verge of being evicted from the cottage for unpaid rent.'

Hope set her cloth down with a frown. 'It's only been a couple of weeks since Keith was fired, and Rhys paid him up to the end of the month. Amelia's working full-time and I know she gives her parents almost every penny she earns, plus Daisy had those extra hours here. How can they be in debt?'

'He's gambled it all away.' They both swung around at the sound of Amelia's voice. She was standing just inside the hallway door, pale and wan as a ghost. 'Mum found out when she spotted a final demand on the doormat. Dad always insisted on doing everything, the bills are all in his name and she doesn't even have access to the bank account.' Amelia closed her eyes. 'I told her so many times she needed to sort that out, but she never was one to rock the boat.'

'Come and sit down.' Ziggy was already moving to put his arm around Amelia's shoulders and steer her towards the chair she'd vacated earlier.

It was only as she sat that Amelia spotted the cloth in front of Hope. 'Oh, God, you shouldn't be doing that!'

'Behave yourself,' Hope said. 'I'm not going to melt from doing a few chores, for goodness' sake.'

'Well, I'll speak to Mrs Davis and find a way to make up the hours,'

Amelia protested.

'No,' Ziggy said, in the firm voice of a man who knew how to put on the mantle of authority when the situation required it. 'You will not.' He glanced over at Hope. 'Will you give Amelia and me a moment, there are some things we need to discuss.'

Hope rather had the feeling it would be a one-way discussion, but Amelia was in the best possible hands. If anyone could find a solution to the current mess, it was Ziggy. 'Of course, I'll take the dogs out.'

Closing the kitchen door behind her, Hope lifted her face to the sunshine and let it chase some of the sadness away. It had only been a matter of weeks ago that she was chafing under the weight of her family's over-attentiveness and craving a space of her own away from them. Though she still wanted to take the step towards further independence, she was more determined than ever to do it with the right amount of grace and appreciation for everything they'd done for her. But for a twist of fate, she could be in Amelia's shoes. She could have been in an even worse situation if her mother hadn't taken the necessary steps to protect her and escape from her own awful marriage.

Still, there was a gap in her mind about the man she owed half her DNA to. Hope wanted to forget all about him, to carry on in blissful unawareness, just as she had for the first twenty-five years of her life. What would it gain her to be like Amelia and know the truth about the people who were a part of her make-up, even with all their faults and weaknesses? Hope didn't know. But like a sore tooth, she couldn't stop poking at the idea of finding out, even if it was likely to cause more pain.

Hope stayed in the yard with the dogs, who were happy to chase a tennis ball for as long as she was willing to throw it. When the back door finally opened and Amelia stepped out, Hope was relieved to see she'd got some of her spirit back. She still looked pale and tired, but whatever Ziggy had said to her had put a bit of steel in her spine and she looked much more like her old self. 'Okay?' Hope asked.

Amelia shook her head, but there was a hint of a smile as she said, 'Not by a long shot, but I will be.'

'I know you will. Hey, I need to head into the village to pick up a few things, do you want a lift?'

'No, thanks. I'm going to walk. I've got a lot to think about.' Amelia glanced over her shoulder to where Ziggy was leaning up against the open doorway. 'Thank you.'

'You don't need to thank me. Give me a call when you've made that appointment and I'll come with you.'

'Okay.' Amelia turned back to Hope. 'I'll see you later.'

'I'll text you next week and maybe we can meet up for lunch one day?' If Amelia was going to get her life back on track, she was going to need all the support she could get. They'd both let their friendship drift and it was time for Hope to be the one to reach out.

'I'd like that.'

As she walked away, Ziggy came to sit beside Hope on the bench. 'I need you to do a couple of things for me when you're in the village, if that's okay?'

'Sure. Whatever you need.' She had a few minutes before she had to get going, so she leaned back against her uncle and let the reassuring weight of his arm settle along the back of the bench behind her. She lifted her face to the sun once more, grateful for the strength and the steadfastness of this man who'd always been there for her. But even in that moment of contentment, she couldn't help but poke at the empty space in her mind.

* * *

Hope was just crossing the road from the shop to the pub when her phone vibrated in her pocket. She paused on the pavement to adjust the bag of shopping she'd paid for – along with the Rileys' outstanding bill, as per her uncle's instructions – and checked her messages. It was Cam, letting her know they were calling it a day at the dig and he'd be back at the lodge within the next half hour and she was welcome to join him whenever she was ready. Deciding that if she was quick, she'd have time to get home, have a shower and still get to Cam's by six so they could chill on the patio before dinner, Hope pulled open the door to the pub and stopped dead at the sound of raised voices.

'I've told you twice now, Keith, you're not welcome in here any more,'

Iain, the landlord, was saying.

'And I'm telling you it's a bloody free country and I want a beer!' Keith yelled back.

Feeling like a coward, but knowing now was not the time, Hope let the door close and turned towards where she'd parked her car. She'd speak to Ziggy and they could make another arrangement to pay off Keith's tab. Her uncle had persuaded Amelia to allow them to settle all the outstanding debt and once the final total was known, they would set up a repayment scheme. It was better than a bank loan, or loading up on credit card debt. The interest on either option would be another millstone around Amelia's neck. Whether or not they'd be successful in implementing the other half of Ziggy's plan to get Keith's doctor on board and try to get him into a treatment programme... Hope glanced back at the pub in time to see a red-faced Keith storm out... well, that was a problem for another day.

Three-quarters of an hour later, she was walking up the porch steps of the lodge carrying a large quiche and a bottle of her favourite rosé. She'd left the dogs at home with Rhys, who'd promised to take them out later when he walked Samson and Delilah. The patio doors were wide open to allow what little breeze there was in, and Cam was sitting at the inside table, his still-damp hair falling over his forehead as he stared at something on his laptop. 'Knock, knock,' she called as she walked in.

'Oh, hey, come and look at this!' His smile was so broad it crinkled the skin at the corner of his blue eyes, and he looked like he'd caught the sun again.

She set the food and bottle down as he scooted to one side of his chair, leaving a space for her to perch on beside him. His arm closed around her waist and he hugged her close as he reached with his other hand to tap the screen. 'Look,' he repeated, sounding more excited than she'd heard him before.

Hope wanted to drink in the joyful expression on his face, but she did as she was told and stared dutifully at the image on the screen. It was mostly off-white with a load of fuzzy splotches and lines. 'What am I looking at?'

'You're looking at what might be one of the greatest undiscovered complexes of buildings in the country!'

'What?' Hope spun towards him so quickly she would've toppled off the chair if he hadn't been holding her. 'Don't joke about something like that!'

Turning to face her, Cam's blazing eyes met her own. 'It's no joke. Whatever we've got here is beyond my wildest imaginings. Here, let me show you.' He reached for his mouse, and the image on the screen switched to a sketched plan. She recognised the curve of the river, the small cluster of walls that were the remains of the chapel and the square compound where the site buildings and even a couple of cars had been drawn in to show the parking area.

'We've only scanned this bit,' Cam said pointing the mouse to a shaded-over red area between the chapel and the boundary of where she'd hoped to build her house. 'I thought it was a busted flush because the results from the magnetometer scans this morning were just interference, but Adam started finding traces of structures within his first couple of sweeps with the resistance meter.' He moved the mouse over to another narrow shaded area beside the river. 'And here's what Barnie thinks might be some kind of drainage system,' he said, tracing the mouse arrow along a dark line leading from the bank.

'You found a drain?' Hope wasn't sure that warranted this level of excitement.

Cam laughed. 'No. We only *think* we've found a drain. Until we can dig some test pits, we can't be sure of anything. It'll be a few days until we can do that, though, as we have to scan the whole area first.'

'But it's a good result so far?' Hope asked.

Seizing her by the waist, Cam dragged her over into his lap. 'It's amazing! You're amazing!' He kissed her and instead of his banked anger from the previous night, he was all playful pecks and nibbles until she was giggling from the sheer infectious joy of his exuberance. When she came up for air, Hope wriggled free from his lap and held out her hand to him. 'Come and sit out on the patio and we can toast your success while you tell me all there is to know about drainage systems.'

She'd been teasing a little, but Cam managed to make it interesting, showing her examples of other systems which had been uncovered in the past from basic ditches and early soakaway systems to the sophisticated underground sewers dating back to Roman times. She couldn't say she fancied the communal toilets he showed her from Pompeii, nor the open channels that had once run through the centre of the streets in London for people to chuck their buckets of waste into. She was glad when he skipped over the details of cholera epidemics caused by contaminated water pumps because they still had to eat. 'I'll never be able to watch a historical film or TV show in the same light again,' she said with a laugh when he rose to refill their glasses.

He grinned down at her. 'Have I put paid to your *Outlander* time-travel fantasies?'

She wrinkled her nose. 'Just a bit.' Though she could lounge there all evening in the shade, her stomach gave her a gentle rumble of reminder, so she followed him into the kitchen. 'Do you want me to heat this up?' she asked, retrieving the quiche from the table and setting it on the counter next to the oven.

'I'm fine with it as it is, if you are.'

Five minutes later, they were sitting at the table with a hastily thrown together salad and huge slabs of quiche before them. Hope couldn't stop her eyes from straying to the dark blobs and marks on Cam's laptop screen. No matter how hard she squinted, she couldn't see what he could obviously read in the data. Perhaps, once they'd had a chance to map the whole site, she'd be able to make more sense of things.

'So, how was the rest of your day?' Cam's question drew her attention away from the screen.

Pulling a face, Hope pushed her salad around with her fork. 'Not great.' Though she'd lost some of her appetite, she forced herself to eat a few bites as she brought Cam up to date with the situation with Amelia.

'I'll never understand men who can treat their families like that,' Cam said, shaking his head.

'It makes you appreciate what you've got all the more, I suppose,' Hope observed, remembering the affectionate way Cam had talked about his father, the way he'd spoken with pride about how hard both he and his mother had worked to give him a good life and help him on his way to university.

He nodded. 'I feel like I'll never be able to thank my parents enough. I still haven't worked out what I'm going to give them for their anniversary in August.'

'It's the bank holiday weekend, isn't it?' She remembered it because he'd mentioned the dig being over before then. Given what they might have discovered, she wondered if those plans would have to change. She wasn't in any hurry to see him leave, that was for sure. 'Do you think they'd like it here?'

Cam blinked at her. 'Here in the lodge? I'm sure they would, but it's only got one bedroom. Unless you mean they could stay next door?'

Hope smiled. 'I was thinking of something a bit more upmarket than that. We've got our light and sound spectacular that weekend so I could speak to Mum about designing a special package for them at the spa. She's brilliant at that kind of thing.'

'That's a lovely idea, but I'm not sure my budget stretches quite that far,' Cam replied with a shake of his head. Hope stared at him, didn't say anything, just raised an eyebrow. 'What?' he asked, appearing genuinely confused.

For such an intelligent man, he could be downright stupid sometimes. 'Do you honestly think I would expect my partner to pay for his parents to come and visit?'

'Partner?' Cam's lips curled up at the corners. 'Is that what I am?'

She shrugged, refusing to acknowledge the slight heat building on her cheeks. 'Well, we're a bit too old for boyfriend and girlfriend, don't you think?'

'I think you can call me whatever you like as long it means I get to keep spending time with you. So, you think there's a good chance we'll make it through the summer then?' She could tell he was teasing, by the tone he used.

Hope paused, as though giving the matter serious thought. 'If you play your cards right, I reckon I might let you stick around.'

Having set his knife and fork aside, Cam rose from his seat and came to stand beside her chair. He extended a hand towards her, and Hope took it, a knot of excitement curling in her belly. 'Where are we going?'

Cam pulled her up and into his arms. 'If I'm going to persuade you to keep me, I thought it was time to get started.'

20

The next few days passed in something of a blur. Ed had arrived and he and Cassie had taken over responsibility for mapping the rest of the site while Cam pored over the seemingly never-ending bits of data they were gathering and tried to make a decision about where to position their first set of trenches and test pits for maximum potential results.

After his wade in the river, Barnie had gone back to the family's archive with a renewed sense of purpose. They'd tried the magnetometer again in a different area but the results were still a puzzle, so Cam had called time on that and put all the team's efforts into the more labour-intensive resistance meter. He was sitting in the site office with Declan, marking up his set of plans with the position of the first trenches, ready for the ground-works team who were due to arrive in the morning, when a harassed-looking Scott came dashing up the steps.

Cam was out of his seat at once. 'What is it? Has there been an accident?'

The wave of relief he felt when Scott shook his head was palpable. 'No, no, everything on the site is fine.' The young man shot an embarrassed look at Declan then back at Cam. 'Can I speak to you about something?'

'I'll stick the kettle on,' Declan said, never one to pass up the opportunity for a cup of coffee. Cam swore he'd never sleep if he drank even a third of the amount of caffeine the site manager got through in a day, but Declan seemed to live off the stuff.

Cam waited until the site manager had headed down the steps towards the welfare unit, then nodded to the seat he'd vacated. 'Why don't you sit down?'

Scott slid into the seat then stared down at his folded hands. 'I don't know how to tell you.'

Trying to ignore a sudden itch of apprehension between his shoulder blades, Cam forced himself to lounge back in his chair. 'Whatever it is, we can sort it out.'

Scott nodded, but didn't raise his head. 'My father wants to visit.'

Cam sat up. 'Here?'

The young man nodded again. 'He called me earlier to say he's booked in for a weekend at the spa the week after next.' His head shot up, his eyes wide as he stared at Cam. 'I begged him not to, but he wouldn't have any of it. Said he wants to see what I'm doing with my wasted summer.' Scott didn't need to put air quotes around the last few words to make it clear he was repeating his father verbatim.

Cam had the feeling it wasn't only Scott the older Mr Willoughby wanted to check up on. 'And no doubt he'll be wanting to look around the site, while he's here.' It was a headache Cam could do without, but putting Scott's father off would likely heap more pressure on the poor kid.

Scott nodded. 'It's my own fault for not keeping my mouth shut about the brilliant results we've had so far.' He cast Cam a stricken look. 'I'm sorry, I know you told us we should keep everything to ourselves for now, but he was going on and on about me wasting my time and I just snapped.'

Cam took a deep breath, knowing he needed to tread carefully. It had been obvious from the start that Scott's father was a bully. He probably knew exactly what buttons to press to get the poor kid to react. 'I'd have preferred to keep things quiet until we have more of an idea of what we're dealing with, but it's not the end of the world.'

Scott lowered his head, the picture of abject misery. 'I've let you down again.'

Oh, Christ. 'No, you haven't,' Cam said. When Scott didn't look up, he stretched a leg out under the table and nudged Scott's foot with his. 'Look at me.' He waited for Scott to meet his eyes before he leaned forward to rest his folded arms on the table. 'We will handle your father together, okay?' As tempting as it was to bar the man from the site and make his unwanted visit a wasted one, Cam knew it would only make things more difficult for Scott in the long run. 'We'll give him a full tour of the site. Put on a bit of a show for him, even let him try out some of the survey equipment if he's so inclined.'

'You'd do that for me?' Cam nodded, wishing there was more he could do, but whatever was going on between the boy and his father, it was something Scott would have to resolve for himself. 'It's pathetic, isn't it?' Scott continued with a sigh.

'What is?'

'The way I let him push me around. I'm almost twenty years old, I'm supposed to be a bloody man by now and be able to stand on my own two feet.'

Cam folded his arms across his chest and sat back again. 'Are those your words, or his?'

Scott shrugged. 'What difference does it make? It's true either way.' He shook his head again. 'He does this every time I try to make a bit of space in my life away from him. I've tried everything to break away...'

'Even cheated on your exam?' Cam kept his voice soft.

'Yes, even that,' Scott said, his voice full of bitterness. 'I was so desperate, I was willing to jeopardise the thing I want the most.' When he met Cam's gaze, it was with eyes brimming with tears. 'I thought if I could embarrass him enough, he'd cut me off and then I'd finally be free.' He swiped at his face angrily as the first tear tipped down his cheek. 'I hadn't banked on his ego, though. "No son of mine can be a failure," that's what he said to me.'

'So he threw money at the problem until he could make it go away?'

Scott sighed. 'And now instead of escaping him, I feel more beholden to him than ever. He rubs my nose in it every time we speak. Reminds me that I wouldn't be allowed to indulge this stupid hobby of mine if it wasn't for him.'

'You could always take a sabbatical,' Cam pointed out. 'Take some time out and go and do something else for a while.'

'If I did that, he'd try and force me to go and work for him which is what he's wanted from the start.' Raising his hands, Scott scrubbed his face. 'Christ, I sound like a child whining when none of this is your problem.'

Scott went to stand, but Cam reached out and stopped him. 'Do you trust me?'

'Of course!'

Cam was almost ashamed at how quickly Scott replied because he wasn't sure he'd done enough to earn that level of loyalty. But he was determined to do what he could to help him weather this storm. The boy was right, he did need to learn to stand on his own, but that seemed like an impossible task with his father constantly breathing down his neck.

'Don't say anything to your father next weekend. We'll put on a nice show for him. Like I said, we'll give him the full guided tour and I'll have a word with Hope to make sure he gets the best of the best at the hotel and spa. Once he's out of the way, we'll work on what comes next.' He had a few ideas, but he wasn't ready to share them yet. He didn't want to promise a way out for Scott until he was sure he could deliver on it.

* * *

He was still pondering over what to do about the situation when he and Hope were curled up on the sofa that evening. He was trying to listen to a podcast with his earbuds, while she read. Realising he'd missed a chunk of the show, he lifted his phone from the arm of the sofa and slid the progress bar back a few minutes. Hope set aside the book she was reading and tilted her head back to glare up at him. 'Can you stop brooding in my ear, please?'

He pulled one of his earbuds out. 'I wasn't brooding!' he protested.

'Of course not,' Hope muttered before she settled back against him. 'Well, whatever it is you are doing, can you do it without sighing every five seconds?'

'I'll try,' Cam promised, and tucked his earbud back in.

Two minutes later and Hope's book slammed closed again. She heaved herself up and turned to face him, arms folded across her chest. 'Come on, out with it,' she demanded.

Cam switched off his phone and removed his earbuds. 'I'm worried about Scott.'

Hope's exasperated expression softened immediately. 'You think his father's going to cause trouble when he visits?'

'I don't know, but even if he doesn't, I'm still bothered by the tension in their relationship. If Scott doesn't find a way to get out from under his thumb, I'm worried he'll have a breakdown of some sort. You should've seen him today.'

'Maybe it'd be better if we didn't let him visit,' Hope posited. 'This is private land at the end of the day, so we are within our rights to withhold access to it. I can speak to Mum about cancelling his booking – we can make up an excuse – tell him there's a problem with the plumbing and that we're fully booked otherwise.'

It was a tempting thought, but wouldn't that just be kicking the can down the road? 'That might cause even more problems for the kid.'

'He sounds like a real piece of work,' Hope said as she reached for a cushion and set it on her crossed legs. 'What with him, and bloody Keith Riley still acting the fool, I should be relieved that I don't know who my father is.'

It was a totally left-field comment, and Cam wondered what had been going on with Hope that he hadn't been aware of. 'Has something else happened between you and your mum?' It was the only thing he could think of that might have unsettled her.

Hope lifted the cushion and hugged it to her chest before setting it back down with a sigh. 'No. She's been amazing. I know she still worries about me, but she's trying so hard not to fuss.' A little smile crept across her lips. 'Honestly, it's almost comical sometimes the way she goes to ask me something and then changes the subject.'

'She doesn't mind how much time you've been spending with me?' It had crossed Cam's mind, but he didn't want to discourage Hope from spending every free minute she had with him. He knew he was being selfish about it, but their relationship was all still so new and he wanted to hold onto every moment he could share with her.

'Not at all!' Hope tossed the cushion aside and came to curl up against him once more. 'She knocked on my bedroom door earlier and said I should get a move on because I was probably keeping you waiting.'

'I did start to wonder when it got to half-past seven and you hadn't arrived,' he teased, even though he'd not got back to the lodge until nearly quarter past.

'Well, you said you were going to be late, so I nipped into the village to see how Amelia and her mum were getting on.' She nestled a little closer and that, combined with her earlier comment about bloody Keith Riley, was enough to tell him all he needed to know.

'It's not the sort of situation that will resolve itself overnight.' As he said the words, he knew they could just as well apply to the problems Scott was facing with his father. 'All we can do is be around to offer whatever support we can.'

'I know, but it doesn't feel like enough.' Hope sat up again and Cam wondered what was going on with her because she wasn't normally this much of a fidget.

'And all this stuff with Amelia and her dad has been making you think about your own father?'

Hope pulled a face. 'Yes... and no.' He'd never been any good at the cryptic crossword, so Cam sat quietly until Hope could figure out what she wanted to say. 'It shouldn't make a difference, should it?' she said at last, which was no bloody help at all.

'What shouldn't?'

'He shouldn't. I've gone twenty-five years without knowing anything about him, why should I care now?'

Ah. 'It's only natural to wonder about him. You really don't know anything about him at all?'

She flopped onto her back with her head in his lap and looked up at him. 'It's ridiculous, isn't it? I see the agonies Amelia is going through, hear you telling me about poor Scott and all the crap his dad gives him, and I know, I *know* that if I looked, I'd probably hate whatever I found out and yet...'

'Do you think perhaps if you knew the truth about him, you'd be able to put it behind you and move on?' The man was dead, so Cam didn't see how much harm it could do her to know the truth.

'I don't know. I tell myself it's a waste of time and will only lead to more heartache and then the next minute I'm cleansing my face in front of the mirror and trying to work out which of my features might be from his side of the family.'

'Have you spoken to your mum about it? Perhaps if you asked her, she'd tell you a bit more about him, help put your mind at rest?'

'Oh, I couldn't.' Hope shook her head. 'I couldn't possibly put her through that!'

'And how do you think you'd feel if you found out who he was and that he'd done something awful?'

'I already know he wasn't a nice man from what Mum's already told me, so I'm not sure anything else I find out would be that much of a shock. And it's not as though whatever I learn about him is going to make any real difference to my life.' She shook her head. 'What do you think I should do?'

It was an impossible question to answer. He tried to put himself in her shoes, but he'd loved digging into his own past and putting together that family tree for his parents. It had given him a grounding, a deeper sense of self and the people who'd come before him. What must it feel like to have a completely blank slate on one side? 'Do you want me to look for you?' It wouldn't be hard, with access to the kind of records he had.

Hope sat up again. 'What do you mean?'

'Well, I could do a search and see what I can find out and then, depending on what that is, I could help you decide whether or not there would be any benefit in you knowing more.'

'So, if you found out he was an axe murderer or something, you wouldn't tell me?'

'Oh, if it was something like that, I'd probably try and persuade you to make a true crime podcast about it with me.'

Hope rolled her eyes. 'I don't know how you can listen to those awful things! That's no one's idea of relaxation.' Her face grew serious. 'How would you go about it?'

'You said your mother was once married to him, right? With an unusual name like hers, it shouldn't be hard to track down a marriage certificate. That would at least give us a name and a date of birth, and we can go from there. Or not. It would be up to you how much or how little information I look for.'

'A name would be good. And a picture, if we could find one. I feel like if I could put a face to him, I'd be able to stop wondering all the time.'

Or it might open a whole can of worms. But Cam didn't say that because this was up to Hope. All he could do was help her navigate things in the least painful way possible.

She looked over towards where his laptop was sitting on the table. 'Could you do it now?'

'If you want me to, then write your mum's full name and date of birth on a piece of paper and I'll see what I can do.'

He followed Hope over to the table, where she jotted the information down on a Post-it. 'Will it take long?' she asked, raising one hand to her mouth. She looked about to chew on the skin on the corner of her thumb, something he'd never seen her do before, and he wondered if it was an old habit long broken. She seemed to catch herself and yanked her hand away. 'Ugh. I'm going to wait outside. Give me a shout when you find something.' She bent down to retrieve her book and headed out onto the patio, where she settled onto one of the loungers with her back to him.

Cam took a seat and pulled his laptop towards him. 'This might be the stupidest idea you've ever had, Cameron Ferguson,' he muttered to himself under his breath. What on earth had possessed him to volunteer to stick his head in the proverbial lion's jaws like this? What if he found something awful and she ended up blaming him for it? Christ, what if her father really *was* an axe murderer? Feeling slightly sick at the thought, Cam opened the database and entered his login and password. He stared at the Post-it for a long moment then tapped in Stevie's full name and date of birth.

Four records found.

Cam stared at the hyperlink for a long moment. It was too late to turn back now. Even if he could bring himself to lie and say he hadn't found anything, it wouldn't take Hope long to find the truth for herself. He'd shown her how to access the database when they'd been going through the desk survey. What were the odds that she'd end up checking for herself? With a roll of his mouse, he clicked on the link and opened up the list of items found. The first was Stevie's own birth certificate. He clicked it open, but only long enough to verify the information was correct. The place of birth was listed as Stourton Hall and he knew he had the right person.

The second record was the one he was looking for – a marriage certificate. There he was, Hope's father, one Benjamin Albert Lawson. Cam right clicked on the document and saved it to his hard drive. He looked at the final two records, and frowned. He'd expected one to be a death certificate, but they were both birth certificates. He opened the first one, read the name Benjamin Lawson and assumed the database had cross-referenced the file until he spotted the date of birth. *Oh, shit.* He quickly saved the document then clicked back and opened the last one. It was Hope's birth certificate, with Stevie's name on it and a blank space where the name of the father would be recorded. Cam saved that too then opened the first two files he'd saved and set them side by side on his screen. The date of birth details from the marriage certificate corresponded exactly with those of the mother and the father on the birth certificate. Stevie Travers and Benjamin Lawson had had a son together, also called Benjamin.

Not only did it look like Hope's father was still alive, she had an older brother as well. And it looked like it was going to be Cam's job to somehow break the news to her.

21

Hope was surprised when Cam came and joined her on the patio not more than ten minutes after she'd sat down. 'That didn't take long,' she said, setting aside the book she'd been staring at blankly. Cam didn't say anything at first, just sat beside her on the lounger and took her hand. 'Oh no, is it awful?'

Cam squeezed her hand. 'I know his name and his date of birth.'

Hope wasn't sure what she'd been expecting to feel, not happy, given what had transpired between her parents, perhaps relieved or a bit nervous. Not this strange sort of numbness that settled over her. 'Tell me.' Her voice sounded tinny in her ears as though it was coming from a long way away.

'His name's Benjamin Lawson and he was born in London in 1967.'

'Benjamin?' Hope felt her breath catch in her chest and she pressed a hand to ease the sudden ache there. 'Like the baby.'

'Oh, thank God you already knew!' Cam burst out. 'I honestly didn't know how the hell I was going to tell you otherwise.'

'Tell me what?' Hope asked. 'Surely you didn't find a record of the miscarriage.' They didn't record stuff like that did they?

Cam's face turned ashen. 'What exactly did your mother tell you?' His voice cracked a little at the end and Hope stared at him in alarm.

'What do you mean what did she tell me? She lost a baby after my father pushed her down the stairs. She told me she would've named him Ben and that when she found out she was pregnant, she wanted to protect me, so she ran away and came back home.'

Cam shook his head. 'That's not what the records say. I've found a birth certificate that says your mother gave birth to a child called Benjamin Lawson, who was born in December, about three years before she gave birth to you.'

'But that's not possible... Mum told me she had a miscarriage.' She pressed a hand to her stomach, feeling suddenly sick. 'She said she tried to save us both, but she couldn't. And then she said, "my Ben, my poor baby".' Hope stared up into Cam's eyes, reading only compassion and sorrow in them. 'She definitely said she lost a baby, though, but it couldn't have been her fault if he pushed her, so how could she have tried to save him?'

Her head was spinning, her mother's words tumbling around and over like the end of a spin cycle. She thought about Rowena's reaction when she'd said her mother had told her about Ben. The way her eyes had widened with shock before she'd moved the conversation to something else. 'What have I done?' she asked Cam, but what she was really thinking was *Oh, Mum, what did you do?*

Cam reached for her, pulled her against the reassuring warmth of his chest. 'You weren't to know,' he said, pressing a kiss to the top of her head. 'It's my fault for blurting it out like that. I'm so sorry.'

Hope curled her arms around him and clung on. 'It's not your fault. I never should've asked you to look him up. I should've been satisfied with what I have. Ziggy and Zap are the best fathers I could've possibly wanted and yet I had to start poking around.' She pulled back, not wanting to accept the comfort. 'I should never have started any of this. Not the house, not the dig, not any of it. It's brought nothing but trouble.'

Cam looked stricken. 'Please don't ask me to stop, Hope. Not when we could be on the edge of discovering something amazing. This could be the find of my career! I could spend the next few years just trying to document everything.'

He was right, of course. She couldn't ask him to do that. It would be beyond selfish of her, and he hadn't asked to be dragged into her mess. 'No, of course I'm not going to do that. It just feels like everything started going wrong the moment the digger uncovered those stones.'

Cam studied her for a long moment. 'I don't know how to say this, but there's something else. I couldn't find a death certificate for your father.'

'You mean he's still *alive*?'

'I don't know, but I think perhaps you need to consider it's a possibility. Did your mother ever actually tell you he was dead?'

'What are you talking about? Of course she did!' Hope hesitated, racking her brain for details. 'She *must* have told me, I mean she wouldn't just let me believe that if it wasn't true...'

Cam nodded. 'I'm sure that whatever your mother did, she was only ever acting in what she thought were your best interests.'

Hope curled her knees up under her chin and stared out across the little garden. *What am I going to do?* Those same six words chattered through her head in a repeating loop like the bump of a train over the tracks.

Whatamigoingtodowhatamigoingtodowhatamigoingtodo?

She sat there until the last of the light faded, until her limbs were stiff and her back ached, but she still didn't have an answer. She thought about going to speak to Ziggy, whose wise counsel she'd always been able to rely upon, but then it dawned on her. If Rowena knew about Ben, then surely Zap and Ziggy must as well. They'd all lied to her, the four people she'd thought she'd be able to trust above all others.

A soft scuff came from behind her and then Cam was there, carrying a mug of tea. 'I'll leave this here,' he said, bending down to place it on the low table beside her before he straightened and turned away again.

'Stay.' None of this was his fault. She'd gone to him for help and persuaded him to get involved with the dig. She'd raised the subject of her father. He might have been the one who'd suggested doing the research, but he'd only been trying to shield her.

Cam sat on the edge of the lounger. 'I'm sorry.' He sounded desperate, and even in the deepening shadows, she could see the regret etched on his face.

'You only did what I asked you to do.' So why was she freezing him out? Because even after all this, she couldn't bring herself to confront her mother. Whatever Stevie had done, Hope never wanted to see her as upset as she'd been that awful night. 'I didn't mean what I said about wishing I'd never started this because we wouldn't have met otherwise. It feels like you're the only good thing that's happened to me lately.'

Cam reached out and stroked her hair. 'Yes, you did. It's okay to regret what's happened, Hope. Anyone in your situation would feel the same way.'

'Not you, though,' she said, pressing a kiss to his palm. 'I don't regret you.'

With a soft groan, he gathered her into his arms. 'I wouldn't blame you if you did.' He pulled back only far enough so he could meet her eyes. 'If you want me to call off the dig, I will. I can have that hole backfilled tomorrow and we'll get some fresh turf to lay over it. Give it a couple of weeks and you'd never know anything was there.'

It was beyond generous of him to offer, but Hope shook her head. 'The past has been buried for too long as it is. I'm going to dig it all up, no matter how much it hurts.'

* * *

After a restless night during which neither Cam nor Hope got much sleep, he dropped her off outside the farmhouse. 'Are you sure you don't want me to come with you?'

The scared little part inside her wanted him to stay, but this was something she needed to do on her own. He would be there later when she needed to talk to him, to cry on his shoulder and let the solid strength of him comfort her. 'I'll be okay.'

'Text me when you've spoken to him?'

'I will.' After a quick kiss, Hope slid from the car and headed towards the backdoor.

Rowena was in the kitchen, a worried look on her face. 'There you are, darling! I don't suppose you've seen my rings anywhere, have you? I can't find them anywhere and your uncle will be so upset if I've lost them.' Her voice rose and she looked close to tears.

Hope's first instinct was to go and comfort her, to set aside her plan and help her aunt look, but if she let herself get distracted, she might lose courage. 'Sorry, I haven't seen them. Is Ziggy up? I need to speak to him.' She'd decided he would be her best chance of getting the truth once and for all.

Her aunt's brows pulled down in a puzzled frown, her dilemma over her rings forgotten at Hope's uncharacteristic shortness. 'He's in his study. Is everything all right?'

Hope shook her head and marched towards the door leading to Ziggy's little suite of rooms. She closed it behind her, walked the few steps to his study and pushed that door open without knocking. 'I want to know about Ben.'

Her uncle regarded her for a long moment before setting down his pen and pointing to the chair opposite his desk. 'I'll answer whatever questions you have, but there's something I want to show you first.'

She'd hoped to catch him on the hop, but it was like he'd been expecting this conversation and was already prepared for it. Feeling as if the wind had been stolen from her rather indignant sails, Hope waited while he rummaged in the bottom drawer of his desk. He withdrew a single sheet of paper and handed it to her. She scanned the letterhead which indicated it was from a firm of solicitors then moved down to the bold header and then the handful of brief paragraphs beneath it.

RE: Benjamin Lawson

I am instructed by my client to request that all further attempts at communication cease and desist. He has attained his majority and has asked me to state that he has no wish to have any contact with Ms Stevie Travers or any other member of his maternal family.

To that end, I am enclosing a number of items of correspondence previously sent by Ms Travers over the past eighteen years.

I trust you will honour my client's wishes, but should further contact be attempted, we will have no option other than to seek a legal remedy which can only bring unnecessary distress to all parties involved.

Hope checked the date. It was sent ten years ago, when Ben would've been eighteen according to his birth certificate. She looked up from the letter to see her uncle had placed a large box in the middle of his desk. 'What's that?'

With a sigh, Ziggy lifted off the lid. 'It's every letter your mother sent to Ben. Every card she sent on his birthday and at Christmas. All returned to her with that letter.'

Letting the letter fall from her fingers, Hope reached for the box and lifted it down onto her lap. The box was stacked high with envelopes, each one addressed in her mother's familiar, neat hand. Beside the letters was a pile of cards, the birthday ones marked with ages, the Christmas cards a mix of funny reindeer, smiling Santas and jolly snowmen.

To my darling son.

To a wonderful son.

To a very special son.

Hope couldn't read any more past the blur of tears and she set the box down at her feet before she could drip on any of them and risk marring their pristine surfaces. 'He just sent them all back?'

Ziggy nodded. 'That letter is the first and last response your mother ever received from him. And it completely devastated her. She never gave up hope, you see?' He smiled sadly. 'She never said as much, but I'm sure that's what she named you for, her hope that one day you'd all be together.'

'Oh, God.' Hope raised a hand to her lips and pressed hard to try and hold back a sob. 'That's why she never told me?'

'We wanted to tell you, but she wouldn't have it. She was terrified when you were younger that you'd want to see your father and she didn't want him anywhere near you.'

'He's not dead, then, that was another lie?'

Ziggy nodded. 'I can't remember how it came about but once it was clear you thought he'd died then we decided the best thing was for you to carry on believing that. I'll apologise for most of my involvement in this, but not for that. Benjamin Lawson isn't anyone you need in your life.'

'That's a decision I should've been able to make for myself, don't you think?'

'Perhaps once you've heard the rest of what I have to say, you'll think differently.' Ziggy sat back in his chair, his chin resting on steepled fingers. 'Stevie tried everything to get your brother back, but Lawson refused. He threatened to take her to court, said he had evidence from their family doctor about her *instability*.' Ziggy's mouth twisted over that last word.

'The only mental problem she had was the suffering he put her through. Still, your mother was worried if she pressed too hard, he'd start digging around the family for anything he could use against her and he'd find out about you. Lawson agreed that if she surrendered full custody, she could write to their son once a month and send cards at birthdays and Christmas. It wasn't much, but it was a straw for her to cling to, so she agreed. All she could do was write, and hope that as your brother grew older, Lawson would relent and allow her access visits, but he never did. She pinned everything on Ben being able to break free of his father's influence when he turned eighteen, but as you can see from that letter, the rot had already set too deep and he wants nothing to do with any of us. It had to be Ben's choice to come home and when he rejected her, she couldn't bear for you to carry the burden of that rejection as well.'

'I still shouldn't have kept it from you.'

Hope turned to find her mother standing in the doorway, her make-up streaked by the silent tears falling from her eyes. She wanted to go to her, to alleviate the guilt she could read on her mum's face, to tell her it was okay. But that would be another lie, and there had been far too many of them already. 'I'm going to try and understand why you did this, Mum,' she said, softly. It was the best she could offer her at that moment because everything was still too raw. She had a brother out there somewhere and regardless of whatever good intentions her family had had, they'd stolen twenty-five years from both of them.

Stevie nodded. 'That's more than I deserve, darling, I know that.'

'I need a little time to try and process all this,' Hope said, rising to her feet. 'I'm going for a walk.' As she approached the door, her mother stepped back and Hope thought her heart might break all over again. As angry as she was, she still loved this woman who had been her everything her entire life. Leaning over, she brushed a kiss on her mum's cheek. 'Just give me some time,' she said again.

When Hope entered the kitchen, Rowena was sitting at the kitchen table. She started to stand and Hope knew what she wanted, but Ro was a part of this conspiracy of silence too. Shaking her head, Hope walked past her and out the door. She kept on walking, following the paths which had been familiar to her since childhood. Past the oak tree where a piece of shredded rope still dangled from a low branch, the remnants of a long-gone tyre swing Zap had rigged up for her and Rhys to play on.

The echoes of their laughter and excited shrieks came to her, but there was no comfort to be found in old memories now she knew there was a child's voice missing. As she stared up at the faded bit of rope, a horrifying thought occurred to her. Had Rhys known too? Had the family trusted him with this secret and not her? Fighting down a wave of nausea, she turned and started running back towards the farm.

'Rhys? Rhys!' Out of breath, Hope had to bend at the waist and brace her hands on her thighs as she sucked in a long draw of air and tried to still her hammering heart.

'I'm here.' Rhys stepped out of his office at the rear of the barn, his face a mask of pure anger. Ziggy was a step behind him, Zap on his heels. 'They've just told me.'

'Oh, thank God you didn't know!' The sobs she'd been holding finally broke free and then her cousin was there, holding her tight, stroking her back.

'Of course I didn't know,' he muttered, still sounding furious. 'As if I'd ever keep something like that from you.'

'Hope, please try to understand.' Through her sobs, she wasn't sure which of her uncles had spoken.

'Leave her alone,' Rhys snapped. 'Leave us both the hell alone.'

Hope cried until there was nothing left inside her. When she finally lifted her head, it was to find she and Rhys were alone. 'Don't be too angry at your dad,' she said. 'He was only doing what he thought was the best to protect Mum, just like you've always protected me.'

Rhys's eyes were like chips of flint, but he nodded once in acknowledgement. 'I don't care what the biology is, you are my little sister and you always will be.'

She hugged him tight again, wanting to believe that but knowing that something had changed irreparably for both of them. 'We have a big brother out there somewhere,' she said against his chest. 'What if he needs us too?'

They talked for a long time before agreeing things would only get worse if they acted without understanding everything. Now her tears were spent and the first wave of shock had passed, Hope felt steadier in herself. Part of her wanted to look Ben up immediately, to jump in the car and race off to London and hunt him down. But it wasn't only him she'd have to contend with. As far as they knew, her father was still alive and Hope wasn't at all sure that she was ready to deal with him.

After discussing it with Rhys, they settled on a plan. They would wait for now, try and do a bit more research and find out what they could. If Ben was happy and settled, he might not want them barging into his life and turning everything upside down. 'He wrote that letter,' Rhys reminded her as they walked back towards the farmhouse. 'He made the choice to cut us off.'

But he hadn't known about her. Hope didn't give voice to the selfish thought. Ben had grown up knowing his mother had chosen to leave him behind. He might not know the truth of why Mum had left him, but that was the reality for him. If he needed to shut the door on her, and the rest of the family by extension, in order to live a healthy, happy life, then they had to respect his decision. It hurt more than Hope had ever thought anything was possible to hurt. Like she'd lost a limb she hadn't known existed and now her brain was torturing her with the kind of phantom pain she'd read amputees sometimes suffered from.

Their parents and Ziggy were all sitting at the kitchen table when they walked in, a united front, just as she and Rhys were in their own way. 'We're not going to do anything about this for now, and we're both still too angry to discuss it,' Hope told them without preamble. 'But when we're ready, the six of us are going to sit down and talk about this, and you have to promise you will tell us everything. No more secrets, no more lies and obfuscation by omission.'

It was her mother who nodded. 'If that's what you want.'

Rhys snorted. 'None of this is what we want, but we all have to deal with the consequences of your actions. Either Hope and I are equals with the four of you, or we're not.'

'You're going to tell us everything we want to know,' Hope reiterated. She cast a questioning glance to Rhys, to see whether he wanted to push their advantage to the maximum.

He returned her look with one of flat determination before he turned to face the four older people. 'And that includes the truth about Uncle Dylan.'

22

Cam found it hard to concentrate as he waited to hear from Hope. Rather than commit to full trenches, he and Barnie had decided to dig half a dozen test pits to check the widest area of the site possible. They'd marked out the one metre-square zones with a can of spray paint and now it was just a case of waiting for Declan's workers to break ground. Cam had divided the team so he, Barnie, Cassie, Ed, Adam and Zoë would each supervise a pit. A couple of junior team members had been allocated to each group, one to record any finds that came out of the pit and the other to help with the excavations once the topsoil had been cleared. He'd assigned Scott to his own team so he could keep an eye on him; with his father due to descend on them next weekend, Cam was growing increasingly concerned about how stressed the boy looked. Stressed and distracted. 'Earth to Scott.' Cam waved a hand.

Scott blushed and shook his head, the glazed look in his eyes fading. 'Sorry, I was miles away.'

'Look, if you're not going to concentrate, then maybe you should go for a walk or something. We can handle this.'

'No. I'm fine. This is important and I promise to pay better attention.'

Cam was pleased to see Scott stiffen his spine a little and he clapped him on the shoulder. 'Look, I'm a bit distracted myself this morning, so let's help each other keep our heads in the game, okay?'

'Okay.' Scott's smile faded. 'Is everything all right? Is there something that I can help with?'

Cam was struck once again just what a good kid he was. 'It's a personal thing but not anything to worry about, I appreciate you checking, though.'

'You ready?' It was the groundworker.

'Whenever you are!'

There was a small cheer as the groundworker stuck the edge of the turf cutter into the soil and worked his way around the highlighted square. Cam was too nervous to join in – his gut told him they were on to something special, but he'd talked down everyone else's excitement at the survey results. One way or another, the next couple of hours would reveal a great deal.

* * *

'I don't understand.' It was Scott who spoke, but he was only echoing what they were all feeling as they stared down into the small hole.

Cam crouched and scraped the soil back until he could loosen a broken brick from the soil and pull it free from the jumble of other rubble and rubbish. He turned the brick this way and that. It was old, not one of the identical ones moulded and fired by the thousands that made up modern homes and buildings, but nowhere near old enough to fit in with the ruined remains of the chapel. 'We still need to get everything out, photograph and record it,' he said, though he couldn't keep the disappointment out of his voice. 'Come on, give me a hand.'

It was only the first test pit, Cam told himself as he tried to keep calm. There could be any number of explanations. Once he'd got Scott started, he decided to check on the others to see how they were getting on.

If the expression on Barnie's face was anything to go by, the answer was not good. Standing next to him, Cam stared down at the jumble of artefacts on the grass at Barnie's feet. There were a couple of pieces of broken brick similar to what Cam had been pulling out of his pit, a lump of clay pottery they'd not be able to put a date on until it had been cleaned up, and part of a decorative carving. 'This looks promising,' Cam said as he knelt down to inspect the carving. It was only a small piece so hard to tell what the design was, but it could be part of a roof boss or some other kind of flourish.

'It's closer in period to what we might expect but it was in the same layer as the brickwork, which makes me much less happy about it,' Barnie said, coming down on one knee beside him. He picked up one of the bricks. 'I don't know what to make of these, they remind me of the raised beds in the ornamental gardens behind the house.'

Cam frowned. 'It's a trek from there to here. I've found similar stuff in mine, though. Do we have a date for the gardens?'

Barnie shook his head. 'Not exactly. I found some plans in the archive but anything relating to the Hall itself I put to one side. I'll pull them out when I go back and I'll take a couple of these brick fragments back with me so I can do a closer comparison. You still haven't been up and had a proper look around the Hall, have you? The family maintained the front façade pretty much as it was originally built, but there's all sorts of quirky additions around the back.'

'I'll try and make time this weekend, but can I leave it with you to look into for now?'

'Sure. Shall I head back there and crack on?'

Cam glanced around at the mess of the site. There were bits of finds everywhere and it would take time to sort and catalogue them all. It was basic work and he could supervise it. 'I can handle things here. Why don't you take Ed and Cassie with you? The sooner we understand what's going on here, the better.'

'Sounds like a plan. Hey, why don't we meet up at the pub later for dinner? Ed and Cassie want to check it out and Meena is at a family birthday, so I'm at a loose end. Bring Hope and we'll have a few beers and chill out.'

'I'll see what she says. Even if she's not up for it, I might try and pop down for a drink.' He was conscious of how much time he and Hope had been spending together. His friends had rearranged their summer plans to support him and he didn't want them to feel like he was taking them for granted.

It was late afternoon before Cam finally heard from Hope. He'd been so busy trying to keep an eye on everyone at the dig, he hadn't stopped for more than five minutes to eat a sandwich someone handed him and gulp down a cup of coffee. The air was thick with anticipation, as though everyone knew they were just a few steps away from discovering the truth about the site, but Cam kept them focused on the tasks at hand. Impatient as he was to make sense of everything, they couldn't afford to be sloppy. Even the groundworkers had wanted to pitch in, so Cam had set them up under Adam's watchful eye to sift through the spoil heap from each of the pits to make sure they hadn't missed any fragments of material.

'It's a bit like panning for gold,' Paul had declared once he got the hang of shaking the large sieve. 'I saw them doing that once on a documentary.'

'If you find a gold nugget, I'll let you keep it,' Cam joked. The kind of treasure he was interested in would be dismissed by most as rubbish, but even the smallest pottery shards could help with dating the site.

He'd moved on and was double-checking the finds each team had bagged so far when his phone rang. Seeing it was Hope calling, Cam dusted off his hands and walked far enough away for privacy while still being able to keep a watchful eye on the site. 'Hey. I was getting worried about you. How did it go?'

'About as awful as you might have expected.' Hope fell silent and Cam wished he'd made the effort to seek her out rather than them doing this over the phone. 'Everybody knew, well, apart from Rhys, and I swear he's even more furious about it than I am.'

'They've told you the truth, though?'

'Yes. Well, as much as I could handle for the moment. There's still some other stuff we need to get to the bottom of, but that can wait for now.' The laugh she gave was a painful, choked noise that broke Cam's heart. 'Ben doesn't want anything to do with us. I can't say I blame him, but I had at least hoped we could salvage something positive from this whole bloody mess.'

Cam listened as she described the contents of the solicitor's letter sent on her brother's behalf. 'Oh, darling, I'm so sorry.'

'Me too.'

'Look, I can finish up here and come and see you if you need me, or you can come and meet me at the lodge if you'd prefer?' He'd wanted to do another hour on site, but if Hope needed him then he could trust Adam and Zoë to supervise closing down for the day.

'That's so lovely of you, but I'd rather be on my own for a bit, if you don't mind.' Hope sighed. 'It's all so awkward here right now, but the estate needs all of us to run properly. We're a part of this place, and it's a part of us. It's where we belong. I'm going to have to find a way to live with what I know.' She gave that sad laugh again. 'Be careful what you wish for, eh?'

'Why don't you come and stay at the lodge with me for a few nights while everyone gets used to the situation?' He could only imagine how hard it would be for her to sit around the kitchen table for dinner and feel betrayed by everyone sitting with her. Except for Rhys... 'I was going to meet Barnie, Ed and Cassie in the pub for dinner. Why don't you and Rhys come and join us? It'd give you both a bit of breathing space. I haven't said a word to anyone about what we found out last night, so you won't have to worry about having to talk about it.'

'I'm not sure I'm in the mood for it. You won't mind, will you?'

'Of course not. And I don't mind if you'd rather stay at the farmhouse either. I just want to help you get through this in whatever way I can. Look, I'll go to the pub with the others and if you decide to join us, then great, if not then text me later before you go to bed.'

'Okay. Look, I'd better go as I need to go and see if Rowena has managed to find her rings. She was beside herself earlier and I kind of brushed her off because I was too focused on talking to Ziggy.'

Cam's heart swelled with compassion and affection. Even with all the shocks that had been dumped in Hope's unsuspecting lap, she still loved and cared for her family. It was going to be a very rocky few months, but he had faith they would find a way through. 'Okay. Call or text me if you need me and I'll be there.'

* * *

'Oh, this is lovely,' Cass said with a delighted smile as Barnie held the door of The Stourton Arms open for her and Ed. Cam followed them into the bar, remembering to duck before he clunked his head on the low beams – something he hadn't managed on his first visit. It was quiet, but then it was a Tuesday night. Still, given how busy the campsite on the estate was, he'd expected more than half a dozen tables to be occupied.

'Table for four?' Barnie asked the barman.

'Better make it for six as we might have company later,' Cam reminded him.

'Oh, yes, of course. Can you manage six?'

'If you want to stay in here, then that's no problem.' The barman pointed to a large table set in the window. 'If you'd rather sit out back in the beer garden, it might not be so easy.'

Cam hadn't realised there was a beer garden. Though the windows were open, it was a bit stuffy in the bar. 'Do you want to try out back?' he asked the others.

'We'll go and see,' Ed volunteered. 'If we find a space, I'll bag it and Cass can nip back in and let you know.'

'Good plan. What are you drinking?'

It took a bit of friendly arguing with Barnie over who was going to buy the first round, which Iain, the man behind the bar who turned out to be the landlord, found highly amusing. By the time he'd pulled three pints and sorted out a gin and tonic for Cassie, Cam and Barnie were still bickering about it. 'How about I open you a tab and you can sort it out later?' he suggested.

'Thanks. Do you need a credit card for that?' Barnie opened his wallet.

Iain snorted. 'It's not like I don't know where to find you if you skip out without paying, is it? Your dig's the talk of the village.'

Cam supposed he should've expected they would be the focus of attention. He remembered the mess up at the site after the break-in and wondered if it was possible someone in the village was responsible. 'I hope we aren't causing too much disruption for anyone.' He kept his tone casual, but it wouldn't do any harm to scope out the general feeling.

'Nobody's said so, although a couple of folks mentioned getting stuck in the traffic the other day behind that big wagon when it took a wrong turn.'

'Yeah, we had an issue with one of the site cabins and had to get it swapped out.' As Declan had suspected, the contractor had wanted to take back the damaged cabin and the only time they'd been able to do the swap was mid-morning. 'I hadn't realised the driver got lost, though.'

Iain shrugged. 'When you live in the countryside, you get used to stuff like that. If it's not a tractor, it's a bloody lorry driver following his sat nav rather than using a bit of common sense. People parking here, there and everywhere doesn't help much either.'

He sounded complacent rather than irritated, but Cam still felt bad. 'We got lost the first time we visited,' he admitted. 'But at least we were only in a car and the roads were quiet.'

'Don't fret yourself about it,' Iain said, offering him one of the pints he'd just pulled. 'We got him round the loop of the village green and pointed in the right direction.' He grinned at Cam. 'And I for one am grateful for the extra business you and your team are sending my way.'

Cassie waved from the door to the beer garden so, after thanking Iain again, Cam and Barnie collected their drinks and a couple of menus and followed her outside. The first thing Cam noticed was the heady scent of the bright pink roses as they passed beneath a trellised walkway. The second was the buzz of chatter and laughter. He stepped out into the evening sunshine to find the garden was much larger than he'd been expecting. Picnic-style benches were set at reasonable distances apart with large umbrellas overhead to keep off the sun from those who wished to avoid it. Ed was at a table in the corner and had just finished putting the umbrella up when they reached him. Cam handed him his spare pint before climbing over the bench seat opposite and sitting down. 'It's nice out here,' he observed, looking around. More roses covered the Cotswold stone rear wall, these a paler shade of pink than the ones on the trellis.

'It's lovely,' Cassie agreed. 'Good idea of yours.' She raised her glass and clinked it against Barnie's. 'What do you want to do about food? Did you find out what time the kitchen shuts?'

Cam hadn't thought to ask so he picked up the menu and scanned it quickly. 'It says here they serve evening meals until nine, so there's no rush unless you're starving?'

She shook her head. 'I'm fine if everyone else is. Let's wait and see if Hope and Rhys decide to join us.'

Cam had only said the pair were busy with chores around the estate so might not make it and the others had accepted that. Having taken a sip of his beer, he set it down and folded his arms on the table. 'So, how did you get on?' He knew he'd set them a hell of a task and spending a hot day cooped up in the old baron's library couldn't have been much fun, so he hadn't wanted to press for an update. Still, they'd let him chatter on about how the site work was going without a word as to their progress in the archives, which seemed a bit odd, even if they didn't have anything much to report.

He watched as the three of them exchanged a look of what could only be described as amused satisfaction. Barnie checked his watch then dug into his pocket and laid a pound coin on the table. 'I make that half an hour, so I'm out as I said he wouldn't last longer than five minutes.'

Cassie reached across and picked up the money then held out her palm to her husband. 'I said twenty minutes, so I'm the closest.' She wiggled her fingers. 'Come on, cough up.'

Grumbling, Ed took a pound out of his pocket and dropped it next to Barnie's coin. 'You let me down, Cam. I said you'd hold out for at least an hour.'

'Ha bloody ha.' Cam mock-scowled at them. 'You were willing to let me stew for an hour before any of you said anything, and here was me feeling bad that you'd been sweltering inside all afternoon.'

'Oh, it was quite nice, actually. With the windows open, we managed to generate a pleasant breeze.' Cassie paused to take a sip of her G&T. 'Besides, once Barnie found the garden plans and we got stuck into unlucky number thirteen's diary then I didn't notice much else.'

'Unlucky number... you mean the thirteenth baron?' Cam sat up straight. 'You found something? Tell me!'

His friends burst out laughing and Cam had to grind his teeth while they got themselves under control. 'Ed? Mate? Come on, I expect this of these two, but you've always been the sensible one.'

Ed grinned. 'Sorry, we shouldn't tease you, but it was too good an opportunity to miss. As Cass said, we found the plans for the garden—'

'*I* found the plans for the garden,' Barnie cut in with a triumphant smile. 'Two sets, in fact, dated less than two years apart. The gardens still resemble much of what was on the later plans.' He pulled a folded piece of paper out of his back pocket and shoved it across to Cam. 'It's a bit rubbish as I had to try and shrink it down on the photocopier, but you'll get the idea.'

Unfolding the A4 square, Cam had to stare at the blurry copy for a few moments before he could start to make sense of it. It didn't help that the original document had yellowed with age, making the sketchy drawing that much harder to decipher. 'It looks like a cloister?'

Barnie nodded. 'Remember when garden follies were all the rage in the eighteenth century? It looks like the baron decided to remodel the gardens and build one of his own.' He tapped a faint scrawl underneath the drawing. 'I'm not sure if you can read it on the copy but on the original plans, it's called the Abbot's Walk.'

Cam's head shot up at that. 'Abbot's? Are you sure it says Abbot's?'

He looked from Barnie to Ed to Cassie who were all grinning and nodding. 'We're sure,' Barnie said.

'In the diary, baron thirteen refers to his plans to take window arches and other stones from the abbey ruins to build it.'

'An abbey, though?' Cam couldn't quite let himself believe it. 'Bloody hell, I never dreamed it'd be anything as grand as that.'

'Oh, it gets better!' Cassie said, clapping her hands together. 'We're not only looking at uncovering the ruins of a site of significance, but it comes with a curse to boot!'

'A curse? I'm not sure I like the sound of that.'

Cassie laughed. 'Oh, it's obviously a load of superstitious old nonsense but it'll be a great yarn to spin to visitors.'

'You'd better tell me all about it.' Cam had just lifted the remains of his pint when his phone buzzed. 'Hang on.' He quickly scanned the message from Hope. 'Hold that thought. Hope and Rhys are on their way and they're bringing Amelia.'

'The woman who's been cleaning the cabins for us?' Ed asked.

Cam nodded. 'She's a good friend of the family and she's been having a tough time of things. I don't want to go into details because it's not really any of my business, but let's keep any personal enquiries to a minimum, yeah?'

'Of course,' Cassie said. 'Shall we go and meet them in the bar and get some more drinks in? They've got a nice sharing platter on the starters as well, so I'll order a couple of those and that'll keep us going until we decide what to do about dinner.'

Barnie patted his shirt pocket, stood to check his back pockets then bent to glance around under the table. 'Damn. Has anyone seen my phone?'

Cam checked the ground beneath his side of the table. 'Can't see it. Are you sure you brought it with you?'

'I always have it on me. Meena was going to text me later.'

'I'm sure she'll forgive you,' Cam assured his friend, but Barnie still looked a little downcast.

'He seems to really like her,' Cassie said as they headed back inside. 'Looks like you're not the only one who's found love here at Juniper Meadows.'

'I...' Cam didn't know what he might have said if they hadn't got caught up trying to squeeze past a family coming the other way. By the time he reached the bar, Cassie was already ordering the drinks and seemed to have forgotten, so he was happy to let the subject drop. There was plenty of time to think about all that later, for now he was happy to enjoy Hope's company and see how things played out.

Iain had just poured the last pint when a cheerful voice called out. 'Another of those please! And a bottle of your finest pinot grigio, good sir!'

Cam turned with a smile to see Rhys filling the doorway with his broad frame. He ducked the beams without having to think about it and came over to shake Cam's hand. 'Thanks for the invite, much appreciated.'

'It's the least we can do when you've given us such a warm welcome. Oh, that reminds me, did your mum manage to find her rings? Hope mentioned earlier that she'd misplaced them.'

Rhys shook his head. 'There's been no sign of them anywhere and we've turned the entire farmhouse upside down. She and Stevie have searched through the hotel as well, trying to retrace everywhere Mum went this morning. She's absolutely beside herself about it. Dad's suggested he commission some new ones for her from the jeweller who has a workshop at The Old Stable Yard, but she can't accept they're gone for good.' He sighed. 'They were heirlooms, you see, and she feels so guilty about it as she wanted to be able to pass them down one day.' Rhys laughed. 'I'm not sure who she thinks she's going to pass them down to because I haven't got time to find a girlfriend, never mind think about having kids of my own one day!' He reached for the pint Iain held out to him and took a long draught. 'God, I needed that.'

Cam wondered what was keeping Hope, and turned to see she was still trying to encourage a reluctant-looking Amelia through the door. In contrast to Hope's shiny dark hair, Amelia's blonde bob hung limp and lank. He caught Hope's eye and they exchanged a quick smile while she continued to whisper to her friend. He turned back to Rhys, not wanting Amelia to feel like she was being watched. 'We weren't sure what everyone wanted to do about eating so we've ordered a couple of sharing platters for now.'

'Good plan because I'm starving.'

Cassie laughed and said to Iain. 'Better make that three platters and maybe a couple of bowls of chips?'

'No problem.'

'Oh, and can I cancel my gin? If the others are having wine, I'll have a glass with them.' She looked over her shoulder and, spotting Hope and Amelia, she made an immediate beeline for them.

'Everything all right with Amelia?' Cam asked Rhys in a low voice so no one else would overhear.

Rhys scrunched up his face in a scowl. 'Not really. Keith made a right stink about going into rehab last week. He only agreed to it in the end when Daisy threatened to leave him, apparently.' He shook his head. 'I think she should do that, anyway, but I've already been told what I can do with my opinions on the matter so I'm keeping well out of it.' He sent a worried look towards the three women. 'Amelia called the clinic today for an update and they wouldn't tell her anything. Said it was in the interests of patient confidentiality, which I think is a load of bullshit. The amount

Ziggy is shelling out on that place, they should be calling with hourly bloody updates if you ask me.'

'At least Keith's going to get the help he needs,' Cam offered, trying to look on the positive side of things.

'We can only hope so.' Rhys didn't sound the least bit convinced.

Deciding he'd poked his nose in more than enough, Cam shifted the topic of conversation. 'Well, hopefully we can distract Amelia with some news about the dig,' Cam murmured as the women approached. In a louder voice, he said to Hope, 'Barnie and the others have uncovered some interesting stuff in the archives and were just about to tell me when you texted.'

Her eyes lit up. 'Oh, really? Well, that is good timing on our part.' She stretched up on tiptoes to give him a quick kiss before looking around the bar. 'Where are we sitting?'

'We've got a table outside. Here, can you take these glasses?' When she reached for them with a nod, Cam picked up the bottle of wine which Iain had helpfully placed in an ice bucket. 'Can you manage this, Amelia?'

She stepped forward. 'Yes. Hey, I hope you don't mind me gatecrashing?'

Cam smiled down at her. 'You're not at all, but you might regret it when we bore you to death with archaeology talk.'

Her smile warmed at the edges and he was pleased to see a spark of interest in her tired eyes. 'I've been dying to find out more about what you're all doing up at the dig. I'll confess I had a quick study of the plans up on the wall in the office when I was cleaning the other day, but I couldn't make head or tail of them.'

'You might regret saying that by the end of the evening,' Cam said with a laugh. 'Ladies first.' It wasn't any conscious design, but the four of them formed a protective circle around Amelia as they made their way out to the garden. Rhys led the way, with Hope and Cassie on either side of the other woman and Cam at the rear. There were a few interested glances turned their way, a couple of nudges and nods, and Cam stepped closer to the three women, when he noticed Hope shooting a hard stare at the people on the table beside her.

Rhys sat down beside Ed and Barnie, leaving Cam to squeeze onto the end of the opposite bench next to Hope. 'I told you I should've stayed at home,' he heard Amelia murmur from where she was sitting between Hope and Cassie. 'Everyone's staring.'

'Ignore them,' Hope said, giving her friend's hand a quick pat before she reached for the bottle of wine. 'Have a drink and forget about them. They'll get bored soon enough.' She poured three glasses and handed one to Cassie. 'Cam says you've got news about the dig.'

23

Hope was relieved when Cassie accepted both the drink and the conversational cue. She was worried about Amelia, but the longer she stayed cooped up at home, the worse she was going to feel. Keith was away at the private rehab facility her uncle was paying for, and Hope was damned if she was going to let her friend skulk around feeling like she was in any way to blame for her father's bad behaviour. Hope didn't fool herself into thinking she held much sway over the community, but what little bit of influence she had, she would put to good use. Amelia being seen with both her and Rhys – particularly when it was her cousin who'd been forced into the position of having to fire Keith – would make it clear to everyone there were no hard feelings between the Travers and the Rileys.

'We were just telling Cam that we found two sets of plans for the Hall gardens as well as a diary belonging to your...' Cassie paused to count off on her fingers. 'Eight or maybe nine times great-grandfather. Assuming there is a direct line of succession for the family title.' She looked to Barnie as though for confirmation.

Barnie shrugged. 'I haven't got around to sorting out a family tree yet, it's on the list but hasn't been a priority.' Because Cam had asked him not to go poking around in the family history, Hope knew, but she appreciated him not saying as much.

'I'm sorry,' Rhys said. 'But what have the gardens got to do with anything? I thought you were confining your work to up near the chapel.'

'We are,' Cam confirmed. 'But we found some unusual materials in the test pits we've dug, including what looks like brick and rubble that match those used in the construction of the ornamental gardens. It's definitely much later than what we were expecting to find, so Barnie and the others have been trying to track down some answers via the records in your family archive.' He pushed a creased-looking piece of paper towards Rhys and traced the outline of something with his finger. 'See here? These are the original designs for the gardens and it looks like your ancestor planned to construct a folly using some of the stonework from the ruins.'

Hope leaned forward, trying to make sense of the blurry photocopy. 'A folly?' She'd heard the term before, but wasn't clear on the historical significance of it.

'It was a bit of a trend in the eighteenth century in particular for the owners of big estates like yours to build elaborate architectural features in their grounds,' Cam explained. 'Mock Grecian temples, fantasy grottos, stone towers that looked out over the parkland.'

'Your great-whatever grandfather decided to build himself a cloister, a covered walkway like you often find attached to large churches or other religious buildings.' He tapped the piece of paper. 'What's unclear at the moment is if they knocked down one that was already part of the ruins up by the chapel and were planning to rebuild it, or if they were just repurposing whatever they could find and cobbling something more fanciful together.'

Hope frowned. 'But surely if there was something that big on the site, we'd know about it? What happened to all the stones, even if they did knock the existing buildings down?'

'That's where the curse comes in,' Cassie said, which didn't make any more sense than the rest of it.

Hope looked up at Cam. 'What curse?'

He grinned. 'This is as far as I got in the conversation earlier, so I'm as much in the dark about it as you are.'

'If you'll be quiet for a minute, I'll explain,' Cassie said, rolling her eyes.

But before she could do just that, two of the local youngsters who helped out in the pub arrived at their table laden down with food.

It took another five minutes for everyone to grab a plate and take what they wanted, hand around napkins, sauces, cutlery and the like. Once everyone was sorted, Hope picked up a chicken goujon from her plate and dipped it in a little ramekin of sweet chilli sauce she and Cam had commandeered between them. 'So, come on then, what's all this about a curse?'

While the rest of them made inroads into the platters, Cassie outlined what they'd found in the old baron's diary. 'At first, it appears that work on the new gardens went smoothly. With the help of local labourers from the village, the architect got the pieces he wanted from the ruins extracted and transported to the grounds at the back of the Hall.' She pulled a face. 'I don't think they took much care with anything they didn't want to use for the new cloister.'

Cam shook his head. 'I dread to think how much destruction they wrought on the site. Folly, indeed.'

Reaching for his hand beneath the table, Hope gave it a comforting squeeze. 'So what happened next? How did we end up with what we have now and not this cloister design?'

'As I said, at first they made good progress and then things started to go wrong. They were working up near what I think is what the family refers to as the chapel. It's not entirely clear, but there is a reference to the oak tree. One of the labourers was breaking up what they thought was a stone floor and smashed right through into an underground crypt.'

'Oh, God, how awful! I had no idea there were even any burials up there.' The family had a private graveyard near the newer chapel next to the Hall, so she supposed she should've considered the possibility of older graves near the original chapel – or whatever it was because from what she could make out from the elaborate design of the folly walk, there had been something much more substantial on the site once upon a time.

'Nobody did, according to your ancestor's diary,' Cassie said in a quiet voice. 'They covered the crypt back up but the next day one of the workers fell from some height and broke his neck. Two days later, there was a storm unlike anything they'd ever seen. The river broke its banks and flooded the site. That's when the rumours started that they'd unleashed a curse by disturbing the dead.'

Amelia shuddered next to Hope. 'Ugh, how macabre.'

Hope stared down at the chips going cold on her plate and she pushed it away, not feeling hungry any more. 'It is a bit grim.'

Her cousin was made of sterner stuff because he continued to wolf down his food. 'Superstitious nonsense,' he scoffed between bites. 'They probably wanted an excuse to down tools.'

Cassie nodded. 'That's what the baron complained about in his diary, particularly when they started asking for more money. He persuaded most of the workers to continue, but a few refused to return. A couple of weeks later, a fever ran through the village and the estate. Your ancestor didn't go into numbers, but several people died, including his eldest son.'

'Oh, that's awful.' A cold shudder ran down Hope's spine as she tried to imagine the despair the old baron must have felt over losing a child, and his heir to boot. Things like that mattered to families like theirs, no matter how much they tried to pretend they'd moved on from such things. If Ziggy didn't have any children, which was looking increasingly likely given he hadn't been out on more than a handful of dates as far as Hope could remember, then eventually Rhys would inherit the baronetcy. She pushed the thought away because even thinking about it felt like inviting disaster down upon the family. Her grandfather and both her uncles were fit and well, so it wasn't something that needed to be worried about for many years. Hope tapped the wooden bench. *Touch wood.*

Cassie nodded. 'He was distraught and things only went further down-hill. After that, no one would come and work for him – and not just the extra labourers he'd got in for the gardens – the farmworkers downed tools and refused to set foot on the estate until the baron promised to do some-thing about it. In the end, they left him no choice and he agreed to knock down what there was of the folly and return all the stones to the site. He was so angry, he razed the entire site to the ground, apart from what was left of the chapel because no one would go near it, and they buried every-thing. He had the gardens redesigned and when they'd finished building them, all the excess soil and leftover rubble and brick was transported up to the ruins and dumped on top until there was nothing left to see but a flat field.'

'I wonder if that's why we don't graze up there,' Rhys put in suddenly. 'I've always assumed we avoided it because the river is open there and it's too much of a risk to the livestock, but there are other parts of the estate where the river has been fenced off from the grazing land.'

'Could be,' Cam agreed, then he rubbed a hand over his face.

'Are you okay?' Hope asked him. 'You're not worried about this nonsense to do with a curse, are you?'

Laughing, he put his arm around her shoulders. 'Not one bit. I was just thinking about how much damage was done and wondering what the site might have looked like before the baron got it into his head to build that stupid folly.'

'What's done is done,' Hope said, resting her head on his shoulder. 'All you can do is keep digging and see how much of it you can salvage.'

The mood around the table took a bit of a nosedive and Hope was wondering whether they should call it an early night. She was still worried about Amelia, who hadn't done more than pick at her food, even before the conversation had turned to dead bodies and curses. The wine bottle was empty, but her friend hadn't taken more than a couple of sips. Hope wondered if they should've been more sensitive about her father's drinking, but if they'd all chosen soft drinks, then what kind of a message would that send to Amelia? We'd better not have a glass of wine in case you end up an alcoholic like your father? Hope shook her head. No. Whatever sins and wrongs Keith had committed, they were his burdens to carry, and his alone. She nudged Amelia's shoulder. 'You all right?'

Amelia managed a small smile. 'Just tired.'

'If you want to go...'

'No, please, I'm fine.' Amelia tipped her head back to look up at the sky, which was a brilliant mass of gold and red with the slightest hint of purple at the edge which augured the approaching sunset. 'It's so nice to be out instead of stuck at home staring at the TV while Mum works her way through all the evening soaps.'

'Shall I get us another drink then?' When her friend nodded, Hope looked down at Amelia's plate. 'Maybe something else to eat – we could split something if you don't want a full meal.' Even if she had a mouthful or two, it would be better than nothing. Not waiting for an answer, Hope picked up one of the menus. 'If we're going to order anything else, we should do it sooner rather than later,' she said to the group at large.

The rest of the evening was much more relaxed. Over another round of drinks and main meals, including a chicken Caesar salad Hope shared with Amelia, Cam and his friends got into exchanging banter about their university days. It seemed they would spare no shame to keep each other laughing, from missed lectures to foolish dares, including one where Cam had slipped an anonymous Valentine's card into Mrs Cotteridge's handbag. 'I thought I'd got away with it all that time,' he said, chuckling at the memory. 'And then I walked into my office the first Valentine's Day after I started working as junior lecturer and there it was, sitting on my desk!'

'The same card?' Hope couldn't believe it.

He nodded. 'The very same one. I spent ages choosing it and it had this sort of red velvet background. I couldn't give Mrs Cotteridge any old tat, you know.'

'Did she say anything to you?'

'Tell her the best bit!' Barnie called out before he turned towards her and carried on speaking. 'He put it back on her desk the year after, and they're still exchanging it!'

Cam shrugged, looking a bit embarrassed but also pleased with himself. 'She's an absolute sweetheart. She really looked out for us when we were students and she's still covering my arse all these years later.'

Hope remembered the way the older woman had considered her request for a long moment before leading her towards Cam's office when she'd shown up looking for help. 'If it wasn't for her, I might never have met you.'

Leaning over, Cam pressed a quick kiss to her lips. 'It's my turn to give her the card next year, I'll have to add a bouquet of flowers and a box of chocolates to thank her.'

While Hope sat there, feeling all warm and fuzzy inside about the idea of the two of them still being together then, Barnie began relaying some outlandish story. He'd gone home with a girl who lived in one of the other halls and ended up getting locked out in the corridor when he'd opened the wrong door, trying to find the bathroom. Even his most frantic knocking hadn't woken her up and he'd ended up sleeping in the communal kitchen with only a tea towel to protect his modesty when her flatmates began to stir the next morning.

Hope clutched her stomach, which ached from laughing, as she pictured him sitting there in a plastic bucket chair with just a scrap of cloth over his lap. 'Stop it, for goodness' sake,' she gasped.

'My pelvic floor isn't what it used to be,' Cassie announced, through tears of laughter. 'If I have an accident, Lysander Barnard, it'll be your bloody fault!'

'Lysander?' Amelia said in disbelief before clamping a hand over her mouth. 'Are you serious?'

Barnie immediately scowled, which only made everyone laugh harder. Cassie heaved herself up from the bench. 'Come on,' she said to Amelia, offering a hand to pull her up. 'You can show me the way to the ladies', and I'll tell you all about it.'

They stayed until the sun was nothing more than a thin strip of red on the horizon, everyone too reluctant to make a move while knowing they all had full work schedules the following day. 'We should go,' Hope said, having drained the last of her tea. The hot drinks had been another delaying tactic, as had the desserts no one had needed but hadn't been able to resist when they saw the people at a nearby table tucking into thick wedges of strawberry cheesecake.

'You said that ten minutes ago,' Rhys said with a laugh.

'And a quarter of an hour before that,' Barnie added.

'Then this time we really need to move,' Hope retorted, but still couldn't quite get herself to stand up.

'Come on then.' Cam stood and held out a hand to her.

'Such a boy scout,' Barnie mocked.

'You're welcome to stay if you want,' Cam said, turning to offer a hand to steady Amelia as she extricated herself from between the bench and the table.

'I might just do that,' Barnie replied. He looked around the others who were still seated. 'Anyone for a nightcap?'

'And that is definitely my cue to go.' Rhys swung his long legs over the bench and rose. 'Some of us have a 5 a.m. appointment with a milking machine.'

'Kinky.' Barnie waggled his brows. 'So you're going to leave me all alone?' He jutted his bottom lip in a good approximation of a pouting child.

'Looks like it, *Lysander*.'

Hope laughed as Cam put his arm around her. 'Don't be mean to him.'

'I'm not being mean,' Cam protested. 'I'm not forcing him to come with us, am I?' He dug his phone out of his pocket and waved it at Barnie. 'Hey, remember earlier when you mentioned you'd left your phone behind?'

Barnie frowned at him. 'Yeah, what of it?'

Cam flicked on the torch app and flashed it in his friend's face. 'Oh, just wondering how you're going to find your way back alone without it, seeing as it's going to be pitch dark in approximately...' He tipped his head back to study the sky. 'About five minutes.'

'Oh, shit!' Barnie scrambled up from the bench. 'And Meena was going to text me! I'm going to be in big trouble, I'm telling her you all held me hostage and forced me to eat pudding against my will.' They left the garden on another wave of laughter.

As they stepped outside the pub, Amelia reached out and drew Hope into a hug. 'Thanks for tonight, it was just what I needed.'

Hope kissed her cheek. 'It was so lovely to spend time with you, and I'm really sorry we've let things slip lately. Let's make it a regular thing, okay?'

Amelia nodded. 'I'd like that.' She huffed out a breath that was half a laugh. 'We're going to be seeing plenty of each other for the foreseeable future. Mum saw the doctor today and her chest infection hasn't responded to the antibiotics as well as they would like. He said if it gets any worse she might end up in hospital for a couple of days for a stronger course of treatment.'

God, that was the last thing they needed. 'Oh, what a shame. Will you keep me in the loop when you find out more? You know I'd be happy to pop in and check on your mum while you're at work.'

Amelia hugged her again. 'Thank you. I feel like we're just such a burden on everyone at the moment.'

Before Hope could answer, Rhys came over and slung an arm around Amelia's shoulders. 'Not that bollocks again? Come on, I'll walk you home and explain for the hundredth and first time why you're not a burden on anyone, especially not your friends.'

'The last thing I need is a lecture from you, Rhys Travers,' Amelia retorted with a snort, but she hooked her arm around his waist. Turning towards the rest of them, she waved with her free hand. 'Night, guys. Thanks for a lovely evening!'

'Night,' Hope replied along with a chorus from the others. 'Do you want us to wait for you, Rhys?'

He shook his head. 'No, I'll only be a couple of minutes. I'll catch you up.'

Hope watched them walk away for a moment then held out her hand to Cam. They fell into step, the others a little way ahead. 'Are those two going to get back together, do you think?' Cam asked.

She shook her head. 'I don't think so, though I'll never say never about anything. I think it was one of those things that burned hot for a while but fizzled out just as quickly. I'm glad they've remained friends, though.'

Cam was quiet for a while. 'Do you think that's what might happen with us?'

The question pulled Hope up short. Was he feeling like they rushed into things and was now regretting it? He hadn't given any indication he wasn't enjoying their time together. Hadn't he said earlier he would be sending Mrs Cotteridge flowers next Valentine's Day for introducing them? That hadn't sounded like someone who was second guessing things. She glanced down at their clasped hands and decided to be brave. 'I don't think so. We're not teenagers in the first flush. I know we've grown close in a relatively short amount of time, but I'm not a silly kid. I know what I want in my life, and for the foreseeable future, I see you playing a very big part in it.'

Cam drew to a halt and took her in his arms. 'I'm glad you feel that way about things, because that's exactly how I feel, too.'

24

The rest of the week passed in what seemed like a blink of an eye and before Cam knew it, it was the weekend again. Now they understood what they were dealing with, the excavation works had begun in earnest. With the aid of the groundworkers, they'd stripped back the turf around where the test pits had been sunk and extended each to around five square metres. Barnie's main focus remained in the archives as he continued to piece together the story of what had happened on the site; in particular, Cam was hoping he could find out more about the location of the crypt. Until they could narrow down a search area, they'd decided to cordon off the area around the chapel and beneath the oak tree to avoid any potential accidents. There was no telling how safely the labourers had covered up the opening of the crypt and the last thing he wanted was a cave-in.

They'd dug down to a depth of about a metre in Cam's trench and he was pretty sure they were through the spoil from the gardens. Large tarpaulin sheets covered the land on all four sides of the hole, their blue surfaces covered in a mishmash of stones, bricks and a jumble of random finds. It was still too early to tell the trash from the treasure, so they'd done their best to group the finds together by appearance and approximate age for now. Straightening up to loosen a knot in his back, Cam stared out over the tarpaulin to his right. It was covered in pieces of stone that matched the general appearance of the walls of the chapel. Here and there, he spotted hints of something wonderful – the curve of an arch, two pieces that slotted together to form the bottom half of what might be a ceiling boss. It was like one of those 'world's hardest jigsaw puzzles' scaled up a hundred times.

He heard his name being called and turned to see Scott waving to get his attention. The young man was holding his phone up and Cam knew immediately what that meant. 'Here we go,' he muttered to himself. Clambering out of the trench, Cam dusted his jeans off and turned to Adam. 'Can you keep an eye on things here?'

'Sure, Cam.' Adam glanced beyond him to where Scott was waiting and pulled a face. 'Try not to punch Mr Willoughby, no matter how hard he pushes your buttons. We can't afford for you to get locked up.'

Cam laughed. From the fierce glare on Adam's face, it looked like he was the one contemplating giving Scott's father a whack or two. He'd grown really protective of the lad and Cam had been pleased to see the way Scott had been thriving under his and Zoë's attention. 'That's good advice, I suggest we both keep it in mind.'

Adam shot him a rueful smile. 'I'll do my best.'

Deciding to try to make a good impression from the off, Cam accompanied Scott up to the Hall to meet his father. They arrived to find both Hope and her mother had already swung into action, the pair of them chatting with Willoughby over tea and cakes at one of the tables and chair groupings which were set at discreet intervals around the impressive entrance hall.

'Ah, here they are!' Stevie said, gliding to her feet with that innate grace she had. 'I was just telling your father what a help you were the other week at the party, Scott,' she continued before turning back to Willoughby. 'Such a delightful young man you've raised, he's a credit to you.'

God bless you, Stevie. Cam hid his smile at the nonplussed look on Willoughby's face. It was clear he wanted to be his usual scornful self, but in the face of a proper lady – a baron's daughter, no less – it was clear he was trying to be on his best behaviour. He would be the sort of man who was impressed by titles, of course, and Stevie was looking every bit the lady in a neat black skirt, a cream silk blouse and a thick rope of pearls at her throat.

Hope was dressed in her usual work gear of a Juniper Meadows branded polo shirt, jeans and boots, but she had that same straight-backed deportment as her mother. She rose as well in one fluid motion, leaving Willoughby floundering for a moment in the deep leather bucket chair before he too stood.

'Mama has arranged for Mr Willoughby's luggage to be taken up to his room. We did offer luncheon, but Mr Willoughby is keen to visit the dig.'

Cam bit his lip at Hope's use of both 'Mama' to refer to her mother and the word 'luncheon'. Both she and Stevie were laying it on with a trowel, but you'd have to know them as well as he did to understand they weren't ones for airs and graces. Though both women were smiling, there was still a tension between them. Not wanting to deepen the rift in the family, Hope had decided against moving in with Cam at the lodge and was splitting her evenings between there and the farmhouse. Given how stilted things were between Hope and Stevie, Cam was beyond grateful they'd still found time to put on this charade for his sake. 'Well, we're ready whenever you are.' Cam looked Willoughby up and down, judged his cords and checked shirt more than acceptable for being on site, he wasn't sure about the leather moccasins, though. 'Do you have any other shoes with you?'

'I've brought some trainers because I wanted to check out the gym, but that's all.' Willoughby glanced between Cam's, Scott's and Hope's boots. 'I don't want to be trekking around in the mud in them. They're Moncler.' The name meant nothing to Cam and that must have shown on his face because Willoughby scowled and snapped, 'They cost me four hundred quid.'

'No one cares about your designer trainers, Dad,' Scott said with rather more bravery than Cam might have expected. 'I've got a spare pair of boots in my locker you can borrow.'

'What you're wearing should be fine,' Cam conceded. 'It's still very early days, so we've only opened up the first few trenches this week. You might have been better off waiting longer for a visit until we've made more progress. I'm afraid you might be disappointed.' The moment the words were out, Cam regretted his choice.

'I'm already disappointed that my son has chosen to waste his time grubbing around in the dirt instead of focusing on a proper course that will set him up for the future,' Willoughby said with that familiar sneer. Just as a leopard couldn't change its spots, it seemed there was a limit to the amount of deference Willoughby could show before his natural arrogance took over. He adjusted the band of the large watch on his wrist, another designer brand, no doubt. 'Come on then,' he barked at Scott. 'Show me what it is that's so bloody special about a few old lumps of stone in the ground.'

Once they arrived at the site, things didn't improve. Willoughby didn't try to hide his impatience as Declan took him through a visitor safety briefing. 'Yes, yes, I'm not an idiot,' he said, trying to cut the site manager off halfway through. 'I do run my own business, you know, and this isn't my first time on a site. Can we just get on with it?'

Declan stared pointedly at Willoughby's footwear then back up at him. 'You have two choices. You let me finish this briefing or you take yourself back to the spa where I'm sure the ladies there will pamper you in the manner you're accustomed to.'

Deciding he didn't want to get caught in the middle of a pissing contest and trusting Declan to deal with the situation, Cam steered Scott towards the door. 'Come on, let's fetch those boots for your dad in case he decides he wants them after all.' Without an audience to perform to, perhaps Willoughby wouldn't need to flex his ego.

They made it into the welfare cabin before Scott burst out, 'God, why is he always like this?'

'Our backgrounds are sometimes hard to escape from,' Cam said as he leaned one shoulder against the row of lockers. He'd been giving the matter some thought since discovering Willoughby had booked a visit, hoping to find some common ground for Scott's sake, or at least to try to understand what made the other man tick. 'Your dad has fought his way up from nothing to run a really successful business. I'm not making excuses for the way he behaves, but I can empathise somewhat because I had to get over some people's expectation I was going to fail because of where I came from. I've tried not to carry the shadow of that with me, though I'm not always successful.'

Cam paused, wondering if he should continue with his train of thought. 'When your dad pulled strings and got you back on the course, I was furious because I saw that as him exploiting the privilege of his position.' When Scott looked downcast, Cam gave him a reassuring smile. 'I'm glad we got you back, even if I don't approve of the methods. I know this stuff with your dad is stressing you out, but give yourself some space and time and you'll find a way to get through it. And don't forget to keep reaching out for help. We're a team. Try and remember that.'

Scott pulled his spare boots out of his locker and closed the door with a decisive click. 'He's going to be embarrassing, we both know that.'

Cam nodded. 'But the only person he's embarrassing is himself. I know it might not seem like that to you—'

'It doesn't,' Scott said, cutting across him. 'But thanks anyway.' And that, Cam decided, was his cue to shut up.

Cam took his time as he walked Willoughby around the perimeter of the site. He started up near the chapel, pointed out the size of the broken window arch still visible and how its dimensions indicated a building of some significance. He pointed to the cordoned-off area and spoke about the earlier discovery of a crypt and how that was one of the things they'd be looking for later in the project. He scrubbed his finger along the soot marks and explained his theory about the potential destruction being down to the recovery of resources like lead from the roof by the local community, explained about the stonework in some of the cottages in the village and how it wasn't unusual for people to use whatever was to hand at the time, even if that seemed incomprehensible to modern sensibilities.

As they strolled back towards where the team was working, Cam continued his explanation. 'Consider a site with the renown of Avebury. It's a World Heritage Site and arguably one of the most well-known prehistoric monuments after Stonehenge. The significance of the site to our ancient ancestors is not lost to us today and we can marvel at its existence. During the medieval and Middle Ages, when people were in the full grip of Christianity, it would've been seen as something strange and sinister, certainly not of God's making. Large parts of the circle and the avenues were destroyed, the stones pushed over, some buried, others smashed up and used to build dwellings. You can see evidence of that in the village today.'

Willoughby thrust his hands in his pockets and glanced around. 'Are you trying to compare a few tumbled stones and a couple of holes in the ground to some ancient wonder of the world?' His tone clearly said he thought the whole thing was a joke.

Cam smiled, though he wanted to grit his teeth. 'Not at all, I was just offering a parallel example of when communities have repurposed historical remains for their own use.'

'So, what have you found then?'

Knowing he'd put him off as long as possible, Cam led the other man towards where Cassie and Ed were supervising the excavation of the nearest trench. 'Honestly, at the moment, it's a bit of a mystery.'

'You mean you don't know what you're doing,' Willoughby scoffed. 'That's no surprise.'

'I mean these very early results are not what we were expecting, so we are in the process of cataloguing what is coming out of the pits while Dr Barnard does some further research into the family's extensive archive to try and give us a better picture of activity on the site.'

'Surely that's something you should've done before dragging everyone here and wasting all this money? I only let Scott come on this blasted wild goose chase because you'd promised there was something worth finding! Look at this junk.' Willoughby aimed a kick that sent one of the brick fragments skittering across the grass.

'Hey!' Cassie protested just as Cam stepped into Willoughby's personal space.

He wasn't nearly as broad as the other man, but he had an inch or two of height on him. Confrontation was not his style, at all, but a line had been crossed and he was not prepared to stand for any more of this idiot and his nonsense. 'Enough. We've done our best to accommodate you, for Scott's sake, not for yours, but I will not have you causing damage to this site. I think it's time you returned to the hotel and spa to enjoy the rest of your weekend. I'm sure the Travers family will do everything they can to facilitate your stay.'

Willoughby's face turned red and for a worrying moment, Cam thought he was going to get a punch in the mouth for his troubles. He dug deep and held his place, refusing to let this man bully him as he had so many other people. With a snort of disgust, Willoughby turned away. Cam's relief was short-lived as the other man rounded on his son. 'Get your stuff. It's clear you've let this charlatan play you for a fool, but I've indulged this pathetic little hobby of yours for long enough. You're coming home with me today.'

Scott turned pale as a ghost, but he shook his head. 'No. I'm staying here.'

Willoughby took a step towards him and immediately the other members of the team moved forward until they formed a semi-circle around Scott. They didn't say anything, but their message was clear enough. 'I said get your stuff,' Willoughby snapped again, but he didn't move any closer.

'And I said no. This isn't a hobby, this is my future career you're trying to jeopardise and I'm sick to death of you trying to push me around. Go home, Dad, you're not welcome here.'

'You'll be singing a different tune when you realise you can't earn a living grubbing about in the dirt. When you do finally figure it out, don't bother to come crying to me, boy, because you've burned your bridges once and for all. I've wasted all the time I'm going to on hauling your arse out of the fire – you're on your own from now on.' Willoughby swung towards Cam, literally shaking with rage. 'And as for you! I'll be speaking to the vice chancellor about you. You might have got away with it last time, but I won't rest until you're out of a job!'

Cam felt sick at the thought of being hauled over the coals by the university administrators again, but just as before, he'd done nothing wrong. 'You've threatened that before, Mr Willoughby. Now why don't you do us all a favour and go home.'

'Don't worry, I'm going!'

Cam let him stalk off as far as the compound, before realising the blasted man had no way to get back to the Hall without walking as he and Scott had given him a lift. 'Make sure he's all right, will you?' he asked Cassie with a quick nod towards where the rest of the team had gathered around Scott, then he jogged across the site for what was going to be a very unpleasant drive.

In the end, Declan agreed to drive Willoughby back, while Cam followed in his own vehicle. He shoved his Bluetooth headphone in and called Hope as he was driving away. 'How's it going?' she asked as soon as she picked up.

'Disastrous, I'm afraid. Willoughby's on his way back to the Hall with Declan. He's leaving immediately. I wanted to give you the heads up in case he causes a scene.'

'Oh no, how awful for you all. Look, I'm still up here, so let me get on to Mum and we'll get his bags brought down from his room. With any luck, we'll be in time to catch him outside and he can go straight to his car.'

Not wanting to leave either her or Stevie to deal with Willoughby when he was the source of the man's ire, Cam pulled up next to Declan as he stopped outside the front of the Hall. 'Hope is already arranging for Mr Willoughby's bags to be brought down so we might as well head straight to the car park so he can load his car.'

'Desperate to see the back of me, eh?' the florid-cheeked man sneered, leaning across from the passenger seat.

In response, Cam pressed the button to roll up the window and turned his car around to lead Declan to the car park tucked behind one of the later extensions at the rear. They'd just parked when the rear door opened and Hope appeared, a smartly dressed young man on her heels carrying a weekend bag and towing a matching suitcase. 'I'm sorry to see you go before you had a chance to fully appreciate our facilities, Mr Willoughby,' Hope said.

'I've already wasted enough of my time this weekend.' Willoughby pointed to a large maroon Jaguar. 'Over there, boy,' he snapped as he pulled a set of keys out of his pocket, pointed a fob towards the car and unlocked it.

If Hope felt the same level of disdain as Cam did for the dismissive way Willoughby spoke to the porter, not a flicker of it showed on her calm face. Cam made a note never to play poker with her. 'Well, you'll be welcome to return any time,' Hope said with a smile as she gestured towards the car.

They'd barely taken half a dozen steps towards the Jaguar when the porter came dashing over and whispered something in Hope's ear. Cam didn't need to see Hope's eyes widen to know there was a problem, the lad's pallid complexion was enough. 'If you could wait here a moment, Mr Willoughby.' Hope didn't wait for a reply, her boots scuffing on the tarmac as she marched over to the car with the porter beside her.

The porter gestured at the side of the Jaguar before turning to point at the car next to it. 'If someone's dented my door, there'll be hell to pay!' Willoughby snarled as he set off after them.

Cam exchanged a quick 'what now' look with Declan before they jogged over to see what the problem was.

It didn't take more than a couple of steps to catch up with Willoughby. Cam took one look at the man's face and genuinely feared for Willoughby's health. It shouldn't be possible for a human to turn that shade of puce and not be having a stroke or a heart attack. Cam glanced over at the side of the Jaguar and wondered if he too might have a medical incident when he saw the ugly, jagged scratch running almost the full length of the body-work. Feeling sick, he met Hope's worried eyes and she nodded mutely towards the black Ford parked next to it. A second ugly gouge traced the side of that vehicle too.

'What the bloody hell?' Willoughby managed to choke out as he bent to stroke the damaged paintwork.

'I'm so very sorry, Mr Willoughby,' Hope said, crouching next to him. 'We will of course pay for the repairs.'

'Damn right, you will!' Willoughby all but roared in her face.

The force of his mottled fury would've knocked most people over, but Hope merely straightened and turned to the porter. 'Check every car in the vicinity. Don't touch anything, though.'

'I'll give him a hand.' Declan pulled out his phone and followed the porter. Cam saw them stop at the next car in the row and knew they had a serious problem when Declan raised his phone and began to take photos.

'I'd better call Ziggy.' Hope's neutral expression hadn't changed, but Cam didn't miss the small tension lines around her eyes. He nodded down at where Willoughby was still crouched to indicate he'd deal with him, and she turned and walked away a few paces to make her call.

'Let's check the rest of your car, make sure there's no other damage,'

Cam suggested. His personal feelings towards the man had no place here. He was clearly upset and had every right to be.

Willoughby pushed himself upright. 'Don't touch my car.' He pulled out his keys. 'I'm getting out of here before anything else happens, now get out of my way!'

Taking a step back, Cam raised his hands. 'I'm just trying to help. I realise this must be very upsetting for you, but the Travers will need to take a record of the damage done.' He pointed along the row to where Declan and the porter were half a dozen cars further down. 'It's not only your car that's been targeted and they'll need evidence to make a report to both their insurers and the police.'

Marching around to the back of his car, Willoughby picked up his abandoned bags and tossed them in the boot. 'That's their problem, not mine.' He slammed the boot closed and swung around to face Hope, who had just come off the phone. 'You'll be hearing from my solicitors.'

'You'll need this then.' Cool as a cucumber, Hope pulled a business card out of her pocket and handed it to him. 'All my contact details are on there, including my email. Submit the invoice for the repairs and I'll see it's paid the same day. I wish you a safe journey home and I'm very sorry again that you've been caught up in this awful business. I trust you'll be willing to give a statement to the police should they wish to speak to you about this?'

'Well, yes, of course. I'm not one to obstruct a criminal investigation. And mind you do make sure the bill is paid.' Apparently expecting her to put up a fight, Willoughby looked a bit disappointed at being robbed of the chance to yell at her some more.

'If you can possibly bear with me a few moments longer, I'd like to take some photos for our records.'

Having just declared he wouldn't be obstructive, there was little Willoughby could do. 'Be quick about it.'

25

Hope watched Willoughby drive away. If he'd honked his horn, he couldn't have reminded her more of Mr Toad in that moment. 'Horrible man.' She sighed.

'I'm sorry I've brought all this trouble to your door,' Cam said, coming to stand beside her. He reached for her hand, and she let him take it, grateful for the support.

She squeezed his fingers for a moment before releasing them. 'It's hardly your fault we've got a vandal on our hands, is it?'

'You think it's vandals, then, and not...' Cam gestured towards the now empty driveway.

'You're not serious?' She knew the man had come looking to disrupt things, but he struck her as too status conscious, too vain to consider damaging an ego extension like his big shiny car.

Cam sighed. 'No, not really.'

Willoughby was the least of her problems, and she couldn't afford to waste any more time worrying about him. They had a hotel full of guests and though she hadn't got a final count yet from Justin, the porter, as to how many cars were affected, a fair number of them were about to have their weekends ruined. 'If it was only his car, then I'd maybe be willing to entertain the idea he'd done it himself to cause trouble, but I think he's just been caught up in something unrelated. He wasn't around when someone tried to break into the site cabin, remember?'

Cam shoved his hands on his hips and sighed. 'No, you're right. I was just trying to tie everything up in a neat bundle. If it's not him, then we've got a serious problem on our hands. This doesn't strike me as kids messing about.'

Hope nodded. She'd struggled to accept that as the explanation for the earlier damage, but now she was convinced there was something more sinister going on. Someone was trying to cause trouble for her and her family. But who? The only person on her suspect list was Keith Riley, and he was safely shut up in rehab. Who else had they upset? It wasn't a nice thing to have to think about, but she'd have to sit down later and try to come up with a list of unhappy customers, guests who'd complained about their previous stays. It felt like she was clutching at straws, but she didn't know what else to do. Still, it would have to wait because there were more pressing problems, such as telling all the guests whose cars had been scratched.

When Cam put his arms around her, she leaned into him, taking strength from his unwavering support. 'I'm sorry this is happening,' he murmured before letting her go. 'Right, what can I do to help?'

She appreciated the fact he was trying to shoulder some of the responsibility, but her family were practised in dealing with problems and having too many people involved would only lead to confusion. Raising a hand, she placed it on his chest. 'I want you and Declan to go back to the site and focus on what you came here to do.' She caught a movement out of her eye and saw both her mother and Ziggy approaching. Her uncle had swapped the jeans and sweatshirt she'd seen him in that morning for a smart suit, and Mum was holding a suit carrier, which Hope knew would contain a similar smarter outfit for her than her current jeans and polo shirt. 'Look, I need to get changed and start speaking to the other guests.'

Cam looked reluctantly between them all. 'It doesn't feel right, leaving you to deal with all this.'

Hope didn't have the bandwidth for an argument with him right then. She was already stretched wafer-thin, and she knew her mother wasn't in any better a state than she was. It would take every ounce of their reserves to face the guests and deal with what was going to be an unpleasant few hours. She pressed her fingers into his chest, feeling the lean strength of him and wishing she could fold herself into it once more. There'd be time enough to seek the comfort she needed in his arms later, but for now, she had to squash it all down. 'Just go, please,' she whispered.

Cam raised his hand to cover hers. 'Okay. You'll come over later.' It wasn't a question and Hope nodded. With a quick reassuring squeeze of her fingers, he released her hand and stepped back. 'Come on, Declan. Let's get back to site and leave the family to deal with this.'

The site manager was already approaching with the porter. 'It's a bloody mess,' he said to Hope. 'Whoever did this needs catching before they do any more damage.'

She nodded. 'I know, and we'll do our best to make sure that happens. Can you email me the photos you've taken?'

'I'll do it the moment I'm back at the office.'

With one final, reluctant glance at the damaged cars, Cam and Declan headed for the vehicles and Hope could forget about them for a few minutes. She took the suit carrier from her mother and on impulse leaned forward and kissed her cheek.

'It's your grey trouser suit,' her mum said. 'I always loved the cut of it on you, so I told Ziggy to bring it.'

Hope returned her smile. 'That's perfect, thank you for thinking of it. We're going to need all the power dressing we can get. Justin has been checking the cars, so I'll leave him to update you on the tally while I go and change.'

They met up in the lobby a few minutes later. While she'd been getting changed in the office, Hope had run a printout of their current guest list. As Ziggy read out the car registrations Justin had written down, Hope checked the list and highlighted the affected guests. 'Eleven,' she said with a sigh as she capped the highlighter. 'Twelve, if we include Mr Willoughby.'

'We'd better start making calls,' Stevie said. 'Do you want to split the list, or shall I speak to them all?'

'I'll help you,' Hope replied. She turned to her uncle. 'What are we going to offer them as compensation?'

'A full refund for their costs this weekend, all repairs and the option to return at another date should they wish,' Ziggy suggested. 'It can come out of the contingency fund.' He stood. 'Can you run off another copy of the list for me and I'll make contact with the police?'

'Of course.' Hope rose and led the way back towards the office. As they reached the door, she hesitated and turned back to her uncle. 'This is really serious, isn't it? It's not just kids messing about.' The break-in at the site cabin had cost enough; even though the hire company had only needed to change the lock, they'd threatened to uplift everything from the site without a hefty deposit as surety against further damage. With that and the installation of security lights and wiring an alarm to the fence, her own small contingency for the dig was already eaten up. This, on the other hand, was going to cost them thousands, never mind the damage to their reputation once word got out, as it inevitably would.

'No. It's not just kids.' Ziggy placed a hand on her shoulder. 'We'll get through this, Hope. I know I have no right to ask this of you given everything, but I want you to trust me now.'

He looked shattered. Though she was still angry with both him and her mother for keeping secrets, Hope needed to make something clear to both of them. 'Someone is trying to break us and I'm not going to let that happen. This is our home, our livelihood, our family.' A family that had several holes in it, but those were problems to be dealt with on another day. 'I'll get you that list.'

* * *

It had taken all of her reserves and most of the day to deal with their understandably unhappy guests. Some, like Mr Willoughby, had packed up their things and left, but a few had been persuaded to stay. Their wine cellar was several bottles of champagne lighter, but given how much the whole mess was going to cost them, Hope had agreed with her mother that it was a small price to pay.

There'd been a few grumbles about lack of CCTV in the car park and it was on Hope's list of things to talk to Ziggy about in the morning. They'd avoided it so far as there'd never been a problem before, but there had to be a way to add some discreet cameras without damaging the exterior fabric of the building. Perhaps Declan could point her in the direction of the security contractor who'd installed the alarm and lights at the dig compound? Hope pulled out her phone and tapped in a reminder. Her head felt so full, she'd reached the point where if she didn't note things down the minute they occurred to her, then they were likely to be forgotten.

She hoped a shower and a change of clothes would make her feel better, but she still felt soiled from the ugliness of the day. Someone had marred the beauty of the idyll they'd created, had spoiled the special weekend of all those poor people at the Hall. As she sat at her dressing table to brush her hair, she tried not to cry as she recalled the tears of a woman whose husband had brought her away for a rest after a gruelling series of cancer treatments; at the brave faces put on by the couple who'd saved all year to celebrate their first wedding anniversary, only to have it ruined.

By the time Hope made her way along the familiar path to Cam's lodge, she was more than ready for the day to be over. She'd let the dogs off their leads and was happy for them to roam ahead, as they knew by now which way she was heading. She turned down the almost hidden entrance to the lodge and let her hand trail through the climbing plants along the wall. The sweet scent of jasmine filled the air and she breathed deeply, letting it soothe all the jagged bits inside her.

The dogs' excited barking stirred her, and a smile came to her lips as she heard Cam fussing and talking nonsense to them. She rounded the corner of the lodge to find him on his knees, one arm around each of the dogs as they returned his affection with doggy licks and nuzzles. 'You look awful,' he said, coming to his feet as she climbed the stairs towards him.

'Gee, thanks. You sure know how to make a girl feel special.' Hope still lifted her head to accept his kiss.

'Upstairs,' Cam ordered when they came up for air.

As much as she wanted to fall into his arms and forget about everything, she was too stressed and wired from the day to be in the mood for anything other than a cold glass of wine and to slump on the sofa. Something of her reluctance must've shown in her face because Cam shook his head with a grin. 'Not that.' He kissed her mouth, just the merest brush of his lips. 'Well, maybe later. Come on, I'll show you.'

Intrigued, Hope let him lead her upstairs. The bed had been made up with crisp white linens and Cam had folded the balcony doors back to let in the soft evening air. She might've faceplanted into the middle of that sea of white cotton if Cam hadn't tugged her hand and led her across the room and through the open door to the en suite bathroom.

'Oh, Cam.' The roll-top copper tub was full of inviting bubbles and a dozen candles had been lit to bathe the room in a soft golden glow. The doors here were open, too, letting that same sultry evening air in. The faint hint of jasmine teased her nose, either carried in on the breeze or from whatever soothing concoction he'd poured under the hot water when filling the tub. A small table had been set next to the bath and a glass of wine stood waiting for her. Tears pricked the backs of her eyes.

'Here, let me help you.' Cam knelt and tugged at the laces of her trainers. She stood still as he carefully helped her out of her clothes. His hands were gentle, his words soft as he urged her to lift her leg or extend her arms so he could pull her top over her head. Too numbed by the sadness of the day, Hope moved compliantly to his instructions. When he pulled a hair scrunchy she must've left there another night off his wrist and combed his fingers through her hair, the first tear fell. As he curled her hair into a loose knot on top of her head and kissed the tender skin of her nape, a second followed it. By the time he'd helped her into the tub and the warm cocoon of the water enveloped her to her shoulders, the tears were falling freely. She didn't sob, didn't hitch her breath, she just let the pain and the ugliness of the day seep away in salty trails that were swallowed by the bubbles. Cam sank to the floor beside the tub, holding silent vigil until with a sigh she dipped her hand into the warm water and washed the last of the tears from her cheeks.

'Do you want to talk about it?' he asked.

Hope laughed, a cracked, slightly wonky sound, but the best she could manage. 'God, no.'

Resting one arm on the side of the tub, Cam grinned at her. 'Then let me tell you all about my equally shitty day and perhaps that'll make you feel better.'

It didn't exactly cheer her up as he outlined Mr Willoughby's awful behaviour at the site, followed by a further afternoon of cataloguing all the rubble and stones they'd unearthed so far from the trenches, but at least it distracted her enough from her own woes. Having taken a sip of her wine, Hope offered Cam the glass. 'Sounds like you need this more than I do.'

Cam took a drink then passed it back. 'I've definitely had better days.'

'And you're still no clearer on what's going on with the site?'

'Nope. It's such a complete and utter jumble at the moment. All we can do is keep clearing them and try to sort out what's coming out.' He scrubbed a hand through his fringe, the way he always did when he was frustrated. 'It's like someone mixed half a dozen jigsaw puzzles together – having thrown away all the corner pieces first.'

Hope offered her glass back to Cam. When he shook his head, she took a sip while she tried to think of other positives she could add. 'It's still very early days.'

He swirled an idle hand through the warm water of her bath. 'You're right, of course, and that's exactly what I've been telling the rest of the team.'

Sitting up, Hope curled her knees up under her chin and shuffled along the tub until there was an empty space behind her. 'If you're going to sulk about it, you might as well join me in here.'

Cam laughed. 'Is that the new rule? Sulking is only permitted in the bath.'

Extending one soapy hand, she nudged his arm where it rested on the side of the tub. 'It is, although it's not the only thing we can do in here.'

'Oh, really? Well, in that case...' He rose and stripped his clothes with fast, methodical movements. 'Scoot forward a bit more,' he told her as he moved towards the back of the tub.

Hope did as he said and felt the water rise against her back as he stepped in. 'Hang on, I might need to let a bit of the water out.' She reached for the chain and lifted a corner of the plug as Cam carefully lowered himself behind her. The water level rose alarmingly, a small amount seeping over the edge of the roll-top. 'Woah, steady!' Giggling, Hope tugged the plug all the way out while Cam braced his weight on his arms.

'Let me know when it's safe,' he said with a laugh.

'Try now.' Hope left the water to drain lower until she was sure Cam was settled then replaced the plug and added a quick blast of hot water.

'Come here.' Cam's arms circled her from behind and she let him ease her back against his chest with a sigh. 'Better?'

Closing her eyes, Hope let the last of the tension drain from her body. 'Much.'

26

After a quiet evening with Hope and a surprisingly good sleep for both of them, Cam walked her and the dogs back to her car early the next morning. 'You really should think about leaving a few things at the lodge,' he said as she came up on tiptoe to claim a kiss.

'I know.' She rested her head against his chest. 'I was trying to make things easier for Mum, but with everything that's been going on, perhaps a bit of space might be just what we both need.'

If she wanted to move in, Cam had no objections, but he also knew Hope and her mother had a very difficult tightrope to walk over the coming weeks and months. 'Whatever is easiest for you is fine by me,' he promised her, dropping another kiss on her mouth. 'What's on your agenda for today?'

She scrunched her nose. 'Home to change and then back up to the Hall. I want to follow up with everyone who was affected yesterday and make sure they have everything they need to continue to enjoy what's left of the weekend. What about you?'

The sulk in the bath had done its trick and Cam was determined to be more positive about everything. He was still concerned about who it was causing trouble for Hope and her family, but there was nothing practical he could do other than make sure his team was safe and taking sensible precautions. The best thing he could do was to try to make some progress at the dig. 'I'm going to extend my trench deeper and see if we can hit on anything that might be left of the original stonework in situ.'

'Sounds like a plan. Right, I'd better make a move.' Hope's cheek remained pressed firmly against his chest and Cam found himself just as reluctant to let her go.

'We could sneak back to bed,' he murmured into her hair. 'It's still early.'

With a laugh, Hope raised her head and gazed up at him. 'You are a terrible influence, and as much as I like that idea a lot more than what I have planned, I'll have to decline.'

Cam pouted, more because he wanted to hear that glorious sunshiny laugh of hers than out of any real sense of disappointment. They both had too much to deal with to indulge themselves. Soon, he promised himself, silently. 'Will you let me know how you get on?'

'Yes. And you'll let me know if you have any news as well?' When he nodded, Hope went up on tiptoe and kissed him. Cam chased her mouth down as she lowered her heels, stealing little pecks and kisses until she was giggling and squirming with delight. 'Get off!' She gave his chest a playful shove then darted back up for a final kiss. 'Go!' She pointed towards where his car was parked then tugged open the door of her own.

Backing up, Cam kept his eyes locked on her as she tugged on her seat belt and started the engine. 'Call me later, yeah?' he called.

'Will do!' Hope backed out of her space and turned her car towards the exit. 'Love you, bye!'

Love you. The words struck him hard in the chest as true as an arrow from Cupid's bow. Could she really mean it? She'd said it so casually, perhaps the words had slipped out by accident. Her family were openly affectionate, and he'd heard them exchange a dozen such off-hand farewells. Did *he* love her? Oh, hell, maybe he did. Should he say it back? Did he want to say it back? He did. He did! Cam opened his mouth, then closed it again. Hope was already halfway down the road and far out of earshot. He reached for his phone, started to message her, then deleted it. A text was no way to say it for the first time, or would it technically be the second time, seeing as how she'd already said it? With his head still in an absolute whirl, Cam climbed into his car and headed up the hill towards the dig.

He tried his best to keep his mind on the job in hand. Having briefed the team about the change in plans, he sent most of the group to continue the endless job of cataloguing their previous finds while he headed out with Declan to review the state of the trench so the groundworkers could get started. Once that was sorted, he was at a loose end until they could start hand digging again, so he went to find Cassie, who was sitting at a table at one end of the welfare cabin reviewing the catalogued records from the previous day to ensure all the finds had been photographed and bagged correctly. Those members of the team who weren't busy bagging the rest of the finds had taken the chance of sneaking an extra cup of coffee and were gathered around the table nearest the door.

'Want a brew?' Adam asked, raising his cup.

Shaking his head, Cam continued to the back of the cabin and sank down in the chair beside Cassie.

'You look like a wet weekend,' Cassie said, sparing him half a glance before returning to her task. Not sure how to put anything into words, Cam began leafing through a stack of record cards. 'Leave those,' she ordered, giving the back of his hand a playful tap. 'I've already checked them, and you'll mess up my system.'

'Sorry.' Cam set the cards back where he'd found them and slumped back in his chair. His determination to put a positive spin on things hadn't lasted long. 'I think I've messed up, Cass.'

'How so?' She sounded half-distracted, her attention still on the card she was reviewing.

'Hope told me she loved me, and I didn't say it back.'

'Excuse me?' It shouldn't have been possible for her voice to climb that many octaves in so few syllables. Her exclamation drew the attention of Adam and the rest of the team, their heads popping up like meerkats as they swivelled around to stare at them. 'Out,' Cassie ordered them, one finger raised to point at the door. 'Right now!'

Cam didn't miss the bemused looks the others exchanged as they trooped out of the cabin and closed the door behind them. 'Way to make a scene, Cass,' Cam grumbled, wishing he'd kept his mouth shut. He should've waited and spoken to Ed about things. Or Barnie, perhaps. No, not Barnie. He wouldn't have been able to deal with that much hysterical laughter in his fragile state.

'Way to drop a bombshell on me, Cam,' Cassie mimicked then waved her hand in dismissal. 'Never mind that, tell me what the hell is going on! I thought you liked Hope. I mean you two are spending an awful lot of time together and I was only saying to Ed last night how well suited the pair of you are.'

He started laughing, he couldn't help himself.

'What? This isn't funny, Cam! You've left that poor woman hanging and now you're laughing about it. Who even are you?' Cassie sounded properly outraged, which only made him laugh harder.

When she opened her mouth to berate him again, Cam held up a hand to give him chance to draw breath. 'Jeez, Cass, I can't tell you what's going on if you don't let me get a word in.'

'Oh.' She seemed to consider that for a moment before nodding her head once. 'Point taken.'

Cam outlined what had happened with Hope earlier. 'My brain was buzzing,' he said as he tried to explain how he'd felt as he stood there watching Hope drive away. 'There were just too many thoughts, too many emotions and by the time I figured out how I felt, it was too late.'

'Why didn't you call her?'

He scrubbed a hand through the back of his hair, trying not to shift awkwardly under Cassie's laser focus gaze. 'I was going to text her, but that didn't feel quite right.'

'Text her?' Cassie raised her eyebrows in plain exasperation.

'I know. I know.' Cam held up his hands. 'I'll go and call her now.'

He hadn't made it out of the cabin before Adam appeared on the steps below him. 'Can you smell that?' Adam snuffled his nose. 'I'm sure it's smoke.'

'Like cigarettes?' As Adam backed away, Cam followed him down the steps, drawing a deep breath in through his nostrils. The groundworkers were the only ones who smoked and they had a fire bucket set up in the far corner of the compound, away from everything else. They were busy with Declan, so any cigarettes should've been extinguished some time ago. Still, he supposed they'd better go and check. He sniffed the air again, there was a faint whiff of something...

'I don't think so,' Adam said, keeping pace with him as they headed towards the smoking area. 'More like a bonfire or something?'

They didn't need to get too close to the fire bucket for Cam to tell it wasn't the source. A handful of butts were sticking up from the sand, but other than that, the area was spotlessly clean. As he turned away, a gust of wind blew in from the west and he curled his lip at the acrid scent. 'God, where is that coming from?' He turned towards the dig. 'Are they crop burning?' It seemed far too early in the season for that, and come to think of it, he couldn't remember the last time he'd seen anyone burning off the stubble. 'Do they even do that any more?'

Adam shrugged. 'I dunno. I guess Rhys would. Shit! Look at that!'

Cam followed the direction of where Adam was pointing towards a thick column of black smoke. 'Christ! Isn't that over where the campsite is?' They started running towards the dig. 'Declan! Declan!' Cam shouted towards the site manager.

The big man took one look at them sprinting towards him and waved his hands at Paul to shut down the digger. The machine shuddered to a halt, the sudden silence almost a shock. 'Wha...?' Declan didn't even finish his question. He must've already caught the smell of the smoke, which was growing stronger with every step Cam took. 'What the hell is going on?'

Cam halted behind him, trying to catch his breath and trying not to cough as the first hint of smoke in the air hit them. 'We don't know, but we think it's over near the campsite.'

'Bloody hell, let's hope not. Come on, we'd better go and check it out.'

Leaving Cassie and a couple of the others to secure and close down the site, the rest of them piled into their vehicles and Cam led their little convoy along the winding estate road towards the campsite. As they drew nearer, it became increasingly obvious that's where the smoke was coming from and it was all he could do to stick to the low speed limit and not race along. The last thing they needed was to have an accident on top of whatever else was going on. The screaming wail of a fire engine reached him as they pulled into the campsite car park and were greeted with a nightmare scene.

People were running everywhere, stuffing their belongings into open boots, kids crying, dogs barking, frustrated parents yelling at each other. Cam jumped out of his car and just managed to grab a young boy of around five or six out of the way of another car which was reversing without any care. 'Watch what the hell you're doing!' Cam yelled at the man behind the wheel. All he got was a mouthful of abuse in return as the man shoved his car in gear and drove off.

Smoke was billowing over the car park now, making it even harder to see, but as far as Cam could tell, it was coming from the other side of the boundary wall from one of the arable fields. *Thank God.* His relief was short-lived, as the kid he was holding began to struggle and Cam had no choice but to let him go. 'Don't run!' he called, to no avail as the boy charged across the car park and into the arms of a woman next to a red estate car. She shot Cam a glare, but he was already turning away to speak to the others. 'Declan, can you take a group and start trying to instil some order here?'

The site manager nodded grimly and beckoned to Paul and Tony, the groundworkers. 'You take this side, I'll take the other. Tell everyone to calm down and to wait in their cars once they're loaded and we'll get them all out as quickly and as safely as possible.' Cam watched the three of them stride off, and silently wished them luck. At least they still had their high-vis vests on, which might give them a modicum of authority.

Cam turned to Adam. 'I'm going to see if I can find Hope.' He was sure she would be down here, drawn to the problem the same way they'd been. 'Take the others over to the campsite and check everything is safe. Grab what you can but only if it's safe to do so. I want you back here in five minutes, okay?'

'Got it. We'll walk the long way round rather than trying to cross the car park.'

'Good idea.' Cam coughed as a gust of wind sent another cloud of smoke overhead. 'Have you got something to cover your mouths with?'

'We'll grab something as soon as we get to the tents.' Adam tugged his T-shirt up over his mouth and nose, then turned to the others. 'Come on, let's get our stuff and get the hell out of here.'

Cam pulled his T-shirt up as well and made his way towards the top of the car park where he could see Declan in his bright-yellow vest talking to three tall, familiar-looking men. A fire engine was parked near the drystone wall which marked the boundary estate while offering what would normally be an idyllic view across rolling fields. Today it was a hellscape of heat and flames. The engine was connected to the campsite water supply and the firefighters had hoses aimed over the wall. From what Cam could make out through the billowing smoke, it looked like they were trying to create a fire break by damping down the wheat nearest the wall. He went straight up to Rhys. 'Where's Hope?'

'She's up at the Hall with Mum and Stevie. The guests up there are demanding to know what's going on, so they're trying to keep them out of the way.' He shoved his hands on his hips and glared out over the wall towards the burning field beyond it. 'When I find out who did this...'

'Calm down, son.' Zap's tone was even, but his face was a mask of anger to match Rhys's. 'We'll worry about the how and the who later, once we've got everyone away safely.' He lifted his head. 'Is it me or is the smoke lessening?'

Instinctively they all looked towards the burning field. It was still well ablaze, but the wind seemed to have shifted direction and was carrying the smoke away from the campsite.

'Right,' said Ziggy, sounding determined. 'Let's not waste this window of opportunity because the wind might change again at any minute.' He turned to his brother. 'You and Rhys go and see if you can get the campervans on their way.'

'Me and my guys can handle the car park,' Declan said and with a nod from Ziggy, he strode away.

Which just left Cam. 'What can I do?'

Ziggy shot him a grateful smile. The strain around his eyes was palpable, but his voice was as calm and steady as ever when he replied. 'Can you head for the tents and help whoever you can see who needs it?'

Cam nodded. 'Absolutely. My team are already there packing up, I'll ask for volunteers to help.'

Ziggy placed a hand on his arm. 'The moment that smoke shifts back, I want you all to get the hell out of there, okay?' His grip tightened briefly.

'You matter to Hope, you matter to all of us. Things can be replaced – people can't.'

Touched by the sentiment, Cam rested his hand on top of Ziggy's for a moment. 'I promise, and you be careful too. Whatever is going on with you and Hope, you are the father she needs.'

'Go on now.' Ziggy's voice sounded gruff, but he was smiling as he headed off towards the firefighter in a white helmet who looked to be the one in charge of the scene. As he jogged towards the campsite, Cam had a choked feeling in his throat that wasn't only down to the smoke.

He arrived in time to find Adam, Scott and the others loading rucksacks onto their backs and tucking bedrolls under their arms. When he asked if anyone was willing to volunteer to assist the other campers, every one of them volunteered. With a bit of reshuffling of loads, half the group went off to stow their gear in the vehicles, ready for a quick exit, while the rest of them split into pairs and approached the nearest tents to see what could be done.

Luck was with them, it seemed, because the worst of the smoke stayed away. A steady stream of campervans trundled past on the far side of the campsite, so it looked as if Zap and Rhys were managing to control things over there. It was a bit more chaotic for Cam and the team because people were trying to pack, keep an eye on their children and break down their tents all at the same time. We can only do our best, Cam reminded himself as he and Scott moved from tent to tent. Some were grateful for the help, others preferred to manage on their own, but all were grumbling about the stink of smoke that clung to everything.

He was trying to comfort a crying toddler with a nose so snotty it was enough to put Cam off fatherhood for life when he heard a sharp whistle from behind him. Jiggling the little boy in the crook of his arm while waving a grubby rabbit with the other, Cam turned to see Rhys waving both arms high over his head. Cam couldn't exactly dump the child down, so he called to Scott. 'Run over and see what's going on with Rhys, will you?'

With a nod, the boy loped away and Cam kept one worried eye on him while he tried to cajole his new little friend. 'It's all right,' he crooned, rocking the boy. 'Look, your mummy is right there.'

The boy's harassed-looking mother glanced up from where she was stuffing clothes into a bag. 'Be a brave boy, Oscar.' She flashed Cam a quick smile. 'I can't thank you enough for this.'

'It's fine, really. I'm just so sorry that everyone's holiday has been spoiled, but at least no one's hurt.'

She nodded. 'I keep telling myself that's the main thing.'

Whether it was the jiggling or the dancing rabbit, or just plain boredom on Oscar's part when he realised he was stuck with Cam for the time being, the boy quieted down and rested his head against Cam's chest. Tucking the rabbit into the boy's arms, Cam continued to rock from side to side as he waited impatiently for Scott to return.

'Cows!' Scott blurted out as soon as he was within earshot. 'There's cows loose on the road. One of the campervans almost collided with the herd but managed to stop in time.' Scott sucked in a deep breath and let the rest of his words out in a fast stream. 'Rhys and Zap have gone to try and sort it out, but we need to hold everyone here.'

'Run and tell Declan as he's in charge of the car park and then find Ziggy, okay?'

Scott dashed off without a word and Cam hugged the little boy close to his chest. 'What the hell else is going to go wrong today, eh, Oscar?'

27

Hope had just finished settling the last of the hotel guests in the conservatory with morning tea and cakes when her phone started ringing. She muted it and smiled down at the couple in front of her. 'I want to thank you again for your understanding and patience. As soon as we have an update from the fire brigade, I'll personally update you.'

'Is everyone safe?' The woman cast a worried glance towards the windows, where a faint haze of dark smoke was hanging in the distance.

'As far as we are aware. The fire is outside the boundary of the estate, we're just keeping everyone inside as a precaution for now. If you'll excuse me for just one moment?'

The moment she was out of earshot, Hope grabbed her phone and returned her cousin's call. 'Rhys? Is everything all right?'

A car horn blasted and she thought she could hear someone shouting. 'Get back in your car!' Rhys yelled and then he spoke into the phone. 'Fucking nightmare! The cows have broken through the fence on the west pasture and have strayed all over the road. Don't let anyone leave the Hall until we've got them contained, okay?' He muffled the phone and yelled something again which she couldn't catch.

'Who's with you to help?' she demanded when he got back on the line.

'Dad's here and a couple of stockmen from the farm. We're okay but there's a bloody queue of traffic from people trying to leave the campsite and... Christ! Someone's trying to cut across the bloody field. I've got to go!'

The phone went dead, and all Hope could do was stare at it as she blew out a breath and tried to keep calm.

A gentle touch on her arm had her turning to face her mother. 'Everything all right?' Stevie asked.

Hope glanced past her mother's shoulder to make sure the guests were still settled in their armchairs and enjoying their tea. 'That was Rhys. The cows in the west pasture have got loose somehow and it's causing chaos for people who are trying to leave.'

Stevie winced. 'How on earth did that happen?'

Hope's attention strayed once more to the dark haze on the horizon. 'I don't know, but I don't like it.' She turned back to Stevie. 'Look, if you and Ro have everything under control here for now, do you mind if I nip over to the campsite and see how they are getting on? I might be able to get an update from the fire brigade while I'm there to see if, or when, our guests will be safe to go outside.'

'That's a good idea, darling.' Stevie gave her a quick hug. 'If it's going to be later, then we'll see about some complimentary spa passes or I'll dig some games and puzzles out of the library cupboard for anyone who prefers to stay here in the conservatory.'

'I'll be as quick as I can.'

Her mother reached for her hand. 'Have you heard from Cameron?'

Hope shook her head. She'd been trying not to think about him and keep her mind on the guests. He and the team were miles away from the fire, at least. 'I'll try and call him once I've been to the campsite.'

'Go steady. Text or call me when you can with an update.'

When Hope arrived at the campsite car park, the first thing she spotted was the cluster of familiar cars, including Cam's battered old hatchback. What was he doing here? Her heart began to pound but then she spotted Declan in a high-vis vest striding towards her and she began to calm again. 'Everything okay?' she asked as she climbed down from her Range Rover. 'Rhys just called me and told me about the cows getting out.'

'It's under control here for now, but people are starting to get restless.' He indicated a queue of cars being held at the exit by two other men wearing high-vis clothing. Declan rubbed a hand over his chin. 'Cam and the others are helping people pack up where they can.'

'They're all safe?' She hadn't realised how worried she was until Declan nodded. 'Everyone's fine. Look, can I borrow your keys? The Range Rover is big enough to block the exit gate and should be enough to put off anyone with the bright idea of queue-jumping.'

'Sure.' Hope placed them in his palm. 'Where's Ziggy?' As much as she wanted to find Cam and see for herself that everything was okay, she had to keep her focus on her job. The guests' welfare was paramount.

'Last I saw him, he was chatting with the scene commander from the fire brigade. Look for the chap in the white safety helmet.'

'Thanks.' Leaving Declan to move her car, she made her way along the queue of vehicles. Wherever she saw a window open, she paused and gave them a quick update.

'How much longer are you going to keep us trapped here?' An angry-looking man had climbed out of his car further up the queue and was marching towards her.

Here we go. Knowing that body language was key, Hope adopted an open, friendly stance with her feet set slightly apart and her hands down at her sides. 'Hello! I was just making my way up the line to speak to you, but you've saved me a job. As you are probably aware, we've got an issue with some livestock getting loose on the estate and we need everyone to remain here where it's safe until we can get them contained again. I'm sure it won't be long.'

'Bunch of bloody jokers,' the man muttered. 'What kind of a tinpot place are you running here? You can't stop us from leaving'

Hope kept her smile relaxed while she silently called the man a few choice names. There was always someone who felt the need to throw their weight around, to make their presence felt the way dogs needed to pee on everything. At least this idiot was keeping his fly zipped, so that was something to be grateful for, she supposed. His antics had drawn a few other people from nearby cars and Hope knew this was the moment when she won or lost control of the situation. 'How much do you weigh, sir?' she asked, pitching her voice loudly enough for those around them to hear.

He blinked, frowned then shook his head. 'What's that got to do with anything?'

'I don't need an exact number.' She studied him a moment and decided to err on the side of flattery. 'About eleven stone?'

The man shrugged. 'Something like that. What's your point?'

She did a quick calculation in her head. 'Eleven stone is 154 pounds. The average weight of a fully grown cow is 1,200 pounds. Add in the fact they are going to be in distress because there are already people shouting and sounding their horns, plus some in the herd are pregnant. You must see that is a recipe for disaster unless the situation is brought under control. We have trained staff from the farm on scene and they are doing everything they can to make things safe for everyone – including our animals. Do you really want to get caught up in all of that, rather than waiting here until we can get you a safe route out?'

'Lady's got a point,' a man sitting in the car closest to them called out. 'I don't fancy my chances against a cow, don't fancy one running into my car, neither.'

Hope shot the man a brief smile of thanks. 'We really are doing everything we can to get you all out of here. Please just bear with me while I get the latest update and I'll be straight back.' She gestured with her hand for the irritated man to walk with her back towards his car.

'My kids are upset,' he grumbled to her.

And seeing him marching around and yelling was going to help that how? Hope merely gave his comment a sympathetic nod. 'I'm sure they are. All that smoke everywhere must have been very frightening.' She glanced towards the fire engine. 'It looks like they've got things under control and at least the wind is keeping the smoke away now.'

'I suppose so. What are you going to do about our ruined holiday, though?'

Hope tugged a business card from her pocket. 'We'll be in touch with everyone about their booking and refunds will be issued as soon as we can get them sorted out. Here's all my details. Send me an email when you get home later, and we'll take it from there.'

'Get in the car, Mick,' an exasperated female voice said through the open window. 'The poor girl's doing her best!' She leaned further forward to address Hope. 'Is everyone okay?'

Hope bent forward and returned her smile. 'No one is hurt as far as I know, which is the main thing. We really will try and get you all on the road as soon as possible.'

'Thank you.' The woman turned to her husband. 'Get in the car.'

Taking the chance to escape, Hope hurried the rest of the way along the line, not stopping to address anyone in particular, just repeatedly thanking everyone for being patient and promising an update as soon as she had one. Thankfully, Ziggy was waiting for her at the top of the queue.

'Problems?' he asked her with a frown.

'Nothing I can't handle,' she assured him, which earned her a nod and a smile that said he'd expected nothing less. 'What's the latest?'

'Zap's just called and said they've got the herd back on the other side of the fence and they've managed to block the hole.' A deep furrow etched into his brow between his eyes. 'He reckons the fence was cut and there's signs of blood. It might be from one of the cows when it escaped as they haven't checked them all over yet, of course...'

'The fence was definitely cut?'

'He reckons there's no doubt about it, so if the blood isn't from one of the animals, then whoever is causing all this might have injured themselves in the process.'

'Good.' Hope wasn't the vindictive type, but in this case, she was willing to make an exception.

Ziggy smiled. 'Fierce little thing, you are. Best the police find whoever it is before you do, eh?'

Hope laughed. 'I might not go that far. So how much longer before we can release the queue?'

'Ten minutes or so. I want to give them time to clear the cars and campervans which are already on the road.'

'That's a relief. What about the fire?' Smoke was still billowing from the field behind them.

Her uncle shook his head. 'The crop is a total loss. All the fire brigade can do is contain it and let it burn out. Luckily, they arrived in time to stop it spreading beyond the one field. There were a few stray sparks, but those were caught and stamped out before they managed to catch. If the wind stays in our favour, this will be the worst of it.'

'Are you going to give people the opportunity to stay if they wish?'

'Not on the campsite. Not until we catch whoever it is. The Hall we can protect if we set a perimeter patrol, but I'm going to close public access to the shops at The Old Stable Yard as well.'

Which would mean more lost revenue for the estate on top of the growing number of refunds and cancellations. 'I'll call Mum and update her. She's going to give out spa passes to keep the guests happy.'

'I'll call her. You go and find Cam. He's with his team, helping people to pack up.' Ziggy hesitated then tucked his hands in his pockets. 'It's not my place to tell you what to do, but if it was, I'd say you've got a good man there and I hope we'll see a lot more of him in the future.'

Stepping close, Hope threw her arms around her uncle's neck. 'It's always your place, even when I'm mad at you about everything.'

Ziggy's arms closed around her. 'If I could turn back the clock and change the way we've handled everything, I'd do it in a heartbeat.'

But they couldn't. Any more than Hope could wish away the lingering feelings of betrayal. 'There's no magic solution for this.'

Her uncle dropped his arms and stepped back. 'I know. I'm just grateful you and Rhys are giving us a chance to make things right.'

Hope wasn't sure they'd ever be truly right again. It was still too soon, no matter how much she wished she could give him the words she knew he needed to hear. 'Let's get through this mess first and then we'll have time to talk.'

'That's all I'm asking for, Hope, just time.'

By the time she'd tracked down Cam, it looked like most of the camp-site had been packed up. She found him and the rest of his team standing next to their tents. His face lit up the moment he spotted her and she walked straight into his open arms. 'Thank God you are okay.'

'I'm fine.' He dropped a quick kiss on her mouth. 'Are you okay?'

She nodded. 'Yes. Rhys has got the cows contained, so everyone should be on the move soon.'

'That's good news. Does he know what happened?'

Hope led him a little way away from the others. 'The fence was cut.'

'Shit. And the fire?'

She shook her head. 'I don't know yet, but I'm not feeling like it's a coincidence given everything else that's happened.'

'I don't want to believe it, but I think you're right.' He glanced over her shoulder at his team. 'What do you think we should do?'

'I don't know. Once everyone is clear from the estate, why don't you all come up to the farmhouse? They won't want to sleep here, and Ziggy wants to close the campsite as it's too exposed. At least the farm and the house will be more secure, even if we have to re-pitch some of the tents in the yard tonight.'

'It'll be a bit of squeeze, we could probably extend the compound up at the site and move the camp up there,' Cam suggested.

'No!' Hope surprised herself with the vehemence of her reaction. 'I don't want any of you out on the estate tonight.' She took his hand and looked up into his eyes, which were full of compassion and concern. 'Please.'

'Whatever you want.'

She leaned forward to rest her forehead on his chest. 'I want all this to go away.'

'I know. Come here.' Cam pulled her close and Hope let herself lean into the solid strength of him, just for a minute.

28

An hour later and apart from a couple of families who were ferrying the last of their stuff to their cars with the help of Scott and a few others, the campsite was empty. His team had packed up their tents and those would be going into the back of Hope's Range Rover next. Hands on hips, Cam looked around them. The place was a mess of abandoned bits and pieces and rubbish. It would take a couple of hours to clear up what was left, but they could come back and do it later. He wanted the team down at the farmhouse for a break first.

He spotted something beneath one of the trees in the corner and wandered closer to investigate. As he got closer, he realised it was a small tent – the kind of thing you might get for kids to camp out in the back garden in. The front was zipped shut. Cam looked around, but the only people in sight were his team. He turned back to the tent. 'Hello? Is anyone in there?' Silence greeted him.

He waited a moment then nudged the tent with his foot and called out again. 'I'm going to open the zip, let me know if there's anyone there.' Nothing. Moving cautiously, he tugged the zip down about halfway, but it was clear almost immediately it was empty. A strong smell of petrol hit him and he froze. Backing away from the tent, he pulled out his phone and dialled Hope's number. She'd gone to speak to Ziggy to let him know they were about ready to leave.

'I'm up by the trees,' he said by way of introduction when she answered. 'Near the far end. You'd better get up here and bring Ziggy with you.'

Five minutes later and they were staring at the contents of the abandoned tent. Alongside one of those small plastic jerrycans people used to refill their cars in an emergency, there was a dirty sleeping bag, several empty bottles of cheap booze and a few bits of clothing. Using a stick he'd picked up, Ziggy flipped over a dark blue polo shirt to show the embroidered logo on the front. It was a match to the one Hope was wearing, only the one in the tent looked as grubby as the sleeping bag.

'Someone could've stolen it.' Cam was clutching at straws, but he couldn't bear the look of pain and shock etched on Hope's face. One of their own had betrayed them.

'I think we should leave this for the police,' she said, when Ziggy crouched down and lifted the edge of the sleeping bag with the stick.

'It's definitely our man.' Standing up, Ziggy stepped to one side so they could see what he'd uncovered.

It was a large screwdriver, the tip of it covered in flecks of burgundy paint Cam just bet would be a match for the paintwork on Willoughby's car. Something red caught his eye in the shadowed corner of the tent and he craned his neck forward for a better look, making sure he didn't touch anything as he did so. 'Shit. That looks like Declan's cash box.' Cam sat back on his heels. 'You definitely need to call the police.'

Ziggy nodded. 'I'll go and talk to the incident commander as well. He'll want to know we've found petrol.' His gaze drifted towards the still burning field. 'No wonder it went up so quickly.'

Feeling useless, Cam walked beside Hope as they followed in her uncle's wake. She looked as tired and as scared as he felt. If the culprit was willing to use petrol to start fires, they were lucky he hadn't decided to target the actual campsite, or God forbid, the Hall or the farmhouse. Shuddering at the thought, Cam reached for her hand. 'The police will find out who it is.'

'I know who it is,' she replied, grimly. 'I recognise those bottles. They're the same brand as the ones Rhys found hidden in the barn.'

Cam stopped in his tracks. 'Keith? But I thought he was away in rehab.'

'So did we all, but who the hell else can it be?' Dropping his hand, she raised hers and began ticking off points on her fingers. 'He knows the estate. He had uniform shirts like everyone else who worked here – and I bet Rhys never thought to ask for them back. He's got a grudge because Rhys sacked him and then Ziggy got him barred from the pub. It has to be him.' Her eyes widened. 'I need to call Amelia and warn her.' Cam watched as she grabbed for her phone and searched for the right number. It rang and it rang until finally switching to voicemail. 'Amelia, it's Hope. Please call me when you get this. I...' Hope's eyes met his and Cam shook his head. It wasn't the sort of thing to say in a message. 'I just wanted to see how you're doing. Call me as soon as you can, please.'

'Maybe she's still at work?' Cam suggested, though it was hard to ignore the sick feeling in his stomach.

'You're probably right. I'll try her again later. Let's go and talk to Ziggy.'

It was early evening by the time they'd got everyone off the estate who was leaving. The shopping area at The Old Stable Yard had been relatively quiet and boards had been posted at the entrance advising that the estate was closing, so Hope's family had decided to let the shoppers already there conclude their visits rather than causing any more alarm. The police had shown rather more interest than last time and were still up at the campsite with Ziggy. The fire brigade had packed up and gone home, the blackened field barely smoking now the blaze had consumed the entirety of the wheat crop.

Cam's team were real troopers about the upheaval and had set up camp in the yard outside the farmhouse back door without a murmur of complaint. They'd drawn up a roster for the various showers and bathrooms and those who were waiting were happy to sit outside with sandwiches and cups of coffee. The smell of smoke lingered, even after a shower and a change of clothes, and Cam wondered if he'd ever be free of it. Telling himself there was no time to be maudlin, he headed downstairs and called out the back door. 'Main bathroom is free, who's next?'

'Oh, that's me!' Zoë hopped up from the bench by the wall, where she'd been sitting next to Adam. 'But my clothes are still waiting for the washing machine.'

'You can help yourself to whatever you need from my room,' Hope assured her, coming up from behind Cam. 'Come on, I'll show you.' There was the sound of a horn from the gate, which made them all jump as they'd locked up once everyone was inside.

Cam exchanged a look with Hope. 'We'd better go and check who it is.' He tried to keep his voice light. There was still no answer from Amelia. Rhys had gone down into the village to check on her, but he had a key to the gate so would surely just let himself in.

'I'll come with you,' Adam said, jumping up, and before they knew it, they had half a dozen escorts as they approached the gate.

Cam felt Hope relax beside him as soon as she spotted the car outside the gate. 'It's Mrs Davis, our cleaner.' She opened the gate and stood aside to let the little red Fiat through. 'What are you doing here?'

'I thought you'd need a hand with washing and the like,' Mrs Davis said, resting one arm on her open window. 'Blooming smoke gets into everything.' She looked past them to the makeshift campsite in the yard. 'And if anyone needs a bed for the night, then I've got a spare room and Iain at the pub says he'll take in a couple. Sandra and Penny said the same.' She looked back up at Hope. 'It was Sandra who rang me after the café closed early.'

Ah, the good old village grapevine had been at work by the looks of things. Cam was touched at their thoughtfulness and he rested a hand on Mrs Davis's car as he bent down to offer her a smile of thanks. 'That's so kind of you. I think we're all right for beds tonight, although I'll ask the team to be sure. As for doing a bit of washing, that would help us out no end, if you really don't mind?'

'Not a bit. Bag up everything and we'll get it sorted and back first thing in the morning. Those that haven't got rooms to offer still said they'd be happy to stick a load on, so it won't be a problem.'

Cam raised his head to look at Hope, who was blinking back tears. 'You didn't have to do this, you know?' she said, her voice sounding raw.

Mrs Davis snorted. 'After everything you and your family have done for this community, it's the least we can do. Now come on, let's get everyone sorted out. There's a box of meat in my boot as well, sent from Charlie at the butcher's, and Rob sent a load of veg that needs using today.'

While Adam and Zoë sorted out a couple of sets of clothes from everyone and shoved them in a black bin liner for Mrs Davis to take back with her, Cam and Hope carried the donated food into the kitchen.

'What's this?' Rowena asked, greeting them with her usual warm smile.

'A little help from the village,' Hope said, setting the boxes down. 'Mrs Davis has summoned the cavalry.' She opened the box and began pulling out carrots, courgettes, peppers and onions. 'At least we won't have to worry about having enough to feed everyone.'

'Looks great. I can rustle up a stir-fry or we can roast them in the oven,' her aunt suggested. She looked to the pile of sausages, burgers and chops Cam was unloading from the other box. 'Or we can do everything on the barbeque like we did for the party.'

'We can cook,' Scott volunteered from where he'd been washing some dishes in the sink. 'Me and the others will sort it out.'

Cam smiled in approval at the boy. No, not a boy, he was a man. There were still things to resolve with his father, but Scott was growing in confidence every day. 'That would be a great help, Scott. Why don't you stick everything in the fridge for now and then you can let the others know the plan.'

It was a polite dismissal, but Scott was smart enough to pick up the hint. 'Sure thing.'

Once they were alone in the kitchen, Cam closed the door.

'What's got you so serious?' Hope asked.

Sighing, Cam sat at the table and faced the truth he'd been trying to avoid. 'I think we should shut down the dig.'

Hope sank into the chair next to him. 'Won't that put you behind?'

'I can't put the team at risk, Hope. Their safety is my responsibility and if someone were to get hurt, I'd never forgive myself.' He'd also be out of a job, but right now that was the least of his worries.

'You're right. I know you're right...' Hope reached for his hand. 'This is going to be terribly selfish of me, but I don't want you to go.'

Cam couldn't stop the warm glow spreading inside him. 'It's going to take us more than one summer to sort out everything that's going on up there, a couple of weeks' break won't do any harm. The team are doing their best to hide it, but I know they're as shook up about all this as I am.' He squeezed her hand. 'Given everything that's happened, I'd feel better if I knew they were off site and safe until the police sort it out.'

She nodded. 'Honestly, I would too.'

Rowena took the seat opposite them. 'Your mother and I were talking earlier and we're closing the hotel and spa as well. We've got enough volunteers from the estate staff to keep an eye on things up there tonight, and most people are due to head home tomorrow. We've already spoken to Ziggy, and he agrees. Stevie and I have been on the phone all afternoon, postponing everyone with a booking for next week.'

She nodded towards the closed doors to Ziggy's office. 'I'm going to check and see how she's getting on.'

'We can't go on like this forever.' When Cam turned to face Hope, her expression was bleak. 'It's a balancing act keeping the various businesses profitable and every day we're without guests will push us further towards the red.'

Cam could only imagine how much pressure the situation had put her whole family under. 'I don't see you have much choice at the moment. Whoever is behind this isn't going to stop until he's caught.' If someone got hurt, or God forbid, killed, that would surely be the end of the estate. Something like that would destroy their reputation.

'Let's hope the police find him sooner rather than later.' Hope did her best to smile, but it didn't quite reach her eyes. 'Let's try to look on the bright side. You'll definitely have to come back next summer now.'

He cupped her cheek. 'You can't get rid of me that easily. I said the team were going home for a couple of weeks, I didn't say anything about me.'

'You're staying?' The way her eyes lit up made his heart soar.

'Of course. I know you're strong enough to deal with everything that's going on with your family, but I want to be here for you. If you'll have me, that is?'

'You don't even have to ask.'

Even with so many awful things going on, he had so much to be grateful for, most especially this wonderful woman. *God bless you, Mrs*

Cotteridge, he thought as he leaned in and gave Hope a quick kiss. When he pulled back, he held her gaze. 'I know this is the worst timing in the world, but I need you to know that I love you too.'

'You do?' Hope's golden sunshine laugh filled the air. 'Oh, Cam, I think you have the best timing in the world.' She flung her arms around his neck and he let himself be swept away on a kiss so right, he knew he wanted to kiss her like that forever. When they broke for air, Hope gave him a puzzled look. 'What did you mean when you said I love you too? I've never said it to you.'

'Yes, you did. When you drove away this morning.' God, was it really only that morning? It felt like a lifetime ago.

'Did I? I certainly didn't mean to.' Her wonderful laughter filled the air again. 'Oh, don't look at me like that!' She cupped his face in her hands. 'I love you, okay? I love you, I love you, I love you!'

The only way he could stop her from saying it was to seal her mouth with another kiss.

EPILOGUE

Amelia parked her car in front of the cottage and grabbed her handbag from the seat. She locked the car more out of habit rather than any fear someone would steal it. Stourton-in-the-Vale wasn't exactly a hotbed of crime, and nobody would be desperate enough to steal a clapped-out old Fiesta with nearly 120,000 miles on the clock. It was getting to the point where it might end up costing more to get it through an MOT than to buy a replacement. She shook her head. Who was she kidding? If the Fiesta broke down, she'd be going to work on the bus.

She hooked her bag on her shoulder, trying to ignore the nagging weight of the phone inside it. She'd had several missed calls while she'd been in the office. One from Hope and another from Rhys. Amelia leaned against her car and closed her eyes. She loved her friends, she really did, but she didn't want to talk to anyone tonight. All she wanted was to slip into a hot bath and crawl under her duvet for an early night. She was beyond exhausted, the kind of tired where she didn't even have the energy to eat, even though she knew she needed to keep her strength up. She couldn't afford to get ill. With all the bloody debt her father had saddled them with, she *literally* couldn't afford it.

Beans on toast would keep her going. She could skip the bath and take them straight up to her room and eat sitting cross-legged on her bed. At least then she wouldn't have to face her mother's constant sighing and worrying over that deadbeat she still wanted to call her husband. It was almost too much effort to push herself upright from the car, but she couldn't stand out in the street all night. The curtains were probably already twitching across the road. That was enough to get her moving.

Heading up the path, Amelia rummaged through her bag for her keys, before remembering they were still in her hand. God, she really needed a decent night's sleep. Raising her key towards the door, Amelia spotted the sliver of light shining past the edge and frowned. Had her mum heard her and already opened the door? Thinking that must be it, Amelia pushed it open and put on the brightest voice she could muster. 'Mum? I'm home. Sorry I'm a bit late, but the traffic was a nightmare.'

Silence.

'Mum?' Amelia chucked her bag on the sofa in the empty living room and walked back through the little house towards the kitchen. Maybe she was in bed? The doctor had warned Daisy to rest, but she wasn't very good at taking it easy, knowing how much of a burden her illness was on top of everything else. 'Mum?' she called again, louder this time.

'In here.' The words were hard to make out and Amelia clenched her jaw. Oh, God, she couldn't be crying again over that useless bastard, could she? It was the last thing Amelia needed to deal with.

'Come on, Mum,' she said, pushing open the kitchen door. 'He's not—' Amelia's words froze in her throat as she took in the scene. Her mother was crouched on the kitchen floor, half-sobbing, half-wheezing, the front of her T-shirt covered in blood.

Daisy Riley raised her eyes from the man sprawled on the floor beside her. 'I can't get the bleeding to stop. He won't let me call an ambulance.' She was clutching a tea towel as red as the front of her shirt, which was wrapped around Amelia's father's arm.

'No ambulance, I'll be fine.' The words were slurred. No doubt he was drunk again.

'You can bleed to bloody death for all I care!' Amelia snapped. 'What the hell happened? Why aren't you at the clinic?'

'Stuck up bastards,' Keith mumbled. 'Tryinatellmewhadado. I bloody showed 'em.' His eyelids flickered and then his head dropped back to the floor with a thud.

'Dad? Dad!' Oh, God, maybe he did need an ambulance! Amelia turned on her heel and ran back into the living room to find her phone, almost bumping into Rhys. What was he doing here? And why was he looking at her with those big puppy dog eyes full of sympathy? Could this day get any bloody worse?

'Get out of the way, I need to get my phone. Dad's had an accident.'

Rhys's expression turned from one of concern to one of anger. 'He's here?'

'Yes!' Amelia grabbed her bag and snatched up her phone. 'He's in the kitchen with Mum. Where are you going?' She blew out a breath. There was no point in talking to his brick wall of back. Jabbing at her phone, she dialled 999.

'Ambulance service. Is the patient breathing?'

The question startled Amelia. 'Yes. I think so. He was a moment ago. Sorry, it's my father, he's cut his arm badly and there's a lot of blood. I think he's lost consciousness.' What if he really was hurt? Was he going to die? Amelia might have wished him gone a thousand times, but the reality of it almost took her knees out from under her.

The operator's calm voice filtered through her panic. 'I've got an address in Stourton-in-the-Vale, is that current?'

'Yes,' Amelia managed to get out. 'Primrose Cottage. We're almost opposite the church.'

'That's useful information, thank you. Help is being arranged. Is the patient there with you? Can you check for a pulse, please?'

'He's in the kitchen, hang on.' Amelia ran through the door to find Rhys on his knees beside her father. He'd taken over from her mother, who was curled up in the corner, still coughing and crying. Amelia needed to get her to bed before they had two emergencies to deal with, but she needed to address the most immediate problem first.

The bloody tea towel was on the floor beside Rhys and he'd grabbed a clean one from the drawer – because of course he knew where everything was kept – and was pressing it hard against her father's forearm, which he was now holding up in the air. 'Is he breathing? The operator needs to know.'

Rhys glanced up at her through his thick fringe and nodded. 'Yes. Tell her the wound is about six inches long and very deep. I've got pressure on it and it's elevated. It'll need flushing out because he did it on one of our fences so there's a high chance of infection.'

Amelia had no idea how he knew all that, but she relayed the information to the operator.

'Thank you.' Amelia could hear her fingers clattering against the keyboard as the woman typed the update into her system. 'We're doing our best to get there as quickly as we can. Is the wound still bleeding?'

Amelia looked at the tea towel. Rhys had folded it into a tight square, but it still looked mostly white. 'Is it still bleeding?'

He raised his hand for a split second. 'Yes, but I think it's slowing down.'

Amelia sank down on the floor next to him, feeling numb and useless. 'It's slowing down.'

'That's great. Keep maintaining pressure on it. While we're waiting for the ambulance to arrive, can you give me as much detail as you know about the patient?'

She couldn't look at Rhys as she relayed her father's medical history and details about his drink problem to the sympathetic woman on the other end of the phone. She didn't know why she felt embarrassed, it wasn't like he didn't know all the gory, disgusting details already. Still, she wished it wasn't him sitting beside her, even while knowing he was the only person she would rely on in such awful circumstances.

It felt like it took the ambulance crew forever to arrive, but was probably less than half an hour, which given the remoteness of the village was something close to a miracle. 'We were already heading in this direction and got diverted onto this call,' the cheerful paramedic who'd introduced himself as Chris told her. 'Right then, what's going on here?'

Amelia got herself out of the way while Rhys calmly relayed the information to Chris. Only once the paramedics had taken over did he go to the sink and wash his hands before coming over to lean against the kitchen wall beside her. Her mum was still huddled in the corner and Amelia knew she should go and help her, but she knew if she did, she'd be bawling her own head off in two seconds flat, so she left the poor paramedics to deal with her as well.

'We'll have to call the police,' Rhys said quietly. 'Your dad's the one who's been causing trouble on the estate. He set fire to one of the fields next to the estate this morning and let a load of cows out on the road. That's how he cut his arm.'

'Oh, my God.' She remembered smelling smoke when she'd driven through the village, but assumed it was someone with a firepit in their garden enjoying the summer evening. Bile rose in her empty stomach and she swallowed it down hard. 'Was anyone else hurt?'

Rhys shook his head, still looking thunderous. 'More by luck than anything. If the fire had jumped the wall, then the whole bloody campsite would've gone up. One of the cows has already miscarried this afternoon. I'm worried she won't be the only one.'

Amelia felt her knees go from under her and she slid down the wall until her bottom hit the floor with a jarring thud. She stared in disbelief as Chris wrapped her father's arm in gauze and tried to rouse him. Keith mumbled something and Amelia felt her breath catch in her throat. He wasn't dead, then. Not sure if it was a good thing or a bad thing, all she could do was watch while the other paramedic coaxed her mother up off the floor and towards the stairs.

Once he had the bleeding under control, Chris turned his kindly smile towards her. 'He's going to be fine, love. We'll have to run him up to the hospital, though, so I'll need some personal details. ID would be useful if you've got something to hand.' He raised a shoulder in an apologetic shrug. 'Paperwork, and all that.'

Amelia roused herself. 'His wallet should be in his pocket.' She stared at her father's bloodied trousers, feeling sick at the thought of touching the dark, sticky mess.

Noting her hesitation, the paramedic extended his gloved hand towards Keith's thigh then paused. 'May I?'

Feeling pathetically grateful, she nodded. 'Please.' Amelia took the wallet when he offered it and flipped it open, looking for her father's driving licence. A folded piece of paper fell to the floor and Rhys picked it up while she pulled the plastic licence card out and gave it to Chris. 'Will this do?'

'Perfect.' The paramedic reached for his tablet and took a screenshot of the licence before handing it back. Amelia watched him tapping away at his tablet; it was easier to focus on him rather than look at her father sprawled on the floor. She didn't think she'd ever be able to look at him again.

'Amelia?'

She'd almost forgotten Rhys was there. 'Sorry.' She tucked her father's licence away then held her hand out for the piece of paper. 'Here, let me put that back.' Rhys was staring at her, his face a blank mask apart from a dark fury burning in his eyes. He'd unfolded the paper and she could see it was a bill or a receipt of some kind. 'What is it?'

'Mum's rings.' The words were ground out between gritted teeth.

'What are you talking about?' Amelia all but snatched the receipt and scanned over it. She immediately recognised the name of the local pawn-broker's shop. She'd grown familiar with the place over the years, going in to reclaim whatever her father had hocked when he was desperate for cash.

Please, no, not that.

The description blurred as her eyes filled with tears. Two Rings. A plain gold wedding band and a diamond and opal engagement ring. 'Oh God, Rhys, I'm sorry.'

'They'd better still be there.' Rhys glared over at her father's prostate form and for a moment Amelia worried what he might do.

'I'll go first thing in the morning and reclaim them,' she promised, reaching for Rhys's arm and drawing his attention away from the target of his anger. 'I'm so, so sorry.'

'It's not your fault.' He'd never sounded so cold, and Amelia released his arm at once.

'I'm sorry,' she muttered again, knowing she sounded like a broken record. They were the only words she had, even though they felt meaning-less in the face of everything her father had done.

She began to fold the receipt, but Rhys took it from her. 'I'll sort it out, you've got enough to deal with.' His voice was softer now, and she wasn't sure what was worse, his icy anger or this tender sympathy.

Amelia sank back against the wall, wondering how on earth she was going to undo all the damage her father had done. The simple truth was that she couldn't. 'You should go,' she said to Rhys, without turning to look at him. 'There's nothing else you can do here. I'll have to go with him to the hospital. I'll make sure the police speak to him before he's discharged.' She swallowed, hard. 'I'll tell them everything, including about the rings.'

Rhys knelt beside her, his anger banked down, though she could still sense the tension in him. 'Forget about the bloody rings, they don't matter. You do. I'm not leaving you to deal with this on your own, not with your mum so poorly, as well.'

She didn't want to, but she could. She had to. 'Go home, Rhys. I don't need you.' It was a terrible lie, but what else could she say? After everything the Travers family had done for them, this was how her family repaid them? The shame of it was too much. 'Go, please.'

His eyes seemed to be burning into the side of her cheek, but she didn't turn to meet them. She couldn't look at him. Couldn't bear to see the pity she knew she'd find in them. The same pity that had killed her love for him when they were younger. She'd never wanted to rekindle that first flush of youthful passion, but she'd cherished him as a friend – him and Hope both.

As she watched him walk from the room, Amelia knew it was time to face the truth. The Travers family would all be better off if they never saw hide nor hair of any member of the Riley family again.

ACKNOWLEDGMENTS

Welcome to Juniper Meadows!

It's always exciting to start a new series, but it's a scary feeling too. I know how much my readers relate to each of the settings for my books so I put a lot of pressure on myself to try and conjure up somewhere gorgeous and welcoming. I feel like I have achieved that with Juniper Meadows and I can't wait to explore it further throughout the series.

Thanks to Cecily Blench (copyeditor) and Susan Sugden (proofreader) for helping with all the fiddly bits and making this the very best story I can bring you. With all our best efforts, the odd mistake might slip through but I hope you can forgive that.

Very special thanks to my fabulous editor, Sarah Ritherdon, who always makes me laugh and puts up with me even when I'm being completely flaky x

To everyone at Boldwood Books for creating the most collaborative, friendly and supportive working environment any writer could wish to have. You make everything so much easier x

Thanks to Alice Moore for the most beautiful cover. We wanted to try something a bit different and I hope you all agree that Alice has absolutely done me proud (as always!) x

#TeamBoldwood! What a dream you all are x

A very special mention goes to Andrew Saporoschenko and Meena Kumari who both made generous donations to the Books for Ukraine auction to have a named character in this book.

Andy, you sure set me a challenge at first by wanting a character called Zap, but in the end it proved to be brilliant inspiration as it gave me the idea for all the elder Travers siblings names, so thank you!

Meena, thank you for always being so generous and supportive. I hope you will approve of Barnie as your 'book boyfriend' x

I couldn't get through the days without my writing gang – Phillipa Ashley, Jules Wake, Bella Osborne and Rachel Griffiths who are always there to cheer me up and cheer me on. I love you all x

Saving the best to last, all my love and thanks go to my husband x

AUTHOR'S NOTE

We will be returning to Juniper Meadows in the autumn when Amelia's determination to avoid the Travers family will be put to the test by the arrival of Ben Lawson, Hope's estranged brother.

MORE FROM SARAH BENNETT

We hope you enjoyed reading *Where We Belong*. If you did, please leave a review.

If you'd like to gift a copy, this book is also available as an ebook, large print, hardback, digital audio download and audiobook CD.

Sign up to Sarah Bennett's mailing list for news, competitions and updates on future books.

https://bit.ly/SarahBennettNewsletter

Why not escape to the seaside with Sarah Bennett's glorious, feel-good Mermaids Point series...

ABOUT THE AUTHOR

Sarah Bennett is the bestselling author of several romantic fiction trilogies including those set in *Butterfly Cove* and *Lavender Bay*. Born and raised in a military family she is happily married to her own Officer and when not reading or writing enjoys sailing the high seas.

Visit Sarah's website: https://sarahbennettauthor.wordpress.com/

Follow Sarah on social media:

- facebook.com/SarahBennettAuthor
- twitter.com/Sarahlou_writes
- bookbub.com/authors/sarah-bennett-b4a48ebb-a5c3-4c39-b59a-09aa9idc7cfa
- instagram.com/sarah_bennettauthor

Boldw**oo**d

Boldwood Books is an award-winning fiction publishing company seeking out the best stories from around the world.

Find out more at www.boldwoodbooks.com

Join our reader community for brilliant books, competitions and offers!

Follow us
@BoldwoodBooks
@BookandTonic

Sign up to our weekly
deals newsletter

https://bit.ly/BoldwoodBNewsletter

Ingram Content Group UK Ltd.
Milton Keynes UK
UKHW041957100323
418368UK00002B/6